THE
PAPER
BOYS

D.P. CLARENCE

First paperback edition February 2024

Cover design by Bailey McGinn

ISBN 978-1-7395509-0-5 (paperback)

www.dpclarence.com

For my partner, Luke, who doesn't read books.
(£20 says someone has to tell him about this dedication.)
And for Hail, who does.
(And inspires me every single day.)

"News is what somebody somewhere wants to suppress, all the rest is advertising."

Lord Northcliffe, newspaper proprietor.

Prologue

Sunny

B ECOMING ONE OF THE least trusted people in Britain doesn't happen by accident. I worked hard to achieve it. Some days I wonder why I bothered.

I became a journalist to make a difference to the issues I'm proper passionate about, like fighting poverty, discrimination, and climate vandalism. In reality, since moving from Leicester to London to work on (the now strictly metaphorical) Fleet Street, I'd spent most of my time parked up outside the Beckhams' house in a cold Vauxhall Astra, waiting for everyone to go to bed so I could sift through their bins looking for "exclusives." Apparently, they're what the people want to read. In eighteen months at the *Bulletin*, I'd spent more time standing outside courthouses shouting "Are you a nonce?" at disgraced national treasures than I had shining a spotlight on the absolute scandal of inequality and the intergenerational hardship it causes in communities like the one where I grew up.

When pollsters ask the people of Britain which groups in society they trust the least and thirty per cent say journalists, I get it. And I can just about take that on the chin. But what they don't tell you when you become one of Britain's least trusted people, what really hurts, is that it makes you proper undatable.

When you tell a boy you're a reporter for the country's most hated tabloid newspaper, they disappear faster than you can say "But I'm a good person, really" or "I would never write that about a member of Girls Aloud, please don't judge me by the actions of my employer." The only people who get it, who understand what it's like being a journalist looking for love, are other journalists. Which is a shame, because if there's one cast-iron rule in this business, it's that you *never* date another journalist. After all, how could you possibly trust them?

1

SUNNY

THE SUN WAS BARELY up, and already my piss was boiling. I threw my strictly-work-purposes-only tablet onto the bed in disgust. It landed right side up, lighting my bedroom in a soft white glow. The picture of my own stupid face shone brightly up at me from my photo byline in the morning's paper, mocking me. "Sunny Miller, Political Reporter." I smacked a pillow over it so I didn't have to stare at the comedy headline the subeditors had put on what had been, when I filed it the night before, a very serious article about the government funding programmes to "save the British countryside." I mean, it was mostly about otters, and who doesn't bloody love otters? "WOTTA LOTTA OTTER NONSENSE," the headline screamed from the page.

This wasn't the first time the *Bulletin* subs had done a job on my attempts at serious journalism. My investigation into the desperate underfunding of Britain's road network was given the headline "Pothole celebrates second birthday." They even published a photo of it with a celebratory cake. My story highlighting the scandalous treatment of peaceful protestors by the Metropolitan Police was published as "Let them eat meat:

Police run out of vegan meals after arresting 145 Just Stop Oil libtards." It didn't matter how serious the story was, the *Bulletin* turned it into a joke. It was proper infuriating and soul-destroying.

A screech of air brakes pierced the air. A bus had pulled into the stop beneath my bedroom window, and the idling engine rattled the cracked pane of single glazing. My phone pinged. I didn't need to check the message. It was Dav telling me he was waiting downstairs. I opened the curtain. Golden early morning sunlight flooded into my room. A few passengers were climbing on board the 260 to White City, bundled up in their puffer jackets against the chilly April air. Dav was jogging up and down on the spot in his blue tracksuit, mist billowing from his mouth, like a turbaned Thomas the Tank Engine. He waved. I threw on my sweats and my trainers, shoved my house key in my pocket, and dashed down the stairs.

"You've got a face like Gordon Ramsay licking piss off a nettle," Dav said.

We bumped fists, and as we set off along our usual route towards Gladstone Park, I told him about the latest comedy headline.

"The worst bit was the strapline: 'They squat on public land and build illegal dams, and now they're getting fat on the taxpayer's purse.'"

Dav's cautious side-eye suggested I'd lost him.

"Otters don't build dams. Beavers build dams."

"Gotcha."

"So now, thanks to some bellend subeditor who's somehow never been forced to sit through an episode of *Springwatch*, not only is Britain's wildlife-loving public going to think I am an idiot, but Jemima Carstairs is never going to trust me with an exclusive again."

Another cautious side-eye. I rolled my eyes.

"She's the environment secretary."

"Gotcha."

Dav's a music journalist for a slowly failing street magazine. He's proper smart, but about things like the feud between Robert Smith and Morrissey and remembering which Gallagher is the douchebag, not politics. Dav and I grew up together. He'd been my best mate since year three, when Mrs Yates sat the (probably queer) new brown kid next to the (definitely queer) unpopular ginger kid, so the class bullies would have all their targets conveniently located in one place. We quickly became thick as thieves, bonding over our mutual love of *High School Musical*. I spent the next decade swapping my free school meal for the delicious and exotic contents of Dav's lovingly prepared lunchbox. We studied journalism together at Leeds; then Dav and his ludicrously perfect boyfriend, Nick, moved down to London while I went back to Leicester to spend two years at the local rag—writing about People's Postcode Lottery winners and barn fires—before eventually landing a job on Fleet Street and joining him in London.

Dav patiently listened to me moan as we jogged along the quiet terraced streets of Willesden Green and through the Churchill Road underpass.

"I should quit," I said, with sudden clarity.

Dav's eyebrows arched like the Maccy D's logo.

"It took you two years to get a job on Fleet Street, and you're gonna pack it in because the subs like a joke? Get a grip, mate."

"I'm embarrassed to work there."

"You knew what the *Bulletin* was like. You knew what you were getting into."

This was true. But I'd only taken the job to get my foot in the door at a national paper. The plan was to work hard, break real news, and hope someone at one of the more respectable broadsheets might notice and give me a shot. Or, if not a broadsheet, at least a paper that not only didn't publish a pair of bare tits on page three but also didn't respond to the criticism of its publishing bare tits on page three by publishing a pair of bare bollocks on page five. How was anyone going to notice my "real news" when it was always turned into puns and parody?

"I'm not sure how much longer I can put up with it," I said.

"Stick it out, princess. It's not forever."

We jogged through the ornate gates of Gladstone Park. There was a light frost, and the grass was white and shiny in the misty morning light. Dav was forgetting about my other huge, intractable problem—my chief of staff, JT Thorpe.

"He proper hates me," I said. "Looks at me like he's one uncomfortable bowel movement away from flushing me completely."

"He promoted you to the politics team, mate."

"Only because he flushed the turd in front of me. He's never really forgiven me for missing that story about the sicko from Leicestershire."

"You mean the bloke from Newton Bardon who was meeting men online, knocking them out with roofies, and cutting off their balls?"

"I should have known about all of it, apparently, as the newsroom's designated 'mincer from the Midlands.'"

"It was one psycho in his attic with his dick in one hand and a scalpel in the other. In a tiny village. *Miles* away."

"If you ask JT, it should have been a *Bulletin* exclusive. And you don't rob a man like JT Thorpe of a headline like 'Bollock Bandit trawled chat rooms for tempting testicles' and stay in his good graces."

We reached the top of the hill. The view across London was obscured by mist.

"I should definitely quit."

"How much money you got in the bank right now, mate?" I knew what he was going to say. "No way you got more than a month's rent saved."

He paused for confirmation, but I wouldn't meet his eye.

"I'll take that as a yes. You can quit, but you'll be back in Leicester five minutes later, mate—sleeping in your old bedroom in your old council flat, watching your old *Glee* DVDs and wanking over Darren Criss, until your mum finally nags you to death."

"I'd be fine for a while," I said. But Dav was right. I had less than £300 in my account to last until payday. If I chucked my job, or if JT finally sacked me, London was over. My heart sank. We jogged in silence for a bit.

"You doing anything for the coronation?" Dav asked.

I groaned. "Are you seriously going to watch that gold-gilded wankfest?"

"It's history, in't it? Come round ours if you want. Nick and I are having a small gathering."

"Some bloke inherits a hat from his old man—not to mention a shockingly unrepresentative role in our democracy and a couple of billion in property and trinkets—and suddenly everyone's a knee-bending Tory."

"You'll never get a job up the posh end of Fleet Street with that attitude, mate. They're proper rigid for King George and Queen Philippa."

"You're meant to be on my side, Davinder."

"Look, do you want to spend an afternoon on my couch eating my mum's bhajis or not?"

Amita's bhajis? I didn't need to be asked twice.

"Does that mean your folks are coming down for the party?"

"Sort of." Dav paused. "They're going down the Mall to watch the King and Queen go past."

I shook my head in disbelief.

"Class traitors!"

Twenty minutes later, we were back at my front door. My wonderful neighbour, Rosie, was hanging out her upstairs window, with a fag in hand, blowing her smoke into the street. We said good morning, and she waved back regally, like she was Queen Philippa herself. Dav put his hand on my shoulder.

"You're a good journo, Sunny," he said. "Just stick at it. It'll all work out."

Dav jogged home, and I went inside in search of a hot shower. I was too late. The rush had already begun. My flatmate, José, was in the bathroom and his girlfriend, Stella, had started a queue—standing in the hallway in her pyjamas, towel over her arm, hair like she'd spent the night shagging in a hedge. When I did finally get a shower, the hot water would be gone. I went to my bedroom, sat on the edge of my bed, and plucked off my socks. Dav's final words rang in my ears. *Just stick at it.*

I opened the BBC Sounds app and put on the *Today* programme. *Today* is basically a taxpayer-funded babysitting service for baby boomers, but it's also essential listening if you're in the news business. The silky-smooth voice of presenter Lucy Veeraswamy filled my tiny bedroom. She was interviewing some woman about the cost of living crisis. While I waited, I watched out the window. The 260 bus was idling at the stop. Its rumble rattled the broken pane and made my floorboards shiver. Old Mrs Patel from number eighteen pulled herself up onto the bus with an effort. She was followed by a fit lad in his early twenties, wearing those proper sexy cargos the tradies all wear these days. I opened GayHoller, the LGBTQ+ dating app, to see if he happened to be on it. Some proper hotties use that bus stop, and I'd scored from there before, so it paid to do a little investigative journalism.

"Let's turn to what today's papers are saying," Lucy Veeraswamy trilled. I turned up the volume. My story getting a mention was about as likely as the BBC namechecking the page-three girl. *And getting her boobs out in the* Bulletin *today, Candice from Carlisle.* It'd never happen. There'd be riots. Rightly so.

"To the big story of the day," Veeraswamy began. "The *Sentinel* leads with allegations that the government is secretly planning to build a new nuclear power plant at Newton Bardon in Leicestershire."

My heart (metaphorically) stopped. I couldn't even draw breath for fear of choking on it.

"Energy Minister Bob Wynn-Jones has denied any such plan exists, but in an exclusive, the *Sentinel* says it has seen documents that suggest negotiations between the UK government and Belarusian energy baron Yevgeny Safin are at an advanced stage."

"Bastards!"

My heart was now racing. How did I not know about this? JT was going to rip my throat out via the far end of my alimentary canal.

"We'll be speaking to *the Sentinel*'s political reporter, Ludo Boche, to get more on that story at a quarter past eight," Veeraswamy said.

That just about finished me off. Ludo *bloody* Boche. I punched the duvet. Then I launched myself onto the bed and punched it again. I hadn't met Ludo Boche yet. He was new on the *Sentinel*'s politics team. He'd only been there for five minutes. I had no clue how this absolute knobber had broken a massive story in my own backyard, but I was willing to bet the fact his father was the *Sentinel*'s editor hadn't done him any harm. Journalism is all about contacts, and the Boche family had a rolled-gold address book. Either Ludo or his old man would have gone to school with whoever dropped them that story. You could bet your nanna's last pair of knickers on it. I punched the duvet again.

The sound of air brakes pierced the morning air once more. Bus stop boy would be disappearing into the vast metropolis of London, never to be seen again. I grabbed my phone again to quickly scroll GayHoller in case the fittie had a profile I could save for later. Nothing. Just my own stupid freckled face beaming back at me from above the words *Ginger* and *Spice up your life*. For the second time that day, I was being mocked by my own electronic image. I threw my phone on the bed and slammed my fists into the mattress. Then I roared into my pillow for good measure.

2

LUDO

NOTHING JOLLY WELL KEEPS your ego in check quite like staring at yourself in a TV-studio mirror under harsh fluorescent lighting at eight o'clock in the morning, nursing a hangover that thumps like two honey badgers shagging inside your skull, while some incredibly patient make-up artist tries to breathe life into your corpse with a bucket of Max Factor. I was being interviewed on telly in half an hour but had to knock off a quick radio interview with the BBC's *Today* programme first—so my phone was clamped to my ear as I sat on hold, waiting for Lucy Veeraswamy to start asking me questions. My father always said journalism wasn't a nine-to-five job, and I always rather planned to take him at his word. Unfortunately, on this particular morning, "not a nine-to-five job" didn't mean rolling into the newsroom at half ten after a long, casual wank and my third macchiato of the day. It meant getting up at six, pouring myself into a taxi driven by a man whose halitosis had soaked into the upholstery, and making my way to South Bank to do a bit of national breakfast television.

I was in demand today, after my first big splash in the *Sentinel*. Everyone wanted a piece of me. My story was set to roll on for days, and there was a good chance the minister at the centre of the scandal would have to resign. Two months into my career and I was about to claim my first political scalp. I should have been on cloud nine. Instead, I was staring at my reflection, trying to summon up the life force needed to sound professional for Lucy Veeraswamy.

She started her introduction, and the phone clicked in. I'd come off hold. As Lucy fired off her first question, I stared at the bags under my eyes. They were so heavy they'd be over the carry-on limit for even the most permissive of airlines—no matter what you promised the boy on the check-in counter you'd do for him on his break. I was feeling very, very sorry for myself. Five minutes later, the interview was winding up, and I still looked like death.

"We should say we have reached out to Energy Secretary Bob Wynn-Jones's office for comment, but we haven't received a reply as yet," Veeraswamy said. That was the BBC's obligatory three seconds of balance—designed to offset the on-air execution that had just occurred and ensure the government kept funding them for another year.

"Ludo Boche, from the *Sentinel*, thank you for joining us."

The audio clicked in my ear, indicating we'd come off air.

"Congratulations, Ludo!" Lucy said. "I bet your mum and dad are chuffed to bits."

Here it comes, I thought.

"I worked with your mum at BBC Hampshire, back in the day."

"Yes, of course."

"Give them both my love, will you? Tell Beverley we must catch up soon. And give Hugo a nudge for me, will you? I sent him an email about a month ago. Not sure if it got through the keepers or not."

There it was.

"Must dash," Lucy said. She was gone before I could say goodbye.

A bookmaker could keep me hostage for a year and I still wouldn't understand how to place a wager, but I was willing to bet Veeraswamy's email was *not* an invitation to lunch. You show me a journalist who doesn't already have a newspaper column in the *Sentinel*, and I'll show you a journalist who *wants* a newspaper column in the *Sentinel*. Lucy Veeraswamy did not, as yet, have a column in the *Sentinel*.

I was just about to put my phone in my pocket when it buzzed. It was a message from my mother, the aforementioned Beverley Barker-Boche. Mummy no longer worked at BBC Hampshire but was now the somewhat institutionalised executive producer of the BBC's equally institutionalised flagship investigative programme, *Compass Point*.

Mummy: *You sounded asleep, darling. Did you do the vocal exercises I suggested?*

Asleep? I wasn't jolly well asleep. I might still have been drunk, but I was very much awake. I had the taxi receipt to prove it. I thought I'd performed remarkably well, considering I'd only had about three hours' kip. After a night at the theatre, I had accidentally ended up at Maxime's, the Soho club, with my little brother until well after two, and I hadn't yet had a drop of caffeine for the day. My phone buzzed again.

Mummy: *You'll need to be a bit livelier on TV or they won't invite you back! Maybe drink some coffee? Good luck darling. Very proud of you. x*

Given six million people up and down the country still spent their Monday nights sitting in front of *Compass Point*, tut-tutting about the state of Britain into their cups of tea, I had to acknowledge Mummy probably knew what she was talking about when it came to appearing on the telly. I would do jolly well to listen to her advice. I turned to the make-up artist, who was buried in her phone—probably googling whatever technique it is morticians use on particularly peaky cadaver.

"Linda, can I get a coffee from somewhere?"

"Of course, pet."

She grabbed her walkie-talkie off the dresser and said something cryptic, or possibly northern, into it. A minute later, one of those cheap airline-style coffee pots arrived. As Linda slapped TV make-up on my face like a builder rendering a garden wall, I wolfed down cup after cup of thin, watery caffeine. It tasted like the kind of thing Thames Water might release undiluted into the sea.

The morning was dragging on. I went to check my watch, but my wrist was bare. My little brother's favourite drunken game is to change the alarm tone in my phone, without me noticing, to some beastly racket. Accordingly, I'd awakened to Blondie's "Heart of Glass" at blistering volume. In a flailing bid to turn it off, I'd knocked over the glass of water on the bedstand, completely buggering my Apple Watch. I also drenched the signed copy of *Wolf Hall* I was definitely (probably) going to read some day. OK, confession: If I'm being absolutely honest, I really only kept it there to make me look cultured in front of any potential boyfriends. If I'm being honestly honest, there had never been a boy with enough boyfriend potential to see it in the first place. But, in principle, if there ever was such a boy, I wanted him to know I was the kind of serious person who read tomes of the literary weight of *Wolf Hall*. As opposed to the kind of person who would spend twenty minutes pumping a make-up artist for gossip about Harry Styles. Which is exactly what I was doing when the door to the make-up room swung open and a fierce-looking fellow with an authoritative clipboard and matching audio headset poked his head through.

"Ludo Boche?" he asked.

I turned from the mirror to face him directly. He was about eight feet tall and lanky, with a sweep of hair that, if you stuck it under a paint shop colour tester, would see you walking away with a tin of white emulsion. He was wearing a figure-hugging blue romper suit and a red bandana, which made him look a bit like an extra from *Made in Dagenham*. I was immediately obsessed with this aesthetic.

"I'm she!" I said, trying to channel a little golden-age-of-Hollywood glamour but falling short and looking like the kind of high camp muppet who might turn up to a house party in velvet trousers and start singing showtunes. (Which, frankly, is *exactly* the kind of muppet I am.)

"Gassed," *Made in Dagenham* said, one eyebrow raised. It was an unreadable expression. "I'm Petey. I'm the AP. If you're ready, I'll take you through to the green room. We've had to move you up. You're on the couch in five."

Linda studied my face one last time and declared that I was, indeed, ready. I thanked her profusely, assuring her that, were it within my gift—and I thought it was possible it might be—she could look forward to a damehood for services to hung-over homosexuals in the New Year Honours List.

"Let's go," Petey said. As I got up from the chair, I felt terribly queasy. All that coffee, on top of no food, on top of a cracking hangover, just wasn't sitting quite right. Petey held his clipboard aloft in what felt like a vaguely threatening manner and ushered me out the door. As I followed him down the hall to the studio, the coffee started repeating on me, all acid, bile, and regret. In the green room, Petey passed me a lapel mic cable, which I threaded under my jersey, and plugged it into a battery pack. He then tried several times to slide the battery pack into my back pocket without success.

"Sorry, these chinos are a bit tight," I said. "I have ballet butt."

"Hench, innit?" Petey said. He gave up and clipped the battery pack onto the pocket instead.

"Gimme your phone, keys, and watch," he said, holding out his hand.

"Is this a stick-up?"

"You have to leave anything that might make a noise or interfere with the microphones here before you go on set."

Thanks to Jonty, I no longer had a watch, but I gave Petey the rest of my worldly chattels. He disappeared into his headset, listening intently. Someone called, "And we're out."

"You're on," he said. I was ushered to the famous yellow *Wake Up Britain* sofa where Sally Quartermaine and Krishnan Varma-Rajan greeted me like long lost friends. Krishnan leant over and touched me on the knee, which would have felt jolly intimate if, firstly, it wasn't for all the cameras and crew and, secondly, it wasn't for the fact I felt like I was about to vomit all over the famous *Wake Up Britain* coffee table.

"Can I have a quick word with you in the break?" Krishnan said.

"Of course."

Krishnan Varma-Rajan had deep-brown eyes that sparkled when he smiled. You could see why they put this man on breakfast television. He was bewitchingly handsome. After he came out a few years ago, one of the papers ran a story claiming the NHS had run out of antidepressants, such was the effect on Britain's housewives. Overnight he went from being Britain's most eligible bachelor to Britain's most eligible *gay* bachelor. Rumour had it the unsolicited underwear arriving in the *Wake Up Britain* postbag switched from Victoria's Secret to FIST overnight. He'd been knocked out cold marching in last year's London Pride when an overzealous autograph hunter threw a dildo at his head. It was all over Twitter. He was off air for a week, waiting for the circular bruise from the suction cup to fade from his forehead. In other words, Krishnan Varma-Rajan was undisputed gay royalty, and he wanted a private word with *me*.

"And we're on in five, four..." a dismembered voice informed me from somewhere. Sally and Krishnan sat up straighter, so I did the same. The next five minutes were a blur, as two of British television's most beloved faces asked me a range of serious questions about surprise nuclear power plants, Belarusian oligarchs, and government energy policy while I tried not to vomit live on national television.

"One last question," Krishnan said. "The government is committed to reaching net zero by 2050. Doesn't nuclear need to be a part of the conversation if we're to make that deadline?"

"The problem here isn't necessarily the *nuclear*, it's the *conversation*," I said, surprising myself with how intelligent I sounded. There was a brain in there somewhere, among the cocktail recipes, West End musical lyrics, and rutting honey badgers. "The problem is that the energy secretary hasn't been having a conversation with the people of Leicester. They're going to wake up to find a nuclear power plant being built in their backyard, and it'll be too late to do anything about it."

"Would they want to do anything about it?" Krishnan asked. "Leicester is a deprived part of the country with high levels of unemployment. They might welcome the jobs." Krishnan sounded like my father: *Sorry your town now has a half-life of two million years, but at least you bludgers will finally feel the dignity of work.*

"They might," I said. Although I wasn't terribly certain how many unemployed nuclear scientists there were just hanging about in Leicester. "But the point is, if this is such good news for the people of Leicester, why is the government being secretive about it instead of shouting it from the rooftops?"

Before I knew it, Sally and Krishnan were thanking me for coming in, and it was all over. Sally turned to a different camera and began reading from the autocue.

"When is a King Edward not a King Edward?" she asked the audience at home. "When it's a King George the Seventh. Gloucestershire farmer Ted Sykes has grown a potato that bears more than a passing resemblance to the new king, who'll be crowned next month at Westminster Abbey. Farmer Ted will be here after the break to show us one not-so-humble spud. See you in a bit."

"And we're out," the dismembered voice announced.

Sally thanked me again for coming in and kissed me on both cheeks. Krishnan, his hand gently touching the back of my arm, indicated I should come with him. We stopped at the side of the set, and he adjusted the knob on his microphone's battery pack so that all the lights on it went out. I tried to do the same to mine, but I was nervous and there were several knobs and, somewhere between my brain and my fingers, something short-circuited.

"Allow me," Krishnan said. He put a hand on my shoulder to turn me around slightly and disappeared behind me to fiddle with the battery pack. Was this flirting? It gave him a marvellous view of the ballet butt. Naturally, I leant forward to accentuate the fall of the curve—because, apparently, I flirt like an alley cat. It seemed to be having the desired effect. If Krishnan stayed back there much longer, he'd have to sign a consent form. My heart quickened. A chorus line of butterflies danced the grand jeté in my stomach. I heard the click of the knob, and Krishnan's hands guided me back around to meet his face.

"I wanted to ask you…" Krishnan said. He was a good six inches taller than me, so I was forced to look up to meet those ravishing eyes. He leant his face close to mine. It felt intimate. His cologne, all spice and musk and manliness, hung in the air between us. I was suddenly very conscious of my breath, which must have smelt like a Caffè Nero dumpster.

"Yes?" I asked, already imagining our future together—the cottage in the Cotswolds, the two corgis, the groundskeeper with arms like Christmas hams.

"I was just wondering whether your dad mentioned anything to you about my proposal for a regular column in the *Sentinel*?"

There it was. Bewitched by the prettiest face on British television, I hadn't even seen it coming this time. The butterflies in my stomach must have been equally blindsided, because they jetéd into overdrive. I threw up, spewing coffee and contempt all down the front of television's most eligible totty.

It was a spectacular and complete disgorgement. I really, *really* got it all out. The bad TV coffee, the imagined corgis and the house in the Cotswolds, the anticipated lifetime of invitations to BAFTA after-parties, the insane belief anyone would be interested in me for me. I expelled it all.

3

SUNNY

THE *BULLETIN* OFFICE WAS in a brutalist concrete eyesore near London Bridge, but it was handy for Borough Market, if you wanted a cheap lunch, and it was handy for the Thames, if life all got a bit too much. Which it often did when your chief of staff was a proper unreformed homophobe, racist, and misogynist bellend like JT Thorpe.

I wasn't looking forward to seeing him this morning. I took the stairs up to the fourth floor and slid into the newsroom, hoping to sneak to my desk without anyone noticing my arrival. I wanted to make some phone calls to my old contacts up in Leicester to find out what the deal was with this nuclear power plant story before facing JT. It was just after eight, but the newsroom was already humming. The website team were beavering away, like the sweatshop automatons they were, unable to go home unless an algorithm told them to. One of the early-shift crime reporters was busy on the phone, jotting down notes.

"Sorry, Sergeant, your phone broke up then. Which part of the victim's head did you say was missing?"

I grimaced. It was a relief to be on the politics team now and not have to do police-reporting shifts any more. All the gory details and dead bodies were hard enough to deal with, but when you worked at the *Bulletin*, every death and trauma was given the full *Midsomer Murders* treatment. Recent headlines we'd carried included "Body in forest eaten by badgers!," "Constable's bellend badly bruised after beating with own baton!," and "Dogger collared! Naked vicar nicked at notorious A12 sex hotspot."

"Miller! My desk. *Now.*" JT's booming voice rolled across the newsroom like thunder, rattling the perpetually clenched sphincters of every journalist on the news floor. I hadn't even reached my cubicle-prison yet. How did he know I was in the building? Was I being tracked with the same microchips he used on the website team?

"Coming," I shouted.

I scooted across to my desk and ditched my bag. The rest of the politics team was nowhere to be seen. Smart tactic. If it was going to be a first-come-first-eviscerated kind of morning, it was better to take your time coming in and let JT exhaust himself disembowelling your colleagues first. Better to return only in the relative safety of that period when he was dopily digesting the blood of his victims but wasn't yet back to full strength.

As I collected my notepad and pen, I noticed Cathy's handbag open on her desk. It seemed Cathy, the political editor and therefore the person who would, in a real workplace, be called my team leader, had come in first. Cathy might already be dead.

When I got to JT's door, Cathy was very much alive and well, sitting opposite the chief of staff in one of his "naughty chairs." They're the chairs you sit in while he calls you a "useless festering cockwomble" and makes you question why you ever thought journalism was the career for you. JT pointed a finger at the empty seat beside Cathy.

"Sit," he said.

I plonked myself down with all the gusto of a man who had just performed his own haemorrhoid surgery. JT Thorpe was a Generation X newsman with the soul of a baby boomer. Not one of the good baby boomers. Not the sort who talk like Dot Cotton and buy Branston Pickle in bulk from Aldi. JT was the kind of baby boomer who thought the concept of white male privilege was a conspiracy pushed by leftards who would not rest until every red-blooded heterosexual man had been forced to wear nail polish and bleach his anus. He had the bearing, manner, and fashion sense of a pot-bellied railway workers' union shop steward from the 1950s. He wore braces and kept his shirtsleeves rolled up to display heavily tattooed forearms that said *If you mess with me, I'll lamp you*. JT also had wildly expressive veins in his neck, and those veins were currently dancing their way up to his head like vigorously copulating snakes.

"How did we miss it?" he asked. He held up a copy of the *Sentinel*, slapping the paper with the back of his hand. I looked at Cathy, hoping she might jump to my defence. You know, like a team leader is meant to do in these situations. She sat there stony-faced, saying nothing, unable to meet my eye. That told me everything I needed to know. Gestapo Officer JT Thorpe had let her live only because she'd given him the names of her collaborators. She had survived by shifting at least some of the blame onto me.

"Boche must have a contact in Energy," I said. "This wasn't on anyone's radar."

"I know it wasn't on anyone's radar," JT said. He slammed the paper down on his desk and drove his fat, sausagey finger into it. "That's the point. I don't know if you've realised, sunshine, but that's what we do here. We find out things, and we put them on people's sodding radars. The question is, Where the hell were you? Off buggering the animals of Farthing Wood while the government secretly planned to irradiate your whole family with strontium-90."

"I'm not sure that's how nuclear power pla—"

"It's your hometown, you arse-fingering pisswizard."

I was painfully aware of that. On the Tube ride in, as I considered which of my contacts to call for comment, I thought about what the jobs might mean for people back home, and what it would mean for them if, once the plant was operational, something went wrong. It didn't bear thinking about.

"There must be a leak from inside the Department for Energy, because if anyone back home knew—"

"A leak? You don't say." The sarcasm dripped from JT's mouth and made a soupy pool on his desk. I changed tack.

"I know we missed it, and I'm sorry," I said. The veins in JT's neck were now so engorged I genuinely thought-slash-hoped he might have a stroke. "If I jump on a train this morning, I can be in Leicester by lunchtime. I know the people, the leadership. I can get their reactions while Cathy gets the political response out of Westminster." I looked at Cathy for support.

"Adib is already on a train to Leicester," Cathy said.

"You're sending Adib?" The hope of taking me mum up the Bells for a cheeky fish supper on the paper's dime while I was in town evaporated. Good job I hadn't texted her.

"Not sending. Sent," Cathy said. "He was on the seven forty-five from Saint Pancras." With our travel budget, I was impressed he wasn't on the Megabus.

"But I know the patch," I protested.

"That wasn't much help to us yesterday, was it?" JT said.

Newsrooms, I had discovered, were a bit like the jungle, or the dark room of a Vauxhall club: it's very much eat or be eaten. I was now fighting for survival. My mind was spinning, trying to work out how I could be most useful.

"So, you want me stay here and help Cathy on the politics?" I asked.

"No, mate," Cathy said. "You're doing PMQs."

Had the pool of sarcasm on JT's desk not been metaphorical, I would have gladly drowned myself in it. Being sent to cover Prime Minister's

Questions was one step up from being asked to review the previous night's episode of *Hollyoaks*. PMQs was a half-hour soap opera absolutely no one was interested in unless they were actually in it. It was performative, predictable, and almost never contained even a single piece of useful information or insight. The only real difference between PMQs and *Hollyoaks* was the main actors in PMQs were unlikely to start an OnlyFans when their careers finally fell apart. Worst of all, there was zero chance of breaking any actual news—of taking a story further, of generating exclusives, of earning a front page—by sitting in the House of Commons watching a publicly televised pantomime.

"You cannot be serious?"

The veins shagging in JT's neck gave me my answer.

"We should probably be watching that," Cathy said, pointing up at the television hanging from the ceiling. On the screen, *Wake Up Britain*'s telegenic hosts, Krishnan Varma-Rajan and Sally Quartermaine, were telegenically interviewing a very telegenic young man.

I had a sneaking suspicion I knew exactly who the lad on the TV was. His clothes were what Americans would call preppy but, where I come from, would get your teeth kicked in. He had round glasses, which he kept pushing up onto his nose, even though they were already on his nose. It was some kind of nervous tic. (Journalism pro tip: always keep an eye out for people's nervous tics.) He also had a mop of black wavy curls, which he kept trying to push behind his ears but which appeared to be completely ungovernable. He was gesturing wildly. Far too wildly for half past eight in the morning. He moved like a marionette, as if his arms were independently hinged.

JT turned up the volume. It kicked in just in time for me to hear the words "nuclear power plant," and I knew for certain this absolute whalluper was Ludo Boche. The product of England's best schools. Someone who had been handed their job as a graduation present. This was privilege in action. This was the British class system operating optimally. I felt resentment rising up inside me as Ludo Boche repeatedly mentioned my hometown of Leicester.

"Get my town's name out of your fucking mouth!" I shouted at the television. Cathy jumped in her seat. JT glared at me, snake-veins pulsating.

"Is he *flirting* with Krishnan Varma-Rajan?" Cathy said.

"Flirting?" I said. "I thought someone had tasered his puppeteer."

4

LUDO

HONESTLY, I DIDN'T EXPECT to walk into the newsroom to a round of applause, but it was a jolly nice touch. Even if that round of applause came from just one man, and that one man was my godfather, the *Sentinel*'s pensionable theatre critic, Ben Diamond.

"Encore, darling boy!" he shouted, standing at his desk and clapping enthusiastically. I curtsied, extending my arms like Margot Fonteyn taking her final curtain.

"Did you watch me, then?"

"Watch you? Darling boy, I was transfixed. Not since Olivier last graced the National's hallowed stage has South Bank seen such a gilded performance. Five stars. Absolutely five stars."

"You didn't give Olivier's final performance five stars," I said.

"Quite true, dear boy. Don't quibble."

I grabbed Uncle Ben's hands and squeezed them, partly in a gesture of appreciation but also because I wasn't sure he'd stop applauding otherwise. It didn't matter how awful you felt, how bad your hangover was, or how violently you'd just vomited all over a sex symbol, Uncle Ben could make you feel as fit and confident as a young roebuck in the first spring of his physical peak. At eighty-eight, Uncle Ben was joie de vivre personified. The man could walk into a morgue and have the bodies up and dancing the foxtrot within five minutes. He was so beloved in our family that we all called him Uncle Ben. Even my father.

"I finally went to see the Lord Lucan musical last night," I said, as Uncle Ben lowered himself back into his chair.

"What did you think?"

I leant in conspiratorially.

"Is it terrible to say that I was relieved when he finally killed the nanny?" Uncle Ben's roar of laughter filled the newsroom. "That Australian accent was terrible," I said.

"Darling, they're lucky it hasn't caused a diplomatic incident," Uncle Ben said. "Australia House keeps inventing emergencies to stop the high commissioner from seeing the show. Last week they told him Shaftesbury Avenue was flooded."

He laughed until he coughed, and I waited for him to pat the phlegm back down into his chest. The man had been smoking at least a dozen cheroots a day since, well, the days when men smoked cheroots. So, his lungs weren't what they could be. His eyes watered with the effort, and it sent his neck scarf skew-whiff. I leant over to straighten it.

"Tell me, dear boy, who did you see the show with? Did you take a sweetheart?"

I didn't mean to sigh quite so heavily.

"Definitely not a sweetheart, Uncle Ben," I said. My brother, Jonty, was meant to be my date to the show, but he'd flaked on me in favour of attending some very Instagrammable opening of some very TikTok-able new rooftop bar in Kensington with a bunch of other influencers. I'd seen the show by myself, my coat folded neatly on the empty seat beside me. It was only after the show, feeling jolly lonely, that I had been cajoled by a series of texts into joining Jonty and his chums at Maxime's.

"Not seeing anyone special, then, darling boy?"

"Only you, Uncle Ben. Are we still on for *Yentl* on Friday?"

"*Kamuvan*, my boy. Of course!"

Someone called my name across the news floor. I was wanted in the small conference room. Uncle Ben gave a playful salute farewell.

***

I N THE CONFERENCE ROOM my father sat at the head of the table in his trademark dark-grey three-piece suit. He thought the suit gave him the air of authority and dignity. I thought it made him look like an East End gangster dressed up to impress a jury. Dotted around the table were the rest of the politics team, faces buried in notepads, newspapers, and laptops. No round of applause this time. My father didn't even stop to say a simple "well done." I slid into a seat next to the *Sentinel's* political editor, Ford Goodall—a man blessed with both the name and the personality of a clapped-out transit van.

"We were just assigning follow-ups to the power plant story," Ford said. "Penny is already on her way up to Leicester for local reactions. I'll be digging into whether there are any questions of corruption, because I've had a call this morning that suggests there might be—"

"Oughtn't I do that one?" I said, feeling somewhat indignant that what promised to be the meatiest follow-up to my story was being given to someone else.

"No," Ford said. "We've got something else in mind for you."

My father leant forward, his reading glasses swinging in his hand.

"We thought, given it is Wednesday, and given the situation in Leicester is highly likely to come up, you might like to—"

"Write the PMQs sketch?" I interrupted, beating my father to his punchline. "Are you serious?"

From the first day I joined the politics team, two long months ago, I had been begging to be allowed to cover Prime Minister's Questions. The hurly-burly of a full House of Commons chamber, the cut and thrust of the debate, the pantomime of jeering and sneering from the back benches—it was as close as politics came to theatre, and I jolly well loved it. But Penny was the *Sentinel*'s sketch writer, and there was no way she was going to give up that prestigious little gig unless she was dead or, well, unless someone had arranged for her to be on a train to Leicester.

"We're serious," my father said. "We think you're ready."

Neither hours in the gym nor highly invasive plastic surgery could have made my chest swell more than it swelled in that moment. I was elated. Adrenaline was shooting throughout my body. If cocaine was as strong a drug as a few of words of praise from my father, no wonder people got addicted to it. I'd be slipping off to the bathroom to snort lines of my father's approval off grubby toilet seats whenever I could.

"I'm ready. Thank you."

Ford suggested I make tracks over to the Palace of Westminster right away, so I could be ready in plenty of time. PMQs started at midday, and it was already gone ten. I had my Westminster pass, and I'd been up to the House before, but Parliament was a rabbit warren and it was easy to get lost, distracted by history, or trapped under falling masonry. I had just stood to leave when I remembered something I needed to tell my father.

"Before I forget," I began, sounding splendidly casual, as if this was the kind of thing one forgot. "I was talking to Krishnan Varma-Rajan this morning."

"We saw the interview, Ludo," my father said. He sounded stern again. He was jotting something down on his notepad and didn't look up.

"You don't like him?"

"If you're telling me you're dating him, then I think you can do better than an overflowing bucket of cock grease like Krishnan. Your mother and I would be very disappointed."

I wasn't quite expecting this level of contempt, but it augured well for what came next.

"That's just as well," I said. "Because I may have, ever so slightly, and with some considerable vigour, vomited on him." At last, Father stopped scribbling and looked directly at me.

"Thank goodness for that," he said. "Your mother thought you were flirting with him. You had us worried." This was not the response I was expecting.

"Has he... complained, or anything?" I asked.

"He won't complain," Father said with certainty. "He'll turn up here hoping to use it as leverage to get the column he's been bugging me about for the past two years. At which point I shall vomit on him myself."

He might have been emotionally stunted by the English boarding school system and harder to please than a Stasi interrogator, but it was always reassuring to know that, when push came to shove, Father had my back.

5

SUNNY

I THREW MY NOTEPAD down on the green leather bench of the House of Commons press gallery in disgust. I had arrived way too early for Prime Minister's Questions. But, like a condemned man shouting at the executioner to bloody get on with it, I just wanted the whole event to be over with. I flopped down onto the bench, sending my notepad somersaulting into the air and onto the floor. The long, padded benches in the House, including the one in the press gallery, had been designed by a proper useless knobber. Every time you sat down, it sent a wave of air billowing along the length of them. I picked up my notepad and put it on the narrow benchtop desk that reporters had been writing at for nearly two centuries.

The press gallery sits high above the heads of the MPs, up in the rafters with the bats, the cobwebs, and the ghost of Margaret Thatcher. David Cameron, when he was prime minister, once said the Palace of Westminster reminded him of school, which tells you everything you need to know both about him and about what's wrong with this place. My school had to close the playground because they found asbestos in the sandpit and had no money to remove it. Cameron's school looked like Hogwarts. There was a stink of privilege on a good two-thirds of the MPs. On the other hand, the leader of the opposition was a single mother from Stockport with a mouth like a dockworker and a right hook to match, so there were at least a few top sorts knocking around who understood real people.

The hum of activity in the House of Commons was starting to grow. Members were finding their places ahead of the prime minister's arrival. The leader of the opposition had taken her seat. I scanned the government front bench. Bob Wynn-Jones, the energy secretary—very much the man of the hour—was nowhere to be seen. If he was smart, he was making himself scarce. My phone vibrated.

Davinder has renamed your group Otter Rewilding.

Our group chat had been called "The Brent Boys" for months, mostly on account of us all living in the London Borough of Brent. But, also, because one of Petey's one-night stands had mistaken their exchange of body fluids for a commercial transaction and had left £200 on the bedside table on his way out the door. That led to both Petey and Jumaane seriously considering trying their hands (and the rest of themselves) at sex work. The dots danced on my screen until a message flashed up.

Davinder: *Otters of Brent, we must rewild. You are hereby summoned to a boys' night out this Friday.*

The messages began to flow into the chat.

Petey Boy: *Gassed for it!!!*

Jumaane: *Yaaaaaassssss! Agenda?*

Davinder: *Drag at the Duncan then Hades for dancing?*

Stavros: *Can we legally call ourselves otters when Sunny doesn't have a single hair on his chest and you've invited Jumaane, who is bald from the eyebrows down?*

Jumaane: *Rude.*

Davinder: *You're the one with the law degree, Stav. You tell us.*

Stavros: *Jumanji, I'm concerned you might have violated the Trades Descriptions Act 1968. For legal reasons, exactly how bald is your bussy?*

Jumaane: *No one likes finding hair in their food, Stavros.*

Petey Boy: *Mad disagree! A hairy bum is bare peng, Jumanji.*

Petey, for some reason unbeknown to any of us, sometimes liked to talk like a proper London roadman. He grew up in a detached house in middle-class Pinner and worked as a producer at ITV, but something short-circuited in his brain when he moved into a share house in Stonebridge. He was like one of those people who woke up from a head injury to find they suddenly drawled their vowels like a heavily intoxicated Texan.

Davinder: *This is not merely a social gathering. Our first order of business is finding everyone a husband!*

Dav was the only one of the five of us who actually *had* a boyfriend. He had been with Nick, a radio DJ, since the second year of uni. Apparently, this meant he had a lot of time to dedicate to finding boyfriends for the rest of us.

Sunny: *Does Nick know you're looking to upgrade?*

Davinder: *Not a husband for me, husbands for you loveless saddos.*

Stavros: *Give Nick my number anyway. Nick is hot.*

Petey Boy: *Def. Nick is FIT!*

Nick: *Nick is here, by the way.*

I was just typing my own appreciation for the hotness of my best friend's boyfriend when some absolute knobber plonked themselves down heavily on the bench beside me. The impact sent a burst of air rippling through the leather padding, lifting my bum several inches off the seat. The shock of it loosened my grip on my phone, sending it flying out of my hands. My phone arced through the air and over the carved wooden barrier and went sailing down into the chamber. It was one of those moments where time slowed down, yet I could not react quickly enough to avoid disaster—like those dreams where you're trying to run but your legs are leaden and you can't move, even though Piers Morgan is right behind you.

"No, no, no, no, *no!*" I said, too loudly. I jumped to my feet and looked down in time to see my phone slap hard against the besuited and athletic chest of Vladimir Popov—the government chief whip and a notorious sadomasochist. I was a dead man walking. Popov looked down at my phone, now on the ground. It was in one piece, but that was little comfort. The chief whip's head turned skywards. His steely gaze locked onto me.

"Sorry!" I mouthed, my hands clutching the sides of my face in a gesture of supplication and apology that suggested if he wanted me to snap my own neck right now, I'd be happy to do so. Popov bent down and picked up my phone. The screen, I noticed, was still unlocked. Popov began scrolling through the messages.

"Oh, that's not good," a voice said beside me, as if reading my mind. I turned. In my panic, I hadn't even checked to see who it was who had just ruined my life. I was greeted by a disobedient mop of dark curls. It was that excitable puppet off the telly. It was Ludo Boche. This overprivileged bellend was haunting my day like the Ghost of Journalism Past. He'd already ruined my morning twice, and now he'd returned to have a crack at my afternoon.

"I wouldn't want old VladPop reading my DMs," Ludo added. "Nothing too saucy in there, I hope? His dirt file is so big he *literally* keeps it on its own server."

I hate people who use *literally* when they mean *metaphorically*. Red flag. I returned my gaze to the cold-hearted political killer who was currently reading whatever banter Dav, Nick, Stav, Jumaane, and Petey were enjoying. I shuddered at the thought. We had just been talking about Jumaane's waxed arsehole. As he scrolled, Popov's shoulders bounced up and down in what I guessed was amusement. I could hear the (presumably metaphorical) dirt file server whirring into action. Could he really just *do* this? Was there no way to stop him reading my private group chat?

"He's typing," Ludo said. Holy crap, he was right.

"This is all your fault," I said.

"My fault?" Ludo turned to me, pushed his round-framed glasses up onto his nose, and swept his curly fringe back with his hand. "How's this my fault?"

"How is this *not* your fault?"

"All I did was sit down."

"You didn't. You threw yourself down like a sack of potatoes and turned the rest of us into a game of press gallery whack-a-mole."

"No one told me the seat was booby-trapped!" His arms entered the electrocuted-puppet mode I recognised from *Wake Up Britain*.

"Why didn't you use your brain?" I said, somewhat unfairly.

"Why didn't you hold on to your phone tighter?" he said, somewhat fairly. I didn't really have an answer to that.

"Look, I'm sorry!" he said, saving me from a fight I wanted to have but couldn't feasibly win. "It's my first time here. I'm Ludovic Boche. From the *Sentinel*. I'm new."

He held out his hand, a bit gingerly, as if I might take the opportunity to pull his arm right out of the socket or fling him bodily into the chamber. I looked at his hand, considering whether to shake it or wave my hand over it to see if I could find the strings. When I shook it, his hand was soft but the grip was firm. His skin was olive against my pale hand. I lifted my gaze to meet his and lost myself in his eyes for a moment. They were a vivid blue. Deep like ink, but sparkly like sapphires.

"Sunny Miller," I said, suddenly aware I'd been shaking his hand for an uncomfortably long time without saying anything. "The *Bulletin*," I added.

"Oh, the *Bulletin*..." he said. I could see on his face he was trawling his brain for something nice to say about the paper but coming up short. "Nice phone hacking" wouldn't really cut it. Although it would be accurate.

"Yes," I said, letting my hand slide out of his. "And before you ask, no. I can't get you the phone number of yesterday's page-three girl."

"Shame," he said. "What about the number of the bloke with the big balls on page five?"

I laughed. I couldn't help myself. Then I was proper annoyed with myself for laughing. This bellend had ruined my day three times now. Still, it seemed wise to be charitable. In an industry as small as the print media, it was *never* a good idea to make enemies of another reporter. Careers took people in all kinds of directions, and you never knew when someone might become your colleague, your boss, or your key to promotion. It was another reason why it was also a terrible idea to sleep with any of them.

"Congratulations on your big scoop," I said. It hurt to say it.

Ludo smiled and thanked me. Several other journos plonked themselves down onto the bench, taking their places for PMQs. I nodded hello to those I knew. Ludo introduced himself to those he didn't. As he leant across to shake hands along the row of reporters, I found myself staring at his arse. For a skinny lad, it was Instagrammably *phat*. I had to force myself to look away before my name got added to some kind of list of people they warn new staffers about.

The atmosphere in the House had changed. The prime minister had entered the chamber and taken his seat. The speaker rose to make an announcement, and the volume settled to a low, respectful murmur. I looked down at Popov, who craned his neck around to catch sight of me. He made a series of hand signals that I took to mean "Meet me in the lobby outside the chamber after PMQs." I sensed there was going to be a high price for this little accident. I nodded at the chief whip and sat back down.

Ludo was already hunched over his notepad, one hand jotting something down in the laziest shorthand I'd ever seen, the other trying to sweep his disobedient hair behind his ear. His Adam's apple bobbed up and down. The muscles of his jawline tightened and relaxed. He had a small constellation of moles on his neck and cheek. Proper sexy.

The leader of the opposition got to her feet to ask the first question. I put the nib of my pen against the fresh white page of my notepad.

"Was the prime minister aware of plans to build a nuclear power plant at Newton Bardon in Leicestershire?" she asked. "When did he become aware of the plans, and when was he planning to tell the rest of us?"

The government benches burst into sham outrage, and opposition MPs bellowed cries of "shame." The great pantomime of democracy had begun. The opposition leader had asked the big question of the day, and everyone wanted to hear the answer.

***

As PMQs DRAGGED ON and question after question hinged on what the opposition was now calling the "grubby backroom deal" to build a new nuclear power plant in my hometown, the shine on Ludo's pretty boy looks tarnished. I started to get angry. This story could have been my big break. It had genuine national significance—something to get me noticed up and down Fleet Street. Something, at the very least, to get JT off my back. I couldn't believe none of my contacts back home had tipped me off. If I couldn't land an exclusive like this one, maybe JT was right. It also proper pissed me off that an old friend of Ludo's father, or someone who used to bugger him senseless in the rowing shed at Eton, had more than likely dropped the story to him. This gold-gilded whalluper was living *my* dream, and it had all been handed to him on a plate. I had plenty of good reasons to hate him. It was going to take much more than an adorable, mutinous boy band fringe and eyes you could drown in to convince me otherwise.

6

LUDO

IT WAS THE MOST important day of my professional life so far, and here I was, covering my first-ever PMQs. Jolly thrilling! I should have been focused on taking down every word of the debate, jotting observations, and conjuring witticisms to make my sketch wazz-your-pants funny. But I couldn't take my eyes off him. I'd never seen Sunny Miller so up close before. I'd seen his photo in the *Bulletin*, obviously, so I knew he was the copper-topped fellow you sometimes saw in the background of press conferences or interviews in the parliamentary lobby. His bright-red hair marked his location like a beacon, which must have been terribly handy for tracking him in a crowd but far less convenient for him if he wanted to disappear into a corner for a private chat with a source. But what you couldn't tell from those grainy images, what I didn't know until I was sitting beside him, was that Miller had the most heavily freckled skin I had ever seen. As I sat in the press gallery, legs jittery with nerves, making notes in my shaky shorthand, I kept sneaking glances at him. He didn't just have the usual small galaxy of freckles, shining out across his nose and cheeks; he had a whole jolly universe of freckles peppering the expanse of his face.

From the top of his forehead to the neckline of his shirt collar, Miller's pale and milky skin was dusted with flecks of cinnamon and ginger and rust. I had never seen anything so unutterably beautiful in my entire life. Miller was stunning. What's more, I'd made him laugh. A cute boy had *genuinely* laughed at something funny I'd said.

As the main business of PMQs wrapped up and the prime minister was answering time-wasting questions from backbenchers about disabled poodle insurance and hostel accommodation for tiddlywinks addicts, Miller stood to leave. I scrambled to gather my things and chased him along the bench, climbing over the rest of press gallery to keep up with him. He darted out the door and down the hall like a spaniel after a duck. He was just about to start down the stairs when I reached him. I tapped him on the shoulder to get his attention, but as he turned, I tripped over a loose bit of carpet, fell to my knees, and smacked my face into his crotch. He reached out and grabbed my arm, pulling me back onto my feet.

"Honestly, mate, you are the clumsiest person I have ever met," he said.

"You have absolutely no idea." He was lucky I hadn't vomited on him yet. I pushed my glasses back onto my face. I felt intolerably dishevelled and, suddenly, couldn't think of a thing to say. I just stared at him, mesmerised by his eyes, which were a brilliant amber green, the same colour as the ostentatiously oversized jewel on my grandmother's peridot ring. My heart raced.

"Can I help you, mate?" he said.

"I'm... lost," I said. I wasn't. The *Sentinel*'s parliamentary bureau was up this flight of stairs and down the far end of the corridor. That was never going to fly, so I ad-libbed. "I'm looking for... coffee."

"Coffee?"

"Yes. I thought you might know where the best coffee is around here." If I were a more confident chap, this was the point where I'd have asked him if he wanted to join me. In this parallel universe, he would have smiled and said "I'd love to," and then we would have chatted and laughed together on the way to find the aforementioned coffee. He would have found me amusing, and I would have found him charming. I would have apologised again for the thing with the phone and the thing with my face in his crotch, and he'd have said don't mention it, and then he'd have asked if I was doing anything later that night. I'd have said, "I am now," and then I'd have gone home and Veeted my freckle in readiness for the first night of the rest of my life. But I am not, alas, a more confident man.

"No idea, mate. Try Portcullis House," he said. "Scuse me. I have to go and extract my phone from a hostile KGB operative."

So, *not* forgiven, then. Miller disappeared down the stairs. I went in the opposite direction, feeling terribly deflated. I turned my mind to the sketch I needed to write. I was almost at the bureau when I heard someone call my name down the corridor.

"Boche!" It ricocheted down the corridor. I knew exactly who it was. I'd been hearing that voice bellow my name down corridors for most of my life. Torsten Beaumont-Flattery was now a special adviser to Environment Secretary Jemima Carstairs but, once upon a time, he had been the head boy and rugby captain of my school. He was tall, handsome, and built like a brick shithouse. He'd lost none of that athleticism since our days at Petersham College. He jogged up the hallway towards me in a grey woollen suit that was pornographically small on a man so impossibly large. The strength of the stitching was a credit to his tailor.

"Can I talk to you for a minute?"

Torsten corralled me into a small meeting room lined with old leather-bound volumes of Hansard, the parliamentary minutes, and closed the door. I stood on a threadbare patch of carpet in the middle of the room. It smelt of rat urine and that special kind of damp that comes with Grade I heritage listing. Torsten perched on the edge of the wooden desk.

"Feels just like school," I observed.

"Congratulations on your big scoop today," he said. He spread his legs wide, unfolding in the way that men with impossibly long legs unfold whenever they have a few square metres of space. If anyone entered the room now, it would look like I was standing between his legs, which would be jolly hard to explain to HR. But as Parliament famously didn't have any HR and I quite enjoyed the proximity, I wasn't going to complain.

Torsten leant back on the desk, stretching the fabric of his shirt across his preposterously thick chest. It was a very big dick energy tableau. In fact, his dick could not have been more at the centre of the room if he'd whipped it out, put a wig on it, and called it Your Honour.

"Thank you for trusting me with the story," I said.

He shrugged, as if mystified by my statement.

"No idea what you're talking about, Boche." He flicked his teeth with his tongue.

Torsten knew exactly what I was talking about. He was the source who'd given me the documents that detailed the nuclear power plant plan. He'd also specifically told me it was terribly important no one knew it had come from him and, specifically, to keep his minister's name a million miles away from the story. I now realised this instruction meant I couldn't even mention him to him, which meant playing silly games like this. Plausible deniability and all that.

"Your story has caused quite a fuss over at Energy. I hear old Bob Wynn-Jones is on the ropes."

Torsten let his knees swing in and out, making his thighs bounce. He knew exactly what he was doing. It looked like he'd convinced someone at the Waitrose deli counter to vacuum seal his cock and thighs into an Ermenegildo Zegna suit. Professionally speaking, this was a problematic flex. But then, we weren't normal colleagues. Torsten Beaumont-Flattery had been playing this game with me for years. He was the college heart-throb. The star of many, *many* teenage wanks. He was my first crush. (Unrequited, obviously, as if I need to clarify that fact. That's the trouble with straight boys these days. Once upon a time they used to beat us up for being gay. Nowadays, they queerbait us into subscribing to their OnlyFans. Torsten was my own personal live-action version of that transaction.)

"How long have you been at the *Sentinel* now?" Torsten asked.

"Two months."

"Two months and you might have already caused your first cabinet reshuffle. Very impressive, Boche."

"Thank you."

I swallowed, unsure what was coming next. Torsten ran a hand through his hair, then let it rest on the vast, rolling expanse of his inner thigh. We were at school again. I was the younger me—the skinny, campy theatre kid—standing in front of the younger Torsten—the handsome athlete who collected virginities like Pokémon. This was a jolly unhealthy level of power for a political aide to have over me. This could become a problem, professionally.

"Is that all you wanted to see me about?" I asked.

Torsten jumped up from the desk and clapped his hands together.

"Absolutely not," he said, towering over me. His eyes lit up. "I've got something else for you. I can't give it to you exclusively, but it's big, and I think you'll love it."

"You sound like a GayHoller profile."

"A what?"

"Never mind." A thought crept into the back of my mind. Did Sunny Miller have a GayHoller profile? I made a mental note to check. "What have you got for me, Beaumont?"

7

SUNNY

I SAT OUTSIDE THE chief whip's office for what could have been several days. It felt like being sent to the headmaster. When, finally, the terrifyingly triangular form of Vladimir Popov arrived to reunite me with my phone, he looked proper chuffed with himself, considering his government had just had a truly terrible day at PMQs. The prime minister had been forced to publicly state his support for Energy Secretary Bob Wynn-Jones, and that was the political equivalent of pulling the pin out of a grenade and sitting on it. The grenade, that is. Not the pin. Speaking of grenades, VladPop had my phone in is hand.

"Oh dear, oh dear, oh dear," he said.

"I'm so, *so* sorry," I said, starting my plea bid early.

VladPop made a tutting noise as he inserted his key into his office door.

"It was an accident," I said, fear rising inside me.

"Let's discuss this inside, shall we? Calmly. Like rational adults."

The chief whip swung his door open, and I stepped past him into the room. He smelt of spice, hair gel, and raw masculinity. His office was a Hansard-lined vault with a view out over the Thames and, at a quick count, at least a dozen pieces of taxidermy. The head of a deer. Some kind of ferret under a glass dome. The cat from the *Pet Sematary* films. Someone had been a bit light-fingered on a visit to the Natural History Museum. It was as ghoulish as a dead-Victorian-aunt convention. Which, I imagined, was the point. VladPop sat down and placed my phone on the green leather lining of his vast wooden desk. I perched myself in one of the naughty chairs opposite.

"I like your friends," VladPop said. He smiled broadly, revealing vampiric canine teeth. "Very much." Then he opened my phone and started scrolling.

"Wait, how did you do that without putting in the code?"

He shrugged. "I disabled the code."

"Don't you need the code to disable the code?"

He shrugged again. I was starting to wonder whether Vladimir Popov really *was* a KGB agent rather than the Very Establishment fourth-generation Old Etonian descendent of a Russian aristocrat who'd fled to England a century earlier to escape the Bolsheviks.

"I'll bring you up to speed," he said. "Peter wanted to go a club in Vauxhall instead of Hades, because there's a new place that's wheelchair accessible for Nick."

This was surreal.

"Do you mind if I ask about Nick? Why does he use a chair?"

"An accident," I replied, shocked to find myself answering this question. "On his bike. First year of uni."

"So young. How sad." VladPop was still scrolling through my phone. This was a gross violation of my privacy, but I was powerless to say anything, given that not an hour ago I'd tried to kill him with it.

"Then Stavros suggested going to Maxime's in Soho, and they held a vote and the others agreed, so you're all going there after drag at the Duncan. You were the casting vote, so I voted in favour. I hope that works for you?"

"Er, yes," I said. Apparently, the chief whip was now my personal assistant and diary secretary.

"Good. I thought, well, Sunny doesn't have a boyfriend, and Maxime's seems like the kind of place you might find the kind of chap who'd put a bit of lead in your pencil. Better than some sleazy club, hey? By the way, I'm worried about Peter's fornicatory habits. Does he visit a sexual health clinic regularly? If not, I can get someone from the Department for Health to give him a call. They're very discreet."

This wasn't just surreal. This was Salvador-Dalí-shagging-a-horse-in-Trafalgar-Square-while-Picasso-fingered-Max-Ernst levels of surreal.

"Can I have my phone back now?" I asked.

"In a minute."

"Listen, I'm really very sorry."

"Don't mention it. It's fine. Accidents happen." He put the phone down on the desk in front of him, lining up the edges to make sure it was square with his blotting pad and pen. Everything in here, I now realised, was fastidiously clean and perfectly square with everything else. Even the taxidermy was remarkably free of dust. These were the hallmarks of a serial killer in almost any thriller you cared to watch. Vladimir fixed me with his steely blue eyes and clasped his hands in front of his chest. Here comes the kill, I thought.

"I did want to ask for your help on something, though," he said.

"Help?"

"Well, not so much help. Let's call it a mutually beneficial arrangement."

I swallowed.

"I could be very useful to you. Professionally," he said. "In my line of work, I come across a lot of... information. And sometimes it's, shall we say, in the public interest for that information to find its way into a respected and august newspaper like the *Bulletin*."

He was taking the piss.

"You want to leak stories to me that could bring down your political opponents?"

"*Leak* is such a loaded word. You should be less judgemental in your line of work. How about we say *share*?"

"Fine. You want to *share* stories to me that could bring down your political opponents?"

"Not necessarily bring down," he said. He raised his eyebrows. "Not necessarily my opponents."

This felt grubby but, I confess, it was proper tempting. If I wanted to get noticed by the respectable end of Fleet Street, an alliance with the chief whip might be just the thing to help me do it. It was probably an arrangement exactly like this that got Ludo Boche today's big splash. If the rich end of town was doing it, why the hell shouldn't I?

"Sure," I said. "Only politics, though. Matters of genuine public interest. Corruption. Misappropriation. Tax evasion. Things of real political consequence. I'm not interested in sleaze just because I work for the *Bulletin*."

He smiled. "Then we have an understanding." He picked up my phone and held it out towards me. But as I leant forward to grab it, he pulled it back. "Speaking of things with real political consequences," he said. He leant back in his chair, tapping my phone against his chest. This was torture. "The government is making a series of big climate change announcements up in the Shetland Islands next week. It's all about reaching net zero by 2050 and so on. It's terribly important stuff. Saving transgender badgers and all that rubbish. Right up your alley. It's not an exclusive, we're giving it to everyone, but it *is* big, and I'd like you to cover it."

"I don't get to decide what I cover," I said. "JT decides—"

"You leave JT to me. Just make sure you're on that plane on Monday morning."

Honestly, this sounded great. My deal with the devil was already paying off. I nodded my acceptance. This had gone much better than expected.

"Good," VladPop said. But just as he leant forward to give me back my phone, the distinctive peal of a GayHoller notification rang out.

"Hello, what do we have here?" VladPop said. To my horror, the chief whip's fingers began rifling through my phone's messages once more. Then they stopped, and his eyes widened in a mixture of disbelief and delight, like a teenage boy surprised by naked breasts.

"You have a message from someone called Cabbage98," he said. More dings rattled out of my phone. "Several, in fact." He began reading.

Cabbage98: *Dear Ginger. When you've finished meeting with Scary, can I buy you that coffee? I wanted to say sorry for the whole phone thing.*

My heart raced.

"Scary," Vladimir said. "I'm Scary. Because you're Ginger. Oh, that's clever."

Cabbage98: *This is Ludo, by the way.*

Cabbage98: *Ludo Boche.*

Cabbage98: *From the Sentinel.*

"Gosh, isn't he sweet?" VladPop continued his unwelcome narration.

Cabbage98: *Dammit, I should have said this was Posh. Can we pretend I said this was Posh?*

"Oh, he's ruining it now," VladPop said.

Cabbage98: *Wait. This is Sunny Miller, right?*

Cabbage98: *God, I hope so. If you're not Sunny Miller, please ignore this.*

"I think someone is sweet on you!" Vladimir said, his voice sing-songing. He was beaming. I could feel my face go phone box red, my heart still thudding. A colleague was flirting with me on GayHoller, and I was sharing the moment with the government's political spymaster. I didn't know what to panic about first. VladPop began swiping enthusiastically through Ludo's profile photos.

"He has very good hair, doesn't he?"

Swipe.

"Here's a picture of him with some old queen. Nice scarf, though."

Swipe.

"Wow. For a skinny guy, he has impressive glutes. Have you noticed his glutes?" VladPop turned the phone around to show me the screen. "Do you think he goes to the gym?" Ludo was wearing ballet tights, bum centre stage, looking back over his shoulder at the camera. His athletic rear was in full view, round as two cantaloupes stuffed into a sock. Jesus. Vladimir turned the screen back to himself.

"I wonder how much he squats."

Swipe.

"Can I have my phone back now?" I asked again.

VladPop looked up from the screen, as if I'd broken a spell. He nodded and handed the phone across to me. I snatched it out of his hand.

"Thank you," I said.

"No problem at all. You should invite young Ludo along to the Otter Rewilding party on Friday night."

This was too much. The chief whip's interest in my private life had to stop right here. He was a source. We were *not* friends.

"I don't date other journalists. It's policy."

"Seems a bit short-sighted. You must have so much in common, surely?"

"I have *nothing* in common with Ludo Boche."

Determined to head off the prospect of VladPop adding a Sunny-and-Ludo folder to his (apparently not metaphorical) dirt file, I reopened GayHoller in front of him and made a somewhat theatrical show of blocking Ludo's profile.

8

LUDO

THE OPENING NIGHT OF *Yentl* was a jolly triumph. Rachel Hoffman, the actor who played the eponymous Yeshiva Boy, took three curtain calls. It was a *lot* of clapping. My hands stung like I'd given a hornet a handjob. When the curtain descended for the final time and the applause had petered out, I turned to Uncle Ben and saw that he had been crying.

"We don't have to go to the after-party if you don't feel up to it," I said.

"You must always show your face at the opening night party, dear boy," he said. "Whether the production was so good you want the cast to go right back out there and do it all again, or whether you know in your gut there won't ever be a second night, you go to the party. Theatre is like family. You show up for the good and the bad. The bar mitzvahs, the weddings, the funerals."

"I note you didn't include the bris."

"No one enjoys a bris, dear boy."

"Especially the baby."

"Quite."

Which is how we found ourselves sitting on a pair of very tall stools in the corner of the theatre's very noisy upstairs bar, teetering over an impossibly small table, sipping bubbles from plastic flutes. Not a single element of the whole ensemble had a sensible centre of gravity. The room was bustling with actors, theatre luvvies, and the assorted glitterati of London's West End. With everyone jostling hither and thither, there was a very good chance of at least our drinks going tits up, if not the whole table and us with it. Especially when I was such a notorious Magnet for Calamity (patent pending).

"I've never seen a stage production of *Yentl* before," I said. "I enjoyed the gender fuckery."

"The what, dear boy?"

"Yentl refusing to conform to society's demands. Dressing up like a man so she can study the Talmud, even though she's a woman. Then there's the attraction between Avigdor and Yentl when she's pretending to be man. That's a wonderfully complicated topic for the time, but jolly relevant and probably quite empowering for a post-gender Gen Z audience."

Uncle Ben looked thoughtful.

"You could develop that idea into a truly remarkable review, dear boy. Although I don't think you should call it 'gender fuckery' in the *Sentinel*."

"We absolutely *should* call it 'gender fuckery' in the *Sentinel*. We should be screaming about the gender fuckery from the rooftops. The LGBTQ+ community needs to know this play exists."

"My darling boy, the gays *absolutely* know this play exists. You're too young to remember this, but we invented Barbra Streisand."

"I wish the play had the songs from the movie," I said.

Unannounced, Uncle Ben burst into the opening lines of "The Way He Makes Me Feel." By the time he was singing about burning like a flame, several people around us had joined in. By the time they reached the line about storms and thunder, Uncle Ben was in the middle of a coughing fit, but a good ninety per cent of the room was singing. This is exactly why theatre people are such jolly good fun to be around. Party guests had their arms wrapped around each other's shoulders and were swaying gently from side to side. Rachel Hoffman, who had not been required to sing onstage and had clearly been desperate for the opportunity to show off her vocal chops, produced a microphone from behind the bar and began leading everyone. At the final note of the song, the room burst into uproarious applause. I joined in, clapping enthusiastically and adding my voice to a chorus of "Encore!"

"Did you set that up?" I asked Uncle Ben when the excitement had died down.

"I didn't have to." He lifted his champagne, entreating me to clink health-and-safety-approved plastic drinking vessels with him. "Welcome to the theatre, darling boy."

I knocked back a huge swig of the quickly warming fizz. I felt so *alive*. I felt like I was a part of something terribly special.

"I'm so jealous that this is your life, Uncle Ben."

"Tepid Asda bubbles in plastic? You need to aim higher, dear boy. Shoot for the stars and soon you might find yourself drinking room temperature Tesco's Finest."

"No, *this*!" I said, waving my arms around to indicate everything around us and nearly unbalancing us both in the process. I steadied myself against the wall with a hand and tried to stop the table from rocking with the other. "Going to the theatre every other night of the week. Meeting fun and exciting people. People who are full of joy and energy, creativity and talent."

Uncle Ben sipped from his plastic glass, then placed it carefully back down on the table.

"It has been a good life," he said. "It's true." He gently turned the plastic stem of the champagne flute between his thumb and fingers. He looked suddenly thoughtful. He'd been doing this a lot lately. I reached a hand across the table and found his.

"What the matter?"

"Sometimes I imagine the life I would have lived if the war hadn't come, if we'd stayed in Poland," he said. "It's a sort of grief, I suppose, for a life I didn't live."

"You don't regret your life here, surely?"

"No, dear boy. Of course not. If my mother and father hadn't brought us here, I would never have met you!" He squeezed my hand. "And I would never have met Michael—and Michael was the very best part of my life."

"I think you'd have still found each other," I said.

"That's a lovely thought, dear boy."

I had never met Uncle Ben's partner. He was one of the many thousands of gay men who didn't survive the decade before I was born. I felt a twinge of regret for saying I envied Uncle Ben's life when his life had also contained such unspeakable pain. That Uncle Ben was talking about Michael wasn't unusual, but all the same, there's nothing more jolly worrying than someone in their late eighties speaking wistfully about what-ifs and the good old days. Despite the champagne in front of us and the revelry around us, the atmosphere at our little table was now primed for Uncle Ben to ask if I was free to go casket shopping with him in the morning, or to hand me a list of music he wanted at his memorial service. I raised the last of my warm champagne.

"To Michael," I said. Uncle Ben raised his glass and repeated, "To Michael." We knocked back our drinks, and when we put our empty plastic glasses back down on the table, Uncle Ben's eyes were watering.

"Do you want another one?" I asked, thinking that by going off to fetch one I might give him a quiet moment to gather himself.

"No, thank you, dear boy. I think it's time this old man went home."

"Are you sure? Jonty has invited us to join him at the club if you'd like to go."

"You go," Uncle Ben said, climbing down off his stool. I leapt down from mine to give him a hand and keep him steady. "I'm tired. It's Saturday tomorrow, and I think I'd like to go to temple in the morning."

Though he lived just around the corner from it, Uncle Ben almost never went to the synagogue. Yentl's passion for the Talmud seemed to have worked some kind of magic on his brain. I gave him my arm, and he threaded his hand through it. I stood a little more upright, because I wanted the man on my arm to see how proud I was to be seen with him, to be his date and escort for the evening. It took us a while to get to the cloakroom because at least two dozen people cornered Uncle Ben to say hello, thank him for coming, or praise him for the glowing preview published in that morning's *Sentinel*.

"Shall I see you home?" I asked, as we stood on the pavement outside the theatre while Uncle Ben finished a cheroot.

"No, my sweet-hearted boy. The night is young, and *you* are young." He put out an arm to hail a black cab that was rolling along Shaftesbury Avenue towards us with its light on. The light flicked off. "You must go out and make the most of it. Go kiss boys. Go do gender fuckery."

The electric cab glided silently up to the kerb and stopped. The door opened, and I helped Uncle Ben climb in, supporting him by the elbow.

"Where to, mate?" the cabbie asked. "Stringfellows, is it?"

The idea of Uncle Ben wanting to go to a strip club made me chuckle. Uncle Ben guffawed, before descending into a coughing fit.

"Connaught Square," I told the driver. I clambered out of the cab and waited for the automatic door to close behind me. I was standing on the footpath, waving like a loon, waiting for the cab to drive off, while Uncle Ben talked animatedly about something with the driver. Suddenly, the rear door window lowered, and Uncle Ben's face appeared at it.

"Did you forget something?" I asked.

"Yes," he said. "I meant to say congratulations!"

"What for?"

"Darling boy, you didn't fall off your stool. Or tip the table over. Or fall down the stairs. Or trip over your own shoelaces. You're not even ending the night covered in champagne! We have made progress, my dear little klutz!"

"Don't be cheeky," I said, pleased to see he had cheered a little. I tapped my hand on the roof of the cab. "Stringfellows, please, driver!"

As the cab took off up the street, I could hear Uncle Ben roaring with laughter.

9

SUNny

M Y EYES WERE STILL adjusting from the fluorescent lighting of the lift to the blue and purple LEDs that gave Maxime's its famously chic atmosphere.

"Where's the dance floor, bruv?" Petey asked.

In front of us were dozens of arty types holding even artier cocktails, bodies draped across an assortment of velvety couches and leather armchairs. A huge bar lined with bottles of alcohol of every colour dominated the centre of the room, where waiters dressed in velvety waistcoats were preparing drinks. This was a far cry from the sticky-carpeted Wetherspoons I was used to. London gifts you these little moments sometimes. The Sunny Miller who grew up on the council estate, stealing cans of Captain Morgan from the offie and drinking them on the swings in the playground, used to daydream about downing fancy cocktails with his mates in a place with a doorman and a dress code. The Sunny Miller who grew up on a council estate, the one who practised talking like a BBC newsreader so he didn't sound like a chav, the one who studied hard to get into uni while his classmates smoked pot and played Xbox, would be dead proud of himself for being here. That Sunny Miller would feel like he had arrived. Although both that Sunny Miller and this one would have to stick to cider if he was paying for his own drinks. Maxime's looked proper pricey.

"There *isn't* a dance floor, Petey," Stav said. "This is a members' club. Tonight, we're looking for husbands, not shags. Remember?"

"Speak for yourself," Jumaane said. "I was promised a rewilding, and this ain't wild. I could do you under the Trade Descriptions Act of 1968, mate."

"You had that one coming, Stav," Dav said.

"It's nice to know Jumaane listens when I speak," Stav replied. "It could save his life someday."

"This gaff is bare buki, though, bruv." That was Petey, obviously. Petey got four A-stars on his GCSEs, including one for English, so you can't blame the education system.

"I'm sorry everyone has their trousers on," Stav said. "But this is *the* place to be. It's so hot on social media right now." When he's not being a lawyer, Stav is a relatively successful food and wine blogger, so I tend to trust his judgement when he says these kinds of things.

"I shaved my pussy for tonight, and I haven't eaten anything since midday," Jumaane said. "I'm *getting* laid, and I don't see any talent in here."

"Sorry fam, we're out," Petey said.

With that, the two of them blew the rest of us kisses goodnight, stepped back into the lift, and disappeared into the night to explore whatever delights the sling rooms of Vauxhall could provide.

Maxime's occupied two floors of an old hospital on a side street around the back of Soho. It smelt of oranges, coffee beans, and the overzealous application of Viakal spray. It was a rabbit warren of a place, with little nooks and alcoves designed to disappear into for trysts or quiet conversations. Me, Stav, Dav, and Nick made ourselves comfortable on a mismatch of blue and green velvet cubes clustered around a coffee table. There was a stage in the far corner of the room. With all the brass instruments set up, it looked like we might get a jazz band later. For the moment, the venue was piping inoffensive generic house music through a sound system at a level that was almost but not quite comfortable enough to talk over. We all picked up a drinks menu, and I quickly realised one cocktail or three ciders would shoot through my budget for the night.

"They've got the Gaia's Rest Vlahiko," Stav said excitedly. "It's from this fantastic little vineyard in Epirus. They've been making wine there for at least four thousand years."

A quick scan of the menu revealed the price of the bottle was almost £100. My heart leapt from my chest and into my stomach without so much as a parachute. Dav's eyes boggled. He must have spotted the same thing.

"If it's all the same to you, Aristotle Onassis," Nick growled out in his deep Aberdonian accent, "we poor media types will stick to a pint of Tennent's, or whatever pish they serve here that does the same job without costing roughly the equivalent of a week-long all-inclusive package holiday to Magaluf."

I laughed. A wave of gratitude washed over me. Relief was written across Dav's face. Stav raised his eyebrows.

"Fair enough, boys. But you don't know what you're missing."

"As long as we're not missing our rent payments, I think we'll survive," Nick said.

A woman in a velvet waistcoat stepped up to our little circle and asked us what we'd like to drink.

***

ABOUT AN HOUR LATER, the night was in full swing. The band was playing a lot of old blues and jazz, which gave the place a proper speakeasy vibe. To my delight, the band had thrown in "When You're Good to Mama" from *Chicago*, which had us all bouncing on our pouffes.

Everything was great, except neither Stav nor I had spoken to any boys except Dav and Nick all night.

"What about that guy?" Nick said, pointing over my shoulder. The three of us turned to see a lanky blond guy standing at the bar, shirtsleeves rolled up, face buried in his phone.

"Too tall," Stav said.

I was just about to offer my own critique when an equally tall brunette woman in a red here's-my-yoni power dress slipped her arm into his and they greeted each other like lovers.

"Too straight," I offered.

Someone somewhere in the club laughed like a jackal. It seemed to pierce through every other noise and machete its way into your eardrum. When the laughter came again a minute later, it was right behind us. A conventionally handsome posh knobber with Hollywood teeth and black curly hair stood surrounded by a gaggle of women in cocktail dresses. It looked like he'd bussed in a job lot of models direct from a Kensington tanning salon. They were taking selfies.

"I can't believe it's really you," one of them said.

"My mind is well blown that you're here!" said another.

"I've never met anyone famous before," said a third.

He was all charm and grease.

"Who the bloody hell is that?" Stav asked.

"No idea," Dav said. "But I wish he'd piss off."

"You want me to roll over his foot?" Nick took the brake off his wheel, playfully.

"I can't take this," I said. "I'm going to the loo." I stood, grabbed my phone off the coffee table, and started weaving my way through the crowd towards the toilets. As I circled around the bar, I opened my phone to check GayHoller. There had to be some other homosexuals in this venue somewhere. I wasn't properly looking where I was going when I walked smack bang into someone. Champagne exploded between us upon impact, drenching my white shirt. It looked like a piss party and an incontinence convention.

"I'm so sorry," I said, shaking alcohol off my arms and brushing it off my chest before it soaked into my white shirt. "That's my fault. Let me get you another."

"No, it's my fault. I wasn't looking where I was—"

I glanced up to see who it was that I owed a drink. At the same time, the stranger looked up from his own champagne-soaked jumper and the two almost empty glasses in his hands. My eyes met his, and I recognised their inky sapphire hues instantly.

"—going," Ludo Boche finished.

Well, this was awkward. He pushed his glasses back up onto his nose. They were flecked with champagne, which must have made it hard to see me clearly.

"You should come with a government warning, mate," I said.

10

LUDO

I F THERE IS ANYTHING more jolly well distracting than the unexpected exposure of a nipple, it's the unexpected exposure of *a pair* of nipples. I was trying desperately not to leer at the two perfectly formed pink circles staring back at me from behind Sunny Miller's champagne-soaked shirt. I had refused to let him replace my spilt champagne, declaring the accident my fault. But he said he felt guilty, and I had a question I wanted to ask him, so I pressed my advantage—insisting he join me for a drink by way of apology.

We were sitting in the booth in the Maxime's VIP lounge that had been reserved for my brother, but Jonty was off cavorting with his legion of followers, doing whatever it was that "influencing" entailed. That left Sunny and me alone with a tremendous amount of champagne that, having been uncorked, was simply screaming for someone to drink it. Sunny sat opposite me, looking wet, unimpressed, and like he'd rather be anywhere else in the world. Booze would fix it.

"I shouldn't really have another drink," I said, as I poured Sunny a glass of the bubbly. "I've got class in the morning."

"You still at uni or summink?" he said. Was that an accent of some sort?

"I teach," I said. "I volunteer at a ballet school. Come eight o'clock to-morrow morning I'll be knee-deep in screaming five-year-olds in tutus and very much regretting every single drop of alcohol I've consumed tonight. Think of me while you're enjoying your sleep-in."

I raised my glass and said cheers. Sunny clinked his against mine, and we sipped at the nectar.

"I knew you did ballet," he said. "I didn't realise you taught it."

I seized on this.

"How did you know I do ballet?" I knew full well how Miller knew I did ballet. My GayHoller profile had a photo of me taken backstage at last year's Christmas show. This was the same GayHoller profile Miller appeared to have blocked within seconds of me sending him a message. OK, a few messages. OK, a barrage of messages. But that was accidental, and besides, I thought I'd been terribly cute.

Sunny visibly tensed in his seat as he realised what he'd let slip. I would have enjoyed his discomfort, but the tensing made his chest and his arms twitch under the damp fabric of his thin shirt, which was clinging to his body as tight as a kidnapper's gag. As he tensed, his nipples bounced. Through his shirt I could see that the sexy rash of freckles on his face and neck continued down over his biceps and across his chest.

"I think someone might have shown me a picture," he said. He had the good grace to blush. He was twisting in his seat like one of my ballet kids when they need the loo and have left it almost too late to ask to be excused. I put him out of his misery and apologised for the spray of messages on GayHoller.

"I didn't mean for it to come off quite as intensely as it must have."

He smiled sheepishly, and I waited for him to apologise for blocking me—or at least to explain it. He didn't. I put the bottle of champagne back in the ice bucket. I lifted my glass.

"To otters," I said. I'd crack this bugger one way or another. Sunny froze, his glass in mid-air.

"Have you been talking to Vladimir Popov?"

"No. Why?" I took a small sip. Sunny did the same.

"Never mind," he said.

"You must tell me what happened when you went to see him. You've still got all your fingernails, I see. Was it just a bit of light waterboarding? Or is he holding your mother hostage until your glowing coverage of his political achievements gets him the knighthood he so richly deserves."

"Remarkably close," Sunny said. I waited for more, but no more information was forthcoming. If that's the way he wanted to play it, I'd come right out with what I really wanted to know.

"Why did you block me on GayHoller?"

There was a beat while Sunny considered his answer.

"Not to be funny, but you're the competition, mate," he said. There was that hint of accent again.

"So, we can't be friends?"

"We can be friends. We can't be *more* than friends."

That unexpectedly stung. This risked becoming more embarrassing than I'd thought. It was time to slip into self-preservation mode.

"What made you think I wanted to be more than friends?"

"You messaged me on a world-famous gay hook-up app. Forgive me for thinking your motives were clear."

"My motive *was* clear. I asked if I could buy you coffee to apologise."

He shook his head.

"You went looking to see if I had a profile. Why did you do that if you weren't interested in being more than friends?"

Now I was the one twisting uncomfortably in my seat. How had he done that? Sunny Miller would make an excellent television interviewer. My glasses pinched my nose. I pushed them back up into place. Both

Sunny's intense amber-green eyes and his blush-pink nipples glared at me accusingly.

"Idle curiosity, initially," I said, hoping I sounded convincingly uninterested. "Are you telling me you don't check GayHoller sometimes to see if someone has a profile?"

"If I want to shag them, sure."

This fellow had so many tickets on himself that if he stood outside Wembley Stadium, he'd get arrested for touting.

"You think I want to shag you?" I asked.

Don't look at his nipples. Don't look at his nipples. Don't look at his nipples.

"I don't care whether you want to shag me or not," Sunny said, seeming agitated. "It's not going to happen."

That was brutal.

"Yes, I think we've established that," I said, trying to rise above the crushing rejection by sounding lofty and indifferent. "Just to satisfy my curiosity, may I ask why there's such vehemence in your assertion?"

"Not only are we professional competitors, which makes it a total no-go zone anyway, but we clearly have nothing in common as people."

It felt like an assassination. I could almost understand Sunny's first point, but the second? I felt unfairly judged, and my back was up.

"You know next to nothing about me," I said.

"I know enough," he said.

"Go on, then." I was holding it together, but there was a lump in my throat that risked triggering my sensitive gag reflex. I felt ill.

"All right, then." He swigged his champagne. "You're a rich kid, so you're probably used to getting whatever you want. Like your job, which, chances are, you got because of who your dad is. That's great for you, but it will have squeezed out some poor kid who could have earned that opportunity based on merit and had their life changed forever." Sunny swept a hand over the table, gesturing at the accoutrements upon it. "You're the kind of person who has VIP-lounge access at fancy clubs and drinks expensive champagne, so I'd say you're probably the kind of person who pushes on doors and they just open for you. That's great for you, too, but where I come from most people push on doors their whole lives, and those doors never open. People like you dream of something, the doors open automatically. People like me dream of something, we have to go make it happen for ourselves—all while people like you hold the door closed in front of us."

This jolly well hurt.

"You really have such a low opinion of me?" I couldn't control the tears welling in my eyes. I was upset, but I was also deeply, wildly angry. I set my teeth, searching for the right words, needing to precisely eviscerate Sunny Miller, but my alcohol-fogged brain was falling hopelessly, desperately short. Then, above all the background music and chatter, a familiar laugh bellowed across the club.

"Who *is* that obnoxious bellend?" Sunny said.

Suddenly, I had all the words I needed.

"That's my brother," I said. "That obnoxious bellend paid for the expensive champagne you're drinking. And for the VIP lounge you're sitting in. I'll grant you, his laugh is a bit grating. But let me tell you something. Jonty is doing a lot more to make the world a better place to live than most people, rich or poor. He spends thousands of hours promoting environmental causes for free. Why? Because he believes in them. He's a goodwill ambassador for the Hazel Dormouse Protection Trust—an endangered species, by the way, and a charity which could otherwise only dream of getting the kind of publicity he gets for them with a single Instagram post. Last year he raised two hundred and fifty thousand pounds for the Great Ormond Street children's hospital, doing something I don't quite understand on OnlyFans but which he assures our parents was absolutely *not* pornography, and I for one believe him because the pictures would have leaked by now. OK, so maybe a few doors may open for him here and there because of who he is, but he's using his influence to drive real change—because you know what, you sanctimonious tosspot, whatever you may think of 'people like us,' *that's* the kind of people we are."

To be fair, my little brother *is* a massive bellend, but it's like Uncle Ben said: you turn up for family, good or bad. I rather hoped I'd put Sunny in his place, but rather than look sheepish, he was shaking his head.

"A bit of charity work. That's your defence of yourself? Of the whole corrupt system you belong to, and perpetuate, and benefit from?" He scoffed. "Mate, you're so privileged you don't even know you're privileged."

I'd had enough of Sunny Miller now. He needed bringing down a peg or two. Fortunately, I found the perfect final flourish.

"Privileged enough to know the difference between an otter and a beaver, at least."

There was, unaccountably, no audience on hand to give me a round of applause, so silence fell between us. Sunny's face was now so red it looked like someone had boiled it in a pot.

"I should go," he said.

"Yes, I think you should."

Sunny shuffled his way out of the booth. He stood for a second at the end of the table, tapping a finger against the wood, avoiding eye contact. His shirt had almost completely dried. The distraction of the slender, tightly muscled body under the fabric was gone. It had lost its lustre, anyway. Sunny tapped his fingers a couple more times, as if summoning the courage to speak. He gave me the briefest flash of those peridot eyes. I raised an eyebrow. His courage failed him. He turned on his heels and disappeared through the crowd. I didn't care if I never saw Sunny Miller ever again.

11

SUNNY

NOTIONALLY, SATURDAY MORNINGS ARE for yoga. Jumaane and I had both joined the Gay Men's Yoga Club as part of our ongoing husband hunt, on the promise that performing regular downward dogs gave you a bum as tight as a drum, vee-gutters so sharp they could cut the waistband on your CKs, and pelvic floor muscles strong enough to shoot a billiard ball out of your arsehole and across a crowded bar. Not that I've tried doing that. Someday, maybe. It's good to have goals. But on this particular Saturday morning, an ashram full of swamis could not have convinced me to haul my arse out of bed and travel into central London, even if they promised to help me avoid the Tube by levitating there. My head was proper thumping. My breath smelt like a fox had curled up in my mouth in the night and died there. But, worst of all, my guts were in knots. I had gnawing regret about my fight with Ludo. While it felt good in the moment, it had been a very, very stupid thing to do, and in the cold, hard light of day, I worried the consequences might be long-lasting.

My phone vibrated on the bedside table. Hurricane Stacey was touching down to leave her regular weekly trail of destruction.

"Hiya, Mum." My first words of the day squeaked out of me like a rusty garden gate. I coughed to clear my throat.

"You sound rough, love. Big night?"

"You could say that."

"Well, I hope you were safe."

"Not that kind of big, Mum. Just hung-over."

"You have to be careful, love," Mum said. "I was talking to Angie Skeggs the other day, and her friend Brenda's sister in-law has a nephew who's gay. Well, apparently, he went to something called a 'fisting party' and busted the laggy band in his bumhole and now he has to shit into a bag. It's proper tragic."

"That didn't happen, Mum."

"It did too. Angie told me. He was up the ospiccle for six weeks. He still can't eat solids."

"Angie Skeggs thinks aliens abducted the real Nigel Farage the day after the Brexit vote and QAnon is covering it up. You should get your news from reputable sources."

"OK, love, I'll get all my news from the *Bulletin* from now on."

My mother could be proper shady when she wanted to be. Fifteen years on the till at the local Tesco supermarket being polite to knobheads is the equivalent of a vocational qualification in sarcasm. She also definitely knew what fisting was. She'd been running the local PFLAG since the year after I came out and knew more about the mechanics of homosexuality than I did. This was just her sense of humour.

"Thanks for your support," I said, sucking the dregs from the glass of water on my bedside table.

"Only joking, love. Had anything good in the paper this week?"

"Nothing worth buying it for, Mum. I had a story on Wednesday about the government giving millions of pounds to some otters."

"Otters? That's nice. I'm glad they've got money for the otters," Mum said. "You remember old Shirley Trimble? They've cut her Universal Credit again. That leg of hers is infected now, and she can't get in to see a GP for six weeks. She'll be tickled bloody pink about the otters. When she comes down the food bank on Monday, I'll make sure and tell her."

Apparently, the answer to the question "Who doesn't love otters?" was Stacey Ann Miller. And, possibly, Shirley Trimble. (Confirmation pending.) The sound of bus air brakes outside scraped around the inside of my skull. I shoved a lazy hand under the elastic of my pants and scratched my balls. You could dig for peat down there. I needed a shower.

"Did you have a reason for calling, Mum?" She called every Saturday. By consent. It was just past time in the conversation for me to wrong-foot her. Just for the variety.

"Just wanted to hear your voice, my lovely. Are you sure you're all right? You sound off."

If my mum had a superpower, it was knowing when something wasn't right. When my first boyfriend dumped me, she was on the blower within fifteen minutes to check if I was OK. It was proper spooky. Though I learned later she'd seen him snogging Derek Potts in the Highcross Costa that morning, so she probably knew something was up.

"I got into a proper mardy with some posh bellend in a club last night, that's all."

"Jesus, Sunshine! What have I told you about fighting?" Mum's voice was so sharp I could feel it in my eyes. "You've got to get that temper of yours under control, Sunny. Is anyone hurt? Are you OK?"

"It wasn't a punch-up, Mum. Although I could definitely have taken him. To be fair, a sock puppet armed with a tube of toothpaste could have taken him."

"But no injuries, no hospital, no cops. Just two idiots with more testosterone in their tongues than their bollocks? No harm done."

I wasn't so sure about that. (Also, ew, Mum, gross.) My stomach twisted. Time for a full confession.

"It's complicated," I said. "He's a reporter. For another paper. Where his dad is the editor. A dad who is also one of the most powerful men on Fleet Street. Oh, and he has a mum who is also incredibly senior at the BBC. I think I might have made myself some very powerful enemies. Of the kind that might come back to haunt me."

OK, so it was *almost* a full confession. I didn't say the reporter in question also had piercing blue eyes and a floppy boy band fringe of black curly hair and the juiciest buttocks outside a Brazilian plastic surgeon's outpatient ward. Or that I found him both beautiful and confusing. Or that he kept creeping into my thoughts, even before I tore his family to shreds in a drunken nightclub tirade.

"If it was just about work, won't it all blow over?" Mum asked.

I cringed. "Not really. I got... pretty personal. I kind of attacked his whole family."

"The family that runs the entire UK media?"

"Um, yeah."

Mum sighed. It was more the thoughtful kind of sigh than an exasperated my-son-is-an-idiot sigh. So that was good, at least. I didn't need a lecture.

"You remember when I got into a fight with Denise from Asda in the Five Bells that time?"

"When she threw her drink at Nan and you slammed her tit into her gravy?" How could I forget? The video resurfaced in my Instagram suggested posts at least once a month.

"I'm not proud of it, Sunny."

"It's had eighteen million views, Mum."

"It's not funny." It was, though.

"The point is, Denise and I will always have our differences. It's not just that I'm a Tesco girl and she's an Asda slag. I'm Wickwar Estate through to me bones. That means something. And she's a horse-faced trollop from the Scriggins Estate who can't stop pinching other people's husbands. Or their sons, to be fair. We're never going to see eye to eye."

Does everyone's mother like to dress up old beef as round-the-houses storytelling, or just Stacey Miller?

"But I'll tell you this for free, Sunshine. That Christmas, when I walked up to her in the Bells and said, 'Denise, we need to put this behind us, because I know you've got points on your Tesco Clubcard you ain't used, and I've run out of the Kiss Salon French Acrylics from the Asda beauty aisle,' it was one of the smartest things I ever did. My conscience was finally clear. We let bygones be bygones once and for all."

"You called her a horse-faced trollop a second ago."

"Yeah, but not to her face."

It was time to wind things up. We said our goodbyes, I went for a pee, and I thought about what to do about Ludo Boche. Then I crawled back into bed with two Tesco brand Nurofen and Berocca and opened GayHoller. I scrolled through the pick-and-mix selection of bare torsos and hopeful faces and the "guess which one of the three of us in this photo is me, yes that's right, I'm the minger" profile pics. Eventually, I opened the app's settings and clicked on my blocked accounts. Cabbage98 was at the top of the list. Possibly the stupidest profile name in the history of GayHoller. I clicked on it, almost without thinking. I just wanted to look at his pictures again. I'd never really looked at them properly. I'd only had glimpses when VladPop held them up for me to see. I wanted to study Ludo's face while I thought about how to clean up the proper mess I'd made. And maybe get another look at that arse in ballet tights?

GayHoller had other ideas.

GayHoller HQ: *To view this profile you need to unblock this user.*

It had two buttons: Unblock User or Cancel. I hit Cancel, closed the app, and threw my phone onto the duvet. If I unblocked him, Ludo would know I was thinking about him. That felt like giving up power, like admitting defeat. But I *really* wanted to look at his pics. I slunk down into the bed, put my hands to my face, and rolled some sleep out of my eye. Then I reached for my phone, reopened GayHoller, and unblocked Ludo's account.

12

LUDO

I SAT ON THE bench outside Miss Tuppence's Ballet School, teaching done for the day. My sunglasses were firmly on. In one hand I held a hair-of-the-dog glass of champagne, in the other, my phone. I flicked through GayHoller. It had been a deathly long morning. There had been some pursed lips and hushed comments of disapproval from parents of kids in every age group, from the tots to the teens.

"You're hung-over, Mr Boche," one mother said, holding her hands over her daughter's ears.

"And yet, here I am. Looking fabulous and giving a BAFTA-worthy performance as an upstanding dance educator."

"These children are seven years old."

"And as long as they're not hung-over, I don't see the problem."

In truth, I had done everything I could to *not* be hung-over. When I got home at two, I'd consumed enough electrolytes to reboot a dead Romanian powerlifter. The problem was I'd had a terrible sleep. Try as I might, I had been unable to get my argument with Sunny Miller out of my mind. I still couldn't. As I sat in the meek April sunshine, saccharine fizz tickling my nose, I kept going over and over everything Sunny had said, everything I'd said, trying to play it differently. In some versions, I put the boot in harder, giving him a good verbal kicking. In others, I avoided the fight altogether. I kept my mouth shut. Or I took a different tone, tried a more reasoned argument, talked through the issues like an adult. But I kept landing back at angry, so I resolved to have nothing whatsoever to do with him. I quaffed my bubbles and returned my attention to my phone. That's when I noticed Sunny Miller had unblocked me on GayHoller.

"Well, that's jolly confusing," I muttered.

13

SUNNY

THE GOVERNMENT HAD STUMPED up taxpayers' cash to pay for a charter plane to get the press pack up to Shetland for the week. There were plenty of commercial flights available. Whatever Environment Minister Jemima Carstairs was announcing, she wanted to make sure the media all got there, and she wanted us controlled. I made a note to dig into the expenses for this trip later.

It was a small jet with maybe a dozen reporters on board, including one photographer and one cameraman, who were entrusted with taking photographs and footage for all the different outlets. It's quite common practice to "pool," as it's called, in the media these days. It saves on resources, and most newsrooms are as cash-strapped as a former *Big Brother* contestant who failed to save during the good times and refuses to admit those good times are over. That's not even an analogy. That's literally what has happened to newspapers all over the world.

I was sitting by a window towards the back of the plane, desperately hoping the seat beside me would remain empty. I knew most of the press pack on the plane. I was on friendly terms with them all, but I had some documents I wanted to read without anyone looking over my shoulder. The one person I didn't see on board was Carstairs. But wandering up and down the aisle of the plane like a lost runway model was Torsten Beaumont-Flattery, the minister's special adviser. He's about a hundred and twenty kilos of pure British beef, and like any sane person, if I were ever called upon to give my life in service of my country, I would gladly volunteer to be crushed between Torsten's thighs.

Torsten's enormous bulk appeared in the aisle by my seat, hand thrusting a folder of papers in my direction. "Miller, have you got a press pack yet?" he asked, in that doesn't-everything-I-say-sound-frightfully-reasonable accent that, where I came from, earned you a brick to the teeth.

I took the papers from his hands. "It's got the whole programme for the week, your accommodation info, everyone's contact details, and a few embargoed media releases with the early announcements, so you can get a head start. There'll be more to follow, of course, during the week, as we make more announcements."

Over the PA the woman who was our lone cabin crew member declared the doors were about to close and anyone not coming with us should leave the plane now. Torsten called over to her and asked her to tell the pilot we were still waiting for one more passenger. I looked around and counted only two empty seats—one up the front with Torsten's suit jacket over the back, and the one next to me. Carstairs wasn't on board.

"Is the minister running late?" I asked.

"No, she's had a few important matters come up that she has to attend to in London. She'll come up tomorrow on another flight."

"Are these newsworthy important matters?" I asked, nudging him in hopes of an exclusive.

"I'm not sure, actually," Torsten said. He flicked his teeth with his tongue. If he were a poker player, this would be his tell.

"Do you want to tell me about these 'matters,' or should I write a story about the environment minister sending *two* fuel-guzzling, climate-destroying jets all the way to the Shetland Islands at taxpayers' expense for a PR stunt, when she could have sent one?"

"Now, play fair, Sunny." Torsten pretended to look wounded.

The cabin crew appeared at his shoulder. We were going to be late if we didn't prepare for take-off now, she said. Torsten leant over me, peering out my window. Heat radiated off him. He smelt of citrus and timber. I wanted to lick the vein in his neck.

"It's OK," Torsten said, pointing out the window. "He's coming now."

Running across the tarmac towards the plane, weighed down by a suit-case, a shoulder bag, and, inexplicably, an oversized airport Toblerone, was Ludo Boche.

"Your seatmate is here," Torsten said, smiling. "VladPop did the seating plan. He said you'd want to sit together." He slapped my thigh, in that way that boys-who-do-sports do to other boys-who-do-sports, winked, and disappeared up the aisle.

Oh, for pity's sake. This was a nightmare. The writers of the *Saw* movies could not have created a more horrific scenario. There was a heavy thud and clatter from the front of the aircraft as Ludo hit the deck.

"It's OK. I'm all right."

Ludo, red-faced, glasses askew, and out of breath, picked himself and his bags off the floor. His Toblerone had taken the full force of the landing and was bent almost at right angles. The cabin crew took his luggage for stowing, and Ludo fixed his glasses. Torsten put an arm around him and ruffled his hair. What the hell was that? I was appalled. But also slightly turned on. Then Ludo spun around to look down the plane and saw the only empty seat was the one next to me. He looked like he would rather have been crushed in the plane's landing gears than sit there. He trudged down the aisle and threw himself into the seat without making eye contact with me. This was going to be a long flight. Worse, clearly, we were going to be stuck together for the next week, which made sorting out Friday night's mardy a priority sooner rather than later. But a small plane surrounded by half the British press pack didn't seem like the right time or place. Until then, and perhaps not even then, it was clear I was going to get the silent treatment. It was two hours to Shetland, but it was going to feel much longer. I slunk down into my seat and looked out the window.

***

AN HOUR INTO THE flight, Ludo hadn't looked up from his laptop except to break off pyramids of chocolate. He wore those noise-cancelling headphones that cost normal people an entire week's wages and was watching something on his laptop. I buried my face in my work-purposes-only tablet, trying to read through background documents about Yevgeny Safin, his energy company, and the history of Britain's nuclear energy industry. In reality, I was running my eyes across the same line of text, over and over again. Not reading it. Not taking it in. My mind was busy war-gaming how to approach Ludo.

Ludo, by contrast, did not appear to be having any kind of internal crisis, although how his stomach was handling all that chocolate was beyond me. He was tapping his fingers and bouncing his feet and occasionally, surreptitiously, conducting an invisible orchestra. To say it was distracting would be selling it short. I could not have been more distracted if he were sitting on my lap twisting ringlets in his hair with one hand and wanking me off with the other. It was entirely possible his strategy was to be as annoying as possible during the flight. I was willing to bet that was his level of petty.

I was doing my best to ignore him when suddenly, *jazz hands*. This was followed by a sheepish sideways glance towards me. Ludo sat on his hands and slunk down in his chair. Were accidental jazz hands even possible? Was this a nervous twitch? I was as curious as a cat with MI5 clearance and nine lives left to burn. When the cabin crew asked Ludo if he wanted a cup of tea, I peered over to see what he was watching. *Hamilton.* He was watching the stage production of the single best musical ever written. A glorious theatrical smoothie of history, politics, and hip-hop. A wet dream of a production for a political junkie like me. Dav, Nick, and I had gone to see it at the Victoria Palace when I first moved down to London. I'd spent my first pay cheque on the ticket. We were all eating pot noodles for a month, but it was worth every penny.

I pulled my phone out of my pocket, opened Spotify, and put on the original Broadway cast recording of the show. I skipped forward through the tracks, trying to get to the same part Ludo was watching. Twenty minutes later, Ludo's hands were loose and tapping again, the cast were singing about "the room where it happened," and I'd just done my own accidental jazz hands.

Ludo hit the space bar on his laptop, pausing the film. He raised his hands to his ears and slowly removed his headphones. Busted. I pulled on my headphone cables, letting the earbuds fall to my lap. Our eyes met for the first time since Ludo had stumbled onto the plane. Ludo's were a stormy blue ocean behind his glasses. There was disdain on his face. A small twitch caught the top of his left cheek. His eyes narrowed.

"Are you mocking me?"

"What? No!" I was on the back foot. "Of course not."

"Then what was *this*?"

Jazz hands.

I didn't know what to say. I plucked an earbud out of my lap and gingerly held it up to Ludo's ear. His eyebrows raised as he recognised the music. He smirked. It wasn't a smile; his lips were pursed, and it didn't light up his face or make his eyes sparkle. It still visibly carried contempt. But then he took the bud from my hand, our fingers brushing lightly, and held it against his ear, as if he were double-checking the evidence. Ludo handed it back, raised his eyebrows, and turned his attention to his laptop. Now seemed like a good time to make peace with him—especially if I wanted to stay sane in the short term.

"I..."

But Ludo's headphones were back on his head before I could get any further.

14

LUDO

WHY DID THE UNIVERSE keep throwing me into the path of this copper-topped pillock? What had I done to deserve being stuck on a remote island with Sunny Miller? A chap with such an enormous chip on his shoulder that he seriously risked spending all week being dive-bombed by seagulls. The fact that he hadn't even pretended to like me to see what he could get out of my family connections was, frankly, the only thing Sunny had going in his favour. OK, that and the fact he looked like a young, freckled Damian Lewis. I had spent the entire flight up trying to concentrate on *Hamilton* but wanting desperately to ask him why, after the scene he'd caused at Maxime's, he had suddenly unblocked me on GayHoller. When he revealed he was also listening to *Hamilton*, I had nearly relented and asked him. But whatever his reasoning, I didn't want his answer tempered by the possibility people might overhear, so I left it.

We hit the ground running in Shetland. The plane touched down at Sumburgh Airport at half ten, and by eleven the whole press pack was lying on our bellies in the grass on a windy clifftop overlooking the North

Sea, jaws on the floor, staring through binoculars at a colony of fabulous seabirds with brightly coloured beaks.

"He looks like the dude on the Froot Loops packet," said Rafiq Farouq, the reporter from the *Guardian*. He and I had buddied up together for our "Welcome to Shetland activity," birdwatching, which apparently had something to do with new conservation funding.

"You're thinking of Toucan Sam," I said. "These chaps are puffins."

"Sam isn't a puffin?"

"I'm pretty sure he identifies as a toucan."

The sea-chilled wind pummelled our faces, making it hard to hold the binoculars steady against my glasses. The coastal air smelt like salt, damp grass, and a parrot cage left too long between cleanings. On a jagged clifftop across a short stretch of silvery sea, a squat white lighthouse stood amid a cluster of other small buildings. Overhead, what seemed like a hundred different species of seabirds circled, squawked, and defecated indiscriminately. The only other sounds we could hear were the sea rhythmically slapping against the cliffs beneath us and the strange growling calls of the puffins.

"They sound like they're pretending to ride motorbikes," Rafiq said. Which was a perfectly accurate summary, if you discounted the noises that definitely sounded like farts.

Our guide from the Shetland Birdlife Trust, Marcia, crept up alongside us on her belly, like an extremely earnest Tough Mudder contestant.

"Remarkable, aren't they?" she said, in the hushed tones seven decades of David Attenborough on our TVs has taught us to use around wildlife. "It's still early in the season. Over the next few weeks about sixty thousand puffin couples will land on Shetland to dig their burrows and lay their eggs."

Cue appreciative noises from Rafiq and me.

"Who are all these other dudes?" Rafiq asked, pointing at the screeching, circling chaos of feathers above us. Marcia, clearly delighted to be able to show off her expertise, began pointing out individual birds.

"That's a guillemot," she said. "He's a razorbill. Those are fulmars. That's a kittiwake. And that one there, the one with the bright yellow on the beak, that's a shag."

"A what?" Rafiq said.

"A shag," Marcia repeated patiently. Marcia, according to her bio in the press pack, had dedicated her entire adult life to studying the birds of Shetland. Marcia must have already heard every joke Rafiq was about to make.

"Is he a good shag then?" Rafiq asked.

"That one's a female, so no. But she's a very healthy specimen."

"Is she looking for a good shag, then?"

"Actually, yes. That's exactly why she's here. See the bird behind her? That's her partner. They're a pair, and they've come here to breed."

"She wants kids? Get out while you can, bruv!"

Marcia politely laughed, then reverse Tough Muddered her way back from the cliff towards the relative sanity of almost any other group of people. It was a testament to her fortitude that she Tough Muddered backwards and not forwards over the cliff to her death.

"Have you ever actually been outside of London before, Rafiq?" I asked.

"You gotta have a laugh, innit?"

I turned my binoculars along the clifftop towards the other reporters. Sunny had paired up with Brody O'Sullivan from the *Sun*, and the two of them were in fits of laughter about something. The probability of shags being involved was, let's be honest, high. The sun shone through Miller's wind-ruffled hair, making it dance like flames of gold and copper. So much beauty all around us—the cliffs, the birds, the sea—yet I found myself staring at Sunny Miller, wanting to understand why he had been so beastly to me, then unblocked me on GayHoller.

"Oh, get in, son!" Rafiq yelled, right in my ear. I turned my gaze to see what Rafiq was so excited about and saw that our shags were, in fact, shagging.

***

WE HAD TWO MORE jolly enjoyable episodes of wildlife voyeurism through the afternoon, one with seals and one with otters, and then what was meant to be a press conference about the government funding protection for all the endangered species we'd spent the day hanging out with. But with no minister around, Torsten fielded our questions. It didn't matter. The whole thing was mostly a reannouncement of Sunny's otters-are-the-new-beavers story from the previous week.

That evening, we wrote our stories in a cosy restaurant that had been booked out for the press group. The sun setting over the North Sea had been spectacular, hued in pinks and oranges—like God was adding a slice of grapefruit to the inky-blue cocktail of the sea. Now, we were back on the coach and heading to our accommodation for the week.

"To get a real Shetland experience, we thought rather than put you all in the same hotel, we'd put you up in some of the island's famous bed and breakfasts," Torsten announced. He was standing at the front of the coach wearing a headset that piped his voice through the speakers. "The coach will pick you up just after nine tomorrow. Be breakfasted and ready and waiting outside your accommodation. Make sure you dress warm. And you will *need* a weatherproof jacket. We've got something rather special lined up for you."

The bus stopped outside a B & B, and Torsten called out the names of the four reporters who were staying there for the night. It was Annabelle Statham-Drew from the BBC and Brody from the *Sun*, and Astrid and Terry, the photographer and cameraman. A minute down the road, the bus stopped again, and two more reporters got off. Another minute down the road, two more jumped off.

"OK, stop four. The Otter's Den," Torsten said. "Miller. Boche. This is you."

The last thing I needed was to spend a week cooped up in the same hostelry as Sunny. This was some top-shelf bastardry. Sunny picked up his shoulder bag, walked past me down the aisle, and got off the bus without making eye contact. I collected my things and, when I reached the front of the coach, quietly asked Torsten if it was possible to swap with somebody else. He looked out the open door towards Sunny and back to me, then switched off his microphone.

"Afraid not, Boche," he said. "The driver dropped off everyone's luggage this afternoon. It's waiting for you in your room already. Your hosts are expecting you. Off you pop."

He ruffled my hair like I was his kid brother. My options were to either make a scene—thereby embarrassing myself in front of everyone in the bus, making myself and my relationship with Sunny the subject of gossip for the rest of the trip, and, worst of all, losing the moral high ground—or suck it up and try to make the best of it. I decided to be British about it. Stiff upper lip. Just because we were staying in the same B & B, it didn't mean we had to spend any time with each other. We were sharing a roof, not a room. Christ, we weren't jolly well sharing a room, were we?

The answer to that question came about five minutes later, when the proprietor of the Otter's Den B & B, the remarkable Mrs Gallacher, showed us to our rooms. Plural. They were separate but directly opposite each other. Sunny and I stood in our respective bedroom doorways as Mrs Gallacher ran us through some house admin. She was a grey-haired, bespectacled woman of the tweedy-tartany sort you meet at riding stables and the Chelsea Flower Show, but with one notable exception.

"What would you boys like for your fucking breakfast?" Mrs Gallacher said with a beaming smile. She had a broad Scots brogue I imagined must be local and a taste for profanity that was decidedly Anglo-Saxon. "Cooked or continental? Tea or coffee? Fucking orange juice, perhaps?"

"Is the orange juice freshly squeezed?" I ventured.

"Is it freshly fucking…?" She trailed off in apparent disbelief. "You're in Shetland, not fucking Seville. It comes out of a box from Tesco. Will that do for you, deary?"

Was she doing this deliberately? Was this experiential theatre? I was entranced. I nodded my consent, desperately wanting the exchange to be over so I could load up Tripadvisor and read the reviews for this place. Sunny, eyes full of wonder, was studying the ceiling like he was looking for hidden cameras.

"The bathroom is the door on the left, up the end of the hall, dearies," she said. "Your towels are on your beds. The Wi-Fi code is on the fucking bedside table. You boys need anything else?"

I said no and thanked her. Sunny, apparently too stunned to form words, shook his head and smiled.

"You're more than welcome to come watch TV in the front room with his lairdship and me, should you wish," she said. "Although there's fuck all on, and we had onions for dinner, which gives us both the kind of gas that melts the curtains. Even the cat has fucked off. But you'd be very welcome, dearies. I could dig you out an N95 mask if it's an issue."

"Tempting. But not for me, Mrs Gallacher," I said. "I think I'll turn in."

"Me too," Sunny said. "Goodnight, Mrs Gallacher."

"Fucking nighty-bye, then, boys. Sleep well."

Mrs Gallacher turned and shuffled up the hall, presumably crop-dusting the corridor with her flatulence as she went. Sunny looked like he'd just won the EuroMillions.

"I love her," he said.

"Do you think the tourist board knows about her?"

"Is it deliberate? Do you think she knows she's doing it?"

"Perhaps it's Tourette's?"

"It's glorious. She's like Mrs Doubtfire, if Mrs Doubtfire were in *Trainspotting*."

I laughed, despite myself.

15

SUNNY

WHEN LUDO BOCHE LAUGHS, his face proper lights up. He has fat, chipmunky cheeks, and they make his eyes squint and his nose crinkle, which makes his glasses lift off his nose. That seems to trigger his nervous twitch, and he pushes his glasses back up onto his face and fixes his hair.

"Can we talk?" I said.

We were standing in the doorways to our respective rooms. I had the sense Ludo had been avoiding me all day—which had at least given me time to build up the courage to ask him to chat. But if I didn't seize the opportunity now, it would drag into another day—which might make things uncomfortable over our eggs and fucking orange juice in the morning. The smile fell from Ludo's face. He stiffened.

"Sure," he said. "You better come in."

I followed him the few short steps into his room. The stone walls had been plastered and whitewashed. It was decorated with the kind of tat you find in seaside gift shops. There were little wooden seagulls, hand-painted pictures of fishing boats, and, inexplicably, a movie poster for *The Dukes of Hazzard* (rated an optimistic fourteen per cent on Rotten Tomatoes). Ludo sat down on the edge of the bedspread. I perched myself beside him. For all I had rehearsed this moment throughout the day, now that the time had come, my body was going into full fight-or-flight mode. My veins were more adrenaline than blood. I put my hands between my knees to stop them shivering and looked up to meet Ludo's stormy blue eyes.

"I was a bit out of line the other night," I said. Ludo's face didn't move. He was waiting for more. Which was fine. I could go further. "I was rude to you. I was rude about your family. I made a lot of sweeping generalisations, and I was a proper judgemental prick. If you're able to forgive me, I'd like to put this behind us." (You horse-faced trollop.)

It was the most complete apology I could muster without a court order and lawyers on standby to hold me to account for every microaggression I'd thrown Ludo's way at Maxime's. Short of uttering the word *sorry*, that is.

"Is that your apology?" he said. "Because it doesn't sound like you're sorry. I see no evidence of a Damascene conversion. I doubt you've changed your opinion about 'people like me' in the course of a weekend. You meant what you said—and, what's more, you still believe it."

I was not off the hook yet.

"I recycled some old class war clichés and stereotypes and packaged them up as targeted insults," I said. "They really weren't targeted at all. I don't know anything about you and your family beyond who your parents are. It was unfair, and I'm sorry."

There. I'd said it. With any luck, I'd saved my career. Ludo took a deep breath and set his jaw. Apparently, we weren't done. I could tell he'd also been rehearsing what he wanted to say and he was determined to say it.

"I want you to know that I wasn't just *handed* my job. I graduated with a first from the LSE. I was the top student in my class. I aced the *Sentinel*'s cadetship exam, but I also had job offers from the BBC, the *Telegraph*, and the *Spectator*. I chose the *Sentinel* because it meant, every day, I got to work alongside the person I admire, respect, and love more than anyone in the world—to see up close how he does what he does. Yes, my father is the paper's editor, but I *earned* my place there on merit."

I nodded. But I couldn't let him get away with that. I swallowed, summoning a little courage as I risked ringing the bell on the start of round two.

"I understand that." My nerves were making my accent slide back, which acted like a flashing neon sign pointing out our class difference. "But as much as you like to believe you got all those offers on merit, having the name Boche on top of all the applications won't have hurt your chances. You must see that, surely?"

I waited for him to get angry, to strike back. Instead, silence fell between us. I looked into Ludo's eyes and realised that what I'd just said had never occurred to him. He seemed, well, a bit crushed. Despite myself, I felt compelled to smooth things over. I only wanted the guy to acknowledge his privilege, not descend into depression.

"To be fair, you *are* proper talented," I said. "Last week made that painfully clear."

It hurt to say, but Ludo brightened a little.

"Thank you," he said. He lifted his glasses and rubbed his eyes with his sleeve. "I owe you an apology too. I'm afraid I felt so jolly embarrassed after you called me out for messaging you on GayHoller that I basically goaded you into that fight. It was petty."

That was a surprise.

"You stuck up for your family," I said. "I would have done the same, mate."

By this point I was feeling proper magnanimous. I'd somehow gotten away with it. Career saved.

"Why did you unblock me on GayHoller?" Ludo asked. Blindsiding your opponent with a left-field question is a hardcore interview technique, and I'd walked into it. But what to say? *I wanted to trawl through your pho-*

tographs because I'm obsessed with the colour of your eyes? I had a Saturday afternoon chub on and wanted to wank off to pictures of your extraordinary arse? I was unsettled after fighting with the Boche family dauphin and was petrified I'd ruined my career? I opted for the truth. Mostly.

"I was correcting a wrong," I said.

"Unblocking someone on GayHoller is not an apology."

"No, the wrong was blocking you in the first place. I only did it because VladPop kept suggesting we'd be great together. He saw your messages to me, and—"

"Oh my *God*. All the stuff about Posh Spice?" Ludo put his head in his hands.

"Also, I guess I wanted—"

Ludo wasn't finished.

"Holy mother of God, the chief whip has seen my profile pictures. The chief whip has seen my butt. Jesus, Bungo, and Great-Uncle Bulgaria, Sunny. What have you done to me?"

I put a hand on Ludo's shoulder. The heat of his body was warm against my skin. He smelt of ironed linen and worn cashmere. Proper cosy.

"I'm in the dirt file," he said. "*We're* in the dirt file."

"There isn't any dirt."

"There's an awful lot of ballet butt."

Indeed, there was. That took my mind somewhere else entirely. Ludo sat staring at the wall, his face in his hands. He sighed heavily but, I noticed, didn't shake my hand off his shoulder. I imagined sliding it around him and pulling him into a hug, as if that might help him feel better. I shook the idea off. Where did that come from? I removed my hand. This was still a Tesco-versus-Asda situation. Ludo sat bolt upright, suddenly perky.

"Is that... Jessica Simpson?" he said, pointing at the poster on the wall.

"Wait, have you never seen *The Dukes of Hazzard*?"

I jumped up and reached for the door, knowing exactly what the evening needed.

"Where are you going?"

"To get my laptop. We're going to watch a film."

***

I T HAD BEEN A long day, and we were both tired, but watching a truly terrible movie together seemed like an excellent way to put everything behind us and make a fresh start. Ludo had come alive at the suggestion, immediately calling it a pyjama party and opening the packet of crisps Mrs Gallacher had helpfully supplied alongside a few individually wrapped biscuits on the tea-and-coffee tray. Before long we were hunkered down on Ludo's bed, computer in front of us, watching the General Lee get airborne and Boss Hogg get his knickers in a twist, laughing our tits off at the Christmas cracker–quality jokes.

"Can you believe the critics panned this film?" I said.

"Clearly they didn't appreciate the subtlety of the performances. Which are so subtle, I'm not even sure they meet the dictionary definition of the word *performance*."

"Who gets the best-actor gong?"

"What's the car called again?"

"The General Lee."

"The Oscar goes to General Lee."

On-screen, Jessica Simpson was flirting with two police officers like someone who had learned how to flirt by watching bottom-shelf offerings on Pornhub. Ludo was in fits of laughter. It shook the bed and made the empty crisp packet crinkle loudly in its hidey-hole between our legs on the duvet. When we got too cold, we had jumped under the covers, propping ourselves up against the headboard with pillows. Ludo's sleepwear was, predictably, proper button-up pyjamas. I normally just wore pants to bed—of the boxer-brief variety, rather than American-style boxers—which seemed a little too revealing for the occasion. So I had pulled on a pair of grey joggers and a sweater, which I'd brought in case the evenings got cold or I felt like walking along a beach giving free dick print to the local lads. (Hey, a girl's got to eat—and I'd be fresh meat up here.)

Ludo roared with laughter. Tears were streaming down his cheeks. We were sitting apart, but I could feel the warmth of him. He might have been a posh knobber with absolutely no idea how the world worked, and we might have had absolutely nothing in common except our jobs, but it felt nice being this physically close to another boy. How long had it been? Three months? Six? The sound of engines revving and wheels spinning filled the room. I felt Ludo move, and I turned to find him looking at me. His face was just inches from mine, his eyes sparkling pools of indigo.

"Do we have any more crisps?" he asked, breaking the spell.

"No, we've eaten all Mrs Gallacher's fucking crisps."

"Right. Onto Mrs Gallacher's fucking biscuits, then," he said, pausing the film and launching himself out of bed and over to the dresser, where the kettle stood. "Cup of tea?"

An hour later, the film was finished and Ludo was fast asleep. I climbed out of bed. He looked cute in his rumpled grampa pyjamas. I gently removed his glasses and put them on the bedside table. Then I grabbed my laptop and slipped out the door, reasonably confident I'd fixed the mess I'd got myself into by making an enemy of Ludo Boche.

16

LUDO

SUNNY AND I SAT beside each other at Mrs Gallacher's kitchen table while she made the kind of fry-up that sends my arteries screaming in search of a salad.

"You boys want any more fucking coffee?" she said.

"Yes please, Mrs G," Sunny said.

"Help yourselves, dearies. The pot's on the side."

It was the kind of filter coffee that sends anyone who *likes* coffee screaming in search of a hipster café. The kind I vomited all over Krishnan Varma-Rajan. My stomach churned. It would have to do. I wasn't terribly sure they did hipster cafés in Shetland. I was pretty sure all the beards and plaid shirts I'd seen around the island were probably just, you know, actual fishermen and farmers.

Sunny was reading the newspapers on his tablet. It was a very domestic, very homely, scene. If you ignored Mrs Gallacher's language. I got up, grabbed the coffee pot, and topped up our mugs.

"What page did you get?" I asked.

"They didn't run it. It might be on the website. You?"

"Picture story on page nine," I said. I'd checked the online edition before coming down for breakfast. "I think the photo of the puffin sold it. They didn't use much of my copy."

"Surely Torsten and Carstairs didn't drag us all the way up here for bloody puffins," Sunny said.

"Language," Mrs Gallacher said.

Sunny was incredulous. Behind her back, we shared a smile.

"Sorry, Mrs G." Sunny stirred his coffee, and I put the pot back on the side.

Sunny continued his train of thought. "We're political reporters. They better have something big for us today or JT will string me up from the rafters in Westminster Hall and use me as bait for a story about sex pest MPs."

"Your mind is a jolly dark place."

***

A N HOUR LATER THE whole press pack was sitting on the coach in the middle of a dreary asphalt car park, high on a windswept hill overlooking a sea whipped up with whitecaps. I was beginning to regret making the nine o'clock deadline for the bus pickup. The morning was overcast and cold, and it was threatening to rain. On the horizon, an oil rig rose from the murky blue of the water, like a rusted Meccano kraken, blighting what would otherwise have been a picture-postcard view. There was a soft rumbling of a helicopter in the distance. On the bus, the reporters all wore serious faces. Annabelle Statham-Drew's mouth was puckered like a Boston terrier's butthole, which certainly explained the breath. Sunny was sitting in the seat beside me, chatting across the aisle to Rafiq about something called Leicester Nirvana, which I thought was a football team but also might have been a hallucinogenic drug. I wasn't paying close attention. Torsten Beaumont-Flattery stood at the front of the bus, as beautiful as the statue of David, wearing a cagoule that fit him like a slightly undersized condom. It could split at any moment. If it did, I was keeping the baby. The sound of the helicopter grew steadily louder.

"Our lift is almost here," Torsten announced. A moment later, the helicopter roared into view over the clifftop, as if this press junket had been produced by Barbara Broccoli and Michael G. Wilson. The sound was deafening, and the wind it created buffeted the bus. The pilot landed the chopper, and the blade rotation slowed to a point where it merely vibrated through the coach rhythmically. It made my tummy feel a little gippy. This was not good news. When I was a kid, Mummy had dragged me along to a military base where she was covering a story for the BBC, and I was offered a ride in a helicopter called a Bell 412. I remember the name specifically because the pilot said he reckoned by the time we finally touched down, I'd done four number ones and a number two. The second and last time I had been in a helicopter was for a joy flight on a family holiday in Cannes. I'd heaved my guts up so spectacularly the pilot had to make an emergency landing on the beach. Father said if the Royal Air Force ever got to hear about my hundred per cent hit rate for downing helicopters, I'd be press-ganged into service.

From his marble plinth at the front of the coach, Michelangelo's Torsten ran us all through the safety spiel.

"We'll be in pairs for the next part of our journey," he said. He pointed at the cammo and photographer. "Terry and Astrid, you'll be going first so you can get whatever shots you want before the rest of us shuttle across to the rig."

Terry and Astrid collected their gear and got off the bus. A minute later, the helicopter took off again. It was a ten-minute round trip to the oil rig. Sooner or later, it would be my turn. My stomach was twisting in knots just thinking about it. How career-ending would it be to soil yourself in front of a dozen colleagues?

"Are you all right?" Sunny asked. "You've gone very pale."

"Not really," I said. Sunny grabbed my hand, which gave me a start because it was the last thing I expected. His amber-green eyes locked firmly onto mine, his blush-pink lips smiling in reassurance.

"You'll be fine. It's an adventure! How often do we get to ride in a chopper?"

It suddenly occurred to me that perhaps riding in a helicopter was not the kind of thing most people did all that often. Sensing an opportunity to confirm Sunny's prejudices about my privilege, I didn't elaborate on my choppy chopper history, but he must have read something in the expression on my face. He leant in conspiratorially. His breath was warm against my ear.

"And I don't know about you," he said. "But I've been waiting for years for a chance to ride Torsten's chopper."

It broke the tension. I burst out laughing. Sunny tried to not chuckle at his own joke but failed. He let my hand go. Apparently, I had been adequately comforted. I wished he hadn't. The heat of him had been reassuring.

"For the record, I saw him first," I said.

"You can't bagsy Torsten Beaumont-Flattery. He's a grown man with rights and free will."

"I'm hardly going to knock him out with chloroform and drag him back to my nest."

"You have a nest?"

"What does it say about your opinion of me that you don't question me having enough chloroform on hand to bring down a man the size of a Charolais bull but you question the nest?"

"So, there *is* a nest."

"It's not a nest, per se. It's a summer house. In my parents' garden. If this is your way of asking me where I live?"

"It wasn't. But now that you've raised it, is it a Kensington nest? A Chelsea nest?"

"It's a Hampstead nest." I spoke without thinking and winced, waiting for Sunny to hit me with more accusations of privilege. Presumably, that's what this entire line of questioning was about.

"Proper posh," he said. The attack flashed in his eyes, but it didn't come. "I don't live too far from you, as it happens. Although my bit of north London isn't posh, obviously."

"Highgate Cemetery?"

"I'm pale, but I'm not that pale."

"You live under a log on Hampstead Heath?"

"I live in Willesden Green. Above the bus stop on the Willesden Lane. But I'm saving up, and I hope to buy a log of my very own someday."

We went on like this for a while until the sound of the helicopter returning finally drowned out the conversation.

"Miller, Boche, this is you," Torsten called out from the front of the bus.

I sat frozen in my seat, unable to will my legs into action. Sunny stood, put his bag over his shoulder, and turned to look at me.

"Come on then, Boche," he said. "England expects, and all that."

"I might be posh, but I'm not the motivated-into-action-by-Admiral-Nelson kind of posh."

"You're posh enough to know that was Admiral Nelson."

"Who did you think it was?"

"Stormzy?" Sunny held out a hand expectantly. "Come on. Chopper fuel isn't cheap, and it's the taxpayer footing the bill for this."

I grabbed Sunny's hand, and he hauled me out of the seat. Once vertical, I let him go, pulled my bag over my shoulder, and followed him down the aisle of the coach, past Torsten, through the front door, and towards the helicopter I was absolutely, definitely about to redecorate with the contents of my stomach.

17

SUNNY

MY HEART WAS THUMPING in time with the thud of the blades. My legs had gone to jelly with the excitement of my first chopper ride. Ludo, though, seemed way less enthusiastic. Instead of his usual olive complexion, he looked as pale as me—and I've had dead people tell me I needed more colour. I was low-key enjoying seeing him so uncomfortable. But all the same, the second our headsets were on and we could speak to each other, I checked in on him.

"All good, mate?" I asked.

He was looking straight ahead, chewing his own face like he was off his chops at Glastonbury, moshing to Anthrax. Or possibly having taken anthrax? I plucked my phone from my pocket.

"We need a selfie!"

Ludo shook his head, but I would not be deterred. I framed up Ludo in the back of my picture.

"Come on, smile! This is awesome!"

Ludo grimaced and raised his hand in a timid little wave. I snapped the picture—Ludo's discomfort preserved for eternity—then spun around and took one just of myself to send to Mum and the Brent Boys. The helicopter lifted off the ground. Ludo gripped his knees.

"You got your WAG Bag?" I asked. The pilot had handed us spew bags the second he saw Ludo's pastiness. Ludo nodded. We shot up higher into the air, tilted, rotated, and flew out over the water towards the oil rig. The second we crossed the cliff face and were over the sea, the air became bumpy, and we jolted and fell and lifted and swayed. I looked at Ludo. He was still in his mosh pit. I burped. My stomach was not enjoying the turbulence either. It was an enclosed cabin, but the smell of aviation fuel was strong, and two minutes into the flight I felt queasy. A minute later, I was chundering up Mrs Gallacher's fry-up into my WAG Bag as intently as if a gameshow host was on standby with a cheque for £100,000 if I managed to fill it. Tears streamed down my face from the effort of puking so violently. I felt Ludo's hand slide onto my knee and squeeze it. What I really needed was terra firma and a nurse to inject Kwells straight into my bloodstream. The helicopter jolted against something solid, and I realised we had arrived on the oil rig.

"Thank God for that," I said, my face still buried in my WAG Bag.

"That was... *so much fun!*" Ludo said.

I looked at him. My cheeks were wet with tears of exertion. My eyes felt puffy, fuzzy, and bloodshot. And there was Ludo, grinning and clapping his hands like a toddler who'd spent the morning mainlining Irn-Bru.

"What a rush!" he said, beaming. Then before I could stop him, he pulled out his phone, framed me up in the background, and took a revenge selfie.

"I hate you," I said.

***

W HEN THE PRESS CONTINGENT was eventually all present and accounted for on the oil rig and I was feeling much better, the conversation among the reporters turned to what the announcement was going to be. None of us had any idea, but the location had raised a few questions in my mind. I jotted them down on my notepad.

The helicopter made its final trip back from Shetland. Torsten Beaumont-Flattery stepped out first, keeping his head low and dashing over like a suited superhero to join us.

"The minister won't be a moment," he said.

The pilot shut off the helicopter's engine, and the blades slowly whirred to a stop. Then, and only then, the lady herself appeared, one hot pink stiletto heel emerging from the door at a time. Jemima Carstairs, the secretary of state for the environment, glorious in a flamingo-pink pantsuit, was the reason we were all gathered on this bleak, remote oil rig. This had the beginnings of an Agatha Christie about it. Would one of us be dead before the press conference was complete?

Jemima Carstairs was smart. She had a reputation as a reformer and an effective minister, and she'd been tipped for the top job. She was in her mid-forties, much younger than most of the cabinet. She had perfectly coiffured long brown hair and eyebrows sharp enough to cut flesh.

"Thank you all for coming," Carstairs said, taking her place in front of the press pack. We all extended our arms towards her to record the audio on our devices. In my free hand, I held my notepad with my questions, clasping it against my chest to stop the pages flapping in the wind. Terry, the cameraman, said he was rolling. Ludo stood beside me, his curls bouncing in the breeze. I could feel the warmth radiating from his body.

"Today, the world stands on a precipice," Carstairs said. "We have a choice. We can continue on the trajectory we have been on. The trajectory that created the modern world, that made Britain great, but which will ultimately cause not only our downfall but that of our entire planet. Or we change course. We can set off in a new direction, harnessing the spirit and ingenuity that saw our small island nation build a great global empire. We take the reins; we seize the opportunities of Brexit and become the world leaders in tackling climate change. We become, once again, through our greatness and our example, a country and a people the entire world looks up to, emulates, and envies."

Holy shitballs, she'd murdered the whole cabinet in some kind of Night of the Long Manolo Blahniks and planned to rule Britain from this oil rig like she was the führer and this was the Eagle's Nest.

"Today, as the secretary of state for the environment, with special responsibility for tackling climate change, I announce the end of the United Kingdom's reliance on fossil fuels. We will aggressively pursue our net zero commitments through whatever means possible, including creating a sovereign wealth fund to heavily invest in new renewable energy projects and technologies—investing in British ingenuity and British companies. We will encourage polluters and the fossil fuel industry itself to make the change to cleaner, greener energy sources and to decommission and rehabilitate outdated, climate-destroying technology like this oil rig, the Viking XI."

The minister continued cosplaying as Winston Churchill for another five minutes, announcing a huge suite of new policies, regulations, and legislation, before we could finally ask questions. Press conferences were a bit of a free-for-all as far as asking questions went. The strategy, generally, was to shout loudest to get the minister's attention, to make eye contact, to keep eye contact, and to keep asking your question even if you could see a madman in your peripheral vision coming at you with an axe. Ministers tended to choose questions based on a vague triage of professional seniority and the likelihood of getting softball questions from friendly outlets. If Carstairs was going on the former, I'd get to ask a question before Ludo. If she went by the latter, he'd get to go first. The minister finished answering a question from Annabelle, and the press pack erupted into a squawking mass, like seagulls on a bucket of chips.

"Ludo Boche," she said, pointing a glossy pink fingernail in Ludo's direction. The noise died down.

"Minister, where does nuclear energy figure in this new policy? Is nuclear good or bad? And what does this mean for the plans for a nuclear power plant at Newton Bardon?"

It was a good question, and one I had written down on my notepad. Bonus: it saved me asking it. I still had one question left, and I was determined to ask it. No one wanted to be the reporter who failed to ask a question at a press conference on a story as big as this. Carstairs nodded, indicating she would take Ludo's question.

"Obviously, many people would like us not to use nuclear energy at all," she said. "I have some sympathy with this view, and I'm sure we will eventually transition away from it completely as new, competitive technologies emerge. But where we do use nuclear—let me be very clear about this—it should be British-owned and British-built, and provide jobs for British people."

Carstairs was now well beyond the usual government talking points. This amounted to a wholesale gutting of her cabinet colleague Bob Wynn-Jones and his dodgy Belarusian business deal.

"So, is the Leicestershire plant on or off?" Ludo said, asking the sensible follow-up question. I felt oddly proud of him. He couldn't have been to too many press conferences. They could be terrifying early in your career. It was like being a newly minted Roman senator on the day they decided to kill Caesar. At first, you're hovering at the back, unsure what's going on. But you soon realise you're going to have to plunge the dagger in yourself eventually, otherwise your career and reputation are toast. It's only then you realise that everyone else is hacking away at the emperor's body so enthusiastically that they're never going to stop to give you the knife. You have to jump in there and grab it yourself.

"Individual projects and investments will go to an independent panel, the make-up of which is yet to be decided," Carstairs said. "But all funded projects must be British-owned and -operated."

I jumped in to ask the last question on my page.

"Minister, this has essentially been an energy policy announcement. Why are you making it and not the energy secretary? Where is Bob Wynn-Jones? And what does this say about his political future?"

"I'm the minister responsible for climate change," she said. "OK, that's enough questions. Torsten will give a copy of the press release with all the details. Shall we get some pictures?"

Just like that, it was over. Carstairs turned her attention to the camera guy and the photographer, and the press pack dispersed across the platform of the rig to make phone calls and brief their bosses back in their newsrooms. Ludo was buried in his fancy-schmancy Dictaphone, saving the audio file of the press conference. I took a moment to process what Carstairs had just said, working out my angle. Could a British government genuinely be taking net zero seriously? Incredible, if true. But something felt *off*. My journalistic radar was pinging. I wandered over to Ludo.

"What did you think?" I said.

"She appears to have lopped off the energy secretary's bollocks and turned them into a jolly haute couture pair of earrings."

"She's certainly emptied his inbox for him."

"Quite."

"Why, though? Why her? And why now?"

Ludo shrugged.

"Bit of good press before a likely reshuffle?"

That was plausible, up to a point. But this kind of announcement required cabinet approval. Where were the other ministers, muscling their way into photos to share the glory? This didn't pass the sniff test.

"Maybe," I said.

Ludo and I wandered off in separate directions and made our phone calls to our newsrooms. JT wanted five hundred words for the website, a page lead for the morning paper, and an analysis piece looking at all the unanswered questions. Cathy and the team would chase up comments from the opposition, oil and gas companies, and environmental groups and keep an eye on Greta Thunberg's socials. When we'd finished the call, I opened WhatsApp and sent VladPop a message.

Sunny: *Why is Carstairs making energy announcements if Wynn-Jones has the PM's full support?*

He replied almost instantly.

Vladimir Popov: *How are my little lovebirds enjoying their island honeymoon?*

This was the text message equivalent of the dead cat strategy: if you don't like the topic up for discussion, throw a dead cat on the table so everyone talks about the dead cat and not the thing you don't want them talking about. I wasn't falling for it.

Sunny: *Unless I hear something very convincing to change my mind, I'm going to write that Bob Wynn-Jones is about to be sacked.*

It took VladPop a little longer to reply this time.

Vladimir Popov: *You must write as you see fit. I would not seek to unduly influence a member of the fourth estate.*

That was as good as confirmation. A second later, another message arrived.

Vladimir Popov: *Come and see me in the constituency office when you're back in London on Friday morning.*

Vladimir Popov: *I want to hear all the gossip about you and Ludo.*

Vladimir Popov: *The kettle will be on.*

I had to kill this off right here and now. It was getting out of hand.

Sunny: *NOTHING IS HAPPENING! I will NEVER get romantically involved with a colleague.*

Vladimir Popov: *Oh, that's a shame. I said to my wife just last night, Ludo is such an adorable helpless puppy of a fellow and you're such a strong and assertive type on the outside, yet such a bleeding heart on the inside. You'd be absolutely perfect together.*

This knobber needed to stop reading Mills & Boon.

Sunny: *Is a Cabinet reshuffle imminent?*

Vladimir Popov: *See you 10am Friday.*

Vladimir Popov: *The kettle. Will. Be. On.*

The man must really like tea.

Sunny: *Fine. But I'm putting the boot into Wynn-Jones in tomorrow morning's paper. See you Friday.*

With that, I followed the rest of the press pack into the oil rig's canteen to write my stories.

***

T HE CANTEEN SMELT LIKE someone had dropped a bottle of cod liver oil and decided to clean it up using a mop soaked in human sweat. I looked around the room for Ludo but couldn't see him. I found a spare table, set up my laptop, logged in to the Viking XI's Wi-Fi, and started tinkering with the opening paragraph of my lead story. A few minutes later, someone tapped on my shoulder. I turned to see Ludo standing beside me, face flushed crimson. He looked adorably flustered. He pushed his glasses onto his nose and ran his fingers through his hair.

"Would you mind sharing your audio from the press conference?" he asked. "I appear to have dropped my Dictaphone into the North Sea."

18

LUDO

FRESHLY SHOWERED AND PYJAMAED back at the Otter's Den, I decided to video-call Uncle Ben. We messaged every day, but sometimes I just needed to hear my godfather's voice and see his face. I'd kept him up to date on *the* situation with Sunny. (Uncle Ben had put the emphasis on the definite article as soon as I told him about our fight at Maxime's.) His advice had been to play nicely. After all, Sunny was a tabloid reporter and could very easily turn our fracas into a juicy titbit for the *Bulletin*.

"How are you fairing up in the fair isles, dear boy? Have you run off with a swarthy fisherman yet?"

"Yes, I am calling you from atop my widow's walk. I am waiting for my lover to return from the sea."

Uncle Ben laughed, coughed, and cleared his throat. In fact, I was calling from my bed, which he could clearly see. Uncle Ben was wearing his silk dressing gown and sitting in his wingback armchair in his drawing room in his Connaught Square flat. Piano music tinkled softly in the background. It was like having a Zoom call with Noël Coward. It was a carefully cultivated image of decadence, which I jolly well envied and made a mental note to emulate in my senior years.

"Did you get the picture of me with the puffins?" I asked.

"I did, dear boy. They looked like good eating."

"You can't eat them, Uncle Ben. They're a vulnerable species. We just photographed them."

"Shame, they're a good size for the oven. I bet they roast up beautifully." Uncle Ben was in a silly mood. I adored him when he was like this. "How is *the* situation? Have you flung Sunny Miller bodily into the North Sea?"

"No, I saved that honour for my Dictaphone," I said.

"What have you done now?"

"We were on an oil rig this afternoon, and I tripped over a cable while running away from what I suspect was an actual albatross."

"Why were you running away from an albatross?"

"It was chasing me. Anyway, when I hit the deck, the Dictaphone slipped out of my hand and skittered over the edge. The albatross went flying off after it. So, I expect it's either swimming with the fishes or it's currently giving an enormous seabird a bout of constipation it's unlikely to forget."

"It's like being godfather to Frank Spencer."

"Who?"

"Never mind, dear boy. If only you could be clumsy on demand, we could book the Palladium and sell tickets."

Uncle Ben sucked back on his cheroot and coughed.

"*The* situation?" he repeated.

"Better than expected," I confessed. I told him about the apology and the pyjama party. "Then this morning he was incredibly sweet and held my knee while I had a minor panic attack about a helicopter ride."

"My God, do you remember Cannes?"

"But then afterwards, he slipped me his MP3.'

"Sounds positively erotic."

I rolled my eyes. "He shared his audio file."

"I'm not sure I understand your generation," Uncle Ben said. "In my day, if you were sweet on a boy, you shared a kiss, not an audio file. Occasionally, you might even share a police cell. But the 1950s were like that."

"What the bally hell makes you think he's sweet on me?" I asked.

"Isn't he sweet on you? You watched movies together. In your pyjamas. In your bed."

"I don't think he is."

"But you're sweet on him."

It was a statement, not a question. I was taken aback. Where had he got that impression? What had I said? Wait, *was* I sweet on Sunny Miller? I didn't think so.

"We're just colleagues, Uncle Ben," I said.

"If you say so, darling boy." He sounded disappointed.

"Put it this way: So far, he hasn't asked me to put in a good word for him with Father, Mummy, or Jonty. So, he might be an overzealous class warrior, but at least he's not using me as a stepladder to a better job. That's more than I can say for most of the other reporters I've met since joining the *Sentinel*."

There was a knock on my bedroom door.

"I bet you that's him now," Uncle Ben said. "Bearing champagne and roses and confessions of undying love."

"It's probably the landlady," I said. "I better go. I'll talk to you tomorrow."

"If it's *the* situation, dear boy, then he's definitely sweet on you!"

I sighed heavily.

"Goodnight, Uncle Ben."

"Sweet dreams, dear boy."

We ended the call, Uncle Ben's words rattling around in my head like a pea in a baby's rattle, demanding attention. I got up and opened the door...

19

SUNNY

LUDO OPENED THE DOOR dressed like after-hours Don Draper from *Mad Men*. All that was missing was the tumbler of whisky. I felt a flush of excitement at seeing him, which disconcerted me slightly. When had that started? Hopefully, it didn't show on my face.

Ludo seemed surprised to see me. I held out my laptop and presented the packet of crisps I had tucked under my arm.

"Mrs G has restocked," I said. "Do you fancy a film?"

"I fancy a fucking cup of tea and fucking biscuit," he said. He waved me in and lifted the kettle to check the weight of it. "I'll just get some more water."

Ludo disappeared out of the bedroom door, turning towards the kitchen. Personally, I'd have filled the kettle from the bathroom sink, avoiding Mrs G altogether. Ludo liked to live dangerously. I put my laptop down on the bed and noticed Ludo's computer was open to whatever he'd been working on. There was text on the screen. There's no greater test for a reporter than this. Should I look? Should I read it and see what he was working on? What if it was a big story, like an update on Newton Bardon or the fate of Bob Wynn-Jones? What if I'd missed whatever it was Ludo was working on and this was my chance to find out about it and ensure I got the story for the *Bulletin*? Proper unethical. But was it any more unethical than trawling through a celebrity's rubbish bin looking for receipts for Botox injections or final-demand notices from Dildos-4-U.com? There's no code of honour between journalists. All is fair. You just mustn't get caught. That was really the only lesson the industry took from the entire phone hacking scandal. But could I do it? Could I really just lean over and read whatever was on Ludo's laptop? *Gah!* Why the bloody hell hadn't it switched to a password-protected screen saver by now? Frankly, it was negligent. It's like he *wanted* me to snoop.

Trust, I thought. He's deliberately testing me to see whether he can trust me. The *Bulletin* might have seen my moral bar sink lower than a Smurf trained in gymnastics could comfortably limbo, but I wasn't going to fail this test and ruin my entire career. Not when I'd worked so hard this week to save it. If Ludo told his parents I'd read his laptop, my reputation would be toast with every single respectable outlet in the country. I'd be stuck at the *Bulletin* for the rest of my career. Worse, I'd get stuck writing for magazines people only buy for the crosswords.

I sat on the edge of the bed and actively looked at almost anything else I could find to hold my attention. On the floor, Ludo's worn clothes were crumpled in a pile. His trousers looked like he'd evaporated out them, his pants still hugging the inside of the gusset. Being caught staring at Ludo's just-been-worn-all-day underpants was almost as bad as being caught reading his laptop. Some guys would love nothing more than to enter a room and find you face down in their dirty briefs, fudding yourself senseless. I suspected Ludo was not one of those guys. And this was not the time to find out. I adjusted my joggers to keep things kosher, in case Ludo walked in.

Ludo walked in.

"Have you been in that kitchen?" he asked. He shut the bedroom door behind him, put the kettle in its stand, and turned it on to boil. "I could have trekked to the gates of hell for this water and inhaled less sulphur."

Ludo noticed his open laptop, closed it, and put it on the dresser.

"What shall we watch?" he asked.

While Ludo made the tea, I searched the streaming services for a film.

"Where does the name Ludo come from?" I asked, making small talk to fill the silence. "I've never met anyone called Ludo before."

"I'm named after Ludovic Kennedy," he said. "Jonty and I are both named after famous journalists. He's named for Jonathan Dimbleby."

Ludo noticed his pants on the floor. He left the tea, rolled his clothes into a ball, and threw them inside his case. For some reason, possibly the faultlessly preppy way he dressed—the cashmere jumpers, the crisp white shirts, the arse-hugging chinos—I had imagined he would be proper neat and tidy. A perfectionist. A kindred spirit with VladPop. But within twenty-four hours of arriving, his room looked like a plane had crash-landed in a field. Based on the evidence, the passengers were all dressed in Ralph Lauren, Rodd & Gunn, and Barbour. Ludo dressed like he was the kind of person who owned a yacht, a horse, and a Labrador but had sent them all to boarding school to get some peace and quiet.

He was stirring the tea.

"And what is the story behind 'Cabbage98,' while we're at it?"

"The ninety-eight is for the year I was born, obviously," Ludo said. "And of course *boche* is short for *caboche*, which means *cabbage* in French, but it also means an idiot. It's what our great-grandpapas called the Germans during the war. Boche, that is. It was a terrific insult, at the time. You probably had to be there."

Diving into the workings of Ludo's brain was like slipping into a parallel universe.

"Cabbage was one of my nicknames at school. Not one of the nicer ones. That was me sort of reclaiming it."

That was probably the most relatable thing Ludo had ever said.

"What about you? Why did your parents call you Sunny?"

"Not parents. Parent. There's only me mum." I caught myself slipping into "Lestah" and corrected course. "The way she tells it, she had been struggling to think of a suitable name when a nurse peered into my crib, saw my fat little face, and said I was 'a little ray of sunshine.' And that was it. Mum called me Sunshine. It could have been worse. I could have been called Ray."

"Sunny is short for Sunshine?"

"Yes," I said. Ludo was wide-eyed. "Are you laughing at me?"

"I most certainly am not! I think it's fabulous. It's like Mary Sunshine, the journalist in—"

"*Chicago*!" I said. Ludo looked at me like I'd made his day. "I proper love that movie," I added.

Ludo passed my tea and sat down cross-legged on the bed, facing me.

"Did you know in stage productions Mary Sunshine is usually played by a man in drag?" he said.

I did.

"Do you like musicals, then?"

"I adore them!" Ludo instantly dialled up the camp to ten. It was like someone had pressed a button. I suspected the only thing restraining him from more jazz hands was the fact he was holding a cup of tea. He was letting his guard down, so I let my walls crumble a little too. I played my ace card—although until that moment I had no idea I'd been holding it.

"My middle name comes from a musical, actually," I said. "I bet you can't guess what it is."

You'd have thought I'd emptied a barrel of kittens on the floor. Ludo was bouncing around excitedly, unable to focus, unable to concentrate. Tea went everywhere. I grabbed his mug and put it on the bedside table.

"Friedrich, for Friedrich von Trapp?"

"Nope."

"Oliver?"

I shook my head.

"Danny? From *Grease*. Everyone's mum loves *Grease*."

"No. It's a lot sillier than that."

Ludo was fanning his face with his hands in excitement. His blue eyes looked up at the ceiling as he searched his brain for plausibly implausible offerings.

"Javert? Sweeney Todd? Simba? Shrek!"

"Steady on."

"You said silly." He pushed his glasses back up onto his nose.

"Do you want a clue?"

"Absolutely not!"

Half an hour later I had a very good understanding of just how deep Ludo's knowledge of musical theatre was. I had been everyone from Sunny Lumière Miller to Sunny Sancho Panza Miller. While I was very much over the game and ready to watch a film, Ludo refused a clue. Then he suggested Wonka, and for the sake of my own sanity, I told him he was close. He nearly jumped through the roof.

"Oh my God! Veruca? Beauregarde? Teavee?"

"So close." He was frantic now, arms in full puppet mode.

"Augustus!"

"You got it."

Ludo leapt up from the bed, punched the air, and did a happy dance. Then he bounced back on to bed and threw his arms around me, nearly strangling me in the process. My face was buried in a mess of black curls. The comforting smell of warm fresh linen, cashmere, and sea salt filled my lungs, and I breathed it in deeply. Ludo was squeezing me and wriggling from side to side like he'd just won the gayest lottery ever invented. I put my arms up and tentatively hugged him back. I could feel his tight, lean muscles moving underneath his cotton pyjamas.

Ludo broke off the hug, drawing away from me just far enough that we could see each other clearly. His eyes studied me. His smile was broad and toothy, creating dimples in the puppy fat of his chipmunk cheeks. One hand was still on my side, the other on my shoulder. He ran it up behind my neck and pulled my face closer to his. I thought he was going to kiss me, and in that moment, for all my better judgement, I was into it. I would have let him. He rested his forehead against mine.

"I can't believe your mother named you after Augustus Gloop." He pulled away, letting his hands drop. I let mine do the same. The moment slipped past us. What *was* that?

"Apparently, it was because I never stopped eating," I said. "But, honestly, show me a baby that doesn't eat non-stop. It's, like, their only job."

"Your mother sounds amazing," he said. "I have to meet this woman."

***

WE WATCHED *CHICAGO*. THE film version starring Catherine Zeta-Jones, Renée Zellweger, and Queen Latifah. We sang all the songs together, although I had to keep begging Ludo to be quieter so we didn't wake Mr and Mrs Gallacher, who by then must have been farting soundly into their blankets up the far end of the house.

"It's nice to see you smiling so much," Ludo said, as the film credits rolled. "I thought you were such a serious person when I first met you."

"You just caught me at a bad moment. In fact, no, wait. You *caused* the bad moment."

"No, I think you're a bit of a grumble-bum. For someone called Sunny, you're very serious all the time!"

"You think because my name is Sunny, I should have a permanently sunny disposition?"

"Sunny by name, sunny by nature?" Ludo offered.

"That's ridiculous," I said. "You don't automatically expect someone called Marina to provide a safe harbour for boats, do you? Or someone called Molly to shaft Ecstasy tablets on a Friday night?"

To be fair, I did actually know a girl called Molly who did that. But that wasn't nominative determinism, that was because her brother Geordie was the local dealer and she got her gear for free.

Ludo laughed. We were tucked up beside one another under his duvet. The heat generated by our bodies and the motor of the laptop had made it slightly sweaty and damp, but neither of us moved to lift the bedspread and let some air in. Ludo was lying close beside me, our legs touching. It felt... lovely. I wasn't quite ready to say goodnight, even though it past midnight.

"You never told me your middle name," I asked. "Do you have one?"

"Benjamin," he said. "For my Uncle Ben. Ben Diamond. He's our theatre critic. If you've ever read our arts section?"

In all honesty, I had never read the arts section of the *Sentinel*, though there was no point telling Ludo that. But Ben Diamond was one of the oldest names on Fleet Street. Everyone had heard of him.

"I remember him being on TV when I was a kid," I said. "He was old even then. He must be ancient now."

"He's eighty-eight, but he has the spirit of someone who's twenty, and I love him for it."

Ludo's whole face was alight, the way a parent's face lights up when they talk about a favourite child. A realisation hit me.

"At Maxime's, when you said you took the job at the *Sentinel* because you wanted to work every day with the man you most admire in the world, I assumed you were talking about your father. But you were talking about Ben Diamond, weren't you?"

"That's right," Ludo said, smiling. "More than anyone else in the world, he's the person who made me who I am."

I grinned. In part at the proper lovely sentiment, and in part at knowledge that Ludo didn't hero-worship his terrifying father and probably wasn't destined to become his clone.

"Uncle Ben sounds amazing," I said. "I have to meet this man."

The idea seemed to please Ludo. He leant his head against my shoulder and shuffled down into the bed a little to get comfortable. It felt more intimate than I was expecting. Like he was testing to see how I would react, whether I was interested in him. And I liked it.

But warning bells were going off in my head. We were entering a danger zone. This level of physical contact was not just well beyond collegiate but beyond simple friendship too. This whole situation was like a box of Guy Fawkes crackers left too close to the bonfire. It could go off at any moment. I could feel the beast in my joggers surging into life. If I didn't put a stop to it now, the beast would be in control—and there would be no telling what the consequences of that would be. Not just on the rest of this trip but on my career long term. This *had* to stop.

"I'm quite jealous of you, working with someone you admire every day," I said, making small talk to buy time while I worked out how to get myself out of danger. "I can't think of anyone I admire at the *Bulletin*. It's a soul-destroying place. It's not what I had in mind when I dreamt of becoming a journalist."

"It has its place in the market," Ludo said. "They're lucky to have you." He smiled up at me, and I got a waft of warm linen and cashmere. So cosy.

"Thanks. Still, I don't want to be there forever. I want to work for a respectable paper. But we all have to start somewhere, right?"

Ludo sighed. He sat up and pulled away. I was grateful for it. He'd unknowingly saved me from myself, from doing something I'd live to regret. All the same, my shoulder felt cool where the heat of his body had been, and I kind of missed it. My cock sent my brain a sad face emoji.

"I'm tired," he said. "It's bedtime, I think."

That was my cue, and I grabbed it, although Ludo didn't smile or make eye contact and it gave me the odd sense he might have been pissed with me somehow. I closed my laptop, picked it up, and crawled out of bed, holding it in front of my joggers to hide any lingering awkward evidence of the beast's recent arousal. I should probably have worn pants, but you just don't with joggers, do you? I tried to find a way to show no hard feelings.

"I had fun tonight," I said, as I opened the door. Ludo smiled, but there seemed to be no joy in it.

"Goodnight, Sunny," he said.

"See you in the morning," I said.

Then I waved—because sometimes, apparently, I am the Forrest Gump kind of awkward—and stepped out of the room and pulled the door shut. I stood in the hall for a moment. All the air emptied from my lungs. It had been a near escape—although I wasn't sure I'd pulled it off without causing collateral damage. Ludo seemed off. Maybe he really was just tired?

I sniffed my shoulder—a completely normal thing to do. It smelt of Ludo. My heart raced. Did I... like him? When did that happen? I shook it off, then took a deep breath, stepped into my room, and closed the door behind me.

20

LUDO

S UNNY SAT OPPOSITE ME at the breakfast table, his beautiful face buried in his tablet. You wouldn't know to look at him just how calculating he was. I felt a twinge of sadness. Mrs Gallacher stood at the stove, the smell of sizzling bacon and frying bread filling the air. Oil splattered loudly in the pan.

"Jesus, would ye get tae fuck," Mrs Gallacher said, leaping backwards from the stove. "Motherfucker."

This was fifty per cent meal preparation, fifty per cent cabaret. Breakfast with a free floor show. I took a mouthful of my muesli and yogurt. On the small television in the corner, I could see the beaming face of a man who, this time last week, I was busily vomiting all over. I hadn't seen Krishnan Varma-Rajan since that morning. I had actively avoided watching *Wake Up Britain*. Seeing him reminded me of the way he'd tried to use me to get to my father, of how small and stupid that made me feel.

I looked across at Sunny, who last night had as good as revealed he was pulling the same stunt as Krishnan. "Someday, I want to work for a respectable paper," he'd said. The words had hollowed me out. I tried to shake off the sadness it created inside me, but I couldn't. I hadn't slept terribly well at all, going over and over it all in my mind. In the end, I had resolved to be serviceably polite to Sunny while I was stuck with him in Shetland, then jolly well have nothing to do with him beyond what was absolutely necessary after we got back to London on Thursday night. I would be distant and professional. We were colleagues. There was no obligation to be friends. This was self-preservation.

The ticker along the bottom of the television screen suggested energy policy was on the agenda again this morning. An image of the Viking XI flashed up on the screen, leading a short package about yesterday's announcements. Sunny and I were in the background in a couple of the shots, which was a cheap thrill. When they cut back to the studio, I was surprised to see Environment Minister Jemima Carstairs sitting on the famous yellow couch, exactly where I had been sitting, chatting to Krishnan.

"She's back in London already," I said, then kicked myself under the table for starting a conversation. Can't even stick to a plan for five minutes.

Sunny looked up at the television momentarily, then back at his tablet, where he was reading the papers.

"What page did you get?" he asked, cheerily.

"The spread on four and five," I said, in clipped tones. The *Sentinel* had splashed with reactions from the big oil and gas companies. This was no surprise. When every news organisation gets the same information, as happens at press conferences, it's the reaction stories that provide the original content that gives readers a reason to buy a particular paper. Even if those reactions are the batshit crazy bile spewed by extremists who would quite happily watch the world burn if they can see how to make a quid out of it. People like the *Sentinel*'s board and shareholders.

"I'm across six and seven," he said. "They didn't splash with it. That honour went to two of the Real Housewives of Tottenham Hotspur knocking seven bells out of each other in a car park outside a Chelmsford nightclub."

To be honest, that did sound more interesting. I said nothing.

"We had the pictures," Sunny added. He flicked through his tablet and held it out towards me, to show me the front page of the morning's *Bulletin*.

"FUR FLIES IN SPURS' BABES BODEGA BRAWL."

It was accompanied by a dark, grainy photograph of two stilettoed women, each tanned the colour of a desiccated satsuma, one wearing a faux fur bolero jacket, going at each other hammer and tongs like two heavily Botoxed ferrets. I half-heartedly smiled in acknowledgement. Something flashed in Sunny's eyes, and I could tell he knew he'd messed up. He was wrong-footed and, I thought, nervous.

"Looks like a fairly solid right hook on the one whose knickers you can see," he observed.

Mrs Gallacher put a bacon butty on the table in front of Sunny.

"Smashing, Mrs G," he said.

"D'ye want brown sauce or the red shite?"

Sunny opted for the red, and she plonked the squeezy bottle on the table. Sunny put his tablet down, ready to get stuck in. He gave me another sideways glance. I pretended not to notice.

"You boys want anything else?" Mrs Gallacher asked.

We both shook our heads. I said, "No, thank you."

"Fine, fine. If you'll excuse me minute, then. Sing out if you need me." She plucked the tea towel off her shoulder and flopped it onto the kitchen counter, then stepped out the kitchen door. A blast of cold air filled the room momentarily as our landlady disappeared outside. She pulled the door closed behind her and shuffled a few steps up the path. I could still see her clearly through the window. I had just taken another mouthful of breakfast when the unmistakable sound of a tremendous fart reverberated through the building. Sunny, mouth full of bacon butty, struggled not to choke for laughter. I swallowed my muesli, feeling faintly ill.

"That was a real window rattler," I said, then kicked myself again. My strategy had, quite literally, gone with the wind. Sunny was hitting his chest, trying to dislodge something. He gulped down a mouthful of orange juice to help it slide down his gullet.

"Is it even safe to eat anything prepared in this kitchen?" he asked, croakily.

"Don't be churlish," I said. "Dysentery keeps you marvellously thin." Sunny laughed, and I inwardly cursed myself. So much for distant and professional.

21

SUNNY

THE DAY WAS OFF to a weird start. Ludo *was* off with me. He sat about as far away from me on the press bus as possible, chatting to Annabelle from the BBC. As the morning progressed, I got the sense he was actively avoiding me, but I needed to focus on the job in hand. The press pack was touring a factory where Shetland locals were employed building wave turbines. The machines, which looked a bit like propeller aeroplanes, were designed to sit in the choppy waters off Shetland, generating renewable energy using the tidal powers of the sea.

"It's a world-first technology, designed and made right here in Britain," Torsten Beaumont-Flattery said. This was interesting, but none of us were science and technology writers; we were political journalists. As we walked around the factory, following the company's founder from point of interest to point of interest, I pulled Torsten aside for a quick word.

"I see Carstairs is back in London," I said. "What's the political announcement out of today going to be? I need to brief the newsroom ahead of morning conference."

Torsten put an enormous arm around my shoulder and walked with me, leading me along behind the rest of the obediently shuffling press pack. With each step his bicep beat against the back of my head like a basketball. I felt vaguely faint. Not from the concussion risk, which was very real, but from the hotness overload. I caught sight of Ludo, who had turned and was glaring at us. Was he actually *angry* with me?

"The minister is on her way back up right now," Torsten said. "She'll meet us at our next stop."

"*Another* trip for the taxpayer-funded jet? This better be good. Talk to me, Torsten."

"The jet had to go back anyway to pick up the secretary of state for education and training."

OK, so that gave me a pretty good steer on the content of today's announcements, but I wanted more information. I punched out a headline in the air with my hand.

"Climate change minister's planet-killing jet-propelled press junket," I offered. I tried another one. "Jemima racks up the Carst-air miles."

Torsten spun me around and gave me the kind of puppy-dog eyes that got actual puppy dogs adopted.

"Now, play fair, Sunny," he said. I went in for the kill.

"Why is Carstairs making announcements about energy policy?"

"The minister answered this yesterday." He flicked his teeth with his tongue.

"You know she didn't. Is the PM about to sack Bob Wynn-Jones? Will he do it this week, or will he wait until Parliament is back next week?"

"You're asking the wrong person," Torsten said, tongue flicking off his front teeth again. "I'm only a special adviser. You'd be better off speaking to the chief whip."

Torsten smiled, then held my gaze for a moment too long. The intensity of the stare would be enough to make a lesser man swoon. Fortunately, I am a consummate professional. I shifted my notepad to cover the front of my trousers. The longer the stare went on, the more I sensed he was trying to tell me something, but I had no idea what it was. He squeezed my shoulder and spun me back around, and we followed along behind the rest of the press pack. Ludo was still looking over at us, his face unreadable. Torsten's bicep bounced against the back of my head as we walked, again. My notepad was still in front of my crotch. As we stopped at the next point of interest, I saw Ludo turn away, slowly shaking his head. Wait, was this about Torsten? Was Ludo *jealous*?

22

LUDO

I FELT JOLLY TIRED and, truth be told, I was getting sick to death of it blowing a gale. Torsten had brought us to a windy knoll overlooking the North Sea. The skyline was dotted with wind turbines, the blades relentlessly circling like in-crowd Soho gays around out-of-town twinks. In front of us, at the base of one of these giant machines, stood Environment Secretary Jemima Carstairs and the secretary of state for education and training, Bimpe Lasisi. Like every other gay boy in Britain, I was *obsessed* with this woman. As always, Lasisi was dressed in traditional Yoruba Nigerian attire. Her hair was wrapped in a magnificent gele of turmeric and gold, and it crowned her face like the halo of a Russian icon. Her hands were clasped in front of her, preventing her shawl from flying off into the wind to join the guillemots and kittiwakes circling overhead.

"Scotland, and particularly Shetland, is a UK leader in renewable energy," Lasisi said. "Today, the government is announcing twenty thousand funded training places for those with relevant skills wishing to retrain and join the renewable sector, annually. We particularly want to encourage those currently working in the fossil fuel industry to retrain, so we can use their valuable skills and experience to help make a cleaner, greener Britain for tomorrow. Today, we also announce five thousand subsidised renewable energy apprenticeships, annually, to encourage young people up and down the country—from Shetland to Penzance—into careers in this exciting, world-beating *British* energy revolution."

Carstairs stepped forward. I heard Sunny clear his throat. I looked over at him, on the far side of the semicircle of the press pack. His notepad was tucked under one arm. The other arm, outstretched, held his phone, catching the audio. The morning sun, peering weakly from behind a cloud, shone red through his hair. It bathed his skin in honey and amber. Why was he so beautiful? Argh!

"We're putting Britain back to work," Carstairs said, looking straight down the barrel of the camera. "Over the next five years, with government support, renewable energy will become *the* major industry across Britain. This government is building a better tomorrow for our children by investing in a cleaner, greener Britain. We are creating the future our children deserve by building the today we all need."

No speech notes. This was all off the top of her head. No wonder people were talking her up as a future prime minister. I knew what my father would say, though. It was claptrap. Non-existent apprenticeships in a non-existent industry. Big announcement, great sound bites, no substance. I was feeling quite cynical about it myself and, to be frank, uninterested in the whole shebang.

Carstairs opened the floor to questions, and the entire press pack began squawking like the birds above our heads. All except me, that is. I couldn't think of a single question. The more I tried to think of one, the less clearly I could think at all. When I finally stumbled across a question, I couldn't seem to keep it in my head, and it slipped away again before I was able to ask it. Ten minutes later, everyone else in the press pack had asked at least one question. Sunny had asked three and was shouting out another one.

"It's a been big week of big, reforming announcements," he said. "Minister, why are *you* making them on behalf of the government, and not the prime minister?"

Carstairs kept looking down the barrel of the camera, not making eye contact.

"This is climate change policy, and I'm the minister responsible for climate change," she said. "OK, everyone got everything they need?" She clapped her hands together, not waiting for anyone to reply. "Torsten will give you a copy of the press release. Shall we get some pictures?"

Just like that, it was over. I stood frozen on the spot, my brain trying to tick over what had just happened.

"Are you OK, Ludo?" It was Sunny. He was standing beside me, a look of concern on his face. I felt the tender tap of his fingertips against my elbow. I pulled away.

"I'm fine," I said. The fingers returned.

"You didn't ask any questions, and I—"

I shook his hand off my arm. Sunny seemed taken aback.

"I'm fine," I said.

"Brain fade in press conferences is really common. It's a good idea to write a few questions down on your notepad before things get started, so you always have a prompt."

Sunny had just mansplained press conferences to a fifth-generation journalist.

"It wasn't brain fade. I'm just tired. I didn't sleep very well."

In fact, I was starting to feel quite light-headed. Over Sunny's shoulder I could see the other journos spreading out over the hilltop, phones clasped to their ears, calling the information back to their newsrooms. I should have been doing the same.

"That's my fault," Sunny said. He had no idea how right he was. "Too many late nights watching movies. I'm sorry." He also had no idea how wrong he was. I smiled faintly. Sunny said he had to call the newsroom and turned and walked away. I looked down at my phone.

"You're still coming to the pub tonight, though, right?" Sunny called out. He was standing about three metres from me, one foot balanced on a boulder like an idealised Victorian image of British masculinity and derring-do. "It's our last night. You don't want to miss it. You can sleep on the plane."

I nodded, just to be polite. Sunny smiled and gave two thumbs up, then turned to keep walking along the rocky hilltop. I returned to my phone and named the saved audio file "Saint Fabulous of Lasisi." I glanced up at the giant turbine above me. The majestic blades spun gracefully, swinging around and around effortlessly, like Margot Fonteyn's pirouettes in *Swan Lake*. My eyes landed on the tip of one blade, following it around as it carved a circle in the air. I felt dizzy. I switched my focus to the horizon to steady myself, took two steps, tripped on a rock, and fell to the ground.

23

LUDO

WHEN I CAME TO, I was lying in the damp grass. I had a thumping headache. There were two blurry figures above me—one with hair that danced and blazed like flames in a hearth, the other with a broad brown face and an aura as gold as the sun.

"Am I dead?" I asked. "Are you Jesus?"

"He's well enough to make jokes, then," Sunny said.

"He's well enough to blaspheme," added Bimpe Lasisi. "That's a fine thing, after the Lord saw fit to save your ungrateful white arse."

Someone called for the minister, and Lasisi hollered back that she was on her way. Her voice boomed across the hilltops with all the authority and lung capacity of someone who'd run a successful comprehensive school in one of London's most deprived areas for two decades before going into politics. I feared I might be permanently deaf in my right ear.

"Praise be to Jesus, you're OK," she said, then made her excuses and disappeared to have her photo taken.

Sunny was crouching over me, his hands firmly pressed into my hip and shoulder. He was still blurry, and I couldn't bring him into focus. I raised an arm to check for my glasses, correctly diagnosing that I was not, in fact, wearing them.

"Don't move," Sunny said. "You've had a fall, and you've whacked your noggin. Your glasses copped it, I'm afraid." I pulled my hand away from my face to find blood on my fingertips. "You did a proper job of it, Ludo Ben," Sunny said.

No one had ever called me that before. I smiled, through the wooziness, at the blur of him, grateful for his kindness.

"Is it bad?" I asked.

"Not too bad. It'll bruise. You might have a black eye for a few days. What happened?"

I tried to get up to rest on one arm, but Sunny told me to stay where I was.

"Torsten's gone for the first aid kit. He won't be a minute. Let's get you patched up first."

"Do you think if I pretended I'd broken my leg, Torsten would pick me up and carry me to the bus?"

"Starting to feel better already, then?"

"Sorry, that's so ungrateful," I said. "You've come to my rescue like a knight in shining armour, and here am I, the damsel in distress, tipping my hat at the nearest meaty squire."

"Mate, if I thought there was a chance of Torsten throwing one of us over his shoulder in a fireman's lift, I wouldn't be sitting here looking after you, I'd have flung you over the cliff, and I'd be trying to snap my own femur between two boulders."

I laughed. It hurt. A gigantic blur came into view, which I took to be Torsten. It was. He wiped my face with cotton pads, mopping up the blood and applying antiseptic. He was so gentle it was almost erotic.

"It's not too bad," Torsten said, speaking with the authority of a man who'd patched up many faces on the sidelines of rugby matches over many years. "You won't need stitches. Just a butterfly plaster. I've seen a lot worse."

He applied the aforementioned butterfly plaster. His enormous fingers, as meaty as the rest of him, were as tender as if he were handling an actual butterfly. Honestly, this man. If I had ovaries, they'd be singing entreaties to him like the sirens sang to Odysseus—and strapping himself to a mast would *not* be enough to save him.

"All done," he said. "You'll be fine now. Just mind out for concussion. We don't want a repeat of the school play, do we?"

Torsten put out a hand and helped me to my feet. My head throbbed with the altitude change.

"Do you need a hand getting back to the bus?" he asked.

"I've got him," Sunny said. To my surprise, Sunny grabbed my arm and put it around his shoulder; then he wrapped his other arm around my waist. "You go deal with that lot." Sunny nodded towards the rest of the press pack, scattered over the blurry hill like blurry sheep.

***

"YOU JOLLY WELL COCK-BLOCKED me just now, Miller," I said, when we were sitting on the bus. "I was as good as wrapped up like a baby in Torsten's arms, and you ripped me out of them, like a nun at an orphanage gate. It's not on."

Sunny laughed. My head was still thumping. Being distant and professional, I saw, was no longer an option. Sunny Miller was now my designated nursemaid—and as it turns out, he was jolly good at it. He was being jolly kind, and it sort of made me regret giving him the cold shoulder all day.

"So, you two went to school together?" he asked.

"We did." I could see Sunny doing the maths in his head, although I wasn't sure exactly what calculation he was making.

"Here you go," he said, passing me my glasses. He'd stuck the broken arm back on with sticking plasters from the first aid kit. When I put them on, Sunny's face came into focus, the white and copper blob of him suddenly a high-definition Technicolor wonder of features and freckles. His brow was furrowed.

"So, what happened at the school play?"

"Bit of bad luck, that's all," I explained. "We did *Les Misérables*. I was Monsieur Thénardier, the landlord. Torsten was my understudy, as it happens."

"I can't really see Torsten in a musical, somehow. Unless there's an *Incredible Hulk* musical I don't know about?"

"Do you want to know what happened or not?"

"I do."

"Do you know the bit at the end of 'Master of the House' when the landlord's wife, Madame Thénardier, hits her husband over the head with a bottle?"

"Please don't tell me she hit you with a real bottle."

"Golly no! That could have killed me. No, I was so into the part that when she hit me with the sugar bottle and I pretended to collapse, I banged my head on the table and knocked myself out cold. They had to carry me off stage."

"That's awful."

"That's not even the bit Torsten was referring to. When I went back on for my next scene, I was so confused from the concussion that I delivered all my lines in French."

"Bollocks, you never!" Sunny said, cackling with laughter. "You're having me on."

"It gets worse. Confused and completely lost as to where we were in the script, I panicked and sang the 'Elephant Love Medley.' Rather well, as it happens, so I was told afterwards. The trouble is, the medley is from Baz Luhrmann's *Moulin Rouge*, not *Les Misérables*."

Sunny was bent over with laughter, slapping his thigh.

"The rest of the cast was so jolly startled they didn't know what to do to get the show back on track, so they let me go on until I'd finished the song. They sent Torsten on to play Monsieur Thénardier for the rest of the show. Except he hadn't bothered to learn his lines, and the only part of the costume that fit him was the hat. So, he went onstage in his dress rugby uniform, with his script in hand, and mechanically read out the lines, like a schoolboy doing a very problematic impersonation of Stephen Hawking."

"OK, that definitely did not go the way I expected."

"It didn't go the way anyone expected. When I saw Uncle Ben in the car park after the show, he said it was 'an avant-garde triumph' and the production was immeasurably better for the changes. Five stars, he reckoned."

"I'm sorry I missed it," Sunny said, still giggling. He dabbed a bit of bandage at my forehead. A sharp pain stabbed through my skull, and I winced. "Sorry, does it hurt? We'll take you to the doctor when we get back into town and get you some painkillers." As Sunny's bright peridot eyes met mine, I could have sworn I saw genuine concern in his expression.

"You're going to look a right mess at karaoke tonight," he said.

"Karaoke?"

"At the pub. It's our final night activity. You can't get out of it now that I know about your singing talents. Will you sing 'Voulez-vous coucher avec moi ce soir' for me?"

I looked at Sunny, bewildered. *Voulez-vous coucher avec moi ce soir*, as any *Moulin Rouge* fan knows, means "Do you want to sleep with me tonight?" Although the song is called "Lady Marmalade," which I was surprised Sunny didn't know. Unless that was deliberate? He was staring back at me, eyes twinkling, cheeky grin on his cocky freckled face. Had I just been propositioned by my nurse? During my convalescence? Where had this confidence come from? Then it clicked.

"You don't speak French, do you?"

"Not a word."

24

SUNNY

PAINKILLERS AND COSMOPOLITANS ARE clearly a proper heady combo. Ludo was (metaphorically) on fire. The minute the karaoke machine was turned on, there he was, channelling Velma Kelly, belting out "All That Jazz" from *Chicago*. It was complete with a dance routine, and not once did Ludo look at the screen with the little ball bouncing over the lyrics. Then Rafiq joined him onstage for "Mamma Mia," and the entire pub was up, singing along and dancing. I had to hand it to Ludo: he knew how to get a party started.

When the song had finished, he popped his mic back into the stand, picked up his sickly pink cocktail, and sashayed across to our table like a drunk in a nightclub. He flopped down in the chair beside me, like his body was boneless. His bruise was coming in well now. He was going to have a shiner.

"Proper impressive," I said. And I meant it.

"Thank you!" He raised his cosmo. I clinked my half-finished cider against it. "We theatre kids keep a few tricks up our sleeves for just such occasions."

As we drank, the unmistakable opening bars of Adele's "Someone Like You" filled the room. Onstage, Rafiq had the microphone in hand and was swaying from side to side, ready for his solo.

"Whoa, this is a big song," Ludo said.

"*Love* Adele."

So did everyone else in the pub, apparently. The crowd hushed in quiet respect as Rafiq's rich, melodious vocals soared over all of us.

"My God, that voice," Ludo whispered. I nodded, spellbound. The song built. Rafiq had the audience in the palms of his hands. When he'd finished, the entire pub erupted into applause. Rafiq bowed deeply, his hands in front of his chest in a gesture of thanks. He was blushing. I stuck my fingers in my mouth and whistled. Ludo's eyebrows went up, his sapphire-blue eyes glassy and incredulous.

"What? We estate kids have a few tricks up our sleeves for just such occasions."

Rafiq bounded over to the table.

"You have a magnificent set of pipes," Ludo said. "Have you been classically trained?"

"Classically what?" Rafiq asked.

"Who taught you to sing like that?"

"Adele." Rafiq looked mystified.

"Yes, it's her song. But who taught you?"

"No one, bruv. I just sing it the way Adele does." Rafiq pointed at our drinks. "I'm going to the bar. Can I get you lads anything?"

Rafiq took our order and bounced off, clearly still on a high from performing.

"He just sings it the way Adele does?" Ludo said in disbelief. "No one just sings it the way Adele does. That takes years of training."

Onstage, some old dude was belting out David Bowie's "'Heroes.'"

"You'd never know Rafiq was sitting on a voice like that," Ludo said. He was swaying slightly. "Like, at the puffins the other day... it was like birdwatching with a frat bro. He seemed like a real *lad*, you know? Beer and football and Nicki Minaj. Then he comes out and sings with the voice of an angel. And he's untrained."

I stared at him, debating what to say. Should I smack him down for making assumptions about Rafiq based on stereotypes and impressions? I could at least point out that Rafiq is an observant Muslim and doesn't drink? Ludo went to sip his cosmo and missed his mouth. He brushed the spillage off his jumper with his hand. With him in this state, there was no point saying much at all. The lesson here was for me, not for him. It was a reminder of the wildly different worlds Ludo and I came from.

In the end, I said, "If we've learned anything this past week, surely it's not to judge a book by its cover?"

Ludo looked up, eyes glassy but intense. He reached over and grabbed my hand, surprising me. His skin was warm and sticky. He'd opened his mouth to speak when three very full glasses appeared on the table in front of us. Ludo pulled his hand away. Rafiq slid into a spare seat beside us. Whatever Ludo wanted to say, it had only been meant for my ears.

We thanked Rafiq for our drinks. His eyes flicked between Ludo and me.

"Am I interrupting summink?"

"Not at all," I said, picking up my cider. We cheersed.

On the stage, "'Heroes'" dude was winding up.

"I'm going to choose another song," Ludo said, stumbling out of the chair and disappearing towards the edge of the stage to flick through the song list.

Rafiq sipped at his Coke.

"You boys banging then, bruv?" he asked.

I spat my cider back into my glass, spilling it all over my face, my jeans, and my shirt.

"What makes you say that?"

"The chirps, bruv. You been proper flirting with each other this whole trip."

"Don't be ridiculous."

"I seen it, bruv. With me own eyes. The way you look at each other. I thought you'd been lipsing at least."

"Absolutely not."

Rafiq shrugged. "You wanna shoot your shot, fam. He's bare gassed for you. And I reckon you are for him too."

"Don't be ridiculous," I said. "He's the competition. Besides, can you imagine me taking him home to meet me mum? I doubt he's ever been in a council flat in his life."

"Who you convincing? You'd be great together, fam."

"Based on what?"

"Chemistry, bruv."

"Someone's spiked your drink, mate. You're high."

Rafiq shrugged his shoulders. "Don't die wondering, bruv. I reckon you should shoot your shot."

***

TEN MINUTES LATER, RAFIQ and I were watching Ludo belt out "Angel of the Morning" with what appeared to be choreographed dance moves. Rafiq put his glass down on the table with a thud.

"If I line up a song, will you sing it with me, bruv?" he asked.

"Nooo. I tried to sing in the bath once, and the water undid the plug all by itself, just to get away."

"You only have to sing the *oh oh oh*s. That's the easy part. I'll do the rest."

I was uncertain. Rafiq nudged me with his shoulder.

"Do it for Leicester, bruv."

"Fine, but if people's ears start to bleed, or if the birds fall out of the sky, or anyone throws a bar stool at us, you're on your own, OK?"

When it came to our turn, and the opening notes of Billy Joel's "Uptown Girl" started to play, Ludo shouted "Tune!" and jumped up onstage with us, joining me in the *oh oh oh*s. Within seconds practically everyone in the pub was dancing and singing along. We bopped and bounced as Rafiq sang the main lyrics and Ludo and I wailed the harmony (if that's what it's called). My singing voice, as promised, sounded like someone had wrapped a crow in aluminium foil and run it through with a chainsaw—but I was having an awesome time. Ludo looked so happy, losing himself in the music. As we *oh oh oh*ed, our eyes met, his sapphire blues sparkling like mirrorballs. He smiled, and I smiled back. I threw an arm around his shoulder, and we swayed in unison, microphones in hand. It felt... *really* good to hold him. To feel the warmth of him beside me. In a few short minutes, it was all over. A couple of locals jumped onstage and grabbed the microphones. We returned to our table. I slid into my seat, safe in the knowledge I had not hit a single note, but more confused than ever about my feelings for Ludo.

25

LUDO

THE NIGHT AIR WAS jolly cold, and the walk back to the B & B was hillier than we'd remembered. The painkillers were wearing off, and with every step, my head throbbed.

"If you're from Leicester," I said, trying not to slur my words, "why don't you sound like you come from Leicester?"

Sunny's arm was around my shoulder. Mine was wrapped around his waist, my thumb hooked into his belt. We were, I confess, rather holding each other up, and weaving all over the road.

"Wossermarrerwiyu?" Sunny said, suddenly. "Got a cob on or summat?"

I stopped and stared at him, leaning backwards slightly, trying to bring his face into focus. Had my glasses come off again? I couldn't seem to un-fuzzy his visage. He was a blotch of pale skin, luminous in the moonlight but featureless.

"How drunk are you?" I said. "You're speaking in tongues."

"Just proving my 'Lestah' credentials."

"Golly. Is that how people speak up there? It's like another language entirely."

"Why do you think I worked so hard to get rid of it?" he said.

"But I don't understand. I thought you were proud of where you come from?"

"I am, mate. But there's terrible accent bias in this country. People hear a West Country accent and assume you're a farmer. They hear a Glaswegian accent and assume you're going to glass them. And if you sound like you come from anywhere north of Milton Keynes, they think you're thick as shit. It's a disgrace, actually. It's part of the ingrained cultural bias and class inequality that robs ordinary people of opportunities."

Somehow, we were back where we started at Maxime's. I feared this could get messy. But how to de-escalate things? My brain was too foggy to think. My temple was throbbing where the bruise was coming in.

"I knew if I spoke like me mum, or the lads where I grew up, I'd never get taken seriously in this business," Sunny continued. "So, I studied the BBC newsreaders and taught myself how to speak properly."

A gust of wind blew across us, and I shivered. Sunny wrapped his arm more tightly around me. It was an instinct. I liked it. And I liked what it implied.

"You're very passionate when you're drunk," I said. "And you're very cute when you're passionate."

"Studies have proven it time and time again," Sunny said.

"That you're very cute when you're passionate?" Which, on the spectrum of distant and professional to "I think you need a bit more lube," definitely qualified as flirting. Strategy be damned. I just wanted to kiss him. Sunny was so pretty and so kind, and I just... wanted... to *kiss*... him.

"You think this is funny?"

"Wait, what?" I'd lost the thread. It was those blush-pink lips. The freckles. The way his nipples were sticking out of his shirt like fingerposts. They were all too distracting. This wasn't going well. I was mentally scrambling around for a way to smooth things over when I tripped on a rock and stumbled. Sunny scooped me up, keeping me vertical with his surprisingly fast reaction time.

"Twice in one day. You've got to pick your feet up, mate."

I thanked him and apologised. My mind swirled with memories of how jolly kind Sunny had been today. He'd been a brick. The way he'd looked after me, fixed my glasses for me. I was still warm with the rush of being on-stage together, having the whole pub singing along with us, dancing, and laughing and enjoying life. Sunny was amazing, and... I'd adored spending time with him like this. It felt right, having our arms around each other like this. I turned to look at Sunny properly, trying to bring him into focus. The moonlight caught the green of his eyes. He was still as unutterably beautiful as I thought him on that first day at PMQs. But he was also still on his soapbox.

"It's all a stitch-up, mate. The Establishment has got it all stitched up."

I searched for something to say but came up empty. Nonetheless, I was pretty sure "the Establishment" meant my lot, and I wondered if Sunny could ever get over this silly chip on his shoulder about coming from an estate.

"I'm sorry," I said. It was all I had. How do you make amends for generations of inequity when, if you're honest, you've never really given it much thought?

***

WE ARRIVED AT THE Otter's Den. Sunny opened the door, and we fell into the house. It smelt like a truck carrying a load of eggs had crashed into the kitchen about three weeks earlier and no one had cleaned up the mess. We staggered our way through the maze of the building to our rooms. Sunny opened my door and helped me into the room, his arms sliding from around my waist as he lowered me onto the bed. I felt the loss of his touch, his retreating warmth. His amber-green eyes seemed to bore into me, and without knowing I had been going to do it, I grabbed his hand to pull him down onto me. Sunny pulled away.

"I don't think that's a good idea," he said. I was mortified. My heart sank. Embarrassment flooded my body. "We're colleagues. And we're drunk."

"Sorry. I got a bit carried away."

He nodded at the poster on the wall.

"It's Jessica Simpson, isn't it? She gets you going."

"It's the General Lee, actually."

I was scrambling for things to say to relieve the tension and get things back to normal. Sunny was clearly doing the same.

"I didn't have you pegged as a car guy," he said.

"Perhaps you shouldn't judge a book by its cover?"

Sunny laughed and retreated to the open door.

"Thank you for today," I said, before he could disappear.

"Don't mention it. Night, uptown girl."

Sunny pulled the door closed behind him. I pulled the duvet over myself, curling up to sleep, still fully dressed.

26

LUDO

THE NEXT MORNING WAS a dark-sunglasses-inside kind of day. My head both looked and felt like someone had popped it inside a rugby ball and given it to Torsten and his mates for a Sunday-afternoon kickabout. Fortunately, we did not have to be up early. Unfortunately, today was travel day, which meant returning to London with a throbbing head and a stomach that might not have the most reassuringly firm grip on its contents. Still, I couldn't wait to get home. Shetland now felt like a holiday that had gone on just a bit too long—when home is preferable to anything a previously longed for destination could possibly hold, when the novelty of the sunshine and snippets of phrase book pleasantries had soured.

We never did meet Mr Gallacher, the master of the house, but just the mention of his name will forever bring the sulphuric stench of that B & B to mind—as clear and pungent as if he were in the room. As we said our farewells to Mrs Gallacher on the front porch, she handed us each a small cardboard box wrapped in pink ribbon.

"What's this, Mrs G?" Sunny said, accepting his gift.

"Otter shite," Mrs Gallacher said.

"Pardon?" I said.

"It's not *actual* otter shite, is it, Mrs G?" Sunny seemed in need of reassurance. He was not alone.

"Och, no, laddie. They're chocolates. There's a place up in Lerwick makes these wee choccies they call puffin poo. They charge like a fucking wounded bull, and I can soon as make them meself. But I cannae call them puffin poo in case they fucking sue us, so I call them otter shite instead, on account of us being the Otter's Den. D'ya ken?"

"I ken, Mrs Gallacher, I ken."

Sunny, already ferreting around in his box (if that's not mixing my mammals too much), plucked out an otter poo and popped it in his mouth. He mawed at it, making appreciative noises, and gave Mrs G a big thumbs up and a cheesy grin.

"Best otter shite I ever tasted, Mrs G," he said.

"I'll save mine for the flight," I said. "I always want chocolate on a plane trip." In truth, I was struggling with the psychological barrier of putting something called otter shite in my mouth.

The coach came rumbling into view.

"That's us," I said. "Thanks ever so much for having us, Mrs Gallacher."

"You're very welcome. We hope to see you back some day. Tell everyone about Shetland and the Otter's Den."

"You can be sure we will, Mrs G."

"Fuckety-bye," Mrs Gallacher said. She waved, turned, and dropped her guts before opening the door and disappearing inside.

The coach pulled to a stop, the air brakes screeched, and I thought my eyes might bleed. The doors opened.

"I really must remember to read the Tripadvisor for this place at some point," I said, as we climbed onto the bus.

When we got to Sumburgh Airport it became clear we were flying home commercial and not by government jet.

"That's my fault," Sunny said. "I kept threatening Torsten with a story about this trip's greenhouse gas emissions."

It made for a much slower journey, including a stopover in Aberdeen, but in the end it wasn't too bad. I sat next to Sunny on the first leg—which was less awkward than I feared it might be, after being rebuffed the night before—and Rafiq on the second. At Aberdeen Airport, I bought a giant Toblerone and shared it with them both—the otter shite having been consumed before we'd even taken off from Shetland. At Gatwick, faced with a train and a Tube and a walk, all of which meant certain death, I said my goodbyes to them both and slipped off to take a cab. If I was feeling generous, I would have suggested Sunny share the ride, seeing as Willesden Green isn't that far from Hampstead. As it was, I felt like I'd had my fill of Sunny Miller for one week. I was feeling a bit tender, my face was black and blue, and all I wanted was my bed.

27

SUNNY

ON FRIDAY MORNING I found myself in Vladimir Popov's constituency office. It was a full-on contrast to his Westminster office, with its stuffed ferrets and strong whiff of empire. His Islington bolthole was painted crisp white, with modern furniture, big windows, and one of those enormous Swiss cheese plants that people went proper apeshit for during the pandemic. Like Westminster, everything in here was immaculately clean. Like Westminster, it smelt of spices, expensive hair product, and that very particular brand of testosterone you get off entitled rich pricks. I had been shown into VladPop's office by Mandy, his assistant, and was sitting in the naughty chair, waiting for the man himself to appear.

"He won't be a minute," Mandy said, popping her head around the door from the reception area. "He's just texted to say he's been held up in Sainsbury's."

"Holy crap!"

"*Delayed*, I should say," she added. "Chatting to constituents. It happens a lot."

She probably meant he was chatting to Lord Sainsbury himself, rather than popping into the supermarket to pick up an egg-and-cress sandwich and a packet of salt-and-vinegar crisps.

"Cuppa tea?"

"Yes, please," I said.

"Bag left in?"

How badly had my accent slipped? Did I sound *northern*? Still, good guess, Mandy. "Please," I said.

She disappeared up the corridor, leaving me alone in VladPop's office. I leant forward in my seat, sneaking a look at what was in his in tray. A couple of crisp manila folders filled with papers. Probably constituent files. But what if they were the chief whip's famous dirt files? This file might contain the mother lode of *Bulletin* front pages.

From up the corridor I could hear the static white noise of a kettle element heating up water and the clatter of mugs and spoons. I craned my neck to look around the doorway. No one was about. I reached over and gently lifted the corner of the topmost folder with the tip of my pen. I could see the purple logo of a company I'd never heard of before, ZephEnergies Limited. On one level, this didn't surprise me. Companies write to members of parliament all the time, and given we'd just had a week of energy policy announcements, there was bound to be a flush of letter-writing activity. On another level, VladPop was the chief whip, not the energy minister, and it seemed unlikely that an energy company planned to build a wind farm or a hydroelectric scheme in his Inner London constituency.

I was curious to know what the letter said. I looked around again to check the coast was clear, then lifted the folder open a little more with my pen. As I stood to get a better view, I heard the front door swing open, and panic gripped me. A gust of cool air filled the building, sending papers flying—including the ZephEnergies letter, which swirled down onto the floor behind VladPop's desk.

"Bloody hell!" the chief whip called out from the entranceway. "Mandy!"

I was in deep trouble if I got caught like this. VladPop would nail me to the door and use my dick as a coat hook. But what to do? The letter could not be safely retrieved. I stared at the piece of paper that had been sitting underneath the ZephEnergies letter, as if it might come up with a plan. It did not. The words "Prometheus Ltd" stared back up at me from the page, laughing at the scrape I'd got myself into. Time slowed down. From the reception I could hear the usually unflappable chief whip, cursing and stomping about, probably picking up scattered papers. That was it! Blame the wind. It wasn't even a lie. I let the manila folder gently fall closed, sat back down in the chair, and waited for the chief whip to make his entrance.

A moment later, Vladimir Popov appeared in the doorway, arms wide, briefcase in hand.

"Sunshine Augustus Miller!" he said, as if that wasn't proper creepy. He popped his case down on his desk. "Come on, bring it in." Was the chief whip about to hug me? I stood. His arms wrapped around me, slapping my back; then his enormous hands grabbed and shook me by the biceps. He gave an alarmingly toothy smile.

"We. Have. *Business*," he said, stretching the words out like he had just ordered a round of margaritas and was ready to gossip with his girlfriends. He released me, walked around the back of his desk, noticed the letter on the floor, picked it up, popped it in the folder, and sat down into his chair.

"But first, I want to hear all about Shetland. *The kettle is on*, as you young people say."

He'd lost me.

"I'm *not* sure we do say that," I said. "I've never heard anyone say that."

"Of course you have! All the gays say it. 'The kettle is on. Let's make the tea.'"

It clicked.

"Spill the tea," I said. "The saying is 'spill the tea.' No one puts the kettle on."

"But then how do you make the tea?"

I was saved by Mandy, who walked in with the actual tea. She put it down on a coaster on the end of VladPop's desk. I thanked her, and she exited the room, closing the door behind her.

"So, tell me, tell me, *tell me*! Did you hook up with Ludo?"

By this point it was clear I had entered a parallel dimension where professional standards and boundaries did not exist. They don't exist at Westminster in our *own* dimension, but this was some next-level intrusion.

"No, I did not."

"Oh, that's a terrible shame. It seems that love is in the air everywhere, but not for Sunny and Ludo."

"Can we get back to the business you brought me here for?" I said, frustration getting the better of me. Vladimir looked hurt.

"Of course," he said. He opened his briefcase and pulled out a tablet, fiddled with it for a bit, and then handed it to me. "Watch this and tell me what you think."

It was grainy CCTV footage, but the figure in it was immediately recognisable as Bob Wynn-Jones. A few seconds later, he was in a clinch with a woman with long dark tresses—a woman I knew not to be his wife. They kissed passionately. The footage went on for about twenty seconds. It was a short clip, but it was explosive. Half the editors on Fleet Street would cream their knickers if they thought they had this story exclusively. Those editors all worked up the trashy end of the street, obviously, but that was *my* end of Fleet Street. JT would definitely want this footage. For me, though, the footage alone wasn't enough.

"There's more. Much more," Vladimir said, eyes twinkling with relish.

"Why are you showing me this?"

"Because you're a journalist, and we have a deal."

"When we made our deal, I said no sex scandals. Things that matter, I said. Things that make a difference. I don't want to be known for writing this kind of trash."

"You do still write for the *Bulletin*, don't you?"

"As a political reporter. I'm not the *Too Hot to Handle* correspondent."

"I love that show, actually."

"It's generally accepted that affairs are private matters. I need more before we can print this. What's the public interest angle on this?"

"Sunny, this isn't just an affair, this is a matter of national security," VladPop said. He pointed at the figure on the tablet. "Yes, he's a cabinet minister. But she"—he pointed at the woman—"is a Belarusian spy. Everyone seems to have known about it except poor Bob."

I gasped.

"Does MI5 know you've got this?" I asked.

Vladimir laughed.

"Where do you think I got it?"

I stared at the frozen image on the screen.

"Are we OK to run it?" I asked. "I can do without being the reason the *Bulletin* offices get raided."

"Sunny, you have a choice. I can either give you the story and you get all the credit, or I can give it straight to JT. Either way, that story will be on the front page of tomorrow's *Bulletin*. How would you like it to get there?"

This didn't need much thinking about.

"Fine," I said. "Spill the tea."

28

LUDO

T O WAKE, SUDDENLY AND unexpectedly, to Ricky Martin's "Livin' la Vida Loca" booming out of every Bluetooth speaker in your bedroom is to understand the desire to stab a knitting needle through your own head, from ear to ear, without fear of the consequences.

"Bastard!" I shouted at the top of my lungs—though from my hideaway in the summer house, there was little hope of Jonty hearing me. When had he managed to arrange this? I reached for my glasses on the bedside table, my fingers finding the fat wodge of sticking plasters that was still holding them together. Sunny's DIY. The bruise on my face throbbed as I slipped my glasses on. I turned off the not-my-alarm alarm. It was six o'clock. By the time I had showered, got into my ballet teaching gear, and made it into the house for a spot of breakfast, Mother and Father were up. Father was boiling the kettle and smearing something fattening on toast, while Mummy was sitting at the kitchen table working her way through the Saturday papers. In the background, the BBC's *Today* programme—radio for the terminally depressed. Father offered to make me a cup of tea, and I readily accepted, because, English.

"Morning, Mummy," I said, kissing her on the top of her head. I plucked the *Sentinel* from the pile, did a pirouette because I could, and sat in the chair on the other side of the table. "Did we miss anything?"

"If you've been scooped, it's not by this lot," she said, pointing at the *Telegraph*.

Father turned up the radio. The lilting sounds of Mum's old chum and predatory wannabe *Sentinel* columnist, Lucy Veeraswamy, filled the room.

"A look at the papers now, and the big story of the day, the *Bulletin* has obtained exclusive images of Energy Secretary Bob Wynn-Jones in what the paper claims is a romantic embrace with a woman MI5 has identified as a Belarusian spy."

"Bastards!" My father, obviously jolly miffed he'd missed the biggest story of the day, dropped a plate.

"Yes, that'll show them, Hugo," Mummy said. She scrambled through the papers until she found the *Bulletin*, right at the bottom of the pile, unfolded it, and stared wide-eyed at the picture. Father, tea towel wrapped tight around his hand in anguish, stood behind her, reading it over his shoulder. In the background, Lucy Veeraswamy continued talking as if she hadn't just completely upended the mornings of Hugo and Beverley Barker-Boche.

"The paper claims the woman, known as Ekaterina Ivanova, used her influence to sway the minister's decision on the controversial Leicestershire nuclear power plant, which was to be built by the Belarusian company Mogilatom, owned by oligarch Yevgeny Safin," Veeraswamy said.

I stood up and walked around the table, joining my father in reading the article over Mummy's shoulder. There it was, staring back up at me from the front page, the photo byline of the beautiful freckled boy with the silly name. The one who'd knocked me back. The one I hadn't been able to stop thinking about since getting home.

"Well done, Sunny Miller," I said.

My father looked at me like I'd just taken a dump in his pocket.

"Friend of yours, darling?" Mummy asked.

"Yes," I said. "We were on Shetland together."

In the background, Lucy was still banging on.

"And we'll be talking to the *Bulletin*'s Sunny Miller about that story after eight o'clock," she said.

I smiled. I couldn't help it. I'd be at ballet by then, surrounded by twenty-two tutued toddling terrorists, trying to turn them into tiny Tamara Toumanovas.

"Someone must have dropped this to him," Father said. "Who the bloody hell dropped it to him?"

"You mean why didn't they drop it to you?" I suggested.

"No, Ludovic. Why didn't they drop it to *you*! This is your story. You've dropped the ball on this. How the bloody hell did you miss it?"

What the? I wasn't having this. I opened my mouth to protest, but Mummy beat me to it.

"Don't be silly, Hugo. You wouldn't have printed something as salacious as a minister of the Crown having an extramarital affair. Sex between consenting adults is a private matter. Isn't that your policy?"

"With a spy, Beverley. It's sex with a bloody spy! Of course we would have bloody well printed it."

"Fine. But would you have given it a headline like this?"

Mummy held the paper a little higher. A grainy image of Wynn-Jones leching all over a woman, one hand ferreting around under her skirt, dominated the left-hand side of the page. Beneath a big red banner that screamed "SEXCLUSIVE," the front-page headline read "BONK WYNN-JONES' SEXPLOSIVE SECRET!" Underneath, in inimitable *Bulletin* fashion, they had chosen the subheading "Revealed: Energy Secretary shagging Soviet honeypot at centre of Leicester nukes deal." That was at least two factual errors and one instance of base misogyny in the space of a dozen words. Remarkable, even by the standards of the *Bulletin*. But the top prize went to the photo caption, which read "POWER PLAY: Bob sticks two fingers up to Britain, while the rest disappear up Belarus."

"This story was *made* for a tabloid like the *Bulletin*," Mummy said. "And whoever dropped this to Sunny Miller wanted Bob Wynn-Jones not just out of the cabinet but out of politics for good."

"Bloody hell!" Father was angry now, balling up the tea towel as if he wanted to strangle it. He threw it hard against the table, but it just kind of flopped there, the perfect symbol of his impotence.

"You took your eyes off the ball, Ludo," Father said. "I knew you weren't ready for the big league."

"Wait, what?"

"You need to lift your game, young man, if you don't want to find yourself stuck down in features writing obituaries and reviewing last night's episode of *EastEnders*. You should have been all over this. It was *your* story."

Father was stabbing a finger at me, his face radicchio red.

"How did you miss it?"

I was speechless. Father ripped the paper out of Mummy's hands, shaking it like he wanted to throttle the life out of it.

"You can bloody well go in tomorrow and clean up this mess."

"It's my day off. Uncle Ben and I are—"

"News isn't a nine-to-five job, Ludo. News is happening *now*—and it's your job to break it!" He slammed the newspaper into the table and marched out of the kitchen and up the hall.

"Don't worry, darling," Mummy said. "It'll be old news by tomorrow, and he'll be outraged about something else. It's just your turn for the firing line today. You and the dinner service."

I wasn't sure what I was supposed to feel in that moment. On one hand, I'd been scooped on a story I had originally broken, by a man I had spent the entire week with and had come to really like—a man who had given no hint that he was working on a story as massive as this. I sort of felt tremendously proud of him. On the other hand, Sunny Miller's rise had apparently led directly to my disgrace—and the end of a long-planned jaunt to the V & A with Uncle Ben. And for that, frankly, I was jolly well annoyed with him. Still, I couldn't deny Sunny was setting the news agenda today. Council estate kid: one. Establishment: nil. I made a mental note to send him a message of congratulations on GayHoller. Later. I wasn't feeling quite that magnanimous just yet.

29

SUNNY

STAVROS: *IF THERE'S NOT an indie band called the Soviet Honeypots by five o'clock this afternoon, youth culture is dead. Congratulations on your big scoop, Sunster.*

Davinder: *Hi, actual music journalist here. Pleased to inform you the Soviet Honeypots formed at ten minutes past midnight last night, when the early edition hit the streets. Their debut album, "Fingerbang," is already topping the UK charts and is Spotify's "most downloaded." If you tune in to PureFM right now, you can hear my talented husband playing their debut single, "Bob Chooses the Nuclear Option and Ends His Career."*

Petey Boy: *Dav, that's peak, man. Sunny, congrats on the splash. If it was a weekday, we'd have got you on the yellow couch, boyo. Believe the hype!*

Jumaane: *Celebrate after yoga, yeah? Miss Timmy's for Bloody Marys and a fat slice of Occasion Cake?*

***

B Y ELEVEN O'CLOCK I had knocked off a bit of national breakfast radio, toned my tummy on the yoga mat for an hour, and was sitting opposite Jumaane in a booth in Miss Timmy's, waiting for the other boys to turn up. I loved Miss Timmy's. As gender non-conforming teahouses go, it was the best one on Old Compton Street. The house specialty was a chocolate torte covered in edible glitter. It looked like a unicorn turd, but the menu said it was perfect for any occasion—hence the name Occasion Cake. Specifically, the cake was "the ideal way to celebrate your birthday, bar mitzvah, coming out, going back in, changing your mind, changing your gender, gay wedding, gay divorce, meeting a new lover, reheating an old lover, getting over a lover, getting over the clap, the release of a new Zac Efron movie, or even just a particularly invigorating wank." They knew their market.

My phone rang. It was that time of the week.

"Hiya Mum, did you hear me on the *Today* programme?"

"I didn't, love. I'm down the food bank cos I done a swap with Wendy from number thirty-three. She's taken Shirley Trimble down A & E, cos that leg of hers has gone septic. I said to Wendy, better you than me. I ain't holding Shirley's hand while they lop her leg off. The doctor'll be hacksawing away at her knee joint, and old Shirl will be rolling her eyes and telling him to stop making such a fuss. You can't help these old dears."

"Mum, a little focus."

"Sorry, love. Well done on your big story. I haven't read it, but I'm sure it'll make a real difference."

"I'm just sitting here with Jumaane. We're having cake to celebrate."

"HELLO, JUMAANE LOVE!" Mum was shouting into the phone. I had to pull it away from my ear.

"Did you hear that?" I said, as if they hadn't heard it three tables over.

"Thanks, Stace," Jumaane said, waving at my phone as if this were a video call. Honestly, the pair of them.

"THANK YOU FOR THE CHRISTMAS CARD," Mum shouted.

"Mum, it's nearly May."

"You're welcome, Stace."

"YOU'RE A VERY WELL BROUGHT UP YOUNG MAN."

"OK, can we call time on this love-in, please? We're meant to be celebrating me today," I said.

"Orright, love. Well, stay safe. When are you coming to visit me?"

"Soon, Mum."

"OK, love. BYE, JUMAANE. And Sunny, remember what I said about fisting—"

I hung up the call. Jumaane looked at me in disbelief.

"Don't ask," I said.

"No, we'll be circling back to fisting in a minute, but does Stace really not read your work?"

"Never has."

"Sod that, babes. My mother has every single copy of *Pastiche Magazine* I've ever worked on. Even if all I did was write the captions."

"I *think* Mum does it to stop me getting ideas above my station."

Jumaane looked horrified. A drag queen rolled up to take our order.

***

I WAS THREE BLOODY Marys and a Long Island iced tea into our brunch when the notorious GayHoller chime pealed from a telephone. Every gay in the vicinity (except Dav and Nick, who had no need of GayHoller because they were unbearably loved up) checked their phone.

"It's for me," I called out, like a teenager in a nineties sitcom who had answered the family phone to find her girlfriend on the other end, ready to gossip. A round of applause went up from nearby tables. Gays were so sarcastic-slash-supportive. It was hard to know which this was. I had so much booze in me, I didn't much care. I opened the app.

Cabbage98: *Bravo, Ginger. You kept that quiet. Father was so jolly miffed he smashed a plate, so you're pissing off all the right people. He's making me work tomorrow, as punishment for missing your "sexclusive." I'd cut the brake cable on your car but I'm not sure if you even drive. Still, well done. Posh x*

That made me smile. I replied telling Ludo where we were and suggested he join us. I wasn't sure why I did that. It might have had something to do with the three Bloody Marys and the Long Island iced tea. It also might have had something to do with the fact that, in the days since getting home, I'd also started to miss his company. I missed the banter, the cosiness, the smell of warm linen and cashmere. I missed hanging out. Was it a good idea to invite him, though? It was too late. I'd sent it. Somewhere across London, the GayHoller chime was pealing a notification for Ludo Boche.

"Er, who is that?" Nick said. I felt the flush of heat in my face, and I knew my skin had betrayed me. I put my phone back down on the table.

"Whoever it is, Sunny's got the hots for him," Dav said. "I haven't seen his face that red since that day he fell asleep on the beach at Hornsea."

"Shut up, I do not. It's just a colleague."

"A colleague texting you on GayHoller?" Stav said. "If you say so, Romeo."

"Your message was proper *long*, bruv," Petey said.

"It's just one of the *Sentinel* reporters saying congrats. That's all."

A quick look at the faces around the table told me not a single one of the Brent Boys believed me. If Ludo did turn up, they'd be unbearable. It was better to rip the Band-Aid off, tell them what I'd done, and let them get it out of their system before Ludo arrived. If he came.

"I *did* invite him to join us a bit later," I said. A chorus of "ooooooh" went up around the table (sarcastic, not supportive). I rolled my eyes. Petey's hands were flapping like a maimed seagull.

"O. M. G. *Which* reporter? Please tell me it in't that Ludo Boche geezer?" he said.

"Why?" I swallowed. "Christ, you haven't slept with him, have you?" While it might be against my professional code to sleep with a colleague, I doubted Petey lived by the same rules.

"Bruv, it in't that! I in't supposed to say nuffin, cos Krishnan made us all sign an NDA right after it happened, but—"

"Spill. The. Tea. Peter," Jumaane said, clapping between each word for emphasis.

"Immediately," added Stav, with lawyerly authority.

By this point, nothing could have prevented Pete spilling the tea on Ludo. Wild horses could not have stopped him, even if they'd been butchered and stuffed into his mouth like some sort of equine foie gras. It all came flooding out. When Petey was done—when he'd finished describing in spectacular detail how Ludo had sat on the *Wake Up Britain* couch and then vomited all over the three-times *Gay Times* Gay Man of the Year, and when my mates were all rolling around on the (metaphorical) floor, howling with laughter—I found myself feeling a bit hacked off.

"People throw up sometimes. It happens," I said. "To be fair, I nearly threw up all over *him* at one point this week, and he was proper supportive. Ludo's a nice guy."

"Bugger me, you *have* got it bad," Nick said.

"I've never seen you like this," Dav said. "And I've known you since we were eight."

"He's just a colleague." Why did no one seem to understand this? "We're covering the same story, that's all. He's still a posh bellend."

"Why would you invite a posh bellend to join us?" Stav asked, with the precision of a jurist.

"To teach you all some table manners?"

"Is that your little arrangement?" Jumaane said. "He shows you what fork to use and when, and you show him what goes where?" The boys roared with laughter. Cake crumbs shot from Stav's mouth and across the table. Gross.

"You've def' been lipsing, I can tell," Petey said.

I rolled my eyes very, very hard.

"See! You have!" He was triumphant.

"We haven't. You know the rule."

Petey wasn't having it.

"OK, Lady Chatterley. Rules are meant to be broken—and you clearly *want* to lips him!" he said. "Good on you, fam. Maybe just give him a Kwell first, yeah? And maybe wear, like, some full-body PPE or sumfink."

The more I protested, the redder my face got, the less the boys believed me. Probably because, well, I *did* want to kiss Ludo. I might have started out being nice to him to undo the potential damage I'd done to my career by insulting his family, but I'd grown to really like him. He was sweet and beautiful and hilarious and great company, and spending time with him had been like putting on a favourite hoodie. But I also couldn't escape that fact that he was also infuriating and entitled and oblivious to his privilege—and giving in to the part of me that wanted to kiss him would only lead to tears. It was why I'd pulled away when he'd tried to pull me onto the bed.

Ludo *was* someone who knew which knife and fork to use and when. I'd never eaten a meal that required more than one knife and fork in the first place. The cold hard realist inside me knew Ludo Boche was a bad idea. But the thing about really bad ideas is they can be proper tempting.

30

LUDO

W HEN I STEPPED OUT of the ballet studio, I felt like a million dollars. It was one of those jolly, bright late-April days when the sun has heat in it, the bluebells and tulips are out, and the trees have turned fully green, even in traditionally Conservative electorates where turning green is still punishable by hanging. I looked up at a big blue sky above me and sucked in a lungful of oxygen (diesel particulate, really; this was London, after all). I had just replied to Sunny's message on GayHoller saying I'd love to join him and his mates at Miss Timmy's when a large four-wheel drive stopped right in front of me, blocking my sunshine. The smooth whirr of an electric window winding down was followed by an all-too-familiar voice.

"Ludo, sweetheart." Mummy never picked me up from ballet class, even when I was seven and taking the class rather than teaching it and the Child Catcher from *Chitty Chitty Bang Bang* could have kidnapped me on the walk home at any point.

"What are you doing here?"

She slipped her sunglasses up onto her head, and I could see she was upset about something.

"You better get in, bubby."

I knew from the crack in her voice it was serious.

31

SUNNY

THE THING ABOUT DAY drinking is, at some point you have to make a decision. Sometime in the afternoon, when the shadows are getting long and the air is beginning to cool, you have to flip a coin. It's still only five or six o'clock. Most people haven't even started their pre-drinks for a big night out yet, but you're already proper wankered. So, do you leave the venue, grab a kebab, walk it off for a bit, and go home to sober up before bedtime? Or do you push on through, order another round of drinks, and try to beat your own liver at a game of who's the hardest? The moment for decision came. I (metaphorically) flipped that coin, and, inevitably, it landed on "stay out with your crew."

I checked GayHoller. Still nothing from Ludo. He'd said he was going home to shower and change and then he'd join us at Miss Timmy's, but he'd never turned up. After inviting him, admitting that fact to the boys, changing my mind, having Ludo say yes, and mentally preparing myself for him coming anyway, to have him jilt me was... proper maddening. I'd messaged to say we'd moved on to the Duncan for the early drag show and to join us there, but nothing. It was clear I had been stood up, which, obviously, the boys ragged me about mercilessly. I was miserable.

"You all right, babe?" Dav said. Onstage, one of the newer queens, Sandy Crotch, was belting out "Euphoria," the Eurovision winning song from 2012. That was the year I missed the final because I was busy losing my virginity to a guy called Gary Bender. Dav had a cob on with me on both counts. No self-respecting homosexual missed the Eurovision final, and certainly not to lose their virginity to someone called Gary.

"I'm fine," I said. "For someone who's been ghosted by London's foremost vomit correspondent."

"You do like him, don't you?"

My heart hurt. I looked into Dav's big brown eyes, pleading for the inquisition to stop. He put up his hands in surrender, then flung an arm around me. He leant his head against mine, the bulk of his turban a soft cushion between us.

"The boys want to hit Vauxhall," he said. "You up for it?"

In a moment of clarity, I put my drink down on the bar.

"I think I might go home," I said.

Sometimes, when you flip a coin, you get the wrong outcome. There's no dishonour in altering course. Minds, like underpants, are meant to be changed occasionally. I hugged Dav goodnight and dropped a metaphorical smoke bomb on the evening. On the Tube ride home, I crafted Ludo a withering GayHoller message.

Ginger: *Dead rude, mate. A text is cheap and manners cost nothing. Bang out of order.*

***

B Y TWO IN THE morning, there was still no word from Ludo and I was lying in bed, smashing GayHoller. I was on a mission. A headless torso at a house party a few streets away was trying to convince me to put some pants on, join him for a few drinks, "and see how it goes." The only thing I wanted less than more booze was to leave the house. All I wanted at this point was to efficiently bust a nut with someone with a full set of teeth, an OK physique, and a face that didn't look like it had been freshly unzipped from a body bag. I wanted shallow, meaningless, transactional sex. I wanted a bus stop boy to come upstairs, swipe his Oyster card against my reader, and piss off back to his own life so I never had to see him again.

My phone chimed.

GayHoller: *Cabbage98 has sent you a message.*

Shit! I threw my phone onto the duvet. I sat bolt upright and rubbed my eyes, trying to sober up or wake up or whatever up it was my body needed to be a normal functioning human being in that moment. I straightened my hair. I checked my breath. Pointless, but standards, and all that. I opened the message.

Cabbage98: *Sunny. Sorry. I've been at the hospital. It's Uncle Ben. They think he's had a stroke. I've only just got home. Sorry to miss meeting your friends. Another day, for sure. I hope you had a lovely time. Ludo x.*

I felt like a proper douchebag. I'd been out partying and celebrating and cruising for an online hook-up, getting angrier and angrier with Ludo, while Ludo was sitting in the hospital, worried sick about his godfather. I thought about my nan when she was in the hospital and how lost I'd felt. I just wanted to comfort Ludo in whatever way I could, to be the shoulder he needed. Suddenly sober, I jumped out of bed and grabbed my work rucksack, rummaging through it to find the folder Torsten had given me on the plane. I rifled through the papers, looking for the page with everyone's contact details on it. And there it was. Ludo's actual phone number. I sat on the edge of the bed and typed it into my phone. My heart was in my throat, waiting for the call to connect, to hear Ludo's voice.

It went to voicemail.

I tried several times, with the same result. If I thought I'd felt like crap before, I'd just found new depths to my misery.

32

LUDO

THE LAST PLACE I felt like being was the office, but Father had insisted my punishment stood. Fortunately, that frightful bore Bob Wynn-Jones resigned at eight o'clock on Sunday morning. It had been inevitable. It was a welcome distraction. It made for a busy shift in the *Sentinel*'s Westminster bureau, but despite being jolly tired, having a face that was more purple than pink and a phone full of missed calls from an unknown number, and being incredibly distracted by Uncle Ben's situation, I was confident I had everything under control. Until, that is, the prime minister went ahead and announced that rather than just replacing his energy secretary, he would be holding a general cabinet reshuffle on the coming Tuesday.

All hell broke loose. It had roughly the same effect as slipping amphetamines into the water supply of an old folks' home. Suddenly, sleepy Sunday Westminster was buzzing with frantic energy. Ford Goodall, our political editor and a man whose personality would be greatly improved by amphetamines in the water supply, came into the office on his day off to write the lead stories and the analysis pieces on the reshuffle. That left me to cover the Wynn-Jones resignation itself. I began working the phones, calling Wynn-Jones's political enemies, looking for any gossip I could get, before moving on to his allies. I'd just been hung up on, yet again, when someone knocked on the bureau door. Ford covered the mouthpiece of his phone.

"Come in," he called.

The door opened, and there stood Sunny Miller, wearing sneakers and a slouchy grey tracksuit that had "lazy Sunday" written all over it. Not literally, you understand. That was the general vibe. What on earth was he doing here? He looked jolly sheepish.

"I thought you might need coffee," he said, producing a small cardboard tray with two small takeaway coffee cups. It looked remarkably like an olive branch. "Can I come in?"

Ford was on the phone, working his contacts, so I didn't think that was a good idea. Whatever was about to be said, Ford didn't need to hear it.

"How about I come out?" I suggested. I nodded to Ford and pointed at the door, indicating I was going out for a minute. He nodded back and waved goodbye to Sunny without breaking off from his phone call.

The corridor was busy with reporters bustling to and fro, half of them looking hung-over and jolly ropeable that they'd been called in, the other half looking thrilled to have got out of ferrying their kids to football match- es or horse riding lessons or whatever familial horrors Sunday usually entailed. Sunny plucked a coffee out of the tray and passed it to me. Our fingers touched as the paper cup slid from his hand into mine, sending a little charge through me.

"Thanks," I said. I suggested we go for a walk, rather than loiter outside the bureau.

"I'm sorry about your uncle Ben," he said. I tried to smile. "Any news from the hospital?"

"Nothing yet today. Mummy is going in after lunch. She'll update us afterwards."

Sunny nodded, his expression uncertain.

After a few paces I felt his hand on my elbow. We stopped on a thread-bare bit of carpet, and he pulled me gently around to face him.

"I'm sorry," Sunny said. "About the text. It was me who was bang out of order. I just—"

"You weren't to know what was going on."

"I tried to call you last night."

My heart skipped. Sunny's hand was hot against my elbow. His peridot eyes looked sad, tired, intense.

"That was you?" I smiled, my mind racing with what this meant.

"I wanted to apologise. And I thought you might need to talk."

"Jolly thoughtful of you," I said. "Sorry. My phone was on silent and, um, I knocked myself out with half a Valium to get some sleep."

Inviting me to meet his friends, digging up my phone number for late-night emotional support, bringing me surprise coffee? My quickening pulse pounded through the bruise at my temple. We ambled slowly along the hallway towards the Victoria Tower, which is the stately mock-Gothic home of the vellum parchments on which Government Acts are still written (because we're English and we can't rush these things). It would have been jolly romantic, if it didn't smell of damp and dead rodents, and if one of us wasn't dressed like an ad for Box Menswear.

"Have you been called in because of the reshuffle?" I asked.

"No, I just thought you might need coffee. You haven't had much sleep."

"You came all the way from Willesden Green just to bring me coffee?" He nodded. "I did."

"You're so sweet. *Insane*, but very sweet." My heart was racing now, my fingers jittery around the cup. At the end of the corridor, I led Sunny down the coiling stairs to the floor below, which was when I slipped, sending my coffee flying over my shoulder like it had been fired out of a trebuchet.

"It's OK! I'm OK," I said.

"I'm not."

I turned around to see the front of Sunny's joggers covered in coffee.

"Buggery bollocks! I am *so* sorry." Flustered, I began brushing at his sweatpants with my hands, as if that might get the coffee out.

"That's my crotch, Ludo," Sunny said. "Again."

I nearly died.

"Oh... bugger me sideways! Ruddy hell! I am so, *so* sorry."

"Hey, don't mention it," he said. He was a couple of steps higher than me, making him monstrously tall. I was still staring at his coffee-stained groin. Sunny put a finger under my chin, gently tilting my head until our eyes met. The tenderness of the gesture made my knees weak. Outside, the sun must have come out from behind a cloud. As the light in the stairwell brightened, fracturing through the stained glass, we were showered in saffron, vermilion, emerald, and cobalt. It was like standing inside a child's kaleidoscope.

"I thought something like this might happen," Sunny said, letting his hand drop from my chin. "So, I factored it into my planning."

He plucked the second coffee out of the tray and handed it to me.

"This is yours too," he said.

Water began to well in my eyes.

"Hey, it's OK," he said. "It's just coffee. Trust me, these joggers have been stained by much worse."

I laughed, sending the tears crashing over the barrier and down my cheeks.

"You're gross," I said.

"I wasn't being gross. If you made that gross, that's on you."

Sunny wiped my tears, his fingers cradling my jaw as his thumb swept tenderly over the wet cheek of the non-bruised side of my face. There was a slight tremble in Sunny's fingertips. Our eyes met. I nuzzled my head into his hand, letting him know it was OK, that I wanted this too. His eyes sparkled, and the corners of his blush-pink lips quivered, ever so slightly.

I took the two steps up towards him. The kaleidoscope turned. We were bathed in gold, ruby, and sapphire, but I was drowning in peridot.

Sunny's fingers slid up into my hair, pulling my face closer to his. I heard him drop the cardboard coffee tray on the floor. His hand found my waist. Then, suddenly, we were kissing. Sunny's lips were soft and gentle at first, then firmer, more passionate, but always deliberate, searching, savouring. He cradled my face with both hands, and between kisses, he breathed in deeply, like he was trying to draw in the whole moment, to take it inside him, make it a part of him. Like this was something that he had yearned for, ached for. Like he wanted to remember every second of it, in case it never happened again. At least I hoped that's how he felt, because that's jolly well how it felt for me.

I had wrapped my arm around him, settling my hand in the small of his back, holding his hips close to mine, as we kissed longer and deeper. And all the while I had this bally coffee cup in my other hand. I reached out to rest it on the windowsill, to free myself to hold Sunny as completely as he was holding me. Eyes closed, returning every caress of the tongue and the lips, I struggled to find the sill. Once. Twice. Three times, I missed. Sod it. I gave up, dropping the cup. It could fend for itself. I heard it land on the stone step, the coffee splashing and gushing down the stairs. I didn't care. I wrapped my arm around Sunny's back and held him tightly. Then his mouth tightened and his shoulders began to bounce up and down. He let his hands slide down to my waist. We opened our eyes. My glasses were terribly smudged, but I could see that he was smiling broadly.

"You're a proper menace to society, you know that?" Sunny said. He was laughing.

"Sorry," I said. "That was a waste of coffee."

"Don't be sorry," he said. Sunny pulled me into a hug, enveloping me in his arms, holding me tightly. It felt safe, reassuring, solid. I looped my arms around his back and nuzzled into his neck, kissing the soft, freckled skin of his hairline, feeling the warmth of his body wrapped in mine, inhaling the smell of him—the intoxicating wood and citrus aromas of his cologne, and, if I was honest, a thick smell of coffee.

"What does this mean?" I said, finally.

Sunny pulled away ever so slightly. Enough to let our eyes meet. We considered each other for a moment. Outside, the sun must have gone back behind a cloud, because the colours of the stained glass began to mute and dull.

"It means I better go find a mop and a bucket before someone kills themselves on these stairs," Sunny said. "And it means next time, I'll bring three coffees. Just to be safe."

"I mean *this*, Sunny. What does *this* mean?"

I could see him pulling away, both physically and emotionally. I felt my heart sink, fearing the worst—that this was a one-off moment, a mistake, a test, perhaps. Something to brush away and forget. Sunny must have read my thoughts on my face. He stepped back from our embrace, but I grabbed his hands in mine.

"Don't overthink it," Sunny said. "You've got a lot on your plate right now. We don't have to name whatever this is just yet."

But my mind was racing, needing to put a pin in this moment, to label it, to define what it was. I couldn't just leave it there. I needed something to hold on to, something that confirmed this wasn't a one-off, that this mattered.

"Are you free Saturday night?" I said, in a flash of inspiration.

"Can be."

"Do you want to come to a thing with me? It's one of Jonty's fundraisers. The people will be unbearable bores who'll probably get massively on your wick, but it's for the Hazel Dormouse Protection Trust, you see, and they're—"

"An endangered species? Yes, I think you might have mentioned it once."

"Will you come?"

Sunny beamed.

"I'd love to come," he said, and I felt instant relief.

Then he leant in and kissed me again.

33

SUNNY

I T WAS TUESDAY MORNING, and I was standing outside No. 10 Downing Street in the cool spring air, press pass and *Bulletin* ID card swinging around my neck, surrounded by TV cameras and the wider Westminster media scrum. We were all waiting for the knobber inside to sort out his cabinet reshuffle. Reshuffles are drawn-out days with long interludes where nothing happens, which gives you plenty of thinking time. And I was thinking about Ludo Boche.

We were in new and proper sketchy territory. I had broken the golden rule and got myself involved with another journalist. I had crossed the Rubik's cube, and there was no going back. (For the record, I know the expression is "cross the Rubicon" but my nanna always used to say Rubik's cube, and using her old malapropisms makes me feel like she's still around.)

Although I had *wanted* to kiss him, I had not *intended* to kiss Ludo. It had just sort of happened. He was so adorably flustered, and there he was, with his bruised face and his glasses still held together with Band-Aids, and, well, his two modes are absolute joy and absolute chaos, and I guess

I thought if I kissed him, it might help flick the switch back from chaos to joy. It had worked. But it had flicked a switch inside me too. And if I hadn't been able to get Ludo out of my mind before, now I could barely think about anything else.

For whatever reason, Ludo hadn't been posted outside Downing Street. The *Sentinel* had sent Ford Goodall, thank goodness, or I might have struggled to get any work done at all. Reshuffles might be long days, but they are also quite good fun. Politicians go through the famous black doorway to learn their fate, faces either stubbornly blank or a rictus, walking like they've forgotten how to walk, and come out again either looking smugly self-satisfied or quietly seething.

When the cabinet appointments eventually began, the big winner was Bimpe Lasisi. She went through the door an education minister and came out as home secretary.

"I thank my Lord Jesus for giving me this opportunity to serve," she said as she walked down Downing Street, dressed for church, to her waiting car. Rafiq Farouq nudged me in the ribs. He leant over to whisper in my ear, so his comments wouldn't get picked up by the TV microphones.

"Bruv, she thanked Jesus," he said. "Who she think live in that building, you know what I'm sayin?"

The next to go in was Jemima Carstairs, who entered No. 10 as environment secretary and left as both environment secretary *and* energy secretary. The PM was creating a new mega-department to drive delivery of the UK's net zero commitments. Vladimir Popov was to remain chief whip. He walked into No. 10 looking like the Terminator, face betraying nothing, and walked out of No. 10 looking like the Terminator, face betraying nothing.

The *Bulletin* being the *Bulletin*, I had an additional responsibility on days like this. It was the other reason I was glad Ludo wasn't there. When the more notorious, scandal-prone or underperforming ministers came out from their meeting with the prime minister—puffy-eyed or with a face like thunder, at the lowest point of their political careers—it was my job to shout something proper devastating at them, and to do so loud enough for all the TV cameras to pick up, in the hopes of getting a reaction.

"Did calling the leader of the opposition a MILF cost you your job, Mr Cocksgrew? Is it true you thought 'hot mic' was an OnlyFans channel?"

"Do you regret spending taxpayers' dollars paying illegal immigrants to power-wash your stables, Lord Busted-Flush? Did the PM sack you today, or did he hose you out with the Kärcher?"

"Is it true you were fired for drinking the PM's wine fridge dry, Mrs Tipple? What's that tucked under your arm? Is that a nice bottle of Pinot Noir? Does the PM know you've got that, Mrs Tipple?"

It's not an honourable way to make a living, but the best ones always get cut up and used by LBC Radio, ITV, and *Private Eye*. Sometimes, if you hit the right note, the BBC might even use one. It's a cheap thrill, but it is exactly the kind of behaviour that makes the public, not to mention politicians, despise reporters. If I'm honest, I really enjoy it. It's a chance to tell the politicians what the people really think of them, to hold them to account for poor behaviour and remind them that power is briefly held and shouldn't be taken for granted.

When it was all over, I leant against the railings next to Rafiq, who was sucking on a vape.

"I heard you been lipsing Ludo Boche."

My jaw swung open like a creaky gate.

"Who told you that?"

Rafiq winked, chuffing out vapour like a kettle.

"Good on you, fam," he said.

"You don't think it's a bad idea?" I asked, relieved to have someone to talk to about it. "We only kissed once, but we've been proper flirty messaging ever since, and I've said yes to a date on Saturday."

"Why would that be a bad idea, bruv?"

"Because, well, the only thing we have in common is what we do for a job, and that's, like, a big reason why we shouldn't be doing this at all."

"Is it, bruv?"

"Don't you think? I mean, I can't imagine taking him home to meet me mum."

"Have more faith in your old lady," Rafiq said. "And in Ludo, for that matter. But what's the hurry, bruv? You in't getting hitched just yet. Calm your tits. You in't had your date yet."

He had a point.

"So, you think going on a date is OK?"

"Gotta shoot your shot, fam." Those were the same words he'd used at karaoke. His smile was broad and toothy. There was a mischievous twinkle in his eyes. I realised I'd been played.

"No one told you I'd kissed Ludo at all, did they," I said. "You just guessed."

Rafiq shrugged, winked at me for the second time in a minute, and sucked back on his vape. I'd just been schooled in grubby tabloid interview techniques by a reporter from the *Guardian*. Proper embarrassing.

***

O N WEDNESDAY, I WAS back at the Houses of Parliament bureau and, for my sins, covering PMQs. As the new cabinet jostled and jockeyed for the best position on the front bench (a competition won by Bimpe Lasisi, who sat there like the mother of the bride at a wedding), someone slid, very gently, onto the seat beside me. I didn't need to look up to see who it was. The smell of warm linen made my heart skip. Ludo playfully nudged his shoulder into mine. I gently nudged him back.

"Did I do it right this time?"

"You mean by not launching my phone into the chamber and nearly killing an MP? You'll be a pro in no time."

As the pantomime played out in the chamber below, from our perch high above it all, Ludo and I scribbled into our notepads. There was real spirit in the House. A government energised by change but uncertain in its new skin, and an opposition that tasted blood in the water. The prime minister bellowed and decried. Lasisi waved her arms in the air like a Pentecostal minister. The opposition leader shook her head and shouted across the dispatch box. Carstairs waved her order papers in her perfectly manicured hands and cried "Shame!" There was a riot down below, but up in the rafters, among the bat droppings and dead Hansard reporters, sat two journalists from different newspapers who were calmly going about their craft, letting their knees touch under the table.

34

LUDO

THROUGHOUT THE WEEK, SUNNY and I kept finding excuses to bump into each other. Texting to check if we were going to a particular parliamentary debate, grabbing coffee together over at Portcullis House, sharing a cab to a press conference in Hackney. We snatched moments, kissing in corridors when the coast was clear, eating our lunch together on a bench in Saint James's Park, sitting by each other in committee meetings and debates. Then, at night, endlessly texting and calling. It was all jolly lovely. There was just one rule.

"We can't ask each other about, or talk about, anything we're working on," Sunny said. "We have to keep our personal and professional lives totally separate, or it'll get messy very quickly."

"I don't want it to get messy," I said.

"Me neither."

I had taken Friday afternoon off to get my glasses fixed and to visit Uncle Ben in the hospital. Before I left the bureau for the day, Sunny met me in our stairwell for a quick kiss goodbye.

"See you at Maxime's tomorrow night," I said.

"I'm looking forward to it. The hazel dormouse will not go extinct on our watch."

"I think Mother and Father might be there."

Sunny, who could ill afford to lose the colour, blanched.

"I haven't actually told them about us yet," I said. "I didn't know what to call... *this*. I think they know something is up, though. Just thought I should warn you."

Sunny took a deep breath.

"It'll be fine. Proper intimidating, but fine," he said.

I kissed him and went to catch a cab.

***

A T THE HOSPITAL I found Uncle Ben sitting upright in bed in pyjamas and a neck kerchief. He was covered in little stickers and wired up to various machines. The room smelt of antiseptic and bleach. He looked tired but cheerful enough.

"Darling boy!" he declared upon seeing me. I put the flowers I'd brought down on the table and gingerly wrapped my arms around him for a hug, trying not to hurt him or accidentally unplug him. He was still looking frail, as he had every day when I'd visited, but he seemed to be in high spirits.

"Your bruise has turned from raspberry to a sort of chartreuse, dear boy," he said. His words were slightly mumbled, one of the after-effects of the mild stroke he'd suffered. I perched on the edge of the bed.

"Careful you don't sit on my cables," Uncle Ben said. "That one's keeping me alive."

I jumped up.

"I'm kidding. Sit." He patted the mattress, and I carefully sat back down.

"What are the doctors saying?"

"Still worried about seizures and fainting, dear boy. My eyes keep going fuzzy. But I swear that's because they won't let me smoke. I'm having withdrawals!"

He spent the next few minutes trying to talk me into smuggling in a packet of Phillies Cheroots for him.

"The nurse says, 'Oh, Mr Diamond, smoking will kill you,' and I say, 'I'm eighty-eight, Nadine, what does it matter now?'"

"It matters to me!" I protested.

"This is a private hospital. I'm *paying* for them to torture me like this. I said to the doctor, if I wanted a lecture on my lifestyle, I could have got that for free on the NHS."

We laughed; then a moment of silence fell between us. Uncle Ben grabbed my hand and squeezed it.

"You look happy, my darling boy. Is it love?"

"I don't know." It was true, I didn't know. But I couldn't jolly well keep the grin off my face. Uncle Ben's eyes twinkled.

"It looks like love to me," he said. "Your whole countenance has changed. You're walking taller. You're glowing."

I smiled.

"Do you think you've found your Michael?"

"I don't know, Uncle Ben. It's too soon, honestly. But I know I think about him every minute of the day. And when I'm with him, it's like that feeling you get when you're sitting in the theatre, before curtain-up, and your stomach is full of butterflies, but it feels warm and safe and like there's no place you'd rather be in that moment. Is that what love feels like?"

Uncle Ben smiled and patted my hand.

"Put it this way, dear boy. Whether it's love or it isn't, it sounds like a very nice situation indeed. Just enjoy it."

Then, I'm afraid, I gushed. For a good ten minutes poor Uncle Ben had to listen to me banging on about Sunny this and Sunny that, until eventually I noticed he was starting to look tired and I feared he might deliberately unplug something just to get some rest.

"I should let you sleep."

Uncle Ben coughed.

"Before you go, dear boy. I'm supposed to be going to the preview of the National's new show tonight. There's a comp waiting for me in the ticket office. Could you sub in for me and write a little review for Monday's paper? Just a few hundred words."

I've never said yes to anything so fast in my life. Uncle Ben withdrew his grip with equal speed.

"Careful, dear boy. You nearly bit my hand off!"

***

I SENT SUNNY A message saying my phone would be off for the next few hours and slunk into my seat in the stalls, my notepad and pen on my lap. There had only been one complimentary ticket, not two, so I hadn't been able to invite Sunny along. As I waited for curtain-up, the seat next to me was frustratingly empty. I imagined Sunny sitting beside me. Holding hands with him. Hearing him laugh at the funny parts. Swapping glances when the play got romantic or sentimental. I was woken from this daydream by Wilhelmina Post, the editor of *Stage* magazine, gliding into the seat beside me. *Stage* was the real theatre enthusiast's journal of choice, read cover to cover by the actors, producers, directors, wannabes and used-to-bes, and fans of London's theatrical community. Wilhelmina, a woman whose dedication to shoulder pads and perms with combed-back fringes was yet to be rewarded by seeing them come back into fashion, was the centre around which this universe circled.

"Hello, Ludo, darling," she said, kissing both my cheeks. "How positively wonderful to see you! Where's my lovely Benny? I need someone to have a cigarette with at the interval."

I filled her in on Uncle Ben, and she promised to swing by the hospital with a bunch of grapes.

"If you really want a few brownie points, sneak him in a packet of Phillies."

She winked.

"Is it your first-ever review?" Wilhelmina asked. I nodded. "Darling, you'll be a natural."

"Any advice for a rookie?"

"Always be honest, but never be cruel. That's the first rule. Not if you want to last in this business. Although perhaps that's less of a concern if it's a one-off. But remember, actors have long memories, and you're only a child. Plenty of time for them to knock you off your bicycle in the King's Road if they're feeling vengeful."

I laughed.

"The second rule. Say whatever you like, as long as you can explain it. If you think the script was weak, you owe it to the writer, whom you're calling out in a public forum, to explain why you thought it was weak. You also owe it to the audience and to your readers. If you can't explain it, then you don't really mean it.

"And the third rule: whatever you say, say it in your own voice. Don't try to be your uncle Benny. Ben Diamond is a legend of the game. His reviews are the stuff of folklore. Laurence Olivier nearly died choking on a chocolate digestive while reading Benny's review of *Long Day's Journey into Night*."

"Is that the one where he wrote something like 'The play is as rickety as the Edinburgh sleeper and takes about as long to get to its destination'?"

"That's the one!" Wilhelmina said. "Well, it was a five-hour play even before Larry fluffed his lines. Anyway, the point is, don't ape your uncle Benny. Develop your own style. Find your own voice."

Golly! It was a masterclass. The theatre darkened, the audience hushed, and I felt the rush of anticipation that comes with curtain-up. A burst of trumpets—an old-fashioned overture. The actors took their places on-stage. I picked up my pen and, in the dark, wrote down Wilhelmina's advice. I might not have got to spend the evening with Sunny, or with Uncle Ben, but learning from one of the industry's all-time greats wasn't a bad way to spend my night. Just for a moment, I let myself imagine that this was my life—and I found I liked it very much indeed.

35

SUNNY

HAVING SUCCESSFULLY NAVIGATED MAXIME's elevator and Jonty's door list, I found myself unsuccessfully looking for Ludo among the noisy partygoers and the swirling waitstaff offering trays of drinks and canapés. There must have been several hundred people, all dressed in their glad rags like they were off to the opera. I felt slightly underdone in my rolled-up white shirtsleeves and skinny black tie, chosen to match my black skinny jeans. The Converse trainers were definitely a mistake. Ludo hadn't told me to dress like we were off to a wedding. This was a fundraiser for a rodent. I had thought the place would be filled with the kind of people who make jam from their own allotment, not the kind of people who bulldoze allotments to build skyscrapers.

At least the crowd wasn't too Westminstery. I hadn't spotted any MPs, just Torsten Beaumont-Flattery, and I guessed he was only there because he knew Jonty from school. He was standing in a corner, deep in conversation with a tall blond man I didn't recognise. I found myself in front of a display of information about the hazel dormouse, pretending I found the literature proper absorbing. I was just about to ask a waiter for a pen to fix some of the grammar when a pair of hands clasped over my eyes and voice from behind me said "Guess who?"

"Noted Hollywood chameleon Meryl Streep?"

Ludo let his hands drop, and I turned around to face him. By this point I was expecting to see him wearing a tuxedo, looking like Timothée Chalamet auditioning for the part of James Bond, but in fact, he was dressed almost identically to me, only in black leather shoes and chinos. Not even a jumper. On closer inspection, he looked slightly dishevelled. I kissed him on the cheek, unsure what the correct etiquette was for greeting each other at a public event, given our unclear relationship status. Let's be honest, mostly I just didn't want Ludo's parents' first impression of me to involve interrupting a snog with their son.

"I couldn't find you," I said.

"I know, I'm sorry. Bit of an accident. Jersey's a write-off, I'm afraid. Unless you know the secret to getting espresso martini out of cashmere?"

"Funnily enough, they didn't cover that at the school I went to. Might be why Ofsted marked us down so hard. Although the knife violence might also have had something to do with it, to be fair."

Ludo paused, clearly tossing up whether I was being serious before deciding the safest bet was to plough on.

"So, I was in the gents, drying my shirt under the hand dryer. I hope you weren't too bored."

"Did you know the French call the hazel dormouse the rat-d'or?" I said, showing off my freshly acquired knowledge. "And in Suffolk they call them sleep-meece, which is proper cute and makes me really like the people of Suffolk."

"Golly, you *were* bored. I'm so sorry."

"Who's that talking to Beaumont-Flattery?" I asked, pointing at the tall blond gentleman in his mid-fifties. Ludo looked around, locating his high school crush with instant, laser-like accuracy that was either adorable or cause for concern.

"That's Dirk Windhoek. Carstairs's husband. Do you want to meet him?"

I declined. I wasn't ready to give up having Ludo all to myself tonight just yet.

"Golly, you haven't even got a drink. What appalling hosts. I'm sorry. Let me—"

Ludo's arms were starting to move like a puppet's. I grabbed his hand before he could run away from me and told him to stop apologising. He pushed his glasses up onto his nose, and anticipating the second half of his trademark twitch, I pulled him closer and pushed his hair behind his ear for him. It bounced back out. I tried again.

"It's totally ungovernable, I'm afraid," he said. "There's a knack to it." He showed me how it was done, twisting the curl and popping it behind his ear.

"See?" he said. It bounced back out again. I giggled.

"I see." I reached for the unruly curl, twisted it, and brushed it behind his ear. It held firm. He grinned. I pecked him on the lips. He tasted like coffee and alcohol. I grabbed his hand and held it.

"Shall we get a drink and make small talk with some of these dormouse people?" I suggested. Ludo nodded, although I imagined we were both more enthusiastic about the first part of the plan than the second. By the time we found a waiter and had scored a couple of glasses of champagne, Ludo's curls were on the loose again.

***

HALF AN HOUR LATER Ludo and I found ourselves chatting to a couple who looked *exactly* like the kind of people I'd expected to find at an event for an obscure endangered rodent. Where most of the crowd were suited and booted, Leaf and Karma were tie-dyed and flip-flopped. I had sort of gravitated towards them out of journalistic instinct. They were clearly the most interesting people in the room. As it turned out, I didn't know the half of it. As it also turned out, they came from my neck of the woods.

"Do I detect a slight Leicester accent there, Sunny?" Leaf asked. He said my name the way my mum says my name, with two soft *o*'s and an *eh* on the end, and it made me warm to him immediately. I told him it was.

"Grew up on the Wickwar Estate," I said, my childhood accent returning to soak my vowels and rinse away my practised way of speaking.

"We run a retreat just outside Melbourne," Karma said.

"Australia?" Ludo asked, a little slow on the uptake.

"Derbyshire," Leaf explained. "Just up the road from Leicester." Ludo blushed. I lightly rubbed his back, letting him know it was OK. He leant back into my hand, so I held it there, pressed into him, the heat of his body against my fingers.

"We do reiki, spiritual healing, chakra balancing, qigong, pranic and crystal healing. You name it, really," Karma continued.

"I do yoga, actually," I said, chipping in what little relevant personal experience I had. (I didn't volunteer that I did my yoga in a room of naked gay men. I felt that might give the wrong impression. Although, to be fair, that wrong impression was exactly why Jumaane and I had joined in the first place.) We chatted about the retreat for a while; then, like a moth drawn irresistibly to a flame, I asked Leaf and Karma what they made of the near miss with the nuclear power plant that had nearly been built less than ten miles down the road.

"What do you mean, near miss?" Karma said. "It's still going ahead."

Ludo and I exchanged glances.

"And it's totally unnecessary," Leaf added. "We don't need it. We should be going renewable. Wind, small-scale hydro, heat pumps, solar. But the politicians will prioritise the big end of town, not the planet."

"But the nuclear plant deal is off," I said.

"Only the Belarusian deal," Leaf said. "It's still going ahead. Just with a different company."

"You sound very certain," Ludo said. "The government hasn't even legislated for the committee that will approve the projects yet."

"You think Carstairs is going to wait for some committee?" Leaf said. "No, this is a done deal."

Ludo straightened up, and I let my hand fall from his back.

"Are you sure?" I said. My heart was racing. If Leaf and Karma were right, this was big news indeed. "Do you have any evidence?"

Leaf nodded. "The government is about to do a deal with a company called ZephEnergies Limited. Their website says they're a renewables company, but that's just greenwashing."

ZephEnergies Limited. I'd seen that name in the file in Vladimir Popov's constituency office. I cursed myself for not having read what the letter said. I'd been too panicked, too rushed. I looked at Ludo. His eyes were on (metaphorical) stalks. If what Leaf was saying was true, it was proper explosive—which is not a word to use lightly when you're talking about nuclear power plants.

"You've seen paperwork?" Ludo asked. "You've got copies?"

"Goodness yes," Leaf said.

"Where'd you get them?" I asked. Leaf said nothing. He pointed at Karma, who was smiling and blushing in equal measure.

"I dabble on the dark web," she said.

I looked at Ludo. His eyes had turned a piercing ice blue. He nodded. We both knew what we had. A massive story—if the evidence stacked up.

Through the sound system came a posh voice I took to be Jonty Boche, welcoming guests to the fundraiser and reminding everyone to pop their business cards into the bowl on the bar for a chance to win "the rat-d'or prize." The formal part of the event was kicking off. I pulled my phone out of my pocket and handed it to Karma.

"Can we get your number?" I asked.

***

AFTER THE SPEECHES, SEVERAL free glasses of champagne, and a good hour of patient small talk with random guests, there was still no sign of Ludo's parents anywhere. Had I got off scot-free? We escaped to what we thought was a suitably private and darkened corner. Massive tactical error. Meeting Hugo and Beverley Barker-Boche would have been intimidating even in the ideal circumstances. Meeting them when you've got their son pressed against the wall of a nightclub, one hand up his shirt and your tongue down his throat, was, let's just say, not the classiest first impression I had ever made. Hugo cleared his throat. I looked up, saw the editor of one of the nation's most respected daily newspapers, and stopped groping his son. I jumped back. Ludo shoved his glasses back on. We straightened ourselves and stood upright like we were two of the von Trapp children, ready for inspection. OK, problematic analogy, but that's the gist.

"Friend of yours?" Hugo asked. Ludo fiddled fruitlessly with the long curls of his fringe, trying to mash them into place behind his ear.

"Are you going to introduce us, sweetheart?" Beverley said, playing good cop to Hugo's bad cop. Ludo seemed stunned into silence. I didn't know what to say.

"Hello, Sunny," Hugo said. "Sunny Miller, this is my wife, Beverley. The mother of the young man whose entire face you've just had inside your mouth. Beverley, this is Sunny Miller of the *Bulletin* and, most recently, our son's tonsils. Sunny's currently enjoying five minutes of notoriety for standing outside Downing Street during this week's reshuffle and shouting 'The PM changes your briefs more often than you do' at old Tubby Kerslake."

I swallowed a laugh. I still found it hilarious.

"That was you!" Beverley shrieked. "I say! Well done."

"Deeply unfair. Tubby is a first-rate chap," Hugo said, his face stern. "Known him since school."

Of course he had.

"Second-rate minister, though, you have to admit," Beverley said. Hugo's face did not admit any such thing. I put out my hand and shook Beverley's and Hugo's in turn.

"Good to see you, Hugo," I said. "Lovely to meet you, Mrs Boche."

"Barker-Boche," Hugo corrected.

"Call me Beverley, please." She was still playing the good cop. Maybe she was just a genuinely nice person? From her demeanour, you'd never guess she produced a TV show that attracted six million viewers each Monday night and had brought down entire governments with its investigations. Beverley wielded her power more subtly than her husband. At least in a nightclub scenario.

"Sorry about that," I said, pointing my thumb over my shoulder towards the scene of the kissing crime. "I'm... from the Midlands."

Beverley laughed a full-throated laugh, and I was relieved my joke had landed. Mums always love me. She leant in conspiratorially.

"Well, I'm from Hampshire, and unless things have changed in the last thirty years, we snog in nightclubs down there too. Only don't tell my mother."

Hugo seemed less impressed.

"Nothing to say for yourself, Ludo?"

Ludo said nothing for himself.

"So, how long has *this*"—Hugo waggled a finger back and forth between us—"been going on?"

I wasn't sure whether Hugo just didn't like me or whether he was also worried I'd compromise his son, that perhaps I was just getting close to him to try to steal leads on stories. It was precisely why journos shouldn't date other journos. I could smell the sense of professional competition on him. I didn't know how to reply. Why was Ludo not speaking? Had he been cryogenically frozen in situ?

"I bet it was Shetland," Beverley said. "Ludo came back from that trip a completely different young man from the one who went up there. Didn't I say to you, Hugo, I said I think Ludo's met someone special."

Hugo grunted.

"Ludo, why don't you bring Sunny over for dinner next Friday night?" Beverley said. "With any luck Uncle Ben will be out of hospital by then, and we can have a double celebration."

The word *celebration* felt premature, a little too serious, a little bit too *big*. The situation was spinning out of our control.

"It's already a double celebration, Beverley," Hugo said. "It's the night before the coronation, remember."

I looked at Ludo. The decision was up to him. He smiled from ear to ear.

"I'd love to," I said, and with all my heart I meant it.

"Any special dietary requirements?" Hugo sneered. "Nut allergy? Vegan, perhaps?"

"I'm just an old-fashioned red meat–eating republican."

Beverley laughed. Hugo's eyes boggled. I felt Ludo's fingers dig into my back.

A few minutes later, party arrangements confirmed, Hugo and Beverley wandered off to make small talk about the rat-d'or with rich folk. I placed my hands on Ludo's hips and guided him back to our spot against the wall. His shirt was untucked, and I slid my fingers up onto the soft skin of his waist. It sent electricity through me, touching this smooth, hidden flesh.

"Now, where were we?" I went to kiss him, but Ludo pulled away, putting a finger to my lips.

"Shall we... go?" he said.

I couldn't say yes quickly enough.

As we waited for the lift, I saw a large glass goldfish bowl filled with business cards, with a sign that said, "Leave your card for a chance to win our rat-d'or prize!" The prize was a weekend away at the Pranayama Retreat, Melbourne. I pulled a battered old business card from my wallet and tossed it in. I was feeling lucky. The elevator dinged. I put my arm around Ludo and waited for the doors to slide open.

36

LUDO

I SLID OPEN THE door to the summer house.

"Wait here," I said, nipping inside.

"Hurry up, it's cold out here."

"I won't be a minute."

Cue me, rushing around madly, making the bed, throwing clothes from the floor into the laundry basket, lighting a few Molton Brown candles, and slipping out of the pants I'd been wearing all evening and into a fresh pair. I checked myself in the mirror, took my glasses off, put them back on, took them back off again, and put them on the bedside table. I ran my fingers through my hair and, finally, flung open the door.

"Here to read your gas meter, mate," Sunny said. I laughed but hoped he wasn't planning to continue this role play once he stepped across the threshold. Not tonight, anyway.

"Nice gaff. The candles seem brave, given, you know, your history."

"Can I get you anything? A glass of water, or...?"

Sunny moved towards me, our eyes firmly locked on each other. His face was beautiful, lit by the golden flickering of the candlelight. I stepped backwards until my legs hit the edge of the bed and I fell onto it. Sunny lowered himself down onto me, the weight of him pressing into me. Our legs tangled. The smell of him filled my lungs and made my heart thump in my chest. My body shivered and tingled. I looked up into Sunny's eyes, his beaming face. Tenderly, he brushed my hair from my face, his fingers gently weaving through my unruly curls.

"You're proper gorgeous. You know that?"

"I'm starting to think you're not really here to read my gas meter at all."

Sunny laughed and lowered his lips to my neck, kissing his way along my jaw towards my mouth. Softly, slowly, like he was savouring every single moment. We kissed, and our hands explored each other's bodies. Within a few minutes, shoes had been kicked off, trousers had been removed and shirts were crumpled on the floor. We rolled around on the bed, kissing and tasting and breathing in every single part of each other, each lost in the other, lost in this delicious, precious moment. I felt more complete, more whole, than I had ever felt in my entire life, just being wrapped up in his arms and having him in mine. My body ached for him, wanted him, needed him, and when I couldn't bear the ache any longer, it welcomed him in.

***

IN THE AFTERGLOW, SUNNY lay back against the pillows and closed his eyes. I lay beside him, studying his body in the candlelight. Wherever the sun had kissed his skin, it was bejewelled with freckles the colours of toast and ochre. The trail of them wound from the neck and across the lean muscle of his chest, where his infamous nipples, the colour of ballet slippers, still stood en pointe. I kissed them. Then I kissed his collarbones and the explosion of auburn and amber gemstones that covered the tight muscles of his shoulders. I rested my head on his chest, my cheek pressing into the warmth of his body. I felt his heart beating beneath me and breathed in the homely, manly scent of him. He smelt of nutmeg and sandalwood and of two boys who had just had sex. He was beautiful, and he was in my bed.

***

I N THE MORNING, WHEN I opened my eyes, Sunny was already awake. He was sitting up against the pillows, one arm around the back of my head, hand resting on my shoulder, the other hand holding my water-damaged copy of *Wolf Hall*.

"Morning, sleepyhead," he said, reaching down to kiss my forehead.

"You're not actually reading that, are you?"

"I'm not sure anybody has *actually* read this. It's impenetrable."

"I only keep it there to impress boys," I said.

Sunny threw the book on the floor and snuggled down into the bed until our noses were touching.

"You don't need a book to impress me, Ludo Ben. You're impressive enough all on your own."

Then he kissed me.

"Hilary Mantel will be rolling in her grave," I said. "All those hours researching Thomas Cromwell, completely wasted."

After round two, and a shower, Sunny suggested we go for breakfast somewhere.

"We've got some serious talking to do," he added.

It was the most deflating thing he could have said.

37

SUNNY

ALARM BELLS STARTED RINGING in my head the instant I saw the queue and the expensive-looking people standing in it. Ludo had suggested breakfast at a posh place on the Hampstead High Street called Arabella McPhee's. It had cute blue-and-green tartan tablecloths and gold lettering on the door and called itself a patisserie.

"You join the queue," I said. "I'll grab a menu."

Ludo nodded. He'd been quiet since we left the house, which I found unsettling.

I found the menu by the door. Fear confirmed. A piece of toast with jam here would clear out my bank account.

I scoured the list for the full English. "Twenty-four quid? Piss off!"

An elderly woman in the queue clutched her chihuahua and glared at me. I apologised. She didn't reply. That decided it. I wasn't eating here. It was time for Ludo to visit the wrong side of the tracks.

"I've got a better idea," I announced, finding him at the end of the queue. "There's a great little caff near mine. Proper full English. Bottomless coffee. You'll love it."

Ludo frowned.

"But this is the most popular place in Hampstead. People fly in from Paris just for the friands."

"Let me take you to the most popular place in Willesden."

He raised his eyebrows. Then shrugged, giving in.

"Fine, let's find a cab."

"Sod that. It's a ten-minute walk to Swiss Cottage, and we can take the Jubilee line to Dollis Hill. We'll be there in no time."

***

HALF AN HOUR LATER we were sitting at a table outside Gloria's, Willesden's best greasy spoon. Your elbows stuck to the table, but it was five quid for a fry-up, and they kept your coffee mug topped up. The waitress came out instantly and took our order. Two full English breakfasts and two bottomless coffees, for the grand total of fourteen pounds. Sweet.

The waitress disappeared back into the caff. Ludo picked up the used ashtray that sat between us, intent on moving it to another table, but fumbled it, and it fell to the pavement, spilling ash and cigarette butts all over the ground and my trainers.

"Bloody buggery bollocks! Sorry!"

It was pretty much the most he'd spoken since we left his house. His quietness had started to proper weird me out. Something was bothering him, but I didn't know what it was. Did he regret last night? Was it something I'd done? I picked up the ashtray and put it on the table over my shoulder.

"How can someone who has done ballet his whole life be so uncoordinated?"

"It only happens when I'm nervous or flustered or in a rush."

Ludo pulled out a wet wipe sachet, which he apparently had in his wallet.

"So, which are you now, nervous, flustered, or rushed?" I asked.

"Well, I *was* nervous, but now I've ruined your shoes and got cigarette ash all over my hands, and I'm flustered as well." He tore open the sachet and began wiping his hands.

"What have you got to be nervous about?"

"You saying we need to have a serious talk." He leant over the table, almost whispering. "Right after we've had sex. That's break-up language, Sunny—and we're not even anything official yet."

"No, it isn't."

"Yes, it is. 'We need to talk.' 'It's not you; it's me.' 'I've been shagging my secretary.' 'You should get yourself tested.' See? It's break-up language."

I laughed. I couldn't help myself.

"I meant we need to talk about what Leaf and Karma told us last night," I said. "It's a huge story, Ludo, and it would be a career-defining scoop for either of us. We need to decide what to do about it."

Ludo's whole body seem to relax. His shoulders dropped; he sighed; the smile finally returned to his face. He passed me the wet wipe, and I cleaned my mitts.

"Can't we just work on it together?" he said, reaching out across the table and sliding his slightly damp hands into mine.

"And publish it where?"

"We could work on it together and each write our own version of the final story and give it to our own papers."

I considered this for moment but dismissed it.

"It's too risky. Someone would publish first, and the one who missed out would never forgive the other. It'd ruin everything."

"You think I'd do that to you?" Ludo said. His brow furrowed. He sat back and pushed his glasses up onto his nose.

"I think our editors wouldn't care a toss about any deal we'd made between ourselves."

Ludo leant forward again, his eyes intense with inspiration.

"So, we jolly well don't tell them we're working on it," he said. "We do all the legwork ourselves, write our stories, and pitch and file them on the same day. Then we tell Father and JT we know for certain the other paper has the story as well and they're running it the next day. That way they'll run it the same day, and no one can gazump anyone else."

I gripped Ludo's hands tightly, enjoying the feel of them in mine—and the public display of affection—while I mulled over his suggestion.

"That might just work," I said, finally. "They'd kill us if they found out, though."

"I sincerely hope my father wouldn't kill me."

"JT wouldn't think twice before killing me. If IKEA sold guillotines, he'd be at the office now, screwdriver in hand, staring at a leftover nut, trying to work out whether the machine was still lethal enough to separate my head from my neck. This has to be a total secret."

Ludo nodded in agreement.

"And it's vital we share everything we discover," I added. "No holding back. Trust is going to be everything if we're going to make this work."

"Name one time I ever held anything back from you," Ludo said. His eyes sparkled, and he was smiling. I almost didn't have the heart to pull the pin out of this grenade. But I did, obviously, because trust requires absolute honesty. And I'd been dying for an excuse to ask him about it.

"You never told me you puked on Krishnan Varma-Rajan," I said.

Ludo pulled his hands away from mine and sat up straight, hands clutched to his chest, like a prairie dog holding a handbag.

"How the hell do you know about that?"

"I have my sources." I was playing it cool.

"No, tell me, because Krishnan made everyone in the room sign an NDA."

Ludo seemed genuinely upset, and I sensed this might be no time to play games. The last thing I wanted was to upset him. Not just because I liked him but because we *needed* to be able to work together on this story.

"Can I trust you?" I asked.

"You know you can. I didn't tell you because, one, I'd signed an NDA, and two, would you tell someone you're sweet on a story like that? When was I meant to tell you? On the helicopter trip while you were chundering your guts up? This morning while your face was buried in my crotch?"

I squeezed Ludo's hands.

"You're sweet on me? How long have you been sweet on me?"

"Stop deflecting," he said. The waitress returned, plonking our mugs of coffee down in front of us.

"Food won't be a minute, boys," she said. We chirped thank yous like hungry nestlings.

"Come on, tell me who told you," Ludo said.

"My mate Petey is a producer on *Wake Up Britain*."

"You're friends with *Made in Dagenham*?"

"Huh?"

"Never mind." He sighed heavily, like the air in the bottom of his lungs had somewhere else it needed to be. "Well, thank you for not telling the *Bulletin*'s infamous gossip columnists about it, at least."

"Are we agreed on the ground rules, then?" I asked.

"Agreed." Ludo squeezed my hand.

"Still feeling nervous? Flustered?"

"No," he said, smiling. "I'm excited for what's to come."

The waitress appeared beside the table.

"Two full English, one with black pudding, one without but with an extra sausage."

I indicated the extra sausage was mine, and Ludo raised a finger in ownership of the black pudding. Was I meant to kiss him after he'd eaten that? His plate connected with the table, and Ludo raised his eyebrows.

"Enjoy, boys," the waitress said, disappearing inside.

"This is a *lot* of food," Ludo said.

I reached for the red sauce.

"This'll set you up for the day," I said.

As we ate, normal, happy, talkative Ludo returned. I looked at the proper stunner sitting across from me, talking about the show he'd seen and the review he had to go home to finish writing. And I thought about the story we'd just agreed to write *together*—against every rule and journalistic instinct—and really hoped that I could trust him.

38

LUDO

FOR ALL IT LOOKED like it had already been passed through the gizzards of one of the larger waterfowl, the Gloria's fry-up was jolly delicious. I studied the clientele inside through the window. Most were tanned, beefy chaps of the sort who wear high-vis uniforms to work. They displayed a level of comfort with the waitress and the furniture that led me to imagine they probably also ate here regularly during the week.

The waitress came out, and Sunny asked her for the bill. As she disappeared back inside, I noticed an old lady creep up to the table behind us.

"What's up?" Sunny said, my face clearly betraying my horror.

"Don't look now, but there's an extraordinary woman behind you, going through the ashtrays."

Sunny, who apparently does not take instruction well, immediately turned around.

"Orright, Rosie. How are you, love?" he said.

What in the Mary Poppins was going on?

The woman smiled, revealing a perfect set of stained teeth, which I took to be dentures.

"You orright, Sun?" she said, with a radiant smile.

Sunny jumped up and hugged her. She had wiry grey hair. Her cardigan looked hand-knitted and beautifully done, except it was unravelling slightly at the pocket. She flashed her eyes at me. I realised I'd been staring.

"Is this your fella?" she said. Whomever this woman was to Sunny, they were on very familiar terms. Sunny smiled.

"Rosie, this is Ludo Boche. He's a journalist, like me. Ludo, this is Rosie. She's a much-loved neighbour—and what we journalists like to call 'a colourful local character.'"

Rosie bellowed with laughter and extended a hand. I shook it. Her fingers were as yellow as her teeth and covered in cigarette ash. I cursed my luck at having already used my emergency wet wipe. Honestly, the thing sits in your wallet untouched for months, and then suddenly you need to use it twice in half an hour. Just like a condom.

I was in the middle of saying that I was pleased to meet her when Rosie's attention was taken by the cigarette butts on the ground. She bent down, picked them up, and popped them in a dirty sandwich bag with dozens of others. What was I witnessing? I looked at Sunny, hoping for an explanation. He frowned and shook his head subtly. He tucked a hand under Rosie's arm and helped her up into his chair.

"You had breakfast, Rosie?" Sunny asked.

"Today?"

Sunny laughed. "Yes, today."

She shook her head. "Not got much in just now, Sun."

"Let's get you a slap-up breakfast, shall we?"

As Rosie smacked her lips and cooed her appreciation, the waitress emerged with our bill. Sunny asked Rosie what she wanted, added a full English to our tab, and paid for the lot. It was an incredible amount of food for twenty-one pounds. With the bill paid, I thought we'd leave the woman to her meal, but Sunny pulled over a chair for himself from the next table, and we sat with her while she ate. They swapped neighbourhood gossip for a while. Somewhere called Churchill Road was having a street party for the King's coronation. Rosie was going. Someone called Mrs Patel had been diagnosed with colon cancer. Sunny promised to call in on her. By the time Rosie had finished her meal, Sunny had agreed to pick up some groceries from the local food bank for her, fetch her prescription from the chemist, and repot her aspidistra—which I'm fairly certain wasn't a euphemism, no matter how sus it sounded.

I looked at Sunny in wonder. Such generosity of spirit isn't something you see every day. My father slams the door on the children who come carolling at Christmas, then watches the footage back on the home CCTV system to laugh at their shocked little faces.

"Have you lived here a long time, then?" I asked.

"Born and raised in Cricklewood," she said, pointing up the street. "My father was a driver out of the Willesden Bus Garage."

"You worked there, too, didn't you, Rosie?" Sunny said, though he clearly already knew the answer.

"For a little while, yeah."

"She's being modest," Sunny said. "Rosie spent forty years cleaning buses. Scrubbing off graffiti, mopping up vomit, scraping up used johnnies. You kept the buses running, didn't you, love? It's people like Rosie that make London work."

Rosie blushed.

***

WHEN ROSIE HAD LICKED her plate clean, Sunny hugged her warmly, and we said farewell. We strolled along the street aimlessly.

"That was a beautiful thing you did," I said. Sunny shook his head.

"She'd do the same for me."

I grabbed his hand and wove my fingers through his.

"Why was she collecting cigarette butts?"

"Tobacco's expensive. Her pension's worth bugger all. She's just doing what she needs to do to make ends meet."

Forty years scrubbing bodily fluids off buses, and Rosie had to spend her hard-earned retirement diving into ashtrays for fag ends? How was this kind of thing allowed to happen in Britain? This was like something from the developing world, the kind of scandal Mummy exposes on *Compass Point* all the time.

"She's had a tough life," Sunny said. "My housemates and I sort of keep an eye on her. She's salt of the earth. She reminds me of my nanna. I enjoy her company."

We found ourselves by the Tube station.

"Do you want to see where I live?" Sunny asked. I turned to face him. "It's in the other direction, but it's not far."

Part of me wanted to, very much. Another part of me had somewhere else it needed to be.

"I need to go to the hospital. I want to check in on Uncle Ben. Then I need to write this review."

Sunny nodded and squeezed my hands in his. Then we kissed, right there in the street, beneath the Underground sign.

39

LUDO

WILHELMINA **P**OST: *FABULOUS REVIEW, Ludo. Congratulations! We'll make a theatre critic out of you yet. W xxxxxx*

Sunny Miller: *Morning, you clever boy. Awesome to come across your sexy face in the arts section this morning. Read it as soon as my boner went down. Great stuff, babe. I bet Uncle Ben is proud. xx.*

Wilhelmina Post: *PS. Saw Benny yesterday. Missed you by a couple of hours. Smuggled in the cigs. I'm way ahead of you on brownie points. As I left, a rather dashing male nurse was wheeling him up to the roof for a smoke! The man is an ICON. W xxxxxx*

Uncle Ben: *Congratulations on your first published review, dear boy! How does it feel? I read it in the early morning sunshine, in a blissful cloud of smoke, on the hospital roof, with my new friend Theodore, who claims to come from Ghana but I'm convinced is the Farnese Atlas come to life. Shoulders the size of my head. Hope to leave hospital Wednesday. May pop a hip so I can hang out with Atlas a little longer. If I succeed, please bring more cheroots. Much love, etc xxxxx*

***

I READ MY REVIEW over breakfast. The subs hadn't cut too much, although one or two of the jokes had been trimmed. I stared at my photo at the top of my review. My name had never been so far back in the paper, yet I couldn't remember feeling so jolly proud to see it in print. Hands down, it trumped scoring the front page with the nuclear power plant story.

Father breezed through the kitchen with his briefcase in hand.

"Are you coming in with me, or are you catching the Tube?"

Parliament was now in recess for the coronation of King George VII, so I was working from the office in the City rather than the parliamentary bureau in Westminster.

"I'll bum a lift, if that's OK?"

I folded the paper and put it on the pile with all the others. Every front page was dominated by the impending coronation. No big news was going to happen this week. Or, if it did, no one was going to be paying any attention to it. This was good news. It bought Sunny and me time to investigate the nuclear power plant deal. I threw my work satchel over my shoulder and followed my father out the door.

Five minutes later we both had our faces buried in our phones as the black cab dashed down Haverstock Hill towards central London. I was replying to texts. Father was doing whatever it was that editors did at eight o'clock in the morning. Putting the fear of God into one of his reporters, probably. As we stopped and started through Camden, Father suddenly put his phone down.

"Is it serious with Sunny Miller, then?"

This was new territory for us. I could not have been more shocked if he'd asked me which Jonas brother I thought was the cutest (Joe, obviously).

I wasn't sure how to answer. I wasn't sure what kind of answer he was looking for.

"I don't know," I said, finally.

"I mean it looked reasonably—and I might say, Ludo, rather publicly—like it was *quite* serious the other night."

"I know," I said. "Are you worried about us going head to head—"

"I don't need to know that kind of detail, Ludo. What you do in the privacy of the summer house is your own business."

"Father! I mean us covering politics. Competing for the same stories."

"Your mother and I did it. Plenty of couples have done it. Some political reporters are sleeping with members of the cabinet. They manage it."

I was not entirely comfortable with this conversation. Normally I appreciated my father taking an interest in my life, but the caveat to that, I now realised, was—not my love life.

That's when Father said the big, awful thing.

"Should I offer him a job?"

I stared at him while I processed what he'd just said. The silence dragged on, and Father felt the need to fill it.

"He's extremely talented. He has a bright future ahead of him. He could be genuinely outstanding if the right people took him under their wing—"

"No," I said. It came out more firmly than I had intended. I apologised. "Sorry, I just don't think that's a good idea." Father looked at me, eyebrows raised in anticipation of further explanation. "If he joins the *Sentinel* and it all goes tits up, I'll still have to work with him every day. I don't think I could stand it."

"Fair enough," Father said. "But I'm telling you now, Ludo, I've got my eyes on that young fellow. If he ever suggests he wants to move to the respectable end of Fleet Street, you let me know. I won't miss out on one of the most promising young reporters of your generation, just to spare your blushes."

It's a bit of a gut punch to hear your father openly put work before his own son. In the past, Father prioritising work over me had come in the form of missed ballet recitals and skipped parents' evenings at Petersham College. They were heartaches at the time, but I could take it. Those parts of my heart had formed calluses. This was the first time my heart itself was a pawn in my father's plans.

The taxi sailed through the lights at King's Cross Station and turned down Farringdon Road towards the Smithfield meat markets. It seemed fitting, given my morning's high had just been butchered like a side of old mutton.

40

SUNNY

WEDNESDAY MORNING, I WAS sitting in a proper dreary coffee shop on the wrong side of London Bridge, with the smiling faces of Leaf and Karma waving good morning to me from my computer screen. They sat in a room of honey-coloured pine walls, light streaming in through a large window, with the Derbyshire forest behind them. It was a stark contrast to the dank café, which I'd only popped into so no one at work knew I was making this call. It smelt of burnt coffee and soggy ham and cheese toasties.

"Summer, come and meet Sunny," Karma said, beckoning someone off-screen towards the webcam. A proper fit blonde appeared. She was probably in her mid-twenties, with the kind of clear skin and clear eyes that only a Spartan-like commitment to training, clean eating, and rude good health can generate. She had probably never consumed anything containing an E-number in her entire life. I self-consciously covered the angry-looking spot on my chin. Summer smiled, and her whole face lit up.

"This is our daughter, Summer," Karma said. "She's a massage therapist, acupuncturist, and reiki healer."

We swapped hellos; then Summer bobbed off to go charge someone £100 to either touch them, push needles into them, or *not* touch them. (Reiki is essentially just being in a room with someone, hovering your hands a few inches above their body. Which is why you never meet anyone on GayHoller who says, "Wanna come over for some reiki?")

"What have you managed to find?" I asked, when I finally had Karma all on my own.

"I've got a few documents for you." She popped on a pair of reading glasses.

I was, quite literally, on the edge of my seat. Partly so I didn't sit on chewing gum. Karma shared her screen, which must have been the first time anyone in human history has successfully achieved that technological feat without ten minutes of faffing about first. A document flashed up with the ZephEnergies logo I recognised from the letter in Vladimir Popov's office.

"These are purchase orders," Karma said. I read them on the screen. "This one is for £96,750 for fencing supplies. Cyclone fencing, plain wire, poles, ready-mixed concrete, it's all here. From a company called Thowden's."

"I know them," I said. "They're a big construction-and-hardware-type company. They've got stores all over the Midlands."

"This is the trade side of their business, not the retail," Karma said. "But why is ZephEnergies putting in a massive order for cyclone fencing with Thowden's?"

"Could be anything," I said, erring on the side of caution. "They could be building a wind farm somewhere nearby."

"I thought that too," Karma said. "Wait until you see this."

Over the next twenty minutes, Karma showed me documents that clearly indicated ZephEnergies had bought and installed fencing around the Newton Bardon site. The paper trail included delivery addresses, quotes from fencing contractors for installation, and—the real icing on the Party Ring—photographs Leaf had taken of the fence going up.

"Why would ZephEnergies be paying hundreds of thousands of pounds to fence off a massive greenfield site at Newton Bardon, a site we already know was earmarked for the nuclear power plant, if they'd not been given the nod that the contract was theirs already?" I asked.

"You can see why we're convinced it's a done deal," Karma said. "As I say, we can get more documents, but they cost a lot of money."

"How much is it?" I said, sliding unavoidably into a Leicester accent. It came out like *owmuchisit*. The answer was £10,000. Daylight robbery. I didn't have any budget, let alone ten grand. This was the price we paid for not involving our bosses in our investigations. That said, unless it involved photos of exposed celebrity boobs, the *Bulletin* wasn't dropping ten big ones on a few documents. We'd have to do without the dark web and its dossier.

"How do you reckon these documents got online anyway?" I asked.

"Could be any manner of ways," Karma explained. "A security breach, perhaps. Hackers. Or there could even be a mole in the business. A whistle-blower. Someone who doesn't like what the company is doing and wants to tell the world but without risking their position or getting caught."

The source of any piece of information is as important as the information itself. What we had here was a nugget. But if history had taught us anything, it was that discovering one little piece of gold is all you need to start a gold rush. These documents were a marker, an indicator. Now Ludo and I needed to keep digging to see what other nuggets we could uncover in the hope that it led to a rich seam of pure gold.

"By the way, Sunny." Leaf suddenly reappeared behind Karma and peered into the screen over the top of his reading glasses. "Do you know someone called Torsten Beaumont-Flattery?"

I said I did and asked why.

"He's coming to pay us a visit. He won the door prize on Saturday night. Know anything about him?"

"Aside from the fact he's built like a rugby player who ate three other rugby players?"

Where should I even begin?

41

LUDO

IN HONOUR OF THE coronation, the Union flag bunting was up, we'd cracked out the Pimm's horrifically early in the season, and a "greatest British hits of all time" playlist was cranking out of the speakers at a genteel-neighbourhood-appropriate volume. It was one of those beautiful May evenings, and Mummy had the folding doors onto the patio wide open. "Letting the outside in and the inside out" was how the architect had sold the idea to my parents before the big renovation a few years ago. Unfortunately, it also gave the local mosquitos the kind of free range that domesticated chickens can only dream of, and I was being eaten alive.

"Where are the citronella candles, Mummy?" She was hooking a string of fairy lights along the fence, which I appreciated because it's always nice to not be the gayest thing at a party.

"Ask your father!"

Father was in the kitchen, his usual weekend haunt, marinating something dead. I didn't really want to disturb him, mostly because it meant I'd have to talk to him, which, today of all days, was a danger to my mental health. Tonight was the first time Sunny would be spending any real amount of time with my family. It was also the first time he'd be meeting Uncle Ben, who was out of both the wheelchair and the hospital now but still weak. I really wanted it to go well.

I turned to Jonty, who was struggling to light the firepit.

"Bet you're now regretting all those misspent afternoons skiving off Boy Scouts to go hang out with girls down by the canal," I said.

"Don't be ridiculous, Ludovic. That was a marvellous investment. I got to touch Laura Pettigrew's breasts."

"Oh, yes! Heavy Pettigrew," I recalled. "Didn't she marry an earl or something?"

"He's a viscount," Jonty snapped. I scratched at my arm, irritating a mozzie bite.

"Only a viscount? How the mighty breasts have fallen. Do you know where the citronella candles are?"

"Cupboard under the stairs?"

The doorbell rang, the buzz amplified through the home security system. Our guests had started to arrive.

"Can someone get that?" Father called out. "I'm in the marinade."

"Need me to hold your head under?" I said, sotto voce. Jonty snorted.

The doorbell rang again. The originally planned dinner party had grown into an actual party, with a horde of guests. But I thought the likelihood of the person at the door being either Sunny or Uncle Ben was high, so I volunteered to answer it. I dashed through the house, tripping on the hall runner and falling hard on my hip and elbow. The doorbell rang again. I picked myself up and inspected the damage in the hall mirror. There'd at least be a bruised elbow in the morning. I straightened my glasses and my hair, tucked my shirt back in to make sure I looked presentable, and opened the door. It was King George VII. Well, it was Sunny, his freckled visage hidden behind a King George mask.

"Hello, lowly subject," he said.

"My liege." I bowed.

Sunny removed the ridiculous mask to reveal a cheeky grin. His coppery hair was either still wet from the shower or freshly gelled. Weekend Sunny was *way* more scally boy than workaday Sunny, and golly, it was unbearably sexy. He was wearing essentially the same outfit as he'd worn to the fundraiser—a white shirt, black skinny jeans, and trainers—but he had added a light-blue hoodie, which was unzipped to the waist. He was holding a four-pack of ciders. He looked like an ASOS model. He looked as hot as hell. He opened his mouth to speak.

"You look—"

I grabbed him by his shirt, pulled him inside, slammed the front door shut behind us, and kissed him against it. Father's voice echoed down the hallway.

"You're on camera, Ludo!"

I rolled my eyes and extricated myself from Sunny. He looked startled. Until a week ago, my parents had never even met a boy I was interested in. Now, they must have thought I was some weird exhibitionist whose fetish was making out with boys in front of his family.

"Better security system in here than a Hatton Garden jewellers," I said. I grabbed Sunny's free hand and pulled him, his ciders, and his exquisite sexiness into the cupboard under the stairs, shutting the door behind us. I yanked the cord to switch on the light, ignoring the throb in my elbow.

"Sex dungeon?" he asked.

"We're looking for citronella."

"Is she the housekeeper?"

"She's a candle. But first, you're going to kiss me without my parents watching for once."

Sunny saluted. "Can do, captain." He put his drinks on a shelf, popped King George into the umbrella stand, and slid his arms around my waist. I let my body sink into his and inhaled the smell of him. Our eyes met, our lips touched, and I tasted the warmth of his mouth. Suddenly, he pulled away.

"You know what? I can't do this," he said.

My heart dropped.

"What's the matter?"

Sunny leant behind me, grabbed hold of King George in the umbrella stand, and turned him around to face the wall.

"That's better. Now, where were we?"

***

T WENTY MINUTES LATER, I'D installed at least twenty citronella candles around the garden. Sunny, meanwhile, had replaced Jonty on firepit duty, and the flames were roaring in furious swirls and eddies, sending sparks high up into the sky above. Sunny stood, sipping at his cider, looking jolly satisfied with his work.

"Good show! What's the secret?" I asked.

"Honestly? Lighter fluid."

"Did they teach you that in the Boy Scouts?"

Sunny laughed. "I was never a Boy Scout. Just a communist garden hoodie." He threw his hood up to cover his head, and I laughed.

"You know the expression is *common or garden*, right?"

"Not according to my nanna," Sunny said, pulling his hood back down and adjusting his hair. He'd definitely gelled it.

Welcoming noises erupted from my parents in the kitchen. I turned to check what the fuss was about. Uncle Ben had arrived. My heart leapt. I slid my hand into Sunny's.

"Come on, there's someone I want you to meet."

In the kitchen, Uncle Ben was lapping up his moment in the spotlight, enjoying everyone making a fuss of him by protesting that everyone should stop making a fuss of him. If they did, he'd be jolly deflated. He was standing with a stick in his right hand, which was new and confronting but better than a wheelchair. The wheelchair, he'd told me, had simply been an abundance of caution on the part of the doctors, but I rather had the impression he just liked being wheeled around by Theodore.

"Dear boy," he said, his free arm spread wide. I slipped inside and hugged him, the sweet, earthy scent of tobacco filling my lungs, the familiar aroma enveloping me like a comfortable cloak. I felt his arm around my back, the squeeze noticeably not as strong as it used to be. My heart broke a little, and I held him too long. "Are you going to introduce me to your handsome prince?" he asked. He was still mumbling slightly.

"Of course," I said, unravelling myself from Uncle Ben, hoping that if he saw the tears in my eyes, he assumed they were tears of happiness. Which, mostly, they were. "Uncle Ben, this is Sunny Miller. Sunny, this is Ben Diamond."

Uncle Ben went in for the hug. Sunny didn't hesitate; he dived right in.

"Now, let me look at you," Uncle Ben said, pulling away but holding on to one of Sunny's hands. Sunny stood back, allowing Uncle Ben to appraise him like he was visiting a stable to buy a thoroughbred. I thought I noticed Sunny stand taller and puff his chest out a little, but he was taking it all in his stride. "He's even better looking than his picture in the paper, wouldn't you say? A face like this should be on television. Beverley, shouldn't a face like this be on the television? He's like a young Robert Redford."

I might have blushed, but Sunny went the colour of a radish.

"That makes two of us, then, sir," Sunny said, a cheeky grin lighting his whole face. Uncle Ben roared into a full-throated laugh, which descended into a cough. He dropped Sunny's hand to cover his mouth. Mummy passed Uncle Ben a glass of champagne. He sipped, swallowing down his cough.

"Can we keep him, Hugo?" Uncle Ben asked, when his coughing fit had subsided. "I like him. His eyes need testing, but I like him."

"That's because you're a terrible old flirt who's easily flattered," my father said.

"At my age, Hugo, when a young man compliments you on your appearance, it's neither flirting nor flattery. It's generosity of spirit. And, believe me, you embrace it with both hands," Uncle Ben said, winking at Sunny and me conspiratorially. He lifted his glass of champagne. "Na zdrowie!"

42

SUNNY

THE PRE-CORONATION PARTY AT the Boche palace was in full swing. The combined wealth of all these posh twats, I reckoned, would be proper staggering. There must have been at least sixty people, milling about, making small talk, jigging to Very British Music and saying "yah, yah" a lot. Jonty was by the firepit, making Instagrammable duck face with some of his influencer mates I recognised from Maxime's. One of the blokes was so fit I found myself pondering the ethics of walking up to a total stranger and asking them if they had an OnlyFans. At the kitchen table, Beverley and Ben were deep in conversation with a group of BBC types, including Annabelle Statham-Drew, who'd been to Shetland with us the week before but had so far blanked me completely tonight. Out on the patio, Ludo and I found ourselves sinking slowly into the lounger, having been cornered by a very drunk Hugo—who somehow no longer seemed to consider me enemy number one. In fact, quite the opposite. It was like the booze had flicked a switch.

"It was bloody marvellous," Hugo said. His arms were moving like someone else was controlling them, and I realised where Ludo got it from.

I wondered if they had the same puppeteer. "Ludo struck the first blow, mortally wounding Wynn-Jones"—he clapped a hand on Ludo's shoulder and shook him, making Ludo visibly cringe—"then you went in for the kill and finished off the useless bastard." He leant over Ludo and slapped his hand on my knee a few times, like he was rewarding a dog. "The future of British journalism is in good hands—and it's sitting right here on my patio sofa."

If I'm honest, I felt as buoyed as I did surprised by the pep talk, but Ludo looked like he'd rather be scraping dog shit from his shoes with his own teeth. Hugo knocked back the last of his red wine and grabbed the bottle to pour himself another. I was nursing my third cider, not wanting to get blattered if there was a chance of a serious make-out session with Ludo later. I was starting to feel cold and couldn't remember where I'd left my hoodie.

"Tell me," Hugo said, "what are your career plans, Sunny? Where do you see yourself in five years?"

"Father!" Ludo's annoyance with his old man spilt over. The two of them exchanged a look. Ludo's was a glare; Hugo's was more dismissive. Whatever this tension was, I had no desire to wade into it. By the same token, one of the most powerful men on (the metaphorical) Fleet Street had just asked me a question about my career plans, and I fully intended to answer it.

"I'm still learning my craft and making my contacts," I said. Always smart to start humble. "And I will always be grateful to the *Bulletin* for giving me my first Westminster gig. But, to be honest, I don't see myself there long term."

Hugo's eyebrows raised, and I wondered if he thought I was being disloyal. It was too late to turn back now, so I carried on. I felt Ludo's hand unwrap itself from around my back, the night air cool where the warmth of his body had been.

"Ultimately, I want to work at a newspaper where I'm respected, both as a reporter and as an individual, and where my work is valued and treated seriously. Somewhere the subs don't add in spelling mistakes, factual errors and, frankly, tits."

Hugo laughed.

"Or beavers?"

"Don't get me started on the beavers."

Ludo stood up.

"Shall we go for a walk?" he said, interrupting what was beginning to feel like an important bonding experience with a man who could make all my professional dreams come true. Ludo must have sensed my hesitation. "I want to show you something," he added. He held out a hand towards me. I looked up at him, his beautiful face framed by Union flag bunting, and heard myself say, "Not just now."

Ludo's face fell. He looked hurt.

"Can we go in a minute?" I said, correcting course. "Your dad and I were just—"

"Never mind," Ludo said, holding up a hand. "You talk. I'm going to get a drink."

He turned and walked away. Every instinct told me to chase after him. To wrap him up in a hug, to apologise for being stupid, for letting myself get distracted by his father's flattery, and to tell him I'd love to go for a walk. But the significance of the conversation I was having with Hugo, the potential effect on my career, was too great. This might be my big shot. In the end, I hedged my bets, wanting to show Hugo I would be a caring partner to his son, not just a good potential employee.

"I should really go check that he's OK," I said.

"Don't worry about Ludo," Hugo said, the dismissive look returning to his face. "He thinks it would be a bad idea for the two of you to work together."

Wait, what? Had they *discussed* this? "Excuse me?" I said.

"He told me the other day, when I asked him if he thought you'd ever consider moving over to the *Sentinel*."

My mind was spinning, struggling to process what Hugo had just said. If I'd understood correctly, Hugo had suggested offering me a job, and Ludo had stopped him.

"He said you had some funny idea that reporters shouldn't get involved with reporters from other outlets," Hugo said.

My heart sank. I picked at the label of my cider bottle, feeling like a proper knobber. I felt the rage growing inside me. Hugo hadn't wanted to offer me a job on merit; he was just being nice to his son. This was humiliating. Something inside me shattered.

"Which is utter nonsense, by the way," Hugo continued. "Beverley and I worked opposite each other early in our careers. You just create a few ground rules. It's not hard. Frankly, it's been the secret to our success. We've pushed each other, driven each other forward. It has lifted us both up, professionally and personally. It's about trust. It's as simple as that."

"Trust," I said. The word echoed around my head, repeating on me, like Hugo had shouted it into an empty canyon. I stood up. "Thank you for the pep talk, Hugo. I appreciate it a lot. I really do. I think I better go and find Ludo."

Hugo drained his glass and stood up.

"I think I better go and find more wine," he said.

43

LUDO

I WAS SITTING ON the wall out the front of the house, looking out into the darkness of Hampstead Heath and jolly well raging. The night was filled with the sound of London celebrating—music, fireworks, and the distant burble and laughter of people. The air was chilly, so I shoved my hands deep into the pockets of my chinos. A fox sauntered across the street, stopped to regard me, then continued on his way—too wily to be bothered with a weeping homosexual. I heard footsteps on the loose gravel path behind me but didn't bother turning around to see who it was. I wished I'd walked farther down the street, or into the park.

"We need to talk," Sunny said. His Leicester accent had been fully deployed, and it sounded alarmingly aggressive. His arms were folded. He looked mad. What the ruddy hell did he have to be mad about? I was the one with good reason to be angry.

"Not here," I said. I nodded in the direction of the heath. "Let's go for that walk." I didn't want anyone overhearing what I had to say, let alone whatever Sunny might be about to say.

We walked in silence along the narrow dirt path for a few minutes, me in front, Sunny behind. He wasn't wearing his hoodie, and I heard him shiver against the cool. I enjoyed his discomfort. Freeze to death, you bastard. I knew this path like the back of my hand. I'd run along it as a child. It was the shortcut from the house up to Parliament Hill, with its sweeping views across London. I'd meant to bring Sunny up here to look at the city lights and see the fireworks going off across the city, from Hackney to Harlesden to Belsize Park. There'd probably be hundreds of people up there right now, all with the same idea. Lovers sitting on rugs, families sharing late-night picnics, groups of teens underage drinking.

I steered Sunny to a quiet hollow by the ponds instead. When I thought my tears had sufficiently dried, I stopped, turned around, and faced him. Sunny had a face like thunder.

"Did you tell your old man not to give me a job?"

There it was. He really was just like all the rest.

"Yes." I let the word sink in like a blade.

"Why would you do that, Ludo?"

"I guess I thought you were different. I should have known better, really." I was shaking now, and I wished I wasn't. "Let me ask you a question: Did you ever like me for me? Or were you just using me to get a job at the *Sentinel*?" I felt the tears spill and roll down my cheeks.

"What? No! I would never do that."

"Everyone else does it. Why the hell would you be any different?"

"What are you talking about?" Sunny was pacing back and forth now, eyes cast down. He looked as tight as a spring.

"Lucy, Krishnan, you. You're all the same. You look at me and you don't see Ludo Boche. You see Hugo Boche's son. You don't see a person, you see a step on a career ladder."

"That's absolute bollocks, Ludo! When have I ever said or done anything to make you think that?"

"In Shetland! When you said you wanted to work for a respectable newspaper."

"What's wrong with that? It's my dream, Ludo. It's all I've ever wanted. It wasn't about you or your family or the bloody *Sentinel*." He was stomping and red-faced. I could see it clearly, even in the dark. His eyes were wet with tears, and I wondered what they were for. "But just so you know, Ludo, I would *never* have taken your father's offer. I am not a *favour*. Wherever I end up, I will earn my place there on merit. Not because of who I'm shagging. But what hurts, Ludo, is that you told him not to give me a shot."

The stress of my situation was causing my brain to glitch, and I was losing track of my own thoughts and arguments. This was how gaslighting worked, but I wasn't sure Sunny was gaslighting me. Had he ever given me cause to think he was using me to get to my father? Or was this all in my mind? Would he really have turned my father down? I had taken too long to answer him.

"This is exactly why I should never have got involved with you," Sunny said. "I knew it was a bad idea."

The words macheted their way into my brain, and anger boiled within me. Tears wrenched from my eyes, hot from rage.

"Is that all I am to you? A mistake?"

"Make up your mind, mate. A minute ago, you were a stepladder."

"A step on a career ladder. Get your facts right!" I was seething now. I went in for the kill. "Oh, I forgot. You work at the *Bulletin*. Facts don't come into it."

Sunny stopped pacing, his eyes connecting with mine. I could see the hurt in them. Mission accomplished. Technical knockout. I expected him to yell. I expected to see the full angry estate kid he kept bottled up inside.

"You know what?" he said. His voice was calm and measured, his vowels long and flat and Leicestery. "Fuck you, Ludo."

We looked at each other for a moment, unflinching. The tears finally spilt from Sunny's eyes. I had broken him. Had I gone too far? Had I been unfair? Sunny set his jaw, hunched his shoulders, shoved his hands into his pockets, and set off across the park.

"Have a nice life," he said. He didn't look back.

I felt something tear away inside me, pulling me apart. I sank to my knees on the grass and cried and cried and cried.

44

SUNNY

I WALKED ALL THE way home to Willesden Green from Hampstead Heath. It took an hour and a half, mostly because I wasted a lot of time trying to jump the railway line at Kilburn. Every step was proper freezing. My nipples were so hard they'd just about cut holes in my shirt by the time I got to my front door. When I got in, I had a warm shower in a bid to stave off hypothermia, but the shivering continued even after I climbed into bed. I was still pure raging, and I couldn't sleep. I lay in bed, awake, going through everything in my mind. Fuck Ludo. Honestly, fuck that overprivileged bellend for the crappy stunt he'd pulled and his crappy reasons for doing it. For all his claims to the contrary, it was just like I'd told him it was that first night at Maxime's. He was just another posh twat, pulling the door closed behind him, stopping people like me getting through.

***

I WAS STILL RAGING about it the next day, as I slouched on the couch in front of the telly in Dav and Nick's flat, watching Westminster Abbey fill up with yet more posh twats ahead of the coronation of King George VII and Queen Philippa. The republican at the feast. Dav was effing and blinding from the kitchen. A loud metallic clatter suggested things weren't going well. The smell of something turning to charcoal wafted across to the living room.

"You better not be burning Amita's bhajis," I called out. More swearing from the kitchen.

Nick glided in front of me, blocking my view of the TV, spun his wheelchair around to face me, picked a can out of his lap, and held it out for me.

"You look like you could use another one of these," he said. I took it. Why did everything always sound kinder in a lilting Aberdonian accent?

"Ta, mate." I leant over. "Has he burnt Amita's bhajis?"

"Let's just say they're very, *very* brown."

I shook my head. Could today get any worse?

Nick wheeled around to the side of the couch, popped his brakes on, and edged himself onto the seat beside me. On the screen, Bimpe Lasisi was navigating her way around the Tomb of the Unknown Soldier, gripping her invitation like it had been signed by God himself. She was dressed in royal blue with gold trim. She would still be the *most* regal person in the abbey, even when the King arrived. Her gele was enormous.

"Imagine being invited to the coronation and missing the whole damn thing because you're sat behind Bimpe and can't see around her hat," Nick said. He cracked his can and held it up to say cheers. I opened mine and tapped it against his.

"You all right, pal?" he said.

"Not really." I gulped at my beer, swallowed, then gulped at it again. I'd already told Dav and Nick what had happened with Ludo. I'd sent them a text saying I wasn't coming because I was still proper fuming. Dav wasn't having it.

"I ain't put up all this bloody bunting and bought a lorryload of sausage rolls just so you can lie in bed all day, crying into your foreskin about how lonely you is," he'd said.

I'm very susceptible to peer pressure where Dav is concerned. Possibly because of the expressive way he likes to paint failure. On the screen, Jemima Carstairs and her husband were walking into the abbey. Carstairs had got the note about not upstaging the monarch. She wore a blue version of her trademark pantsuit, with a fascinator that looked a lot like a wind turbine. Was she ever not on message? Take a day off, Jem.

"I get that you're angry with Ludo right now," Nick said. I sighed, waiting for his enduring sensibleness. "But can you see where he's coming from? Like, if people are constantly using him to get to his parents, just to further their careers."

"I wasn't using him." I spoke too quickly. There was a snarl in my voice. "Sorry," I said.

"That's not how it'll look to him, though, is it? That must have been really triggering for him when you and his old man started talking about you joining the paper."

"Hugo started it!"

"That's not really the point, though, is it?"

"The point is, I've never given Ludo any reason to think I'm using him to get into the *Sentinel*."

"And it was never in the back of your mind? Really? Not even a tiny bit?"

The defensive answer was no, it wasn't. But in the moment, I wasn't sure if that was true. I'd apologised to Ludo after Maxime's to avoid the potential career damage. Was that as good as the same thing? And was there a part of me, deep down, that knew working with Ludo on the nuclear power plant story would get Hugo's attention? I didn't want to be offered a job just because I was shagging his son, but I'd proper jumped at the chance to talk with him about my career at a party I'd only been invited to *because* I was shagging his son. I started to feel uncomfortable.

"Either way, you've buggered it now," Nick said. "You've lost Ludo and probably any chance you had of ever working at the *Sentinel*."

"Thanks," I said. "You're a real mate." Nick was the straightest talker I'd ever met. Losing the use of your legs will do that to you, I guess. Nick had zero time for nonsense. Which was ironic, because what he did for a living was interrupt music to talk crap on the radio.

"What do you actually *want*?" Nick said. "Like, how do we fix this?" I sucked on my can. It was a good question. I didn't have the answer. "Like, does Ludo literally have to make his dad sit you down, offer you a job, and swear on a copy of *Horse & Hound* that it's based on merit, for you to forgive him? Because that's mad."

"It's too late for that," I said. "My reputation is going to be toast up and down Fleet Street once Ludo's version of events begins to spread through his father's media contacts. They'll close ranks around him. Hugo will never give me a job. Nor will anyone else."

"Nor would I, pal," Nick said.

"Oh, cheers, mate."

"If I was Hugo, I mean. Think about it. If he gives you a job now, he's introducing a ton of complications and toxicity into the workplace. That's before you get to the all-points clusterfuck it'd cause at home. Hugo Boche might be a chinless walloper, but he's not a total melt."

On the telly, senior foreign leaders were filing into the abbey. The US first lady, the Canadian and Australian prime ministers, the German chancellor. In the kitchen, Dav was swearing at the fridge, which had started to beep. We needed Stavros. He normally catered for our Brent Boys events, but he, Jumaane, and Petey had all gone down to the Mall to watch the gold-gilded knee-bending jizz-fest first-hand.

"This is exactly why you should never get involved with a colleague," I said. "What hurts is, I proper cared for him, you know? Despite the rules, despite my better judgement, I took a shot on him." I took another swig from my can. If Dav didn't bring some snacks through soon, I was going to be hammered before old George even left the palace.

"You need to work out what the endgame is here, Sunny," Nick said. "What do you want? The job? Or the boy?"

The pause while I considered this question could not have been more pregnant if it had its legs in stirrups and a midwife crouching between them with a net.

"Both, maybe?" I said, unsure of myself. Nick lifted his can to his mouth.

"Right. And you currently have neither." Brutal. He took a sip of his beer, giving his words time to sink in.

"What do you suggest I do?"

"I'd probably start by apologising to Ludo, you daft bawbag."

The TV coverage cut to a picture of the Mall, lined with hundreds of thousands of cheering people. A loud roar went up as the gate to Buckingham Palace opened, the crowd anticipating the King's procession. Somewhere in amongst them were Dav's parents, Stav, Jumaane, and Petey.

Dav came through the living room carrying an overloaded platter of meats, fruits, and cheeses in each hand and plonked them down on the coffee table. No bhajis, I noted. The decision was made. If I couldn't fix the fix I was in, I'd comfort eat until I was too fat to see my bellend over my belly.

"Did I miss anyfink?" Dav said, dashing back to the kitchen without waiting for an answer.

"You missed Bimpe Lasisi making the archbishop of Canterbury look underdressed," Nick called after him.

"Yaasss, my queen. Iconic," he said, returning with a bottle of Tesco Finest cava and three glasses.

"And you missed Sunny realising he's made a terrible mistake."

45

LUDO

I FOUND MYSELF UP the palace end of the Mall, pinned between a lamp post and a rather jolly woman called Bertha. She was from Southend-on-Sea, probably in her late sixties, and was wearing a happy and glorious Union Jack waistcoat. Her husband, Dave, was wearing what I took to be the matching trousers. Barking mad, I thought, then caught myself. If anything could be salvaged from my disastrous flirtation with Sunny Miller, let it be not leaping to snap judgements about people based on first impressions. As it turned out, Bertha and Dave were delightful.

"Kettle crisp?" Bertha slid an open packet of mature-ched-dar-and-red-onion potato crisps under my nose, hand cupping the bottom of the bag.

"Thank you," I said, gingerly dipping my paw into the proffered packet and picking out a solitary salty offering.

"Take a handful, love," she said, in a broad Estuary accent. "Ain't you brung nuffin?"

"Afraid not," I said, grateful for Bertha's generosity. "I didn't really plan to come down. Spur-of-the-moment decision."

In my head, going down to the Mall to join the eleventy billion well-wishers hoping to catch a glimpse of the new King and Queen bobbing past in a golden carriage seemed like a great idea. After all, when you felt like a miserable pillock because the boy you had a massive crush on turned out to be an unapologetically grasping wanker, what better way to cheer yourself up than with a bit of good old-fashioned British pomp and ceremony? In reality, my nose was full of dust, my feet were killing me, and the smell of the Portaloos kept drifting over to remind me just how awful life really was. Thank heavens for Bertha. I plucked a crisp from the little stack in my hand and popped it into my mouth.

"They're good, in't they?" Bertha said. I nodded enthusiastically, mouth full of mushy potato. "We don't normally buy the posh ones, do we, Dave, but it's a special occasion, in't it?"

"Don't normally buy the posh ones," Dave confirmed. I noticed he was missing two fingers on his left hand. "But if you in't gonna push the boat out for a coronation, when are you ever?"

It was the kind of exchange that only happens in Britain. The only reason the British education system doesn't have a GCSE in small talk is because by the time you finish secondary school, you're already an expert in it. I'm convinced it's given along with the measles-mumps-and-rubella shot they give us in infant school. They probably regularly test our sewage for small-talk levels, like they do for polio, cocaine, and Jeremy Clarkson's opinions.

"One hundred per cent, Dave," I said, lifting another crisp to my mouth. "Thank you for sharing them with a blow-in like me."

"You're very welcome, mate.'

"Ow old are you, Ludo, if you don't mind me asking?" Bertha said.

My crisp hovered. "Not at all. I'm twenty-four." I popped the crisp in my mouth.

"He's a good age for our Emilia," Bertha said. I inhaled in surprise, nearly choked on my crisp, coughed, and found myself crouched on the ground with Dave banging his fist on my back. By God, he was strong. I lifted a hand to signal that I was fine before he could beat a vertebra right through my chest. Bertha popped the top on a can of Diet Coke and passed it to me. I accepted gratefully, taking a big hit of the sickly cola.

"You stepping out with anyone special then, Ludo?" Bertha asked when I had recovered. The question squeezed like a fist around my heart.

"No," I said. "Sadly not. I thought I was, but... it wasn't to be." I could feel myself starting to well up, and I feared I might cry in front of these perfect strangers, and that, to be British about it, would be a bit much. I took another swig of the Diet Coke.

"Sorry. It's all a bit recent."

"Never too early to get back on the horse," Dave said, gripping my shoulder like a vice. He only had a thumb and two fingers, but he could jolly well crack my clavicle if the fancy took him.

A roar went up from the crowd further along the Mall, and everyone stood on their tippy-toes and craned to see, ensuring no one saw anything at all. Someone started singing "God Save the King," and we all joined in. Dave saluted. I felt terribly proud to be British. When we'd finished, Dave's arm dropped to his side. I was staring, and I caught his eye.

"Fifteen years in the Royal Navy," he said.

"Emilia's at university in Sheffield," Bertha said. "We're very proud of her. She's studying to be a psychopath."

"A psychotherapist, not a bloody psychopath. Jesus, Bertha. He won't want to take her out now, will he?"

I've never been terribly good at working out when to come out to people. Sometimes, it's safer, quicker, or easier just to let things slip. But if an Englishman shares his crisps with you, surely you can trust him with your essential truth? I mean, if not then, when?

"Actually, I play for the other team," I said. I was about to say, "So, if you have a grandson who's studying to be a psychopath, give him my number," but Bertha was way ahead of me. Bertha had a grandmother's eye for matchmaking.

"Oh, you'd be just perfect for our Harry!"

"He's eighteen, and he's just gone into the navy," Dave said. I bloody bet he had. Lucky old Harry. Probably being buggered around the mizzen mast from one side of the Atlantic to the other even as we spoke. Did the navy still use mizzen masts? What even *was* a mizzen mast?

"We're very proud of him," Bertha said.

Another roar of cheers worked its way up the Mall, and once again everyone craned fruitlessly to see what was happening. This time the crowd kept cheering.

"Looks like interval is over," I said. "Show's back on."

A few minutes later the start of the King's procession marched past us, horses and natty uniforms and brass bands, then carriages and royalty and the dawn of a new era. The cheering of the crowd was deafening. People waved flags and shouted hip hip hooray and sang "Rule, Britannia!" Children sat on parents' shoulders watching history roll past—a story to tell their own grandkids one day. *I was there. I remember when.* Bertha and Dave were in tears. He stood behind her, his tattooed arms wrapped around her shoulders. He kissed her cheek, his tears and hers making a wet mess of their faces, and she turned and kissed him and then turned around completely and wrapped him in a hug. Smiles beamed across their faces, eyes as full of joy as they were full of tears. A peck on the lips, a peck on the cheek. Then I heard Dave say "I love you, sweetie" and Bertha say "I love you, too, bubby."

I wasn't sure I'd ever seen adults show each other actual affection like this before. Not in real life, at least. Onstage, yes. Porgy and Bess. Anya and Dmitry. Danny and Sandy. Even Bonnie and Clyde. (Come on, who wouldn't take a hundred bullets for a love like the love between Bonnie and Clyde?) As far as I could tell, my father's idea of a romantic gesture was stacking the dishwasher. I'd never seen my parents hold hands in public, never heard them say "I love you" to each other, and certainly never seen them climbing all over each other in public like teenagers in love. Most of their interactions seemed to involve petty bickering. I wanted the Bertha-and-Dave kind of love. The wonderful, visible, stick-a-flag-in-it kind of love. I wanted a no holds barred kind of love. Dave winked at me, and I realised I was crying.

"It's a bit overwhelming, isn't it," he said. "Watching history unfold."

But I hadn't been watching history unfold at all. I'd been watching something no marching band or gilt carriage could ever match. Love. And I ached to have someone I loved as much as Dave and Bertha loved each other, who I could share this moment with.

"I think I'm going to go," I said.

"But they ain't come out on the balcony yet," Bertha said.

"We ain't offended you, have we?" Dave added.

"Very far from it," I said. "It has been an absolute joy to meet you. I can't thank you enough for everything. It's been jolly splendid."

"It were only a few crisps, but you're very welcome, love." Bertha wrapped me up in a hug, then apologised for wetting my cheek with her tears. Dave extended his hand, and I shook it.

"If you're ever in Southend, come down the fish shack on the estuary at Old Leigh," Dave said. "The cockles are on us." I thanked him and promised I would. "Mind how you go, lad."

If I weren't so British, I might have told them I thought they were wonderful role models for their grandchildren, or even thanked them for being so unconditionally loving to their grandson that they tried to land him a date. But I am *quite* British. So, instead, I thanked them again for the crisps and the Coke, turned on my heels, and made my way back through the crowd towards Mayfair.

46

LUDO

"**T**ELL ME AGAIN WHY you're sitting on my chesterfield, in front of the television, instead of celebrating the coronation with your sweetheart?" Uncle Ben said, his words mumbled.

The thing about being eighty-eight is you tend to have zero patience for the kind of tiptoeing social niceties that govern these kinds of exchanges for everyone else. Uncle Ben blew a ring of smoke and eyeballed me intently. It was evening, and the velvet curtains were drawn. Benjamin Britten was playing on the gramophone (yes, really), and the telly was repeating gilded scenes from the big day. Bimpe Lasisi popped up on the screen, and I remembered regaining consciousness on a Shetland hilltop and momentarily asking myself if the Church of England had it completely wrong and God was, in fact, a Nigerian-born British woman. I thought of Sunny and how wonderful he had been that day. I thought about last night. Sunny was so incensed, so vehement. Was he telling the truth? What if he *hadn't* been using me to get to my father after all? Would he really have turned down the job? What if he really did just like me for me? Had I made a bally pig's breakfast of it all? Uncle Ben blew a puff of smoke into my face.

"Wakey-wakey, dear boy."

"I met this most tremendous couple down on the Mall," I said.

"George and Philippa?"

"Bertha and Dave."

"Let me guess! Union Jack hats and blazers? Commemorative tea towels to wave at the TV cameras? A thermos in their rucksack filled with mother's ruin?"

I nodded. "That was the general vibe." I felt a twinge of discomfort.

"They always look like they're having so much fun, those people, when you see them on the telly."

Uncle Ben meant no harm, but it would have felt disloyal not to defend my new friends.

"They were jolly good company. Salt of the earth. They'd give you their last penny. Tried to give me their grandson, actually."

Uncle Ben laughed.

"And you declined?"

"I did. But if their grandson is as loving and generous as his grandparents, some boy out there is going to be very lucky someday." I smiled, thinking about Bertha and Dave, and sipped at my sherry. "Honestly, Uncle Ben, they were proper in love. After more than forty years of marriage, they were still holding hands and sneaking kisses like they were in sixth form."

"*Proper* in love, were they?" Uncle Ben said, eyebrows raised. I hadn't even realised I'd said it. Uncle Ben drew on his cheroot, not letting his eye contact drop for even a second, then blew the smoke out dramatically, like he was in an old Hollywood film. "Did you pick up that kind of language from Bertha and Dave? Or is that the influence of that sweetheart of yours?" I decided to ignore this.

"I want someone I can be like that with, Uncle Ben. That's all I want."

"Someone to be barking mad with?"

"If that's what love is, then yes! I want someone I can share the things I love with, like going to the theatre, or spending Sunday morning reading the newspapers and caffeinating a hangover into submission, or singing show tunes on a little jolly to the seaside."

"Can't you do all that with that ginger bit of rough you abandoned on Hampstead Heath?"

Uncle Ben had seen me come back to the house the previous night, had seen the floods of tears. He'd seen me slink along the fence line to avoid everyone at the party and shut myself in the summer house. He'd knocked on my door, coaxed me out like a rat with cheese, and sat on my little porch with me, looking out over the firepit, listening to me pour my heart out.

"I'm through with Sunny, and you jolly well know why," I said. I sipped my sherry. "He was using me."

"Was he, though? I've been thinking about what you said last night, and for a journalist, you didn't really present any ironclad evidence."

"Evidence? My father was practically offering him a job right in front of me. Sunny *told* me he wanted to work for a paper like the *Sentinel* someday, and that he hated working for the *Bulletin*."

Uncle Ben coughed and took a gulp of his sherry to clear his pipes.

"So, when you fell and he looked after you, that was part of some scheme to get a job at the *Sentinel*, was it?"

"Well, no—"

"And when he went all the way into Westminster on his day off to bring you coffee—two coffees, in fact—that gesture was just an elaborate job application, was it?"

"Well, I don't think—"

"Has he actually, at any point, given you any real reason to doubt him? To not trust his motives in befriending you?"

"But Father—"

"That doesn't count. That was on your father, not on Sunny. What did you expect Sunny to say when the great Hugo Boche told him he's wasted at the *Bulletin*? Oughtn't you be pleased for Sunny that Hugo has recognised his talent? Have you ever known your father to give a job to anyone unless they were supremely well-qualified, whether you were dating them or not?

"But—"

"But? But? But nothing. You listen to your godfather, dear boy. Learn from the wisdom of the ancients. Why are all the men in this family such fools when it comes to love? For all that expensive education, not one of you ever seems to see what's right in front of your eyes."

That left me speechless. We paused while Uncle Ben had a coughing fit. He picked up the sherry decanter to top up his glass. His hands were shaking too much to pour, so I jumped up to do the honours. With our glasses refilled, I slipped back into the brown leather of the armchair and asked Uncle Ben what he meant.

"Your father was a blethering idiot when it came to your mother."

"Really?" This was the first I'd heard of this.

"Oh, yes. All I heard for weeks was Beverley this and Beverley that. She was working down in Hampshire at the time but was often up in London. He wouldn't shut up about her. He was absolutely devoted. Hopelessly in love with her. Wouldn't bloody well pluck up the courage to ask her out on a date, though."

This did not sound like the Hugo Boche I knew. A man so confident he could wear a three-piece suit unironically.

"Why not?"

"Oh, he had a million excuses. She's too good for me. I'm not good enough for her. She's all the way down in Southampton. I don't dress snappily enough for a woman like that. She works for the BBC, and it could get complicated. Her parents are socialists."

"Granny and Grandad are socialists?"

"They voted Lib Dem *once*. In a parish council by-election. So, we had months of this mooning. Then one Saturday afternoon, your father was sitting in the very chair you are sitting in now, dear boy, banging on and on about how beautiful Beverley was, how smart she was, how talented she was, and how she'd never go out with him. And your uncle Michael was sick of listening to it. He stormed out the door in a fit. Your father barely noticed, he was so absorbed in his self-pity, until Michael returned forty-five minutes later with a train ticket to Southampton for the following morning and said 'For Christ's sake, Hugo, either put up or *shut up.*'"

My jaw was on the floor. How had I never wheedled this story out of anyone before?

"You make Father out to be a hopeless romantic."

"He was certainly both of those things, dear boy."

"But I've never so much as heard him tell Mummy he loves her."

"My darling boy, there are many different ways to express love. You have *no idea* what happens once they close that bedroom door."

"Ew. *Ewww.* Stop."

Uncle Ben blew smoke theatrically towards the ceiling, once again.

"Will you listen to an old man who knows a thing or two about love and heartache and loss?"

"Of course I will. You know that, Uncle Ben."

"I think this fight you had with Sunny was rather silly."

I opened my mouth to protest, but Uncle Ben lifted a finger to silence me.

"Listen. You've been triggered, as you kids like to say these days, not by something Sunny said or did but by something your father said to him. If you look at what Sunny has done rather than what you've imagined he said or thought, he clearly cares for you as much as you care for him." He paused, letting his words sink in. This man had seen a lot of theatre. He knew how to pause for effect. "You are being, if I might say so, darling boy, a blethering idiot." He sucked on his cheroot, then blew out the smoke. "It's time to put up or shut up."

I put my glass of sherry down on the occasional table and stared blankly at it, processing what Uncle Ben had just said.

"Do you need me to call you a black cab, or..."

47

SUNNY

I WAS PROPER SHATTERED. It had been a long day with very little sleep the night before, so climbing into bed at half nine on a weekend evening didn't feel like the crime it might have. I'd drunk myself sober at Dav and Nick's place, and now I just wanted to sleep. Still hot from my shower, hair still damp, dressed in my favourite slouchy sleeping pants, I slid down into the covers, put my phone on charge on the bedside table, and turned off the lamp. A firework went off outside, then half a dozen more. I was just about to get up to look for the earplugs I had saved from a holiday to Benidorm when the GayHoller chime rang out from my phone. The notification illuminated the room.

GayHoller: *Cabbage98 has sent you a message.*

I sat bolt upright in the bed. I wanted to check the message, but my fingers no longer seemed to work. It took several goes to open it.

Cabbage98: *Hey. Can we talk?*

I considered not answering, but Ludo would know that I'd seen the message already. I thought about what Nick had said. I thought about how miserable today had been and how much I really didn't want to be fighting with Ludo. I thought about the fact that... HOLY CRAP CABBAGE98 IS THREE METRES AWAY. I jumped out of bed and flung open the curtain. Sitting in the bus stop, staring up at my window, was Ludo Boche. He waved, his adorable little face all sad and sorry. He was wearing the blue hoodie I'd left at his house. I waved back. Then he gestured for me to come outside, and in my excitement, I dashed out my bedroom door, tore down the stairs, and opened the door before realising, as the rush of cool evening air hit me, that I was still only wearing my underpants. Ludo's eyes (metaphorically) boggled. I decided to style it out.

"How did you know where I lived?" I asked, leaning casually against the door frame with all the dignity I could muster, as if I'd meant to come out into the street in my pants, as if absolutely everyone did it. Ludo made the few short steps onto the porch.

"You said you lived above a bus stop on Willesden Lane."

"Have you been standing outside every bus stop on this whole street checking GayHoller?"

"Call it investigative journalism?"

"Sounds better than stalking. Which is what this is, to be clear."

"And Rosie was hanging out her window having a cig. So, I asked her which door was yours. That was about half an hour ago. I've been sitting here trying to pluck up the courage to knock."

A couple of lads across the street wolf-whistled.

"Are you going to invite me in?" Ludo asked. "I don't really want to do this in the street. While you're in your pants."

"Of course," I said, stepping aside.

One of the lads across the street shouted, "How much for a BJ?"

"Subscribe to my OnlyFans," I called back. "It's free for incels." It was braver than I felt. My door would probably be egged by morning. Who cared? Ludo was here.

"You have an OnlyFans?" Ludo said, when we were both safely inside.

"Of course," I said. "How do you think I afford this place?" Right on cue, a strip of wallpaper unravelled itself from the hallway wall and curled up on the manky runner carpet. All we needed now was a knock on the door from a payday moneylender, or to find a couple of rats playing backgammon in the kitchen, and Ludo's vision of life on the wrong side of Finchley Road would be complete.

"Can I get you a drink of something? I promise the mugs are cleaner than the kitchen."

"Is there tea?"

"Of course there's tea."

"Earl Grey?"

I rolled my eyes. "I can spray deodorant on the English breakfast if you like?"

We walked through to the kitchen, and I put the kettle on. I was just about to dart upstairs to get dressed when Ludo started in on his apology.

"I'm so sorry. I was a total blethering idiot."

"No, I'm sorry. I shouldn't have—"

"I think we've been a bit silly," he said.

Ludo took a step towards me and grabbed my hands in his. They were warm and clammy, either from nerves or from being shoved too long in his pockets. His blue eyes searched mine. Then apologies and explanations tumbled out of us both, and before I knew it, I was wrapping my arms around him and pulling him close. He smelt of strong tobacco, and I nuzzled my face into his hair and neck and his shirt collar in search of the usual scent of him. When I found it, I sucked it into my lungs like it was oxygen itself. I felt movement in my pants and was deeply conscious that I had nowhere to hide it. At least my flatmates were out. I kissed my way up Ludo's neck and under his jaw and chin until my lips found his lips, and then we kissed and kissed and kissed like sixth-formers at a bus stop.

48

SUNNY

LUDO AND I SPENT the rest of the coronation's long weekend to-gether, bouncing between Ludo's place and mine, watching musicals and cheesy films, walking on the heath, and shagging until our knobs were raw. By Monday night all my cock could produce was puffs of dust. Time well spent, to be fair. I was sitting up against the pillows of my bed, bare-chested, reading a document on my phone. Ludo nuzzled into me. I leant down to inhale the scent of him, expecting warm linen, and got a bit of a shock.

"These sheets are screaming for a wash," I said.

"I think it's too late for that. The only course is to burn them and start afresh."

"Bourgeoise!"

He kissed my nipple and ran his hand across my chest.

"What are you reading? Mao's Little Red Book?"

"Just a piece about this new National Infrastructure Committee Carstairs is setting up. I think we need to knuckle down if we're going to get to the bottom of what's really going on with this nuclear power plant deal. Time is getting away from us."

Ludo agreed.

"OK, let's work out our plan of action," I said, dropping my phone and kissing my way down Ludo's forehead and cheeks before stopping to (metaphorically) suck the lips right off him.

"Come on, Henry Hoover," Ludo said, breaking free. "Plan-of-action time."

"You're proper sexy when you put your foot down."

"Right, that's it." Ludo jumped up and put on his shirt.

"Aw!"

***

PMQs was back on the Wednesday, and it was full of the kind of knee bending and toadying you expect from politicians, wanking on about the coronation and the event putting the *Great* into Great Britain. What would really put the *Great* into Great Britain was a functional health service and jobs north of Hertfordshire. I sat next to Ludo, our legs pressed firmly against each other under the table.

A backbench MP began her Dorothy Dixer question: "Does the prime minister agree with me..." Ludo put down his pencil and slid his hand down against my leg. I did the same and looped my little finger through his. He smiled at me. A beautiful, beaming, conspiratorial smile. There were hundreds of people in this room, but there was only the two of us. I winked at him and tried to hide the stupid grin on my face so the rest of the press gallery reporters didn't begin to think anything was up.

***

O N THURSDAY, I PAID a visit to my new "friend" and co-conspira-
tor, Vladimir Popov. When Ludo and I had divided the research
and interviewing tasks for the nuclear plant story between us, I had taken
VladPop, and he had taken Torsten Beaumont-Flattery. We needed to find
out what they knew, whose side they were on, and whether they were
likely to leak anything in our direction. I sat in VladPop's Westminster
office, wondering if he actually paid someone to vacuum the taxidermy.
He entered with two cups of tea.

"How are my little lovebirds?" He sat down, passing me a cup and
saucer. One coronation and suddenly everyone had gone parody levels of
English. What next, bowler hats?

"I'll tell you as long as you tell me something first," I said.

"Oh, you're getting good at this game. Look at you, flexing your muscles." VladPop made his overdeveloped pecs bounce under his shirt to
really underline the point. It kind of felt like flirting, but I didn't want to
think about that for too long. "What do you want to know, Mr Miller?"

"What do you know about a company called ZephEnergies Limited?"

If the question threw him, Vladimir didn't let on. I suppose you don't
get to be chief whip unless you know how to hold a hand at poker. He
shrugged.

"I don't recall ever hearing that name before," he said, and he must have
caught a glimmer in my eye or something because, just as I was about to
tell him I knew he was lying, that I'd seen a letter from the company on his
desk, he changed his answer. "No, wait. I think they wrote to me once. It'll
be on file in the electorate office if they did. Mandy will know. Why, what
have they done?"

I needed to play my cards close to my chest here. I didn't want to disclose
what I knew, but if I was going to stand up my theory that ZephEnergies
had effectively been given the go-ahead on the Newton Bardon nuclear
plant, then I needed to know how deep the conspiracy went. Was the

entire cabinet in on it, or was Carstairs freelancing? And, either way, why? VladPop was my best source in cabinet.

"Their name has been mentioned in relation to Newton Bardon," I said. "Is there any truth in it?"

"We've only just announced the new National Infrastructure Committee," VladPop said. "It hasn't even met yet. It'd be premature to comment."

"Has the prospect of ZephEnergies taking over the project been discussed at cabinet?"

"You know I can't tell you that. There's such a thing as cabinet confidentiality."

"Cabinet confidentiality means you can't tell me if something has been discussed. Surely you can tell me if something *hasn't* been discussed."

"I don't think that's how cabinet confidentiality works," he said.

"Rubbish. I was told the cabinet spent two hours last month debating whether Paddington Bear would beat Winnie the Pooh in a cage fight."

"We certainly did not!"

"See, you *can* tell me about things that weren't discussed. So, is ZephEnergies the government's preferred partner on the Newton Bardon project?"

"It has to go to the committee."

"But has a deal already been done?"

"Whoever is feeding you this information, Sunny, they're jumping at shadows. There's nothing to see." He twisted in his seat, plucked his cup of tea off his desk, and stared directly into my eyes. "Now, I've answered your questions; you have to answer mine."

On the face of it, VladPop hadn't answered my questions at all. In reality, whether he knew it or not, he'd told me exactly what I needed to know. There were two reasons a politician avoided answering a direct question like this one: either you were right, and they didn't want to confirm it, or they had no idea, so they hedged their bets. There was no way the chief whip didn't know what was going on at Newton Bardon. He probably knew what colour underpants the prime minister had worn to the coronation. I slumped back in my chair. VladPop sipped his tea and put the cup back into the saucer.

"So, are you and Ludo on together, then?" He put up a hand. "Before you answer, let me warn you, the CCTV evidence says yes."

"Are you spying on me using the Palace of Westminster security cameras?"

"I wouldn't call it spying, Sunny. I'm just taking a genuine interest in your welfare."

"Why, exactly?"

"Come on, get to the good bit. Are you an item? Has my little plan to throw you together worked? You'd be so perfect for each other!"

I sighed and caved in. He already had the evidence, so what was the point in holding out?

"Yes, I suppose we are an item."

VladPop squeed like a schoolgirl, and I let him have his moment. Why not? After all, he wasn't the only one who'd been collecting evidence. And the evidence I was collecting would soon be on the front page of every newspaper in the country. My own moment was coming very soon. I was sure of it.

49

LUDO

ON FRIDAY AFTERNOON I waited for Sunny in our stairwell in the Victoria Tower, bouncing up and down with excitement. It smelt slightly of caffeine and spoilt milk from where my coffee had seeped into the cracks of the masonry, dried, and gone crusty. The sound of rushed footsteps came first; then Sunny's head appeared at a level below my feet, his face lit by a cheesy grin. He finished coiling the steps, and he stood before me, his face to mine. I grabbed him by the back of the neck and pulled him into a kiss. He kissed me back but pulled away more quickly than I'd have liked.

"VladPop has cameras everywhere," he said. I could still taste Sunny on my lips, and I found myself licking them unconsciously. "How'd you go with Torsten?"

"He was in a bit of a hurry. He's off to Leaf and Karma's retreat this weekend and wanted to beat the traffic out of London. He's proving jolly loyal to Carstairs. I don't think the old school tie is going to be enough to crack him."

"Do you think he knows the truth?"

"I'm sure of it," I said. "When I asked him whether Newton Bardon was a done deal, he denied it, but..." I clicked my teeth with my tongue.

"His tell?" Sunny asked.

"Yeah."

"We should really invite him to a poker game some night."

I was so excited I was shivering; the adrenaline was rushing through me. The proof we needed felt jolly close.

"It makes sense that he would know," Sunny said. "He's been running around like an obedient lapdog, doing everything for her this whole time. If she's up to no good, she'll have outsourced the dirty work to Torsten to keep herself at arm's length. He's a useful idiot."

"I agree. We have to find a way to appeal to his sense of right and wrong."

"He works in politics, Ludo."

"Yes, but he's not a bad person. Not deep inside."

Sunny was bouncing on his feet. I grabbed his hand and held the tips of his fingers in mine, trying to calm him, trying to calm myself. I studied the pebble-dash of freckles that decorated the back of his hand and re-membered that hand working its way around my body, how good it felt to have it on me, how much I wanted it on me now. All the excitement, the adrenaline, was making me feel reckless. I wanted to kiss him.

"You know him better than anyone," Sunny said. "How do we seduce him to our side?"

"I don't think either of us has the boobies required for that," I said.

Sunny froze, his eyes wide.

"Ludo, you're a genius!" I finally got my kiss. It was long, passionate, illicit, and probably being live-streamed to VladPop's dirt file server.

***

S UNNY'S PLAN WAS AN old-fashioned tabloid honeytrap, and I wasn't happy about it. However, I didn't have any other ideas, so I went along with it on the condition that the person on whose boobies the plan depended did so with her eyes wide open and her consent freely given.

That evening, Sunny and I sat tucked up on the summer house bed, outlining the plan to Leaf, Karma, and their daughter, Summer. The plan was for Summer to get close to Torsten during his weekend's retreat and get him to talk. The redoubtable duo had been jolly keen to do their bit, but what really mattered was what Summer had to say.

"I'm in," she said without hesitation when Sunny finished explaining the plan. Was I suddenly out of touch with feminism? "Anything I can do to stop a nuclear power plant on our doorstep, I'll do it. I have just one condition."

"What is it?" Sunny asked.

"If the story of how you got this information ever comes out, I don't want to be called a 'Derbyshire honeytrap,' or anything like that, on the front page of the *Bulletin*." The look on Summer's face was intense. "Or I'll hunt you down and seriously misalign your chakras, mate. You got that?"

"Loud and clear."

"How would you like us to refer to you, if we ever need to refer to you at all?" I asked.

"How about... environmental justice warrior."

"We have a deal," Sunny said. It was the promise of a tabloid journalist. The kind that had earned reporters everywhere our reputation for being untrustworthy. Sunny had absolutely no power to make a promise like that. When our call ended, I took him to task over it.

"We'll just have to make sure no one ever learns about Summer's involvement," he said.

50

SUNNY

THE WEEKEND WAS PROPER tense while we waited for news from Summer, Leaf, and Karma. On Saturday afternoon, almost twenty-fours into Operation Atomic Kitten (a name Ludo point-blank refused to use but I thought was five-stars-very-clever), we finally got a text.

Karma: *All mostly going to plan. Not really a hiccup, just a surprise. T & S seem to have a deep and genuine spiritual connection.*

Well, yes, I thought. Put single naked He-Man and single vegan She-Ra in a confined space for a weekend and give them nothing but fluffy white towels and essential oils to play with, and some kind of deep connection does seem like the logical outcome.

Karma: *S says T's an old soul who feels things very deeply. He's holding on to a lot of trauma from past lives. She's determined to help him discover a new inner peace.*

Imagine hanging on to trauma from past lives. It was bad enough dealing with the crap that happened to us in this one. Like dealing with a father who bought a one-way bus ticket to fuck-knows-wheresville before I was even born, or being the queer ginger smart-arse in a community where being just one of those things is enough to get you lamped on a daily basis.

Sunny: *Any news on the Newton Bardon plant?*

It was only a slightly impatient message.

Karma: *Nothing specific. But T's soul is clearly troubled about it.*

Twenty-four hours later, Karma messaged again.

Karma: *Long reiki session this morning to promote healing and guide the flow of T's life force energy. He has decided to pay to stay a couple more days to complete a gonging course and crystal healing. He is so receptive to therapy.*

This was bloody agony.

Karma: *T & S forming a beautiful bond. What a blessing it is to witness two souls that clearly recognise each other from a past life reunite like this. We feel he was meant to find us.*

It was like watching one of those TV shows where they build up the big reveal, then cut to an ad break. I was ready to jump on a train to Derbyshire and strangle Karma with my bare hands, and I didn't care how it buggered up my chakras.

Karma: *Nothing else to report.*

The good news was that we now had a couple more days up our sleeves for Summer to find out the information we needed. Assuming Summer was still on our team, which I was starting to feel unsure about. I needed a backup plan. It was time to deploy another time-honoured tabloid trick.

***

B IN DAY WAS A Tuesday in the part of the Royal Borough of Kensington and Chelsea where Jemima Carstairs and Dirk Windhoek lived. Which was how I found myself parked up just off Gloucester Road in Jumaane's battered and cold Vauxhall Astra on a drizzly Monday night, working my way through a box of Tesco Express Krispy Kremes, waiting for the lights to go off in the Carstairs-Windhoek household. It was one in the morning before the windows finally plunged into darkness and I got my chance to go dumpster-diving in search of incriminating documents.

Half an hour after lights out, dressed in latex gloves and an old black hoodie, I was in full cat burglar mode, trying to silently get the lid off the first bin. It was an old-school metal trash can. Who even owned one of these except Oscar the Grouch? I found chicken bones, potato peelings, and plastic wrappers, but no documents. I abandoned it, leaving the bin on the side and the lid off so it would look like foxes had done the damage. The second bin was filled with recycling, but no papers. My last chance was a black bin liner, top tied in a knot, resting against the fence. When I picked it up, it was suspiciously light—and squishy like a pillow. I tore a little hole in the side. It was filled with shredded paper.

"Bingo."

51

LUDO

"T HIS JIGSAW PUZZLE IS jolly pants," I said. It was Tuesday evening, and thin strips of white paper were strewn across the summer house floor. The soundtrack to *Yentl* tinkled away softly in the background. I find Barbra helps me concentrate. I was sitting on the rug, trying to sort together any strips of paper that looked like they matched, based on font, paper weight, or ink colour. "When you said you had a surprise for me, I thought you might be taking me out to dinner or something."

"I brought you curry," Sunny protested. He was sitting at my desk (where our laptops were now more or less permanently set up side by side), glue stick in hand, studying a handful of strips of paper.

"Correction. You went to the house and brought out two bowls of the curry Father made."

"Did I lie?"

"Stop trying to wind me up."

"But you're so cute when you're annoyed."

"Don't upset me in front of Babs. She doesn't like it."

I spotted a flash of red on a strip of paper and extracted it, adding it to a pile of similarly marked strips.

"I think I've just about got all this logo on this letterhead," I said.

Sunny jumped up and joined me on the floor, his shoulder leaning into mine as we studied the pieces. My heart still raced whenever his body touched mine. Like it was illicit. Like someone might tell us to stop it at any minute. He smelt of glue and spices.

He picked up the pieces and shuffled them around, being careful to flatten them against the rug so they didn't tangle or tear.

"That's it. We've got it," Sunny said.

"I've never heard of Prometheus Power, have you?" I asked, but he wasn't listening. He was running his fingers down the length of the portion of shredded page we had managed to piece together. "Dear Mr Windhoek... This prospectus for... investors to raise... a more renewable..."

"No mention of Newton Bardon, nuclear power, or ZephEnergies," I said. "It looks like an ordinary covering letter for an initial public offer to me. Prometheus Power must be about to list on some stock exchange or other."

"Maybe," Sunny said. "But I've seen this logo before. In VladPop's office. I didn't think anything of it at the time. I just caught a glance of it."

"Does it mean anything?" I nuzzled my head into Sunny's shoulder and kissed the soft, freckled skin of his neck.

"I don't know," he said. "But this letter isn't addressed to Carstairs; it's addressed to her husband."

A text message pinged Sunny's phone, and he pulled it out of the pocket of his hoodie. The screen illuminated his face as he studied the message, his green eyes growing wider with every passing second.

"It's Karma," he said. "Torsten has talked."

***

I MIGHT NOT QUITE have approved of Operation Atomic Kitten, and I might not have enjoyed spending three nights piecing together strips of shredded paper, but I had to hand it to Sunny—his dirty tabloid tricks had got results. By Thursday evening, Sunny and I were sitting at our laptops, side by side, writing our separate stories, cross-checking every fact, making sure we could prove everything we'd discovered, and generally making our stories as watertight as possible. When we were done writing, we read our articles out loud to each other. The information was exactly the same, but the tone was jolly different. This was my opening paragraph:

The Government has done a secret deal with British renewables firm ZephEnergies to build and operate a 3.2 gigawatt nuclear power station at Newton Bardon in Leicestershire. The Government had said that any proposals for new net zero energy projects would have to go before the new National Investment Committee, but the Sentinel *can confirm the Leicestershire plant was given the go-ahead before the committee was even formed.*

Whereas Sunny's report had a bit more colour:

The grubby soviet nuclear power plant deal that ended the career of sexpot former energy minister Bob Wynn-Jones has been reheated, with the Government secretly giving the multibillion pound contract to UK-based "renewable energy" company ZephEnergies. The Leicestershire project exploded in a mushroom cloud of scandal last month when the Bulletin *revealed Wynn-Jones was having an extramarital affair with a Belarusian spy. In the fallout, the Government announced it would create a National Investment Committee to decide which net zero projects would get the go-ahead. But today the* Bulletin *can reveal that ZephEnergies was awarded the contract to build and operate Newton Bardon within days of the Cabinet reshuffle that saw the creation of Jemima Carstairs' mega-department.*

"By Saturday morning, this will be all anyone in Britain is talking about," Sunny said.

I passed him a USB stick with his copies of all the evidence we'd collected.

"You'll need this."

We sat back in our chairs and smiled at each other. There was nothing left to do now but for us to pitch our stories tomorrow morning.

"You hungry?" I asked.

"Starving," Sunny said. "Shall we go up the chicken shop?"

"That's not *quite* what I had in mind." I brushed my socked foot against his leg playfully, without dropping eye contact for even a second. It was dark, and we were lit by our computer screens. There had been a rush of adrenaline as we wrote and as we read, but it gave way to something else now. Where there should have been exhaustion, a kind of thrill shivered through me, a nervous energy. Sunny's eyes twinkled, little emerald sparkles shining out amid the peridot. I let my foot stray a little higher. He raised his eyebrows. I smirked. Sunny shoved his hands in his pockets and spread his legs. I crept my foot higher and found the spot where his body was responding to my touch. I realised, then, what this new feeling was. It was power, and the anticipation of power. And it was a *rush*.

Sunny pulled off his hoodie, revealing his beautiful pale skin dashed with the amber and umber of a million freckles. He was lean, and the intercostal muscles of his ribs created tiger stripes that curved around to his back. His blush-pink nipples were as hard as shot in a roasted pheasant. Still, I held his gaze. He did not move. We were playing a power game of our own now, and the anticipation was too much for me. I let my foot fall to the floor. I took my glasses off, crept out of my chair like a predator stalking its prey, crouched on the floor between Sunny's knees, and gently tugged down his joggers.

"Bugger me rigid, Sunny. Do you ever wear pants?"

***

H ALF AN HOUR LATER, we were both sprawled out naked on the rug on the summer house floor, jolly exhausted, completely sated.

"I think I have at least a thousand tiny paper cuts on my back and butt," I said.

"Let me check," Sunny said.

"If I roll over, I'll get them on my front too."

"Roll over."

I did as I was told. The room was dark, lit only by the bluish light from my laptop screen.

"I can't see any," Sunny said.

"I can feel them."

"Do you want me to kiss it better?"

"Yes, please."

Sunny kissed the nape of my neck, his warm breath making my skin tingle.

"Where does it hurt? Does it hurt here?" He kissed my shoulder blade, his lips lightly grazing the flesh, giving me goosebumps all over.

"Yes," I said. "Everywhere."

"Even here?" He kissed the small of my back.

"Yes."

"Here?" He kissed the round of my butt.

"Yes."

"All better?"

"Yes."

"You really have a smashing arse, you know that?" He smacked it, and I rolled over, theatrically kicking a leg high and straight into the air.

"It's all those years of ballet," I said, secretly enjoying the sting where his hand had been. Sunny climbed up the rug until his lips met mine. We kissed. His mouth was warm, and his lips tasted of lube and sex.

"We should shower," I said. Sunny nodded.

There was a knock on the sliding glass door of the summer house.

"Bollocks!" Sunny said, a look of panic on his face. He commando-rolled buck naked along the floor and behind the bed.

"Ludo?" It was Father.

"Just a minute!" I called out, scrambling to throw on some clothes. Fortunately, the curtains were drawn. We were in the middle of a top-secret mission, after all. But considering this was a top-secret mission, we had evidence scattered absolutely everywhere. How were we meant to explain all this shredded paper? Some bizarre kitty litter role play? He knocked again.

"Do you boys want supper?" Father said.

Somewhat dressed, I pulled the curtain around myself, hiding the room from view, and slid the door open a little. I straightened my clothes. I say *my* clothes; I was in Sunny's sweatpants and hoodie, which had been the nearest things to hand. My father rolled his eyes.

"Are you boys hungry? It's leftover curry, I'm afraid, but then curry is always better a few days later."

"Actually, Sunny has promised to take me to the chicken shop. But thanks all the same."

"You're foregoing my famous beef massaman curry to eat at some cockroach-infested high-street fast-food joint?"

Sunny wasn't having this culinary delight disrespected. "High-street chicken shops are our cultural heritage," he called out from behind the bed. "They're iconic institutions, like seaside penny arcades and Miriam Margolyes, and we must use them or we will lose them."

Father frowned. "It's a chicken shop, not the English National Opera," he muttered. He tried to peer into the room, but I pulled the curtain tightly around me.

"You heard Sunny," I said. "It's my patriotic duty as an Englishman to go to the chicken shop."

"There's a better class of cockroach this side of the Finchley Road," Sunny added. "The Hampstead ones wear hairnets."

Father squinted.

"You've got a piece of shredded paper in your hair," he said, plucking it free. I snatched it from his hand.

"How strange."

"What are you boys up to in there? You've been cooped up in here every night this week."

I felt my face flush. My heart pounded in my chest.

"I don't think you actually want an answer to that question, do you?" I said. "If you really think about it."

Father looked down to see I was wearing Sunny's sweatpants. He raised his eyebrows and slowly nodded.

"Right you are," he said, eyeballing me suspiciously one last time. Then he turned on his heel and walked back to the house. "Enjoy the chicken shop."

It was a lucky escape.

Sunny and I showered together in the tiny summer house en suite, almost until the water ran cold. I turned the big light on so we could find our clothes and get dressed. The room was a disaster zone of shredded papers, dirty plates, and strewn clothes. Sunny packed his laptop into his rucksack, making sure he had his USB stick with the copies of the primary evidence. As we left, I looked around at the mess. I wasn't sure I could face coming back to clean this up. I turned off the big light, leaving the room illuminated in the soft blue light of my laptop screen.

52

SUNNY

I WOKE TO THE sound of bus air brakes outside my bedroom window. My arm was dead. I tried to carefully slip it out from under Ludo's neck without waking him, but the arm really wasn't cooperating. He looked so cute, with his hair all mussed-up and dried dribble in the corner of his mouth. As I extricated myself from under him, he stirred.

"What time is it?" he said, without opening his eyes.

My alarm went off. It was a quarter past six. I yanked myself free and tried to reach for my phone, but I had no control of my arm anymore. I had to bounce onto my other side and grab it with the wrong hand.

"I think you've killed my arm," I said, turning off the alarm. I opened the BBC app and put on the *Today* programme.

"Rise and shine, sleepyhead. We've got a big day," I said, kissing Ludo on the forehead.

"Five more minutes."

"OK, mister. I'm going to go shower before my flatmates steal all the hot water. You sleep. I'll be ten minutes."

He reached out a hand and pulled me down to him. I kissed him on the lips, crusty saliva and all. I ran my fingers through the knots of this hair, tucking his unruly curls behind his ear. Then I got up, pulled on some sweatpants, and went to the bathroom.

***

L ESS THAN FIFTEEN MINUTES later, freshly showered and feeling far more alive than I had in forever, I opened my bedroom door expecting to find Ludo still fast asleep. He was gone. His pile of clothes was gone; his phone and glasses were gone. The bed was still unmade. I touched it. It was still warm from his body. Perhaps he was downstairs making coffee? From my phone, the lilting voice of Lucy Veeraswamy announced the news headlines.

"It is being reported the government has done a secret deal with renewable energy firm ZephEnergies to build and operate the proposed nuclear power plant at Newton Bardon in Leicestershire."

What. The. Hell.

"The government had previously said that any proposals for major energy investments would have to go before the new National Investment Committee, but reporting by the *Sentinel* claims the Leicestershire plant has secretly been given the go-ahead already."

WHAT. THE. ACTUAL. HELL.

A deep, angry bellow growled out from the pits of my gut. I tried to call Ludo. He didn't pick up. I threw my phone onto the mattress so hard it bounced off the bed into the wall, cracking the screen. Every doubt I'd ever had about Ludo rushed from the deep recesses of my brain and flooded my body. I fell to my knees. My hands formed fists. I punched the mattress. I punched it, and I punched it, and I punched it. Then I beat the crap out of it with my pillow. When I finally stopped, I was shaking. Still on my knees, the towel fallen from my waist onto the floor, I looked at myself in the mirror. My face was red, my cheeks flooded with tears, my eyes puffy and bloodshot. Snot was streaming from my nose.

"Why did you think you could trust him?" I asked the naked, disfigured creature in the mirror. "This is what you get for breaking the rules. This is what you get for jumping into bed with the likes of Ludo Boche." I spat the words out with scorn. "You're a stupid bloody bellend, Sunshine. And you only have yourself to blame."

I had never been so angry in my life. I had never felt so betrayed in all my life. I had never felt hate quite like the hate I felt in that moment for Ludo Boche. The deceit. The back-stabbing. The cynicism. The contempt. The sheer piss-taking cowardice of running away. I shouldn't have been surprised. His sort never stuck around to face the music. What a prick.

53

LUDO

I T WAS THE LONGEST taxi ride of my life. I had run out of Sunny's flat still pulling on my jersey, arm outstretched, trying to flag down just about any vehicle that might conceivably offer me a lift to the hospital. Except a bus. I did not have time for a bus. Mummy had called about thirty seconds after Sunny had gone for his shower. I knew by the tremor in her voice as she said my name that the news was bad.

"It's your Uncle Ben, sweetheart." The words would haunt me until the day I died. "We're at the hospital. You need to come quickly. There isn't much time."

***

I RAN THROUGH THE corridors of the hospital, trying to follow the instructions Mummy had given me on the phone and asking absolutely anyone in a uniform for directions to Ward D. Completely out of breath, I rounded the corner into the private room to see Uncle Ben unconscious on the bed, surrounded by my mother, my father, and Jonty. Mummy and

Jonty had been crying. Their faces were sunken, the colour drained out of them.

"How is he?" I asked, approaching the bed. It was eerily quiet. "Where are all the doctors? The monitors?"

Mummy stood, opened her arms, and flung them around me. I couldn't remember the last time she'd hugged me.

"I'm sorry, my darling," she said. "He left us a few minutes ago."

My legs gave way. The only thing keeping me from the floor was my mother's arms. I was a dead weight. She let me slump to the hospital linoleum. I heard a blood-curdling noise and realised it was coming out of my body. I was making it, and I had no way of stopping it.

54

SUNNY

I WALKED INTO THE *Bulletin's* concrete brutalist monstrosity at London Bridge. I'd tried calling Ludo at least twenty times on my way to work. I kept getting his voicemail, and I refused to leave what I wanted to say in a message. I wanted him to hear the words coming out of my mouth. I wanted to hear his response. To be fair, I wanted to lamp him. The newsroom was humming. Cathy was already at her desk. She looked *pressed*.

"He's on the warpath," she said, nodding in the direction of JT's office. "How did we miss it?"

I shook my head, unable to even make eye contact with her, let alone explain that we hadn't missed it at all.

"Miller! Get in here, *now*." My shoulders slumped.

"Coming," I shouted. I plucked my laptop from my bag and made my way to the naughty chair in the chief of staff's office.

***

"**D**O YOU MEAN TO SAY," JT said, his snake-veins twisting vigorously, throbbing in time with his pulse, "that we had this sodding story, and you gave it to the *Sentinel*?"

"That's not what happened."

"Do you think I'm an idiot? I'm not the sodding idiot here, you piss-guzzling shit crumpet. You had the story. You worked on it with your little bum buddy from the *Sentinel*. And now the story is on the front page of that sodding Tory-boy wank rag and not, you may have noticed, splashed across the front page of our own august journal. The one that pays your sodding wages."

My laptop was open on JT's desk, cursor blinking at me from the end of the article on the screen, like a relentless middle finger from Microsoft Word.

"Pack your bags, Sunshine. You're out of here. You're through."

My jaw hit the (metaphorical) floor. This was a cock-up. It was unfortunate. I had been stupid. I'd been betrayed. But was it a sackable offence? I mean, I could easily have come in here and *not* told him that we'd had the story. Upon reflection, that would have been the smarter way to play it. I refused to beg for my crap job at a crap newspaper from a crap chief of staff. But I did, at least, want to stand up for myself.

"You need to give me three written warnings before you can sack me."

JT's eyes boggled. His ocular nerves were probably being strangled by the engorged veins pulsing throughout his head. He was boiling like a kettle.

"If you want three sodding warnings, I'll give them to you now," he said. I did not enjoy the look on his face. "Warning number one. You spent company time and resources to investigate a story without informing us. You didn't have permission. We didn't know what you were working on. If anything had happened to you, we'd have been liable, and you wouldn't have been covered by our insurance."

"I didn't use company time and resources!"

"What the fire-pissing ball-cyst is *this*, Sunshine?" He hit the back of my laptop, sending it flying across the desk.

"Warning number two. You shared that information with a journalist from another publication. A sodding competitor, you shit-stabbing arse-womble. Information we've paid for, through your investment in time and effort. And don't tell me you did it all in your own time, or I'll get IT to go through your sodding internet history and match it up to your time sheet. So, you better be unbelievably confident if you want to test me."

When he put it like that, I wasn't *entirely* confident I'd done it all in my own time.

"Warning number three. Then you went and sodding lost it, you cock-swallowing dickwit, and it made the front page of another paper. Now, do you need me to write that down, or have I spelt it out sufficiently that even the tiny sodding maggot you've got crawling around on the hamster wheel you power your brain with can process it?"

It was a complete takedown. He had me bang to rights. JT slammed his fist into his desk, making his computer monitor and keyboard jump—and me along with them.

"Pack your things. Get out of here. You're done."

55

Ludo

I T WAS MID-AFTERNOON BEFORE I surfaced from a miasma of grief and checked my phone. Twenty-four missed calls from Sunny. Ruddy hell. He was mad. Two dozen calls did feel like overkill, though. I slumped into a chair in a hospital waiting room that stank of bleach and heartache. Mummy and Father had gone to find some food for us all. Jonty was being surprisingly helpful and making phone calls to people we needed to notify of Uncle Ben's death. I flicked through my notifications. For all the missed calls, there was only one text from Sunny.

Sunny Miller: *Go fuck yourself.*

OK, I was prepared for mad. I didn't anticipate that level of mad. I called him, hoping to explain everything and, when I had done apologising for disappearing unannounced, frankly, get a little apology of my own for such a jolly rude text. It clicked through to voicemail. I tried again. Nothing. I waited a few minutes, then tried again. Still nothing. I sent a text.

Ludo Boche: *Sorry for disappearing. Sorry I missed your calls. Bit of a big morning. Can we talk when you're free? x*

My parents walked around the corner, laden with paper bags and a tray of coffees.

"It's sandwiches, I'm afraid," Mummy said, spilling open the contents of the bags on the waiting room coffee table. I didn't respond. She looked across at me. "Ludo?"

"Sunny isn't answering my calls." My cheeks were wet again. I was crying.

"He's probably in an interview or something," Father said, flopping himself down in the chair beside me, wrapping his mouth around an egg-and-cress sandwich. Come the apocalypse, all that will be left of Britain is cockroaches and the factory that makes those bloody egg-and-cress sandwiches.

"I missed twenty-four calls, and his only text says 'go fuck yourself.'"

Father burst out laughing, nearly choking on his sandwich.

"Is this a joke to you?" My eyes were on fire, raw from a day of crying, stinging with the addition of yet more tears. Father coughed, hit his chest with his fist, and downed a thick gulp of his coffee.

"He's probably just annoyed about today's front page."

"What front page?"

"I meant to say, Ludo. Very well done. You played a blinder, digging up all that stuff on the Newton Bardon deal. Why didn't you tell me you were working on it? We could have thrown some resources at it for you."

My aching heart now stopped beating entirely. My bowels turned to water.

"What?"

"Your piece on the nuclear power plant. I saw it on your laptop last night when I went in to collect all the dirty dishes. You've been living like a pig in there, by the way. You could at least bring the plates in."

"You read what was on my laptop?"

"The company's laptop, Ludo. It and, need I remind you, anything on it is *Sentinel* property."

"And you just... *printed* it?"

"All the evidence was right there in the paperwork on your desk. I went through it with Ford on the phone, we ran it past the lawyers, and we managed to splash with it on the late edition. It's been all over the news all day. I thought you'd be thrilled."

He took another mouthful of his sandwich.

"I'm terribly proud of you," he said, egg and cress peering at me from between his teeth. I could have punched him then and there, just to wipe the smarmy grin off his face. If my father's pride was indeed a drug, I had just discovered how to rapidly detox.

"Do you have any idea what you've done?"

He swallowed.

"Probably sold an extra fifty thousand copies up and down the country, got a huge amount of free publicity, and put yet another rocket under my son's growing reputation as a promising future Fleet Street heavyweight?"

"That wasn't my story!" I stood up, surprising myself with how angry I was. "Sunny did most of the work on that story. He did all the investigating. He only shared it with me because we got the tip-off together. We were *supposed* to publish it together. We had a deal."

"Sunny did all the investigating?" Mummy said, clearly missing what was important here.

"I told you he was good, Bev. Didn't I tell you?"

"I didn't need you to tell me, Hugo."

I was shaking, my whole body, every cell, quaking with rage.

"Does anyone even care that my boyfriend now thinks that I've used him, deceived him, and run off into the night like a cold-hearted killer?"

"So, call him and explain everything, darling," Mummy said.

"He's not answering my calls!"

Mummy stood, put a hand on my shoulder, and pushed me back down into my chair. This was what passed for affection in our family.

"Calm down, darling. You've had a stressful day."

"Stressful? *Stressful?* I started the day with everything, and now I have nothing. Absolutely *nothing*."

"You have a great front page," Father said. I screamed and lunged for him, enraged. I found myself pinned back by my mother's arms. Tears burnt my cheeks. I was filled with anger, but not the fight I needed to go with it. I was exhausted, powerless, helpless. I sank to the floor, sliding from my mother's arms, my knees crumpling under the weight of me. The will had completely left my body. I had no energy left.

56

LUDO

"JUST HERE PLEASE, DRIVER," I said. "By the bus stop." The black cab glided up to the kerb; I paid and got out. I looked up at the first-floor windows. There was no light on in Sunny's bedroom. He still wasn't answering my calls, so in a last-ditch act of desperation, I had trekked out to Willesden Green to confront him and explain. I was tired, broken, and in desperate need of a hug. I knocked on the door. No one answered.

"If you're looking for Sunny, darling," a voice called from somewhere, "he's gone home to Leicester." I looked around to see Rosie hanging out of her upstairs window, freshly lit ciggy in hand, head wrapped in a scarf like it was still the 1950s.

"To Leicester? But he was only here this morning."

"Got the sack, didn't he."

"He what?" My broken heart broke again. This was awful—and it was all my fault.

"So, he's gone back to Mummy for a bit of home cooking and comfort. Can't say I blame him." She sucked on her cigarette. I edged along the pavement until I was standing directly underneath Rosie's window.

"Did he say when he will be back?"

"Don't expect he's coming back, love. Can't afford the rent on that place without a job. Came to say ta-ta to me this afternoon. Right muddle he was in. I really felt for him. Salt of the earth, that boy."

Those words again.

"Shame on you, if you don't mind me saying so, darling," Rosie said. I stood there, shocked, like I'd just absorbed a right hook to the jaw. The tears started to flow. This was more than I could take today. I looked up at the woman in the window, her eyebrows raised in what I interpreted as disappointment. "He didn't deserve that. Did you think about what would happen to him? Do your lot *ever* think about what happens to the pawns in your little games?"

I was shaking. It was more than I could bear. The tears were rolling down my cheeks and inside my shirt collar. The air was cool against my wet skin. I tried to speak, but no words came out. I lifted a hand in thanks for the information and in farewell, and turned back towards the high road to find a cab. In the end, unable to find one, unwilling to cry on the Tube, unable to work out the buses, I walked all the way home. I was cold, exhausted, devastated. In less than a day, my life had shattered.

57

SUNNY

IN A BID TO cheer me up after the shittiest day of my life, the Brent Boys descended on Crucifix in Vauxhall—a twenty-four-seven homosexual meat market. The club lights were pulsing in time with some proper banging beats. The dance floor was a sweaty mass of shirtless, muscular, hairy men. Some bald, some with beards, some sweating their faces off in puppy masks. A couple of blokes beside us were making out, hands groping at flesh, boners stretching against tiny pleather shorts.

"But why are you leaving?" Dav said, shouting to be heard over the thumping bass. "Bit of a knee-jerk reaction, isn't it? Why not stick around and try some of the other papers?"

"Or TV," Petey added. "You've got a good face for TV, bruv. I've always said that. Believe."

"Would you employ someone who was sacked by the *Bulletin* for unethical behaviour?"

Stavros returned from the bar, fingers stretched around the base of four plastic cups, the liquid in each swirling and lapping and spilling.

"Thanks for the help, boys." Such sarcasm. We each grabbed a cup.

"What am I, chopped liver?" Nick rolled into a clear space to join the group, plucked a cup from between his legs, and handed it to Dav. We cheersed.

"I just can't believe you're *choosing* to go back to Leicester," Dav said. "We spent our entire lives trying to get out of there."

"At least you can take the people there at their word."

"Yeah," Dav said. "If they say they're going to lamp you, they lamp you."

"Let's just dance," I said. "I've got a train to catch in eight hours."

***

W AS IT AN HOUR later? Two hours? I don't know. Time had ceased to mean anything. I was so smashed I'd peeled my T-shirt off and tucked it into my joggers—a skinny, translucent ginger boy among all the muscle Marys and leather bears.

"Here we go, lads!" Petey said, adding a "whoop, whoop" and a finger point. I grabbed his hand and dragged him towards the mysterious black vinyl curtain that led to the dark room.

"No, no, no. You're not going in there. Are you even on PrEP, babes?" Petey said.

I marched on in. Inside it was inky black. The music pulsed through from the dance floor, but the sound was deadened, muffled. I blinked while my eyes adjusted.

"Seriously, though?" Petey said.

I looked at him, smiled, squeezed his hand, and let it go. I knocked back the last of my drink and threw the cup on the floor. A swarm of men huddled in front of me came into focus, their flesh a mass of swaying and writhing. I walked slowly over towards them, my legs feeling heavy, my brain foggy.

At the centre of the crowd of men, a muscled lad with a horse cock was getting a blow job from yet another guy in a mask pretending to be a dog. Did the RSPCA know about these people? I felt a hand on my arse, looked around, and followed the arm up to a shirtless guy with thick stubble and black curls that were slick with sweat. They tumbled across his face, and an image flashed into my mind: me trying to push Ludo's ungovernable curls behind his ears, his blue eyes looking tenderly into mine.

The hand on my arse worked its way up to the back of my neck, and I realised I was staring into the brown eyes of the man whose hand was on me. He glanced down at his cock, which, I hadn't realised, was hard, in his other hand, and leaking. His hand on my neck gripped tighter, the pressure an attempt to coax me to my knees.

I was wasted. I was hurting. I thought this was what I wanted. Confronted with it, however, it was the last thing I wanted. I shook my head, expecting the lad to be pissed off. My hands tightened into fists, ready to square up to him if I had to.

As it happened, he pulled a sad face, removed his hand, and whispered into my ear, "It's a shame, because you're very beautiful." His accent was Spanish, I think. Wherever he came from, he understood consent. I thanked him, said goodbye, and went to sit down on the edge of a nearby box. Before my bum could touch the surface, a hand grabbed my arm.

"For Christ's sake, don't sit down in here," Petey said. "God knows what you'll sit in. You can catch super-gonorrhoea from the handrails, babes. Believe." He yanked me up to my feet.

"I don't feel well," I said.

"OK, soldier. I think it's time we took you home."

I nodded. When Petey Boy was calling time on a night out, it was definitely time to go home.

It was time to go home, full stop.

58

LUDO

A WEEK AFTER HE died, we laid Uncle Ben to rest. His funeral was a fittingly theatrical affair. Rachel Hoffman led the cast of *Yentl* in "Papa, Can You Hear Me?"—their soft, sweet voices filling the Central Synagogue London and leaving not a dry eye in the room. Wilhelmina Post told a few of the more legendary stories about Uncle Ben, which had everyone rolling in the aisles—like the time he accused Doris Day of peeing in his kettle (she hadn't; she'd cleaned it with vinegar) and the time he was evicted from the House of Commons Strangers' Bar after standing on a table and reciting his favourite party piece, Peter Sellers's "Setting Fire to the Policeman."

"The parliamentary police officer on duty had been happy to play along, right up until Benny started flicking lit matches at him," Wilhelmina said.

Father, the consummate storyteller, did the eulogy.

"We are blessed to have had Ben Diamond in our lives at all," he said. "History appeared always to have an appointment with Ben. In 1940, Ben's parents, David and Ester, fled across Europe on foot, with five-year-old Ben and his ten-year-old sister, Ruth."

Not a noise could be heard as father recounted the story of the Diamond family travelling at night, hiding in barns, fleeing when those barns were set alight by Nazis, and being smuggled across borders and through guard posts by a network of resistance volunteers until, finally, they arrived safely in England.

"David took up a professorship at the London School of Economics," Father said. "And young Ben quickly discovered his passion for theatre. Starting with Punch and Judy shows in Covent Garden, before graduating to the West End shows of Shaftesbury Avenue and the theatre district, which would go on to become his life's work."

As Father told of Ben Diamond's early career in newspapers, including several years editing *Stage* before finally joining the *Sentinel* in 1976, it occurred to me just how long Uncle Ben had been in his life too.

"It was my late father, Sir Percival Boche, then editor of the *Sentinel*, who spotted Ben's talent and poached him for the paper," Father said. "While sitting in a dentist's waiting room, he'd read one of Ben's reviews in an old copy of *Stage* and laughed so hard he nearly swallowed his dentures. When my father got back to the office, he handed his secretary the review he'd torn out of the magazine and told her to arrange a meeting with the man who'd written it. Two nights later, my father and Ben dined at the Savoy. Ben had agreed to join the *Sentinel* before they'd even finished the soup course. By dessert, he was an honorary member of our family."

Father spoke about Michael, about the AIDS years in London and the terrible toll of the eighties and nineties on the communities Uncle Ben loved—the queer and the theatrical.

"Ben Diamond was the very best of men," my father said, and there was a crack in his voice, like he might be showing actual human emotion. "He was the life of the party, the heart of any group of people, and the joy in any room. He was my lifelong friend. My confidant. The godfather to my son Ludovic. In some ways, he was a godfather to me, too, because he gave me the love my own father, brilliant as he was, could not. Ben Diamond was, quite simply, the best man I have ever known. And I miss him."

Tears were streaming down my face, a balled tissue disintegrating in my hand under the weight of my grief. For the first time in my life, I was seeing my father as a person. Layered on top of everything else, it was more than I could bear.

"Let me leave you with the best piece of advice Ben ever gave me. He said, 'If you feel something with all your heart, dear boy, go for it. God put it there so you couldn't ignore it. So that with every heartbeat, you'd be reminded of it. To meet our destiny, we must follow our heart.'"

My father was in tears. I was a wreck. I thought of Sunny. I thought of the hundreds of calls and text messages he had ignored. I thought of his hard muscle and his soft skin. I thought of the tenderness of his kisses and the way we laughed constantly whenever we were together. I thought of the hurt I'd caused him. How he must be feeling now. And I thought perhaps, just this once, Uncle Ben might have been wrong. No good had come from Sunny and me ignoring all the warning signs and following our hearts. No good at all.

***

AFTER THE SERVICE, a smaller group of mourners got into a string of cars we'd booked to take us to the cemetery, which was right across London in East Ham. I was meant to jump in one with Mother, Father, and Jonty, but I couldn't face it. I'd seen enough of their faces in the days since Uncle Ben had died. Our conversation had run out. Out of the corner of my eye, I saw Wilhelmina Post hailing a black cab. I trotted down the street towards her.

"Mind if I bum a lift with you, Willy?"

"My darling Ludo, I can't think of anything I'd love more."

59

SUNNY

MUM THREW OPEN THE door to my childhood bedroom, where I was propped up on the bed in just my pants, challenging the stamina of a laptop I had not used since I left university and listening to Lana Del Rey on repeat.

"Jesus Christ, Sunny, have you been wanking in here?"

"NO!" I protested. Obviously, I had been. But I wasn't admitting that to me mum. We might be close, but there are limits.

"At least open a bloody window. It stinks of boy in here." She crossed the room, throwing open the window and saving me the bother. She was wearing her faded pink PFLAG T-shirt from about ten Prides ago. It was a miracle it had survived the washing machine for so long.

"Have you asked Jazmyn about a job yet?"

"I can't go back to the *Mercury*, Mum, it's embarrassing."

Mum stood in front of me, hands on her hips, eyes all serious.

"Then what are you doing back here instead of being down in London where all the jobs are?"

She had a point. "Indulging in a little parental love and sympathy?"

"Right, well, get up and get dressed." She grabbed my wrist and yoinked me off the bed.

"Oi!"

"You've been moping around up here for two weeks, Sunny. Wallowing in your own filth. If you're not going back to the *Leicester Mercury*, then you're coming down the food bank with me. You need a job."

Mum started picking up dirty clothes from the floor.

"I'll do that," I said, remembering the sock I really didn't want her to find. "I know how to do laundry."

"Then get dressed!" A finger topped with bright-red Asda-brand false nails pointed towards the neatly folded clothes in the wardrobe. I picked out a pair of joggers and a hoodie. "No son of mine is sitting around wasting his life on benefits. I raised you better than that, Sunshine Augustus."

"It's not like I've signed on!" I climbed into the joggers.

"It's the principle."

I pulled on the hoodie. "In't the food bank voluntary?"

"Course it is," Mum said. "Then after the food bank we're popping into Tesco, and you can ask Doug about night stacking."

"No, Mum. Come on!" Mum stood bolt upright, eyes wild, the static electricity in the room making the strands of flaming hair she'd failed to snare in her tight ponytail stand on end. It felt vaguely threatening, like a sort of ginger Medusa.

"Tesco too good for you, is it?" she said. Uh-oh. I'd screwed up. "It were Tesco what fed you when you was a kid. It were my wages from Tesco what clothed you. What sent you to that fancy university."

"In that case, why do I have tens of thousands of pounds of student debt that I'll be paying off for the next twenty years?"

"Tesco was good enough for you then. It's good enough for you now."

"It's not good enough for your nails, though, apparently."

"Right!" I'd *really* screwed up. A fistful of red fingernails gripped the neck of my hoodie like a vice as Stacey Ann Miller dragged me bodily out of my bedroom and onto the upstairs landing.

"Car. Now."

"So much for parental love and sympathy."

"If you can't see that parental love is *exactly* what this is, Sunshine, then you in't got the brains I thought you had."

60

LUDO

THERE'S SOMETHING JOLLY GHOULISH about the reading of a will. Obviously, a person's worldly possessions need to be disposed of and distributed somehow, but gathering in a lawyer's office to hear these instructions from beyond the grave read aloud felt terribly cold and grasping. Like grief had given way to greed. Mummy, Father, Jonty and I sat in a semicircle in front of a reassuringly wooden desk. Behind the desk sat a woman in her fifties in red-framed glasses and dangly earrings, which were much cheerier than the occasion called for. Her name was Sarah, and she told us she had inherited Uncle Ben when she had inherited her father's practice.

"Mr Diamond made this will just three years ago. After his sister died. Are we ready?"

We all nodded.

She began "I, Mr Benjamin David Samuel Diamond" and read out all the formal bits about addresses and executors and then, suddenly, stopped.

"Look, I can save us all a lot of time here," she said. "Ludo, Mr Diamond has left everything to you."

"I'm sorry?" My brain didn't trust my ears. I felt my face flush with blood.

"The flat in Connaught Square, last valued three years ago at £1.75 million, all its contents, and a sum of about £750,000 in various accounts, bonds, and investments. There will be death duties to pay, of course, which will take a chunk of that. But the cash should cover it. I'd say you're pretty well set up for life, if you're smart with it. Congratulations, Ludo. You're a young man of independent means."

"Golly," I said, stunned.

"Congratulations, Ludo!" Father said, standing and putting out a hand for me to shake, like that was a completely normal human reaction. Sometimes the alien lizards that control him really give the game away.

"Is it just me, or is it hot in here?" I felt woozy. I loosened my tie. Why was I wearing a tie? "Can someone please open a window?" The room went fuzzy. Then it went black.

61

SUNNY

TWO HOURS INTO SORTING cans of beans and packets of pasta into boxes, I'll admit, any enthusiasm I had for volunteering at the food bank with Mum was drifting. My phone pinged in my pocket. I stopped to check the notification. Through the cracked screen I read the sender's name. It was Ludo. Again. The heat of rage boiled inside me, like it did every time he sent me a message. I deleted it without reading it. Again. It was my default setting.

"Orright, Shirl?" I heard Mum saying from the front counter. "How's the stump, love?"

"They ain't took the leg off yet." I hadn't heard Shirley Trimble's smoke-aged voice moaning for at least a couple of years. Proper nostalgic.

"Got a surprise for you, Shirl," Mum said. "Guess who's here?"

"Noted Hollywood chameleon Meryl Streep?"

I laughed—and slapped a hand to my mouth to smother it.

"No, Shirl. Why would Meryl Streep be on the Wickwar Estate?"

"You told me to guess. Sorry you don't like my guess, love. I'm not a bloody clairvoyant."

I giggled into the crook of my arm.

"It's Sunny, Shirl."

"Who?"

"My boy. Sunny."

I shoved a balled-up plastic bag in my mouth to muffle my laughter and peered through the shelves to watch the scene at the counter play out.

"The poofy one?"

"We don't call them that anymore, Shirl."

"Right you are. The bender, then?"

Mum sighed. She was giving up. "That's the one. He's come home to me, Shirl."

"Boyfriend dumped him, did he?"

Jesus Christ, Shirl. Be gentle with my heart, will you? A twist of pain pierced my chest as I thought of Ludo, what the back-stabbing bastard had done, and my own stupidity in telling JT the truth about what had happened.

"You wanna be careful, Shirl. Sunny's packing your box for you. Play nice, or he'll give you the peach-flavoured yogurts." Mum turned to find me hiding behind the shelf with my lips stretched around a crumpled blue plastic bag. I froze. She glared at me. I tried to smile, but there was too much plastic in my mouth. I spat it to the floor. Mum rolled her eyes. "Get Shirley's box, will you, Sunny?" she said. I grabbed Shirley's box and walked around to the front counter.

"Orright, Shirl?" I said. "Shall I put this in the car for you?" Shirley definitely did not have a car. She barely had teeth.

"Still not wearing underpants then?" she said.

"Touché. How's young Geordie?"

"Up before the parole board next week. We're very hopeful."

"That's good news for the neighbourhood, then."

"Cheeky sod."

"You want me to carry this home for you?" I said, tapping the box with my thumb.

"Yes please, love."

62

LUDO

THE LAWYER, SARAH, HAD said it could be months before I got the keys to Uncle Ben's flat. The joke was on her. I'd had keys to Connaught Square for years, letting myself in and out as I pleased. It was different being here now, though, surrounded by Uncle Ben's things. The smell of his tobacco clinging to the wallpaper and upholstery. The dent in the seat of his favourite armchair. The tumbler of whisky, half-drunk, on the occasional table beside it.

At some point, I was going to have to sort through all this stuff. Not now, though. For now, I just wanted to sit in the happy little bolthole Uncle Ben had created for himself, his retreat from the rest of the world, a little velvet-and-gold-braid-adorned sanctuary. It always felt part palace, part theatre. No one decorated like this anymore. Except the King, possibly, but he had an excuse.

I sank into the chesterfield armchair, pulled out my phone, and composed yet another message to Sunny. He hadn't replied to a single one of them so far. Not the dozens of messages where I explained what Father had done, when I had begged him to speak to me, explained that I hadn't stabbed him in the back. Though he had sent flowers to the house when he'd heard about Uncle Ben, the card was addressed to the whole family, and he had not replied to my messages of grief at all. The ones where I had been crying so hard I could barely type, wanting nothing more than to hear his voice, to have his arms around me, to feel his comfort. Nor the ones where, all cried out, I had poured my heart out about the unfairness of life, the emptiness in my heart, the desolation I felt at losing both my godfather and my boyfriend in the same day. He had not replied when I had messaged him about being sacked by the *Bulletin*, nor when I asked whether he wanted me to get Father to give him a job, nor when I asked if he was coming back to London. The message was loud and clear.

I sat in Uncle Ben's chair and typed out my last-ever message to Sunny Miller. I had done a lot of thinking in the weeks since Uncle Ben's death. It was time for the curtain to come down on this part of my life. I just needed to tie up a few loose ends, starting with Sunny. I opted for text rather than GayHoller because, you know, standards. I did, however, check GayHoller to see if Sunny was actively using it because, you know, I liked to jolly well *feel* my heartbreak. He wasn't online. But he was still a hundred miles away and therefore, probably, still in Leicester.

I finished my message and hit send without reading it back through. It was like ripping off a Band-Aid. I put my phone down on the arm of the chair, stood, walked to the drinks cabinet, and poured myself a whisky. I drifted over to Uncle Ben's armchair and clinked my glass against his, against the glass he'd been drinking from the night before he died.

"That's one big job done," I told the ghost of him. "Just Father to do next. He might be a bit tougher, mind you. Father's likely to reply."

I threw the whisky down the back of my throat and swallowed, like I'd seen people do in the movies, like Paul Newman in *Cat on a Hot Tin Roof*. The air left my lungs, replaced by the burning heat of rocket fuel.

"Christ! Who makes this stuff, NASA?"

I coughed and coughed and coughed.

63

SUNNY

THE THING ABOUT BEING a journalist is it can be proper hard to let things go. It turns out that's the case even if you're no longer employed as a journalist. I was curled up on my childhood bed, heritage-listed laptop on my knees, searching for information about ZephEnergies Limited and Prometheus Power. There was plenty of publicly available information about ZephEnergies, but I thought it was still worth a bit of a dig around. Their interests were certainly well beyond wind energy. They were on the shareholder registers of a couple of other nuclear power facilities. Prometheus Power was more of a mystery. I'd called Stav, who'd used his lawyerly dark arts to help me dive a few levels deeper than simple Companies House searches. He was a divorce lawyer, so he was used to digging around to find where the money was hidden. Although he specialised in gay divorces, so his expertise was mostly in mediating joint custody arrangements for pugs.

"It's a shell company," Stav said. "It's a UK company with fifty-one per cent UK ownership, but the remaining investors are based in the Channel Islands. That's not uncommon."

"Because it's a tax haven?"

"Correct."

"Can we find out who owns those offshore shares?"

There were some keyboard taps at the other end. "Major shareholding is a company called Highveld Industries. Also based in the Channel Islands."

"And who owns that?"

"My friend, you are now in the realm of layering. You could be at this for days and never find the name of an actual traceable human."

"I have time," I said. "That's the one thing I do have."

"Well, I'll leave you with it, then," Stav said. "I'm meant to bill by the quarter hour, you know."

As we hung up, my phone pinged. It was Ludo, again. Seeing his name twisted a knife in my heart. He had cost me everything, and he *still* wouldn't leave me alone. I couldn't deal with it. I had to maintain focus. I threw my phone on the bed and kept digging through the layers of Prometheus Power's investment structure.

64

LUDO

A FEW DAYS LATER, I sidled up to my father in the kitchen while he was doing the dishes. Always best to approach him with something like this while his hands were busy.

"Daddy, can I have a word?"

He gave a world-weary sigh.

"You're about to say something unspeakably daft. I urge you to stop, rethink, and say nothing."

"What makes you say that?"

Water sloshed around in the sink.

"Because last time you called me Daddy, you asked for a horse, and we all remember how that ended."

I certainly did. I think we still had the plaster cast up in the attic, somewhere. It had been signed by Vanessa Redgrave at the stage door of Wyndham's Theatre. A treasure not to be thrown away. I swallowed, not to be deterred.

"I've been talking to Wilhelmina Post. About my career. And I've come to a decision. I don't want to be a political reporter anymore. I want to be a theatre critic."

I heard the distinct sound of a plate snapping in two.

65

SUNNY

I HAD TO GET out of the house. Mum was driving me nuts. She'd also found the stash of proper manky socks under the bed that I'd definitely meant to launder and given me a lecture about personal hygiene and respecting people's property. She seemed less keen on me lecturing her on respecting people's privacy.

"It's my house, Sunshine."

"I think you'll find the council owns it."

The fact she lived in a council flat was one of her triggers. It was a low blow, and it didn't go down well. Which was how I found myself twenty miles up the M1, lying in my pants in a crystal pyramid with a tiny white towel over my arse while Summer realigned my chakras or something. It might have been reiki. There was acupuncture involved at one point, hence the state of undress. I didn't really care for some of this stuff, if I was honest, but Karma had refused to teach me how to surf the dark web until I'd been suitably cleansed.

"You're holding on to a *lot* of anger," Summer said now. I was also holding on to a fart, but I didn't tell her that. If this went on much longer, she'd soon find out. "You need to practice forgiveness. It will free you of a lot of this negativity that's weighing you down. Do you anger quickly? Do you tend to find you're quite hot-headed, *in the moment*?"

Wow. How did she know that? Summer was *good*. This was probably how she got her claws into Torsten.

"Ah, yeah," I admitted. "You know what they say about redheads."

"How we react is a choice. I'll teach you some breathing exercises you can use to pause, to slow down your reactions, so you can make better choices in difficult moments."

"That sounds... great, actually."

"Are you a very spiritual person, Sunshine?"

She full-named me, like I was in trouble. My tummy rumbled.

"I like the *Ring* films," I said. "And *Paranormal Activity*."

"You know what I mean. Do you believe in something bigger than yourself? A guiding force? A great universal energy?"

I did. I was guiding the great force of a Dorito fart as far back up my bum as I could muster without visibly clenching. This torture went on for several hours and would probably have cost a fortune if I was paying for it.

Once she'd taught me her breathing exercises and I was finally free, Summer suggested I take a walk in the forest to spend time in nature. I took her up on her offer and, at a safe distance, fired out a cannonball of wind that not only nearly blew the arse out of my joggers but knocked out a family of rabbits.

***

THAT EVENING, AFTER DINNER, I found myself in the wood-lined office that I had seen so often on Zoom. The late-evening sun streamed in through the big window, filtered by the forest outside. I was sitting in front of my antique laptop, Karma by my side, getting a tutorial on how to use the dark web.

"Now click in here," Karma said, pointing. I clicked. "Right, now you're in the forum. Go down to the categories section."

"You can buy people's internet history? That could ruin a few marriages. Whoa! Weapons? Medical records? Are people really selling all this stuff? Is it even safe for me to be here?"

"You're in the Tor Browser, it's completely anonymous."

"Need any Kalashnikovs while I'm here?"

After a few hours messing about and learning the ropes, I was gaining confidence. I began searching for information about Prometheus Power, Highveld Industries, and the Newton Bardon nuclear power plant deal. I made some progress. I now owned some sort of crypto coin and had drained just over £600 from my bank account—most of what was left of my payout from the *Bulletin*—to pay for sketchily acquired information. I had pieced together a long paper trail to cut through the layering Stav had warned me about.

By four in the morning I was finally so battered that I took myself off to bed. Karma and Leaf had put me up in one of their empty chalets. It was pleasantly rustic. There was plenty of incense but, away from the main house, absolutely no Wi-Fi or 5G.

Out of habit, I flicked through my phone as I lay in bed, waiting to drift off to sleep. Pointlessly, I opened a few different apps, before finally opening my messages. Whether it was the influence of my freshly aligned chakras, the unblocked negative energy, or boredom, I do not know, but when I saw a message from Ludo that I had somehow failed to delete, I decided to open it and read it.

Ludo: *Sunny, I've been trying for weeks to explain what happened and to let you know what I've been going through, to no avail. It has been the hardest few weeks of my life. Harder than my first term at Petersham College, which is saying something, because I got thrown from a pony, landed face first in* *horseshit, and broke both my arms. I couldn't wipe my own bum for six weeks. I don't know who was less pleased, me or the school nurse. I never could quite bring myself to look her in the eye after that.*

I just wanted to say, this is the last time I will try to contact you. I have got the message, loud and clear. Whatever we had, whatever I thought we had, it obviously isn't enough to overcome what you think I've done to you. I wish you would talk to me, let me explain properly about Father going behind my back, and how sorry I am for it, and for everything that followed. But I understand you're angry. I suspect, or perhaps hope, that, like me, you're heartbroken. Because I have never been so jolly heartbroken in all my life. I have felt empty these past weeks. Devoid of purpose, of meaning, of happiness. But I've had enough of wallowing. I'm putting all that behind me now. It's time to move on. Stiff upper lip, and all that.

I just wanted to say thank you. Thank you for seeing something in me, at least for a little while, that made me feel special, worthwhile, valid, and whole. Only two people have ever truly made me feel that way. You and Uncle Ben. It is a terrible misfortune, a tragedy of Shakespearean proportions, that I should lose you both on the same day. What we had meant the world to me. I hope it meant something to you, too.

Ludo. x

I was crying. You'd have to be completely heartless to read a message like that and not feel something. I felt sadness for what had happened. I felt regret, too, for what we had lost. I didn't like thinking of Ludo all alone, helpless, grieving, probably tripping over his own feet. But for all that, there was one line that kept drawing my eye, that I kept rereading. *Let me explain properly about Father going behind my back.* What was that about? Was this some excuse he'd tried on earlier? But then, if so, what was to be gained by repeating it in his farewell message?

For the first time, I wished I'd read some of Ludo's earlier messages—if only for the context. I'd deleted them in anger, and now I had questions because I hadn't read them. I wiped my tears on the duvet cover and began to type a reply. Then I deleted it. I was too tired to write, unsure what to say, and had no way of sending it anyway. But as I put my phone down to charge on the bedside table, I made a promise to the great universal energy that I *would* reply. I owed Ludo that much.

66

LUDO

IN A BOX IN the back of a wardrobe in the spare bedroom in Connaught Square, I found a stack of Uncle Ben's old diaries. They ran, fairly consistently, from 1953, the year he turned eighteen, until 1966. Then there was a gap of a few years, picking up again in 1971 and continuing until 1999, a year after I was born. When I discovered them, 1974 was on the top of the pile. I opened it, expecting to find a calendar of appointments, shows, and birthdays to be remembered. What I discovered was a detailed journal of Uncle Ben's thoughts, experiences, and day-to-day life. Thoughts on the latest production of this or that production, gossip about this or that actor, information about what was going on in the world and his views, and, most alarmingly, particulars about his love life. I slammed the journal shut. As the day progressed, however, I found myself going back to the box to peer into the journals again and again. They were irresistible. A treasure trove of history and witticism.

25 March 1954

They got Peter Wildeblood. The "honourable" beak gave him a year and Montagu and Pitt-Rivers eighteen months each for buggery. This arcane legislation must be wiped from the statute books. I've written to Peter saying he should campaign, upon release, for the decriminalisation of homosexuality, and offering to give him every support I can. I've no idea which prison to post it to, but I shall send it first class so that at least whoever reads the mail before they give it to the convicts knows the calibre of the pansies they're up against.

20 December 1965

Have just seen "Twang!!" Possibly the worst production ever to disgrace the West End. Writer apparently strung out on LSD throughout rehearsals. Director quit before opening night. Songs bore no relationship to the script. Musical director collapsed at interval and didn't come back. House lights kept going up and down throughout the show. Could <u>hear</u> the cast and crew arguing backstage. Take every copy of the script, put them in a hessian sack, weigh it down with two bricks, and fling it into the Thames!

24 November 1991

We lost Freddie Mercury today. Just a day after his statement to the press confirming that he had tested HIV-positive and had AIDS. He said he had wanted everyone to know the truth, that he hoped everyone would join him, the doctors, and the gay community in the fight against this terrible disease. The world has lost a musical legend. When I think of his bravery, I cry. He spoke for all of us. His hopes are my hopes. Vale, Freddie.

Visited Michael in the hospital today. Sat with him for four hours until the nurses turfed me out. He's in and out of consciousness and angers quickly when he's awake. No sign of improvement. Put in a good word for him, will you please, Freddie. He's a good man. He needs friends in high places right now.

One minute I was laughing, the next I was in floods of tears. There was enough here for a dozen books. I felt a pang of regret that Uncle Ben had never written a memoir of his remarkable life. It would have been a bestseller. I wondered why he never had.

My phone chimed with a notification. Mummy. It was eight o'clock, and she, Father, and Jonty were waiting around the corner at Le Gavroche. She wanted to know if I was still coming or whether they should order. I was just about to leave to join them when a thought struck me. I dug through the box and found one last diary, flicking through to the correct date.

28 August 1998

Welcome to the world, Ludovic Benjamin Barker-Boche. Your Uncle Ben already loves you very much. I held you in my arms today, fresh from the oven. A burbling mass of pudgy flesh, whisps of black hair caked to your head, and the bluest eyes God has ever seen fit to bless upon a little boy. You gripped my finger with your tiny hand and spoke directly to my heart. I am honoured that your wonderful parents, just children themselves, to my mind—whip smart but still feckless—asked me to be your godfather. A thousand times yes, my dear little soul.

I promise you this, Ludovic: every day for the rest of my life—which may not be long, I grant you, with the booze and smokes and bacchanalia—will be dedicated to making sure you want for nothing, so that your life may be even more blessed than mine. And my life has been truly blessed. May you know good health and happiness. May you know success. May you know love, dear boy. May you have the wisdom to see how rare true love is, the good judgement to recognise it when you find it, and the sense to hold on to it for dear life—and to fight for it when it's slipping through your fingers. And may you know this: You can always rely on your Uncle Ben—whether you need a warm heart, a firm shoulder, or a wise head. I cannot wait to watch you grow up. My heart is full today—truly full—for the first time since we lost Michael.

I caught sight of myself in the wardrobe mirror. I was a blubbing mess. I washed my face, turned off the lights, and pulled the front door shut behind me. As I cut through Hyde Park to get to the restaurant, I knew one day I would use those diaries to write the story of Uncle Ben's life, so everyone would know just how amazing he was, and how fully he lived.

67

SUNNY

S POILER ALERT: WHEN I woke up at eight that morning, I did not message Ludo. Mostly because Summer pulled me into a wrinklies' yoga class, where I was younger than the average age by at least fifty years and, embarrassingly, about ninety per cent less flexible. Are metal hips double-jointed or something? By the time I'd had breakfast, I just wanted to get back to my computer. I was changing strategy and tackling the layering from the bottom up rather than the top down. I went searching for information on Carstairs and her husband, Dirk Windhoek. An hour or two passed, but I'd discovered nothing. Then I remembered you could buy people's internet histories and, on a whim, typed in the name of my old "friend" and confidant Vladimir Popov.

"Only twenty quid to see everything he's ever googled?" I muttered to myself.

It was worth the splash of cash. A proper bargain. But I wasn't quite prepared for what I found.

"Bloody hell. It's the mother lode."

I called through to the other room for Karma to come take a look at my computer. My heart was racing like a greyhound after a rabbit.

"Look at this. Popov's internet history. It's like a breadcrumb trail. The names of all the companies, the investors—it's all here."

She sat on the edge of the chair, reading glasses low on her nose, scanning the screen. As I reread it along with her, I realised Popov had been using me as a part of this scheme. I was nothing more than a useful stooge. I had been to VladPop what Torsten was to Carstairs. But where she'd used Torsten to find out information, VladPop had used me to disseminate it in the press. I felt like a proper mug. And I wanted nothing more than to take the bastard down.

"How could he be so indiscreet?" Karma asked.

"I reckon he was looking for dirt on the others, in case it all went tits up."

Karma smiled, her face as happy as the one on the buddha I'd been using as a paperweight.

"This is our Rosetta Stone," she said. "You've found the key to the entire paper trail."

She threw her arms around me in a proper rib-cracking hug, her flip-flopped feet stamping up and down in excitement.

"You clever, *clever* boy!"

I laughed. A full-bellied, full-throated, uncontrollable laugh. The kind of laugh they make incontinence commercials about. Karma laughed, too, and I feared I might now actually be *in* an incontinence commercial. She sank back into her office chair.

"We've got them," she said. "We've got the lot of them."

"I need to cross-reference everything, and I have a few more searches to do now to tie it all up in a neat bow. The question is, then what do we do with the information?"

"You're the journalist, Sunny. You tell me."

68

LUDO

A FEW DAYS AFTER I sent Sunny my farewell text, I still hadn't had a reply. It hurt, but I'd expected no less. The silence left everything all feeling rather unresolved, somehow, and that was jolly frustrating. Then a message came through from the Government Media Office saying Carstairs was holding a press conference at the Newton Bardon site in Leicester at two o'clock, and, well, it felt like fate was telling me to go to Leicester.

I had asked to go, but my father was refusing to let me cover it. We were having a stand-off over it in the *Sentinel*'s small conference room.

"But the nuclear plant story is mine," I protested.

"I'm sending Ford," Father said. His suit jacket was unbuttoned, and he had his hands on his hips, giving me what the newsroom called Full Waistcoat. When Father went Full Waistcoat, you jolly well knew you'd lost. My head was thumping from downing too much champagne at Le Gavroche, and I was tired and grumpy because I'd woken at seven, thanks to Jonty's latest surprise alarm, Sheena Easton's "Morning Train."

"Is this because of Sunny?" I said. "Is he the reason you're not sending me to Leicester?"

Father put one hand to his temple, pressing into it with the heel of his thumb, as if he felt a headache coming on and the only way to prevent it was to act like he was in a 1920s silent film.

"I am acting as your editor, not your father," he said. His voice was softer. The grandstanding of earlier now gone. "As your father, yes, I can see sending you to Leicestershire might be a bad idea, given the situation with Sunny Miller."

Sunny was "the situation" again.

"But speaking as your editor, Ludo, you must understand that you have informed me of your desire to leave the politics team. As a result of this frankly mystifying, if not downright ungrateful, decision, I must now think about what is best for the paper. And today, that means sending Ford to cover Newton Bardon."

We were back to Full Waistcoat. My phone pinged in my pocket; I didn't dare check it.

"Now, my question to you, Ludo, is why do you *really* want to go to Leicester? Is it my reporter asking? Or is it my son?"

Ouch. That was irritatingly perceptive.

"You think I'm still hung up on Sunny?"

"Ludo, you literally spoke about nothing else at dinner last night. You briefly mentioned your idea about Uncle Ben's biography, then segued straight onto Sunny. All night. You were a tedious bore, squawking on and on like a lovesick goose whose partner was presently roasting in the oven."

"I didn't talk about him that much, did I?"

"Ludo, your mother, brother, and I now all have honours degrees in Sunny Miller studies. You're clearly not over him. And, frankly, I'm not sure it's very healthy." Father paced stiff-legged from one side of the room to the other, as if his ankles were in calipers, hands still stridently upon his hips. I was silent, unsure what to say or do. He came to a stop at the head of the table and craned his head towards me. He looked like a rooster squaring up for a fight. If roosters wore waistcoats. Which, arguably, they should. Father eyeballed me directly. "The question is, Ludo, what are you going to do about it? Because this mooning *must* stop."

I wasn't sure if he was asking as my editor or as my father, so I kept my trap shut. On the walk back to my desk, I checked my phone. A small piece of me hoped the text was from Sunny. It wasn't.

Government Media Office: *Press Alert. Information Only. Not For Publication: Torsten Beaumont-Flattery is no longer special adviser to the Secretary of State for the Environment and Energy. A replacement will be announced soon. In the interim, please forward any enquiries to Rebecca-Jo Farley in the Minister's office.*

That was a bolt from the blue.

"Penny, did you see the message about Torsten?" I asked, when I got back to the politics desk. "What do you think happened?"

"Didn't you hear?" Penny lit up, eager to share the gossip. "It's all terribly romantic."

"Spill. The. Tea," I said. "Immediately."

"He's chucked it all in for some bird. He's moving up to Derbyshire to live with her in some retreat in the forest."

Golly, Summer moved fast.

"He's only known her a month," Penny added. "But I guess the heart knows what it wants."

If you feel something with all your heart, dear boy, go for it. God put it there so you couldn't ignore it. So that with every heartbeat, you'd be reminded of it. To meet our destiny, we must follow our heart.

"Yes," I said. "Yes, it does."

May you have the wisdom to see how rare true love is, the good judgement to recognise it when you find it, and the sense to hold on to it for dear life—and to fight for it when it's slipping through your fingers.

I picked up my coat, threw my satchel over my shoulder, and sprinted towards the door.

"Where are you going?" Penny called.

"Saint Pancras. I have a train to catch."

69

SUNNY

MY HEART WAS PROPER thumping as I picked up my phone and scrolled down my contact list to the letter *L*. I was the kind of nervous you get when your whole body feels cold, your fingers don't work, and your hearing goes funny. Full jelly bean–dick territory. I found Ludo's name and hit the call button.

"Here we go," I said. Karma and Leaf gave me two thumbs up.

It started to ring. My hands were shaking. I could feel my pulse in my balls. Which is probably cause for alarm, now that I think about it. Karma gestured for me to take a deep breath, and I did.

"Sunny! I'm so glad to hear from you!" My heart nearly burst a valve just at the sound of Ludo's voice. "You'll never believe this, but—"

"Ludo, I'm sorry to interrupt. I know we have a lot we need to talk about and, I promise, we will. But right now, this is more important. Carstairs, Windhoek, Popov—they all stand to make a fortune if the nuclear plant goes ahead. I have all the evidence. The entire paper trail. But someone needs to put the questions to Carstairs."

"Do you mean me?" He was quick on the uptake today.

"Yes, Ludo, I mean you. I've sent you all the documents to your personal email address in a file transfer link, along with lists of questions for Carstairs and Popov. I've done all the legwork." Karma cleared her throat. "Sorry, Karma and I have done all the legwork. We just need someone with access to Carstairs to ask the questions. The story is all yours if you want it."

There was silence on the other end of the line. Well, not silence. It was actually really noisy. But Ludo wasn't saying anything.

"Why don't you ask her yourself?" Ludo said.

"Ludo, don't be like that. Please. I'm sorry I haven't replied to your messages, but—"

"No, no! I mean Carstairs is giving a press conference at the Newton Bardon site at two o'clock. Literally, why don't you ask her yourself?"

I looked at my watch. We had half an hour. My brain was already on logistics. If we drove foot to the floor in Leaf and Karma's Prius and didn't get stuck behind a tractor on the country roads between here and the M1, we could just about do it.

"Thank you," I said. "Thank you, Ludo. I will." I began piling up paperwork into a stack. "Just a sec." I relayed the information to Leaf and Karma. Leaf grabbed the car keys; I gave Karma the pile of papers and grabbed my pen and my notepad with my questions on it. We made a dash for the car. When I was strapped in, I put the phone back to my ear.

"You still there?"

"It's so good to hear your voice," Ludo said, and I thought he might be crying. "I didn't think I'd ever hear from you again."

"I've been going to message you." I was breathing heavily, heart pounding, adrenaline coursing through my body.

"You'll never—" He cut out. "I'm actually—" He cut out again. "Be there in just—"

"Ludo, you're breaking up." Leaf spun the wheels, sending gravel flying everywhere.

"I didn't know where—"

"Listen, Ludo, I've got to go. I'll call you after the press conference."

I hung up. Karma plugged her phone into the CarPlay system as we sped down the driveway.

"We need some car chase music," she said, and put on the *Dukes of Hazzard* theme tune. Did she always have that lined up in case she needed car chase music? All signs pointed to yes.

70

LUDO

I DASHED OUT OF Leicester train station and nearly got cleaned up by a
cyclist whizzing past. Who puts a cycle path that close to the entrance
of a major transportation hub?

"Taxi!" I shouted, out of breath with nerves. "Taxi!"

"There's a rank over there," a woman said, pointing towards the street
corner.

I thanked her and ran for a cab.

"Newton Bardon, please," I asked through the cab window. "How long
do you think it will take to get there?"

The taxi driver, a distinguished-looking Sikh gentleman with a magnificent beard, carefully consider his calculations.

"Please, I'm in a terrible hurry."

"About twenty to twenty-five minutes."

Buggery bollocks. I was going to miss the press conference. I had read
through the questions Sunny had emailed me while I was on the train, and
they were jolly explosive. I was going to miss Sunny giving the performance
of his lifetime. I was going to miss the downfall of Jemima Carstairs. I was

going to miss curtain-up on a thrilling journalistic spectacular. I jumped in the cab.

"If you can get there in fifteen, I'll triple the fare."

"Right you are, sir."

I felt like we needed some chase music. The gentle traditional Hindi music coming from the stereo was completely incongruous. Still, you work with what you've got. I reached across and cranked up the volume as my driver ran an amber-but-tinged-red light.

71

SUNNY

THE PRESS CONFERENCE HAD already started when the Prius screamed to a halt by a gate in the cyclone fence ZephEnergies had built around the Newton Bardon site. I could see a scrum of reporters, camera operators, and photographers across the field and made a dash towards them with my notepad and the most important documents held tightly in my hand. Carstairs was wearing a green pantsuit today. I slipped into the back of the press pack and listened to her speak.

"This project will secure the energy future for people right across the Midlands, as we transition to our exciting low-carbon future," she said. She prattled on for three or four minutes; then the questions started. I edged forward, trying to get close enough to catch her attention. She took a question from Ford Goodall. Good old Ford asked for clarity on when the deal with ZephEnergies had been done, and Carstairs fudged it, just as she had been fudging it since Ludo broke the story—our story—in the *Sentinel*. Crouching, I squeezed in beside Rafiq Farouq, whose eyes bugged wide at seeing me. I put a finger to my lips to stop him saying anything. I winked, because that's the kind of thing people do at moments like this in movies.

In among all the suits, I suddenly realised I was still wearing the old blue hoodie and sweatpants I'd chucked on after yoga. The fact I wasn't meant to be here was going to stand out like dog's bollocks. After a question from the BBC's Annabelle Statham-Drew, I popped my head up and shouted my first question.

"Minister, as an investor in ZephEnergies, isn't it a massive conflict of interest for you to be approving this nuclear power plant?"

Flashes went off, and camera shutters whirred. A murmur went through the press pack. There was blood in the water. Carstairs's left eye twitched, just a little, a nervous tell. But she composed herself quickly.

"I don't hold any shares in ZephEnergies, and frankly, that's a libellous accusation."

The atmosphere had completely changed. The lions were turning on the ringmaster. I stepped forward and held up the documents I'd brought with me.

"Not directly, but you do. Through a series of shell companies, many of which are registered offshore, but you *are* definitely an investor in ZephEnergies. As is your husband, Dirk Windhoek, and the chief whip, Vladimir Popov."

"Rebecca-Jo," Carstairs said, summoning an aide, "I don't believe this man is a serving member of the press. Did you check his press pass?"

Rebecca-Jo shook her head.

"I'm sorry, it's accredited members of the press only, I'm afraid." Carstairs flicked her finger towards her government-issue police protection and then towards me. I was being removed. "You'll have to take your baseless conspiracy theories elsewhere. I'm sure you could start a podcast or something."

A voice came from somewhere behind me.

"What about me? I'm an accredited member of the press. Can I ask a question?"

I turned to see Ludo, chest heaving, a line of sweat on his brow. Where the hell had he come from? The sun was shining off his glasses, an unkempt curl bobbing in the breeze. He looked beautiful.

"Ludo Boche, the *Sentinel*," he said, flashing his press pass at Rebecca-Jo, who knew perfectly well who he was. He lifted his notepad to his chest and peered at it.

"Does the prime minister know you and your family stand to personally earn millions of pounds if this project goes ahead?"

More flash photography. A hum from the reporters.

"Where are you getting this?" Carstairs said.

"Is there a reason you haven't listed these shareholdings on your MP's register of financial interests? Why were you trying to hide it from the British people?"

Carstairs looked flustered now. The photographers were swarming like flies on shit. I showed the documents I had with me to some of the other reporters, proving the information was good. They began chiming in with their own questions. Rebecca-Jo declared the press conference was over. She and the minister turned on their heels, and the press pack upped stumps and followed, squawking like seagulls. Ludo shouted his last couple of questions above the din.

"Have you lied to the British people, Minister?" and, finally, as car doors slammed and engines revved, he banged on the window and said, "Will you do the decent thing and resign, Minister?"

We'd make a tabloid reporter out of him yet.

The car sped away, and a few of the press pack chased after it, as did Leaf and Karma, who played up to the cameras in the spirit of people who loved a good protest.

"You're a crook, Carstairs!" Leaf shouted, waving his fist.

"Lock her up! Lock her up!" Karma chanted.

Ludo watched the car disappear down the road, a vision of calmness among all the pantomime. The wind buffeted his hair. He was still clutching his notepad to his chest. He pushed his glasses up onto his nose. He looked... content. Satisfied at a job well done, perhaps. Like he'd proven something to himself. He seemed to have found a confidence I hadn't seen in him before. In that moment, I forgot everything else he'd made me feel and just felt proper proud. I swept around low in front of him and scooped him up off the ground with my arms around his legs.

"Careful! Put me down. I'm too accident-prone for this kind of thing."

I was laughing.

"You were bloody fantastic," I said.

"I know; put me down."

I loosened my grip and let Ludo slide down my body until his feet touched the ground and our eyes met. All around us was a chaos of media—of radio reporters doing live crosses, of journos calling their stories back into their newsrooms, of Leaf and Karma being interviewed for the TV cameras. But for all the anarchy around us, there was, just for a second, only the two of us.

"I'm sorry," Ludo said. "Father found the article on my laptop in the summer house and—"

I put a finger to his lips. They were soft and plump, and touching them sent lightning through my body.

"It's OK," I said. "I'm sorry I ignored your messages. I was *so* angry. It's something I'm working on. Summer's teaching me—"

"You lost your job because of me, and I'm so, *so* sorry."

"I'm not." And I meant it.

Everything we needed to say hung in the air between us, waiting to be said, but for the moment, we'd said enough. Our eyes spoke for our hearts. They sought forgiveness, expressed sorrow, asked for permission. I let my finger drift along Ludo's cheek and down to his neck. My hand cupped his jaw, and he nuzzled into it, his eyes never leaving mine. My fingers combed their way around the back of Ludo's neck and up into his hair. I pulled him into me, and we kissed. And we kissed and we kissed and we kissed until, finally, Ludo pulled away. He opened the flap of his shoulder bag.

"How did you get here so fast?" I asked.

"I'll explain later," he said, pulling out his laptop. "Right now, you need to write."

72

LUDO

MY FATHER, UPON SEEING footage of me on a news bulletin, one hundred miles from where I should have been and hectoring a secretary of state, called and demanded I file the full story, with backgrounders and information for graphics, in time for the first edition.

"It's not my story," I said. "It's Sunny's."

"Where's he going to publish it?"

"I think he was talking about the *Beano*, but we weren't sure if that was even still in publication. Perhaps *MAD Magazine*?"

"Look. Jesus. Ludo. Just put him on, will you?"

Two minutes later, Sunny had agreed to a jolly handsome freelance fee, consented to send over all his research for legal checks, and knuckled down to write in Leaf and Karma's office. Five minutes after that, Sunny's phone rang. He looked at the caller ID but didn't pick it up. He stopped typing, closed his eyes, and took a series of slow, deep breaths.

"Do you want me to answer it?" I said, hoping to be helpful.

"It's JT Thorpe." He smiled. "He can go to voicemail."

"Don't you want to hear him beg?"

"No. I wouldn't mind hearing the explosion when he gets so angry he overheats and boils in his own piss. But knowing he lowered himself enough to call is all the satisfaction I'll ever need, in this life and the next."

I thought Summer probably still had a bit of work left to do sorting out Sunny's chakras.

While Sunny wrote, I put in a few calls to various MPs to get reactions to go in the story. I had just hung up the phone to a particularly vociferous Bimpe Lasisi when a familiar voice called my name.

"Boche!" Torsten Beaumont-Flattery was standing in the doorway. He was wearing Lycra leggings and a vest, and I damned near passed out. "What are you doing here?"

I'm staring at your crotch like a hypnotised pervert, I thought but did not say.

"Apparently, this is where all the reprobates hang out these days," I said. "You know, disappointing sons, anarchists, people on the run from careers in politics. Congratulations on your retirement, by the way."

"Thanks. Just drove up from London this afternoon, actually. Bit of a relief, really."

"It's the talk of Westminster. Everyone thinks it's so romantic."

"I imagine they're all talking about Carstairs instead now." Torsten looked nervous, standing in the office doorway. "Have you got enough to sink her?"

"Safely, I'd say. And VladPop. And about eight junior ministers and backbenchers. It might well bring down the government."

Torsten scratched his calf muscle with his foot. His junk shifted around like a hare stuffed into very tight sack.

"What are you going to do?" I asked. "Here, I mean."

"My degree was in physiotherapy, so it sort of works quite well for the retreat. And Summer's been teaching me about restoring the soul through shamanic healing, and I think that's a path I'd like to follow, you know? See where it takes me."

"You two really hit it off, huh?"

Torsten smiled.

"It's like Summer says. Our souls just recognised each other. Like, immediately. You know?"

I glanced over at Sunny, face buried in the crustiest laptop I've ever seen, one hand down his joggers, scratching his nuts. I felt my face flush.

"Yeah. I do know," I said. "Although sometimes the souls take a little while to get their act together."

"I should really thank you both," Torsten said, finger pointing between Sunny and me. "Without you two, I wouldn't be here."

Sunny looked up from his screen.

"Winning the door prize had nothing to do with us," he said, feigning innocence.

"I know you asked for Leaf and Karma's help to get information out of me."

Well, this was jolly awkward. Sunny and I looked at each other, then back to Torsten's junk, then up to Torsten's face.

"What you couldn't have known was that I had been carrying, like, this incredible burden that I needed to share. I knew what Carstairs was asking me to do was wrong, using me as a mule to ferry secret documents around half of London. I knew she was up to no good. And the way they brought down Bob Wynn-Jones was just *ruthless*. But between the Official Secrets Act and Vladimir Popov's dirt file, I couldn't just come out and tell any journalists what I knew."

"Wait, what's VladPop got on you?" I asked.

"Summer could see the weight I was carrying." We can all see the weight you're carrying, I thought. Your crotch is at face height, and that thing must weigh at least a kilogram. "When she invited me to unburden myself, it all just started to flow out of me. I let it all go. I'm not weighed down by it anymore. And now, with Summer's guidance, I can begin to heal and find myself."

I've always been jolly cynical about all this spiritual mumbo jumbo, but Torsten looked so sincere, and so *happy*, I wondered if perhaps it was yet another thing I'd jumped to conclusions about.

"So, thank you," Torsten said. He opened his arms and stepped forward to hug me, and as his bulge dug into my stomach, I passed out.

73

SUNNY

WE FILED THE STORY just after eight o'clock.

"Your first-ever *Sentinel* front page. Jolly wonderful," Ludo said, pulling me into a hug. I kissed him.

"How come you don't faint when *I* hug you?" I said.

Then we sat around the retreat's kitchen table with Leaf, Karma, Summer, and Torsten. Leaf had cooked a scrumptious vegan dinner. I was exhausted. I think we all were. But everyone was also smiling and happy, like we'd all had a weight lifted from our shoulders. Before we could tuck in, Karma stood, raised a glass of organic red wine, and tapped it with the back of her knife. The table hushed. She faltered, voice croaky. She tapped her chest.

"Sorry, I'm a bit emotional." Karma's eyes welled with tears. Leaf reached across and held her hand. "I just wanted to thank you all for the beautiful energy you've brought into our lives. Leaf and I have had so much fun, and feel so blessed for everything that has happened these past couple of months. I'm so grateful to the universe for bringing us all together. I just wanted to thank you for coming into our lives and sharing this part of our journey."

Karma was crying, Leaf was crying, Summer was sobbing. Torsten was a blubbering wreck. No one said healing was pretty.

"And to think, as a result of all the fun we've had, we might yet get rid of both that stupid nuclear power plant and a barrowload of corrupt politicians."

Leaf raised his wine glass above his head.

"To changing the world for the better," he said.

"To having clever friends who help you change the world for the better," I said, nodding at Karma and Ludo.

"To fearless journalism and the relentless pursuit of truth," Ludo said, winking at me.

"To the great guiding energy of the universe for bringing us all together," Summer said. She kissed Torsten on the forehead—the only bit of his face not wet with tears.

"To soulmates," Karma said. And, finally, we drank.

***

LATER THAT NIGHT, IN the chalet, it was finally just Ludo and me. Freshly showered, exhausted from a crazy day, we climbed into bed, Ludo wearing nothing but a pair of my pants.

"I can't believe you planned this big romantic gesture and you didn't think to pack."

"Surely that makes it even more romantic?"

"I never realised I was so attracted to other boys wearing my pants. Maybe that's my kink now? The jury is out." I shuffled a little closer and rested a hand on Ludo's hip, sending a (metaphorical) charge of electricity through my body. Ludo smiled. We hadn't really had a chance to talk properly yet, and there were things that needed to be said.

"I'm so sorry about Uncle Ben. I know how much he meant to you. I should have been there for you. That was unforgivable. I'll always regret that."

Tears welled in Ludo's eyes. "Thank you for saying that. But it's fine. Really."

"It's not."

"It wasn't at the time. But it's fine now. I know you were angry, and I understand why." Ludo sat up on one elbow. "What I don't understand is *why* you would think I would do that to you? Publish early and ruin everything."

I squirmed, embarrassed.

"Because we're *journalists*. Because journalists can't be trusted. You were still the competition. I thought you been using me to get the exclusive."

"Why would I do that?"

I shrugged. "Kudos? Reputation? To get ahead?"

"Is this the same guy who told me at Maxime's I got my job because of who my father is?" I looked into Ludo's sapphire eyes, holding his gaze.

"I know. I've been an idiot. I'm sorry."

"I think if we trusted each other more, we could have saved ourselves a lot of pain," he said.

I lifted my hand to Ludo's face, tucking an unruly curl behind his ear.

"You mean if I trusted you more," I said.

"I didn't exactly trust that your motives for being nice to me were pure. I was waiting for you to fail. I'm sorry for doing that."

I forgave him and girded myself for a confession of my own.

"So... I originally apologised to you for our fight at Maxime's because I was terrified you'd trash-talk me to every editor in the country."

Ludo squawked like a parrot, ripped the pillow out from under me, and hit me with it.

"I knew you didn't mean that apology!"

"I'm sorry!"

He was laughing, thank God, and I laughed too.

"In the end, we made a pretty good team," he said.

"We did." I looked up into Ludo's eyes and lifted myself onto an elbow so I could kiss his soft, sweet lips.

Ludo's phone pinged. How on earth did he have reception this far from the house? I'd be taking this up with Vodafone. To my astonishment, he checked the message.

"Father wants to know if you're free for dinner at the house tomorrow evening."

"Me?"

"Unless he meant to invite Stormzy and autocorrect changed it. I expect he's going to offer you a job. There's a vacancy on the politics team."

"At the *Sentinel*?" My pulse quickened.

"No, at Arabella McPhee's Café. Yes, at the *Sentinel*." Ludo replaced his phone, took off his glasses, and plonked them down on the bedside table. "And when he offers it, you should take it. You'd be brilliant. And it's what you've always wanted."

He rested his head against the headboard, his stunning blue eyes shining like sapphires from behind his uncontrolled curls. He was beautiful—and I'd only just got him back.

"I know how you feel about that," I said. "I'm not going to lose you again. The price is too high. Besides, I don't want the job if I'm only being offered it because we're together."

Ludo put his forehead against mine and looked deep into my eyes.

"My father doesn't give someone a job unless they deserve it. I told you that at Maxime's." His eyes sparkled.

"You wouldn't mind working together?" I said.

"Sunny, it's my job. I'm leaving."

Ludo's expression was absolutely sincere. I sat upright in disbelief.

"Why would you leave? You're brilliant."

"I've had a lot of time to think lately. Politics isn't for me. I want to write about something I actually care about."

The penny dropped.

"You're filling your uncle Ben's old seat? Ludo, that's perfect. I'm so happy for you."

"*Noooo*, I'm certainly not ready to fill Uncle Ben's shoes. No, Wilhelmina Post is going to be the *Sentinel*'s new theatre critic. She'll be jolly magnificent. I'm joining *Stage* as a junior reporter. It's well-read and respected, but it's also somewhere I can learn my craft. Earn my stripes. Work my way up."

I kissed him, then. Firmly. Passionately.

"I'm so proud of you." I slid down into the bed and pulled Ludo closer to me, our bodies pressed together under the covers.

"Is that what you call it?" Ludo said, squeezing me through my underpants. "In that case, I look forward to making you jolly proud indeed." Then he kissed me. He kissed my lips, and my jaw, and my neck. He followed the line of my freckles across my shoulders, then pushed me onto my back and kissed his way across my chest to my hardening nipples. He kissed his way down the midline of my stomach, to the place where the freckles disappeared beneath the hair. His mass of black curls vanished beneath the bedclothes, and Ludo kept on kissing.

74

LUDO

"**S**TOP HERE PLEASE, MATE," Sunny said. The cabby pulled over to the side of the road outside a row of mostly boarded-up shops. A splash of graffiti on a closed shop grille declared that "Derek Jones has warts on his knob."

"Jolly public-spirited to let everyone know," I said to Sunny, pointing.

"Welcome to the Wickwar Estate." He winked and climbed out of the cab in search of a newspaper. We hadn't passed a newsagent all morning. Karma and Leaf had dropped us off at their local train station, which was too small to have a shop, so we hadn't seen the *Sentinel* yet. By the time I'd paid the cabby, Sunny was coming out of the shop with three copies of the paper in his hands, head down, staring at the front page. He took a couple of steps, then stopped, his face swirling with emotions. He looked like a tough kid, in his hoodie and grey sweatpants, trying not to cry. Probably because that's exactly what he was.

"Your first *Sentinel* byline," I said, wrapping my arm around his back and pulling him into me. I kissed him on the side of the face. "I'm sure it'll be the first of many."

"Not like this one. This one's special." He held the paper up so I could read it.

Under the headline were the words "By Sunny Miller and Ludo Boche."

"One for the scrapbook, I reckon?" he said, finally looking up to meet my eyes. His smile was as broad as the British Midlands. My God, he was adorable. I went to kiss him, but he put a hand to my chest to stop me.

"Are you trying to get us stabbed?" he said. "You're on the Wickwar now, mate."

"You didn't tell me I'd need my Kevlar vest, or I'd have come more prepared."

Sunny looked at me, one eyebrow cocked.

"Prepared? Yeah, you're a regular Boy Scout. You're literally wearing a pair of my underpants right now."

"Someone may as well wear them," I said, theatrically sweeping a hand in the direction of Sunny's dick print.

"Touché," he said. He folded the papers in half and put them under his arm. "You ready to meet Hurricane Stacey?"

***

I CONFESS, I'D HAD hopes of sneaking a peek at Sunny's childhood bedroom. No such luck. We met his mum at the local food bank instead. She was busy when we arrived, a whirlwind of activity, so I got to see her in action for a few minutes. It was jolly impressive. A tight ginger ponytail bobbed around in her wake as she sent customers off with boxes of groceries, a lashing of banter, and a warm smile.

"What are you doing down here on a Friday, Mam?"

"I done a swap with—"

"Wendy from number thirty-three?" Sunny said. "Does she ever actually turn up for her shift?"

"She's taken Shirley down the ospiccle again. Only her leg has gone proper purple now, right up to her flaps. Wendy said the left lip's swollen up to the size of a grapefruit. Reckons it looks like a Muppet eating its own face. Who's this then?"

Sunny stood a little taller, which pleased me somehow, and took a breath—because someone had to, and it clearly wasn't going to be Stacey—before introducing me.

"Mum, this is Ludo."

"The one you come up here shouting and moaning about?" she said.

"Er—"

"And then spent two weeks moping about the house mooning over and stalking on social media between crywanks?"

"Mum!"

Stacey winked at me. "Lovely to meet you, Ludo." She flung her arms around me in an all-enveloping hug, then, as she released me, said, "Call me Stacey."

"Likewise."

"You want me to call you Stacey?"

"No, I mean, it's—"

Stacey burst into peals of laughter.

"Only teasing, love," she said. Sunny rolled his eyes.

"Did you bring my things?" Sunny asked, somewhat impatiently.

"Your bags are in the kitchen," Stacey said. "I've done your laundry. Not your socks, though. I'm sorry, love. They're still having trauma therapy."

"Enough, Mum. Behave." Sunny glared at his mother, then smiled at me. "Back in a tick." He trotted off in a direction I took to be towards the kitchen, presumably to collect his bags. Stacey leant over conspiratorially.

"Are you two on together now, then?" she asked bluntly. This woman was as ruthless as a KGB officer.

"I, um, I, er. I *guess* so," I said. "I certainly hope so. We're definitely heading that way. I mean, I'm literally wearing his underpants right now."

Shut up, Ludo. *Shut up*. Stacey's eyebrows went up. "Sorry. Not sure why I said that."

"Don't worry, love. Just stay away from his socks, and you'll be fine."

"What's going on with Sunny's socks?"

"Here, listen," Stacey said, and she leant even closer towards me. "Tell me summat, would you? Sunny promises me he's not into summat called fisting, but I don't know whether to believe him. Do you boys do any fisting? I'm worried about his laggy band, is all."

Had I stepped through a looking glass somewhere between the newsagent's and the food bank? Fortunately, Sunny came back, weighed down with rucksacks and bags, and I didn't have to answer. Stacey, upon seeing her son, changed the subject.

"Are you sure you won't stay the night?" Stacey said. "The whole gang's going up the Bells for a knees-up tonight. Denise from Asda will be there. The horse-faced trollop."

Was this a test? She was testing me.

"Sorry, Mum, I have a meeting with the editor of the *Sentinel* tonight."

"You mean your boyfriend's dad?" She hooked a thumb in my direction. Boyfriend? Wow. I mean, I liked it, but, um, boundaries? Sunny and I hadn't had that chat yet.

"Yes, Mum. But he's also a very powerful man, and he might just be willing to give me a job... on account of the *massive* national story that I broke that is on the front page of today's *Sentinel*... and I've left a copy in the kitchen, so you can actually read it for once." It was one of those slow, hint-dropping sentences with drawn-out words designed to give the other person enough time to catch on. It didn't work. Stacey was staring at me, hand gripped in an unsubtle fist, face demanding an answer to her earlier question. Sunny's single-minded drive was starting to make a lot more sense to me now that I'd met his mother.

"Mum, are you even listening?"

The fist was whipped behind her back.

"Of course I am, love. Well done. I'm very proud of you. I just meant if it's your boyfriend's dad, then he won't mind waiting a day so you can spend an evening with your old mum."

Sunny looked ready to blow, so I rode into what I hoped was the rescue.

"Alas, it's my fault," I said. "I have a hundred and twenty-two toddlers in tutus relying on me to turn up and help them perfect their pliés tomorrow morning. Can't let the kiddies down."

"All right then, love," Stacey said, pulling Sunny into a hug. He hugged her back. Less reluctantly than I might have imagined, given this jolly bizarre exchange. Stacey's eyeballs were on me, and the fist was back. I raised a hand and shook my head, silently reassuring her that her son's laggy band, whatever on God's green earth that was, was safe. She smiled and gave me a thumbs up. I've always been good with mothers.

75

SUNNY

L UDO AND I WERE sitting on the Boche family patio, too shy to hold hands in front of his parents but letting our knees touch. Given they'd interrupted us practically banging in a nightclub, this level of modesty might have been over the top, but I was potentially here for a job interview. For the same reason, Ludo had made me wear a collared shirt and chinos. And pants. I was basically dressed like him. Beverley reached over to the coffee table and grabbed a handful of nuts, then sat back on the lounge.

"So, what are you going to do now, Sunny?" she said, popping a pistachio into her mouth.

"Anyone need a top-up?" Hugo waltzed out from the kitchen, tea towel over his shoulder, a spring in his step. I politely declined. This was no time to get buzzed. Beverley and Ludo held up their champagne flutes. "Everything's done," Hugo said. "I'll fire up the barbecue shortly, if everyone's hungry?" This news was greeted by an enthusiastic chorus.

"I was just asking Sunny what he planned to do next," Beverley said.

"Ah, well done, darling," Hugo said. He sat in the chair opposite me. Ludo silently slipped his hand into mine, gripping it tightly, reminding me that it was OK to go for what I wanted.

"Sunny, everyone has been so impressed by the stunning job you've done on the nuclear plant story," he said. "Absolutely first rate." He was leaning forward, elbows on his knees. This was surreal. One of the most powerful men on (the strictly metaphorical) Fleet Street was blowing smoke up my arse, and he was wearing Crocs while he did it. How did you go from three-piece suits during the week to Crocs on the weekend? "You've single-handedly—"

"Not single-handedly," I said. "I had some excellent help." It was my turn to squeeze Ludo's hand. Our eyes met, and he smiled.

"That's as may be, but you had the energy, drive, and skill to follow this story through. Like a dog at a bone. And now Carstairs and Popov have resigned, the government is in disarray, the PM is facing his second major cabinet reshuffle in as many months, a dozen MPs are being hauled before the Privileges Committee, and several are facing recall elections from their constituents. The government may yet fall. This is *real*, consequential journalism."

"Newton Bardon might still end up with a nuclear power plant," I said. "And I've done nothing to improve job opportunities in the Midlands or address raging inequality. Or, arguably, even do anything to stop climate vandalism."

"Is that the kind of journalism you'd like to do?" Beverley asked.

"One hundred per cent."

"You may have heard we have a vacancy on the politics desk at the *Sentinel*," Hugo said, glancing at Ludo before looking back at me. "The job is yours if you want it. We'd love to have you on board."

My heart was thumping. Ludo tightened his grip on my hand, his thumb rubbing along the length of mine.

"Before you answer, Sunny," Beverley said, sitting upright, "there's a researcher position available at *Compass Point*." My ears pricked up.

"Beverley, that's enough," Hugo said. "Sunny's a newspaper man." He smiled at me, looking for confirmation.

"Now, I'm only the show's executive producer," Beverley said, "and I can't promise anything. You'd have to apply for the position like everyone else. You'd need to be the best person on the day. But with your talent and your portfolio, I don't see that being a problem."

"Beverley, for Christ's sake. You're buggering everything up."

"Would I be doing real investigative journalism?" I asked Beverley.

She nodded. "Of course."

"On TV?"

"You wouldn't be on TV just yet, but the on-air role would come. I've seen your press conference performances, and you're a born TV interviewer. And, as Uncle Ben said, a face like that deserves a wider audience."

I looked at Ludo. He smiled and raised his eyebrows, asking me what I planned to do. I shrugged my shoulders. This was a lot to take in. I thought about the little ginger kid on the estate and his dream of one day becoming a respected journalist. He would never have believed he would be in a situation like this, choosing between two of the best jobs in journalism.

"Thank you," I said. "I'll certainly think about it."

"Sunny, you don't want to work at the BBC," Hugo said. "They're all bloody civil servants governed by checkbox exercises—"

"Oh, tell us what you really think, Hugo," Beverley said. "Is that what you think of me?"

"Don't be stupid, Beverley. That's not what I meant."

"It's what you said. How long have you felt like this?"

It was starting to get quite heated. Middle-class voices were being raised, and it looked like these two were settling in for a proper mardy.

"Shall we go for a walk?" Ludo asked. I nodded.

"Good idea."

***

W E DRIFTED UP THE hill of Hampstead Heath, hand in hand. The sun low in the sky, the air and the earth still carrying the heat of a summer's day.

"Do your parents often fight like that?" I asked, as we followed along the path.

"Only about work."

"It must be terrible not to be able to trust your partner like that."

"Just quietly, I think they enjoy it."

We paused by a bench and looked back out over the view across London, the glass towers in the distance shining golden in the light of the setting sun. I pulled Ludo's body closer to mine and rested my hands on his hips, putting my fingers through the belt loops of his chinos. He put his hands around my neck.

"You know I trust you completely, don't you?" I said.

"I know you do. And I trust you too."

The lights of the city reflected in Ludo's glasses. As if reading my thoughts, he gently took them off and slipped them into his pocket. I looked into his inky-blue eyes and brushed a rebellious black curl behind his ear.

"I love you, Ludo," I said. And my heart felt full for saying it.

"I know," he said. "I love you, too, Sunny."

"I know," I said.

Ludo's lips gently brushed against mine, sending electricity through my entire body. I kissed his bottom lip, teasing it. He ran his hands up through my hair. We kissed, and everything about it felt right. I loved Ludo with every cell in my body. When our lips finally parted, we rested our foreheads together. Ludo smiled that beautiful, fat-cheeked, chipmunky smile, and I smiled right back. I had never felt so whole.

EPILOGUE

LUDO

W̲E̲ ̲A̲W̲O̲K̲E̲,̲ ̲S̲U̲D̲D̲E̲N̲L̲Y̲ ̲A̲N̲D̲ unexpectedly, to Sonny & Cher's "I Got You Babe" at eardrum-shattering volume. I slapped an arm out towards the bedside table to find my phone and knocked over my glass of water, drenching my battered, weathered, and decidedly unread copy of *Wolf Hall*.

"Oh, bloody hell," I said. I felt the warmth and weight of Sunny's body on my back as he leant over me, his naked skin against my naked skin. I'd adopted Sunny's night-time attire and had started wearing just pants to bed. Mostly because I liked to feel his body against mine when we cuddled. Sunny grabbed my phone and glasses and handed me both. I turned off the alarm.

"I have no idea how Jonty does it," I said. "My phone is locked."

"Do you want me to show you how?" Sunny asked.

"You know how to break into someone's phone? Is this some dirty tabloid skill you're now taking to a respectable programme like the BBC's *Compass Point*?"

"VladPop showed me how to do it. It's pretty simple."

"We should get up," I said, kissing Sunny's plump blush-pink lips. "Happy anniversary, baby."

Sunny smiled. "Two months. Where did the time go?"

"Let's get up. I have a full day planned."

"You haven't told me what we're doing," Sunny said.

"That's generally how surprises work."

I climbed out of bed and looked at the watery mess on the bedside table. I picked up my signed copy of *Wolf Hall* and dropped it into the wastepaper basket, then opened the summer house curtains. It was a bright, beautiful late summer's day.

"Perfect weather for the seaside," I said, dropping a jolly subtle hint.

"Yes! Penny arcade!" Sunny said. "Get in, son."

***

The sun was beating down from a wide blue sky. Seagulls circled over-head, squawking and calling. People milled about: women in flowing summer dresses, men in shorts with their shirts unbuttoned to the waist—including Sunny, who, for a freckled guy, was jolly keen to get his nipples out. I was *not* complaining.

We walked between the two little rows of stone and weatherboard buildings along the meandering cobblestone road. The air smelt of salt and mud and fish. It was lunchtime, and the tide in the Thames Estuary was low, so the boats were tilted on their sides on the honey-coloured sand, waiting for the water to come back in and refloat them.

As we rounded a corner, I saw a small wooden building made of shiplap boards, surrounded by picnic tables. It was painted in dark blue and had big white writing that said "Fish Shack."

"This is the place," I said.

"Fish and chips at the seaside? Proper amazing," Sunny said. "I hope they've got cockles."

"You grab a table. I'll go order."

I stepped up to the counter, and Bertha's arms flew open, accompanied by a shriek.

"Ludo! You came to see us!" She ran around the counter and wrapped me up in a big hug. "Dave! Dave! Look who it is."

"Ludo! Hello, son. Fancy a pint of cockles?"

Bertha released me, and I reached over to shake Dave's hand. It was his good hand, which had even more crushing power than his bad hand. Bertha looked over my shoulder, then back at me.

"Is the pretty lad with the freckles 'ere wif you?"

I nodded.

"He's ever so handsome, in't he? He should be on TV. Don't you fink, Dave?"

"What's that?"

"Don't you fink that lad over there should be on TV?"

"Born for it, I should have said," Dave said, darting back behind the counter to pull a basket of chips out of some oil.

"Are you stepping out together, then?" Bertha asked.

"Yes. That's Sunny. He's my... boyfriend," I said, feeling a flush of pride, the smile nearly breaking my face.

"Oh, Harry will be disappointed," Bertha said. "We told him all about you."

"If only every gay man had a wingman as wonderful as you, Bertha, we'd all be set."

"Well, thank you for comin' to see us, love. You're a very thoughtful young man. Are you hungry? What can I get you boys?"

***

SUNNY

IT WAS THE PERFECT day for the seaside. I stood, leaning over the wooden railing at the water's edge and scrolled through the digital wallet in my phone, checking for the thousandth time that the tickets were still there and had not magically disappeared. My surprise for Ludo? We were off to the evening's showing of *Hamilton*. He was going to lose his mind. We'd both seen it already, of course, but that wasn't the point. The point was, we'd never seen it together.

As I waited for Ludo to come back with our lunch, my phone buzzed.

Stavros has changed the name of your group to Stav's Greek Gap Year.

Stavros: *I've been summoned to Greece for family stuff. Who wants to join me for a big blowout in Mykonos before I start my big fat Greek gap year?*

Petey Boy: *I'm in, bruv!!!*

Nick: *Definitely sounds wheelchair accessible!*

I was just about to type a reply when Ludo came trotting towards me, a brown paper parcel under his arm and two ciders and a pint of cockles held in his hands. He looked so handsome in his tinted sunglasses, his curls bobbing in the breeze.

"Can you grab one of these?" he called out. Then he tripped on a cobble-stone, slamming into me, drenching me in cider and sending cockles into the air. My phone flew out of my hand and over the edge and plopped into the shallow muddy waters of the estuary. A thousand seagulls descended on us from nowhere, fighting over the cockles. At least the fish and chips were still wrapped. I put out a hand for Ludo to grab, and I pulled him up.

"Thank you," he said, pushing his glasses up onto his nose and brushing his hair back. He looked over the railing at the watery riverbed. "Sorry about your phone."

"Forget about it," I said. "At least the tide is out. I can probably just put it in some rice, and it'll be fine."

"I hope it still works." So did I. I'd spent a fair whack of my first pay cheque from the BBC on those tickets. They were good seats.

"What was it this time? Were you nervous, flustered or in a rush?"

"I think I've discovered a fourth trigger for my clumsiness," he said.

"What's that?"

"Love?"

I pushed a curl behind Ludo's ear and hugged him.

"We could be in real trouble, then," I said.

The End

Want to know what happens next?

Sunny and Ludo's adventures don't stop here.
Get a copy of your FREE novella, *The Silly Season*, when you subscribe to D.P. Clarence's newsletter.
To claim your FREE book, follow the link below and pop in your email address. Once you've replied to the confirmation email, you'll be sent a download link for *The Silly Season*.
https://BookHip.com/RXKVSXS

EXCLUSIVE: What happened when Hugo met Stacey?

It's Stacey versus Hugo in this festive adventure for fans of *The Paper Boys*!

It's eighteen months since Sunny and Ludo got together and life is as wonderful as a West End musical. The boys have settled into their new jobs and have built a fabulous, mostly pants-free life together in the Mayfair flat. There's just one big scary thing they've never quite got around to—introducing their chalk-and-cheese families.

So, what better time to do it than Christmas?

Stacey has made the trip south for the occasion and if she's unimpressed with the capital's famous sightseeing, she's even less impressed to be missing her traditional Christmas Day volunteering responsibilities in Leicester.

Meanwhile, in Hampstead, Hugo is planning a Christmas lunch worthy of a Michelin Star and eagerly awaiting a very special present in the King's New Year's Honours List. It's just the kind of pretentious rubbish that Stacey has zero time for.

A cultural clash seems inevitable, but Sunny and Ludo are desperate for Christmas to go well. After all, they've got a big announcement to make.

Get your FREE novella here: https://BookHip.com/RXKVSXS

ACKNOWLEDGEMENTS

Thanks must first go to my dear friend, the writer and critic Beejay Silcox, who encouraged me to write the kind of book I wanted to read, and gave me the belief that this story could be something. I knew you were a keeper the day you walked into our high school back in 1996 and told the straight boys that playing football was just an outlet for their latent homosexual tendencies. It is a privilege to be your friend.

Huge thanks also to the little band of professionals who helped me get this off the ground: my incredibly insightful and generous development editor, Natasha Bell; my talented and patient cover designer, Bailey McGinn; my wonderful and eagle-eyed copy editor, Elyse Lyon; my incredible proofreader and dear friend, Wendy Wood; and fellow author Valerie Gomez (author of *Cover Story*) for the beautiful chapter illustrations. These women are all extraordinary and highly recommended to any author who is self-publishing.

Thanks to my great team of #bookstagram beta readers for their invaluable insights and advice, including my Leicestershire expert, @danieljlacey—who was the first person to read this book—@jeffstookey1923, @bookspines.and.roses, @valeriegomez_writes, @booksandtatts, @kemery82, and @born_this_way2. Go give them a follow.

Thanks also to the very special gang from my Jericho Writers' Group, the Nashers, who provided encouragement from day one: Yvette, Nia, Dervla, Derek, Ann, Lou, Bec and our much-missed friend Wendy Williams (her brilliant book, *One Call*, has been published posthumously. If you like thrillers, give it a go).

And thank you especially to *you*. This is my first novel and having a reader like you take the time to read it is a privilege. If you enjoyed it, please consider leaving a review or telling a friend about *The Paper Boys*.

Be queer and mighty, always.

D.P. Clarence

ABOUT THE AUTHOR

D.P. Clarence (Dan to his friends—including you, dear reader) was a journalist for a long, long time before finally deciding to bite the bullet and do the thing he always wanted to do—write books about boys kissing other boys.

The Paper Boys is his debut novel.

He is an avid reader of everything from rom-coms to literary fiction—but he especially loves LGBTQ+ fiction. You can see what he's been reading lately on Instagram and Goodreads.

Originally from Australia, Dan lives in London with his partner and their very smiley corgi.

Printed in the USA
CPSIA information can be obtained
at www.ICGtesting.com
LVHW090016100624
782788LV00027B/497

9 781739 550905